Behind Garroway, the *Samuel Nicholas* was fast dwindling to a lopsided disk as the War Dogs hurtled toward Objective Reality. Fusion bursts and antimatter warheads, positron beams, gravitics disruptors, and lasers at x-ray and gamma frequencies crisscrossed the gulf of space between the worldlet and the asteroid-sized spaceship, eliciting dazzling flashes and twinkles of light, expanding clouds of dust and white-hot plasma. Chunks of molten rock and hull metal boiled off into hard vacuum. The *Nicholas* wouldn't be able to take that kind of point-blank bombardment for long.

Which was why, several seconds later, the *Samuel Nicholas* vanished, rotating back up into normal four-D space.

And the cloud of Marine fighters, strikepods, and twelve heavy naval vessels were left alone to confront the Xul world.

"Bastards!" Dravis Mortin said over the squadron channel.

"Belay that," Captain Xander's voice snapped. "Pay attention to your approach."

Garroway knew, with the *Samuel Nicholas* gone, none of the Marines of 1MarDiv would be going home.

We are now on our own . . .

By Ian Douglas

Books in the Inheritance Trilogy

Books in the Legacy Trilogy

Books in the Heritage Trilogy

SEMPER HUMAN

BOOK THREE OF **THE INHERITANCE TRILOGY**

IAN DOUGLAS

An Imprint of HarperCollinsPublishers

EOS
An Imprint of HarperCollins*Publishers*
10 East 53rd Street
New York, New York 10022-5299

Copyright © 2009 by William H. Keith, Jr.
Cover art by Fred Gambino
ISBN 978-0-06-123864-2
www.eosbooks.com

First Eos paperback printing: June 2009

HarperCollins® and Eos® are registered trademarks of Harper-Collins Publishers.

Printed in the U.S.A.

10 9 8 7 6 5 4 3 2 1

For Brea, as always, my patient and loving muse

Timeline of the Inheritance Universe

Years before present

50,000,000–30,000,000: Galaxy dominated by the One Mind, sentient organic superconductors with hive mentality. They create the network of stargates across the Galaxy, and build the Encyclopedia Galactica Node at the Galactic Core.

30,000,000–10,000,000: Dominance of Children of the Night, nocturnal psychovores. They replace the One Mind, which may have transcended material instrumentality.

10,000,000 TO PRESENT: Dominance of the Xul, also known as the Hunters of the Dawn. Originally polyspecific pantovores, they eventually exist solely as downloaded mentalities within artificial cybernetic complexes.

Circa 500,000 B.C.E.: Advanced polyspecific machine intelligence later called variously the Ancients or the Builders extends a high-technology empire across a volume of space several thousand light years in extent. Extensive planoforming of Chiron, at Alpha Centauri A, of Mars in the nearby Sol System, and of numerous other worlds. QCC networks provide instantaneous communications across the entire empire. Ultimately, the Builder civilization is destroyed by the Xul. Asteroid impacts strip away the newly generated Martian atmosphere and seas, but Earth, with no technological presence, is ignored. A Xul huntership is badly damaged in the battle over Mars; it later crashes into the Europan worldsea and is frozen beneath the ice. Survivors of the Martian holocaust migrate to Earth and upload themselves into gene-tailored primates that later will be known as *Homo sapiens*.

10,000 B.C.E.–7500 B.C.E.: Earth and Earth's Moon colonized by the Ahannu, or An, who are later remembered as the gods of ancient Sumeria. Around 7500 B.C.E., asteroid strikes by the Xul destroy An colonies across their empire. Earth is devastated by asteroid strikes. One colony, at Lalande 21185, survives.

Circa 6000 B.C.E.: Amphibious N'mah visit Earth and help human survivors of Xul attack develop civilization. They are later remembered as the Nommo of the Dogon tribe of Africa, and as civilizing/agricultural gods by other cultures in the Mideast and the Americas.

Circa 6000–5000 B.C.E.: N'mah starfaring culture destroyed by the Xul. Survivors exist in low-technology communities within the Sirius Stargate and, possibly, elsewhere.

1200 B.C.E. [SPECULATIVE]: The Xul revisit Earth and discover an advanced Bronze Age culture. Asteroid impacts cause devastating floods worldwide, and may be the root of the Atlantis myth.

700 C.E.: The deep abyssal intelligence later named the Eulers fight the Xul to a standstill by detonating their own stars. This astronomical conflagration of artificial novae is seen in the skies of Earth, in the constellation Aquila, some one thousand two hundred years later.

The Heritage Trilogy

2039–2042: *Semper Mars*
2040: 1st UN War. March by "Sands of Mars Garroway." Battle of Cydonia. Discovery of the Cydonian Cave of Wonders.

2040–2042: *Luna Marine*
2042: Battle of Tsiolkovsky. Discovery of An base on the Moon.

2067: *Europa Strike*
2067: Sino-American War. Discovery of the Singer under the Europan ice.

The Legacy Trilogy

2138–2148: *Star Corps*
2148: Battle of Ishtar. Treaty with An of Lalande 21185. Earth survey vessel *Wings of Isis* destroyed while approaching the Sirius Stargate.

2148–2170: *Battlespace*
2170: Battle of Sirius Gate. Contact with the N'mah, an amphibious species living inside the gate structure. Data collected electronically fills in some information about the Xul, and leads to a Xul node in Cluster Space, thirty thousand light years from Sol. A Marine assault force uses the gate to enter Cluster Space and destroy this gate.

2314–2333: *Star Marines*
2314: Armageddonfall
2323: Battle of Night's Edge. Destruction of Xul Fleet and world in Night's Edge Space.

The Inheritance Trilogy

2877: *Star Strike*
2877 [1102 м.е..]: 1MIEF departs for Puller 695. Battle of Puller 695 against Pan-Europeans. Contact with Eulers in Cygni Space. Battle of Cygni Space. Destruction of star in Starwall Space, eliminating local Xul node.

2886: *Galactic Corps*
2886 [1111 м.е.]: Raid on Cluster Space by 1MIEF. Discovery of stargate path to major Xul node at Galactic Core.
2887 [1112 м.е.]: Operation Heartfire. Assault on the Galactic Core.

4004: *Semper Human*
3152: Volunteer elements of the Marine third Division enter extended cybernetic hibernation.

3214: Formation of the Galactic Associative.

4004 [2229 A.M.]: Dahl Incursion. Contact with the Tarantulae. Attack on Xul presence within the Quantum Sea. Xenophobe Collapse.

4005 [2230 A.M.] Re-establishment of the United States Marine Corps.

SEMPER HUMAN

Prologue

Some three hundred fifty light years from the exact center of the Milky Way Galaxy, the Marine OM-27 Eavesdropper *Major Dion Williams* forced its way through the howling storm.

The howl, in this case, was purely electronic in the vacuum of space, a shrill screech caused by the flux of dust particles interacting with the *Williams'* magnetic shields. But since the tiny vessel's crew consisted of uploaded t-Human minds and a powerful Artificial Intelligence named Luther, all of them resident within the *Williams'* electronic circuitry, they "heard" the interference as a shrieking roar. The tiny vessel shuddered as it plowed through the deadly wavefront of charged particles.

"Sir! There it is again!" Lieutenant (u/l) Miek Vrellit indicated a pulse of coherent energy coming through the primary scanner. "Do you see it?"

"Yeah," Captain (u/l) Foress Talendiaminh replied. "Looks like a gravitational lensing effect."

"Yeah, but it's not noise! There's real data in there!"

"What do you make of it, Luther?"

"Lieutenant Vrellit is correct," the AI replied, as the data sang across the ship's circuitry. *"There is data content. I cannot, however, read it. This appears to be a new type of encryption."*

"But the signal's coming from inside the event horizon!" Talendiaminh said. "That's impossible!"

"I suggest, sir," the AI said, *"that we record what we can and transmit it to HQ. Let them determine what is or is not possible."*

"Agreed."

But then, as seconds passed, Vrellit sensed something else. "Wait a second! Anyone feel that?"

"What?"

"Something like . . ."

And then circuitry flared into a white-hot mist, followed half a second later by a fast-expanding cloud of gas as the *Williams* began to dissolve.

The monitor's faster-than-light QCC signals were already being received some twenty-six thousand light years away, on the remote outskirts of Earth's solar system. The last transmission received was Lieutenant Vrellit's electronic voice, a shriek louder than the storm of radiation.

"Get! Them! Out! Of! My! Mind! . . ."

"Star Lord, you are needed."

Star Lord Ared Goradon felt the odd, inner twist of shifting realities, and groaned. Not *now*! Whoever was dragging him out of the VirSim, he decided, had better have a *damned* good reason.

"Lord Goradon," the voice of his AI assistant whispered again in his mind, *"there is an emergency."* When he didn't immediately respond, the AI said, more urgently, *"Star Lord, wake up! We need you fully conscious!"*

Reluctantly, he swam up out of the warmth of the artificially induced lucid dream, the last of the sim's erotic caresses tattering and fading away. He sat up on his dream couch, blinking against the light. His heart was pounding, though whether from his physical exertions in the VirSim or from the shock of being so abruptly yanked back to the rWorld, he couldn't tell.

The wall opposite the couch glared and flickered in orange and black. "What is it?"

"A xeno riot, Lord," the voice told him. *"It appears to be out of control. You may need to evacuate."*

"What, here?" It wasn't possible. The psych index for Kaleed's general population had been perfectly stable for months, even with the news of difficulties elsewhere.

But on his wall, the world was burning.

It was a small world, to be sure—an artificial ring three thousand kilometers around and five hundred wide, rotating to provide simulated gravity and with matrix fields across each end of the narrow tube to hold in the air. Around the perimeter, where patchwork patterns of sea and land provided the foundation for Kaleed's scattered cities and agro centers, eight centuries of peace had come to an end in a single, shattering night.

The wall revealed a succession of scenes, each, it seemed, worse than the last. Orange fires glared and throbbed in ragged patches, visible against the darkness of the broad, flat hoop rising from the spinward horizon up and over to the zenith, and down again to antispin. Massed, black sheets of smoke drifted slowly to antispin, above the steady turning of the Wheel, sullenly red-lit from beneath. That he could see the flames against the darkness was itself alarming. What had happened to the usual comfortable glare of the cities' lights, to their power?

"Show me the Hub," he ordered the room.

Cameras directed at Kaleed's hub fifteen hundred kilometers overhead showed the wheelworld's central illuminator was dead. The quantum taps within providing heat and warmth had failed, and the three extruded Pylons holding the Hub in place were dark. There appeared to be a battle being fought at the base of Number Two Pylon, two clouds of anonymous fliers, their hulls difficult to see as their nanoflage surfaces shifted and blended to match their surroundings, were swarming about the base and the column, laser and plasma fire flashing and strobing with each hit.

Damn it . . . who was fighting who out there?

"Administrator Corcoram wishes to see you, Lord," his assistant told him as he stared at the world's ruin. *"Actually, several hundred people and aigencies have requested direct links. Administrator Corcoram is the most senior."*

"Put him through."

The System Administrator appeared in Goradon's sleep chamber, looking as though he, too, had just been roused from sleep. His personal aigent had dressed his image in formal presentation robes, but not edited the terror from the man's face. "Star Lord!"

"What the hell is going on, Mish? There was nothing in the last admin reports I saw. . . ."

"It just came out of nowhere, sir," Mishel Corcoram replied. *"Nowhere!"*

"There had to be something."

The lifelike image of Kaleed's senior administrator shrugged. "There was a . . . a minor protest scheduled for nineteen at the public center in Lavina." That was Kaleed's local admin complex.

Eight standard hours ago. "Go on."

"Our factors were there, of course, monitoring the situation. But the next thing socon knew, people were screaming 'natural liberty,' and then the Administrative Center was under attack by mobs wielding torches, battering rams, and weaponry seized from Administratia guards dispatched to quiet things down." The image looked away, as though studying the scenes of fire and night flickering in the nano e-paint coating Goradon's wall. "Star Lord . . . it's the end of Civilization!"

"Get a hold of yourself, Mish. Who are the combatants? What are they fighting about?"

"The stargods only know," Corcoram replied. He sounded bitter. "Reports have been coming in for a couple of hours, now, but they're . . . not making much sense. It sounds like r-Humans are fighting s-Humans . . . and both of them are fighting both Dalateavs and Gromanaedierc. And *everyone* is attacking socon personnel and machines on sight."

"A free-for-all, it sounds like."

"Pretty much, yeah."

Goradon shook his head. "But why?"

"Like I said, Lord. It's the collapse of Civilization!"

Which Goradon didn't believe for a moment. Mish Corcoram could be hyper-dramatic when the mood took him, and could pack volumes of emotion into the utterly commonplace. He was a good hab administrator—the effective ruler of the wheelworld known as Kaleed—but Ared Goradon was the administrator for the entire Rosvenier system . . . not just Kaleed, but some two thousand other wheelworlds, cylworlds, rings, troider habs, toroids, and orbital cols, plus three rocky planets, two gas giants, and the outposts and colonies on perhaps three hundred moons, planetoids, cometary bodies, and Kuiper ice dwarfs. His jurisdiction extended over a total population of perhaps three billion humans of several subspecies, and perhaps one billion Dalateavs, Gromanaedierc, Eulers, N'mah, Veldiks, and other nonhuman sapients or parasapients.

He could not afford to become flustered at the apparent social collapse of a single orbital habitat.

"Star Lord," his AI assistant whispered in his ear. *"Other reports are beginning to come through. There was some transmission delay caused by the damage to the Hub. It appears that similar scenes are playing out on a number of other system habs."*

"How many?"

"Four hundred seventeen colonies and major bases so far. But that number is expected to rise. This . . . event appears to be systemwide in scope."

On the wall, a remote camera drone captured a single, intensely brilliant pinpoint of light against the far side of the Wheel, nearly three thousand kilometers distant . . . perhaps in Usila, or one of the other antipodal cities. Gods of Chaos . . .

he could see the shockwave expanding as the pinpoint swelled, growing brighter. Had some idiot just touched off a *nuke*? . . .

"Star Lord," his assistant continued. *"I strongly recommend evacuation. You can continue your duties from the control center of an Associative capital ship."*

"What's close by?"

"The fleet carrier Drommond, *sir. And the heavy pulse cruiser* Enthereal."

Seconds ago, the very idea of abandoning Kaleed, of abandoning his home, had been unthinkable. But a second nuclear detonation was burning a hole through the wheeldeck foundation as he watched.

The fools, the bloody damned fools were intent on pulling down their house upon their own heads.

"Mish, on the advice of my AI, I'm transferring command to a warship. I recommend that you do the same."

"I . . . but . . . do you think that's wise?"

"I don't know about wise. But the situation here is clearly out of control, yours and mine."

"But what are we going to—"

The electronic image of the Kaleed senior administrator flicked out. On the wall, a third city had just been annihilated in a burst of atomic fury—Bethelen, which was, Goradon knew, where Mish lived.

Where he *had* lived, past tense.

Goradon was already jogging for the personal travel pod behind a nearby wall that would take him spinward to the nearest port. He might make it.

"What I'm going to do," he called to the empty air, as if Mish could still hear him, "is call for help."

"What help?" his AI asked as he palmed open the hatch and squeezed into the pod.

"I'm going to have them send in the Marines," he said.

It was something Goradon had never expected to say.

1

2101.2229

Associative Marine Holding Facility 4
Eris Orbital, Outer Sol System
1542 hours, GMT

Marine General Trevor Garroway felt the familiar jolt and retch as he came out of cybe-hibe sleep, the vivid pain, the burning, the hot strangling sensation in throat and lungs as the hypox-perfluorate nanogel blasted from his lungs.

The dreams of what was supposed to be a dreamless artificial coma shredded as he focused on his first coherent thought. *Whoever is bringing me out had better have a damned good reason. . . .*

Blind, coughing raggedly, he tried to sit up. He felt as though he were drowning, and kept trying to cough up the liquid filling his lungs. "Gently, sir," a female voice said. "Don't try to do it all at once. Let the nano clear itself."

Blinking through the sticky mess covering his eyes, Garroway tried to see who was speaking. He could see patterns of glaring light and fuzzy darkness, now, including one nearby shadowy mass that might have been a person. "Who's . . . that?"

"Captain Schilling, sir. Ana Schilling." Her voice carried a trace of an accent, but he couldn't place it. "I'm your Temporal Liaison Officer."

"Temporal . . . what?"

"You've been under a long time, General. I'm here to help you click in."

A hundred questions battled one another for first rights of expression, but he clamped down on all of them and managed a shaky nod as reply. With the captain's help, he sat up in his opened hibernation pod as the gel—a near-frictionless parafluid consisting of nanoparticles—dried instantly to a gray powder streaming from his naked body. He'd trained for this, of course, and gone through the process several times, so at least he knew what to expect. Focusing his mind, bringing to bear the control and focus of Corps weiji-do training, he concentrated on deep, rhythmic breathing for a moment. His first attempts were shallow and painful, but as he pulled in oxygen, each breath inactivated more and more of the nanogel in his lungs. Within another few seconds, the last of the gel in his lungs had either been expelled or absorbed by his body.

And his vision was clearing as well. The person-sized mass resolved itself into an attractive young woman wearing what he assumed was a uniform—form-fitting gray with blue and red trim. The only immediately recognizable element, however, was the ancient Marine emblem on her collar—a tiny globe and anchor.

Gods . . . how long had it been? He reached into his mind to pull up the date, and received a shock as profound as the awakening itself.

"Where's my implant?" he demanded.

"Ancient tech, General," Schilling told him. "You're way overdue for an upgrade."

For just a moment, panic clawed at the back of his mind. *He had no implant!* . . .

Sanity reasserted itself. Like all Marines, Garroway had gone without an implant during his training. *All* Marines did, during recruit training or, in the case of officers, during their physical indoctrination in the first year of OCS or the

Commonwealth Naval Academy. The theory was that there would be times when Marines were operating outside of established e-networks—during the invasion of a hostile planet, for instance.

He *knew* he could manage without it. That was why all recruits were temporarily deprived of any electronic network connection or personal computer, to prove that they could survive as well as any pretechnic savage.

But that didn't make it pleasant, or easy. He felt . . . empty. Empty, and impossibly alone. He couldn't mind-connect with anyone else, couldn't rely on local node data bases for information, news, or situation alerts, couldn't monitor his own health or interact with local computers such as the ones that controlled furniture or environmental controls, couldn't even do math or check the time or learn the freaking date without going through . . .

He started laughing.

Schilling looked at him with concern. "Sir? What's funny?"

"I'm a fucking Marine major general," he said, tears streaming down his face, "and I'm feeling as lost as any raw recruit in boot camp who finds he can't 'path his girlfriend."

"It can be . . . disorienting, sir. I know."

"I'm okay." He said it again, more firmly. "I'm okay. Uh . . . how long has it been?" He looked around the room. A number of other gray-clad personnel worked over cybehibe pods set in a circle about the chamber. Odd. This was *not* the storage facility he remembered . . . it seemed like just moments ago. His eyes widened. "What's the date?"

Schilling leaned forward slightly, staring into his eyes. Her eyes, he noted, were a lustrous gold-green, and could not be natural. Genetically enhanced, he wondered? Surgical replacements? Or natural genetic drift? She seemed to be looking inside him, as though gauging his emotional stability.

"The year," she said after a moment, "is 2229 *Annum Manus,* the Year of the Corps. Or 4004 of the Current Era, if you prefer, or Year 790 of the Galactic Associative. Take your pick. Does that help?"

He wasn't sure. His brow furrowed as he tried to work through some calculations without the aid of his cerebral implant. The numbers were slippery, and kept wiggling out of his mental grasp. "I went under in . . . wait? I've been under for something over eight hundred years?"

"Very good, sir. According to our records, your last period on active duty was from 1352 through 1377 A.M." Her head cocked to one side. "I believe you called it 'M.E.' in your day. The 'Marine Era?' "

" 'A.M.' means . . . *meant* something quite different. Antimatter. Or morning, if you were a civilian."

She looked puzzled. "Morning? I don't think I know that one."

"From 'antimeridian.' Before the sun is overhead."

"Ah. A planet-based reference, then." She dismissed the idea with a casual shrug. "In any case, you were promoted to brigadier general in 1374, and were instrumental in the victory at Cassandra in 1376. The following year—that would be 3152 by the old-style calendar—you elected to accept a promotion to major general and long-term cybe-hibe internment in lieu of mandatory retirement."

"Of *course* I did. I wasn't even two centuries old." His eyes narrowed. "How old are you, anyway, Captain?"

She grinned. "Old enough. Older than I look, anyway."

"Genetic antiagathic prostheses?"

"Some," she admitted. "There are a fair number of people alive in the Associative now who are pushing a thousand, and that's not counting uploaders. Partly genetic prosthesis, partly nanogenetic enhancement. And I've spent two tours so far inside one of those pods."

"Really?" He was impressed. "In the names of all the gods and goddesses, why?"

She shrugged again. "Cultural disjunct, I suppose."

"Copy that." The gulf between civilian life and life in the

Marine Corps had been enormous even back in his day. It might be considerably worse now.

"The Corps is my home," she added. "Most of my family was on Actinia."

He heard the pain in her voice, and decided not to question her further on that. Evidently, he'd missed a lot of history. Eight centuries' worth.

The numbers finally came together for him. "Okay. I've been out of it for 852 years. I take it there's a crisis?"

Again, that perplexed look. "What makes you think that, sir?"

"An old expression, ancient even in my day," he replied. " 'In case of war, break glass.' "

"I . . . don't understand, sir."

"Never mind." He looked around the chamber that had changed so much in eight centuries. Eleven other pods rested quietly in alcoves around the oval space. His command constellation. The other waking personnel appeared to be working at reviving them. "What'd they do, rebuild the place around us?"

"Moved you to a larger facility, about three hundred years ago. You're in Eris Ring, now."

"Huh. We got hibed in Noctis Lab. On Mars."

"That facility was closed, sir, not long after they brought you up here. The whole of Mars is military-free, now. The Associative's been downscaling all of the military services for a long time, now."

"I see." He was looking forward to catching up on history. It promised to be very interesting indeed. "Eris? A planetoid?"

"Dwarf planet, Sir. Sol system . . . one of the scatter-disk objects."

"TNO," Garroway said, nodding. "I know." Trans-Neptunian Objects was a catch-phrase for some thousands of worlds and worldlets circling Sol beyond the orbit of Neptune, most beyond even the Kuiper Belt. Eris, in fact, according to history downloads he'd scanned, had been responsible for down-grading another dwarf planet—Pluto—from its former status as a full-fledged planet. That had been over a thousand years ago—no. He stopped himself. *Two* thousand years ago.

He nodded toward the other personnel working on the silent cybe-hibe pods. "They're recalling my people?"

"Yes, sir. But the orders were to wake you first. Then your command staff. Protocol. Your brigade will not be revived until you've received a full briefing, and give the appropriate orders."

"Okay. You know, you didn't answer my question, Captain."

"Which one, sir?"

"Is there a crisis?"

"So I gather. I don't have any details, though. You'll get that in your briefing download."

"I expect I will." Carefully, he swung his legs out of the pod recess, his bare feet reaching for the deck. Most of the nanogel was gone, now. He glanced down at himself, then at Captain Schilling. "Hm. I trust there are no nudity taboos in this century."

She smiled. "No, sir. Nothing like that. But I have a uniform for you, if you want to be presentable for your constellation when they come around."

"Good idea. But food first, I think. Uh, no . . . maybe a shower . . ."

"Both are waiting for you, General. Do you feel like you can stand, yet?"

"Not sure. But I sure as hell intend to try." His feet found the deck. He swayed alarmingly, but with Schilling's help, he managed to stay on his feet. She had a floater chair waiting for him in case he needed it, but full muscular control reasserted itself swiftly and he waved it away, preferring to do this on his own if he could. The cybe-hibe procedure permeated the body with molecule-sized machines that did everything from arresting cell metabolism to keeping muscle groups healthy, if inactive. There was some stiffness, and a few unsteady moments as he relearned how to keep his balance, but surprisingly few aftereffects of an eight-century sleep.

Eight centuries? How much had the world, the *Galaxy,* changed? How much had *Humankind* changed? When he'd entered cybe-hibe—it seemed literally like just last night— there'd been the bright promise of a new, golden age. The dread, ancient enemy, the xenophobic Xul, had been defeated at last. Across a Galaxy that had seemed a desert in terms of sentient life—where only a handful of reclusive or unusually sequestered intelligent species had survived the Xul predations—more and more nonhuman cultures were being discovered, contacted, and invited to join the loose and somewhat freewheeling association that was then being called the Galactic Commonwealth.

Now it was being called the Associative? There would be other changes, of course, besides the name. He found himself anxious to learn them . . . as well as a bit afraid.

The shower proved to be a transparent cylinder giving him a choice of traditional water at any temperature, high-frequency sound waves, or total immersion in a thin, hazy nano-parafluid programmed to cleanse his skin while permitting him to continue breathing normally. He chose water, more for the stimulation of the pounding on his skin than anything else. Garroway found he needed the liaison officer's help, though. Without his implant, he couldn't interact with the damned shower controls.

When he was clean and dry, Schilling gave him a button-sized pellet that, when pressed against his chest and activated by her thought, swiftly grew into a skin-tight set of dark gray neck-to-soles utilities. It was, he thought grimly, downright embarrassing. Here he was a Marine major general, and he couldn't even bathe or dress himself without the captain's help.

Then she led him into the mess hall, and he realized just

how much things had *really* changed as he'd slept down through the centuries. . . .

The compartment was large and spherical, with much of one entire half either transparent, or, more likely, a deck-to-overhead viewall with exceptional clarity. The view was . . . stunning, a blue and white swatch of dazzling light, a sharp-edged crescent, arcing away beneath a brilliant, pinpoint sun.

But for a moment, Garroway was utterly lost. It *looked* like Earth, with those piercing, sapphire blues and swirls of cloud-whites. But the sun was all wrong, far too tiny, far too brilliant, a spark, not a disk.

For just a moment, he wondered if something had happened to the sun during his long sleep. Then he wondered if he'd misunderstood the captain, that *this* Eris was not the frigid dwarf planet in Sol's outer system, but an Earthlike world of some other, utterly alien star.

"That *can't* be Earth's sun," he said, squinting at the pinpoint. "It's way too bright." He could see a distinct bluish tinge to the intense white of its glare.

"No, sir," Schilling told him. She smiled.

"And since when do tiny little icebox planetoids have their own atmosphere and water?"

"Terraforming has come a long way, General," Schilling told him. "That's not Sol. It's Dysnomia."

"Dysnomia." He blinked. In his day, Eris had been an ice, rock, and frozen methane worldlet 2500 kilometers in diameter, about eight percent larger than, and 27 percent more massive than, Pluto. Discovered in the early twenty-first century, it had a highly inclined, highly eccentric orbit, but he couldn't remember the exact numbers without his implant. He knew the place was cold, though, down around twenty-five Kelvins or so, a scant twenty-five degrees above zero absolute. Dysnomia had been a tiny satellite of Eris, like Pluto's Charon, but smaller, a rock only 150 kilometers across.

"The Eridian satellite," Schilling told him. "About five hundred years ago, they planted a quantum converter on it and turned it into a microstar. It's tiny, but it's only about thirty-seven thousand kilometers from the planet. Orbits once in fifteen standard days. The converter provides enough heat to warm Eris, and the nanoforming matrix is doing the rest."

"You're losing me, Captain. They turned a 150-kilometer asteroid into a star, and then . . . what? Nanoforming?"

"Terraforming, using nanoreplicators and assemblers. Breaking methane, ammonia, and water ice into water, oxygen, nitrogen, and carbon."

"And the star goes around the planet, instead of the other way around?"

"Exactly. Eris still rotates beneath it, though, and has a day . . ." She paused, closing her eyes as she checked a data base through her implant, "of twenty-eight hours and some."

He looked into the achingly beautiful blue of the planet's crescent. "Terraforming a planet doesn't happen overnight. How long before people are living there?"

"Oh, they're living there now. Not many . . . a few hundred thousand. Mostly military at this point. Most of them are Eulers, actually, in the Deeps. The atmosphere won't be breathable for another few centuries, and the storms are still pretty bad, but they started colonizing it as soon as stable continents emerged from the world ocean."

"Continents."

A globe appeared in the air as Schilling sent a request through her implant, blue and brown, without cloud cover.

"Three main continents," she said, and each highlighted itself on the projection in turn as she named it. "Brown, Trujillo, and Rabinowitz. Those were the discoverers of Eris, way back when. Two minor continents over here . . . Xena and Gabrielle." She paused, then frowned. "Strange. No data on where those names came from."

Garroway thought about this as Schilling led him to a table and two chairs that seemed to grow out of the deck as they approached. The technology *had* changed, and changed tremendously if Humankind was able now to create *stars*, even small ones. That was only to be expected, of course. Human technology had been in a rapidly upward-lunging, almost logarithmic curve since the eighteenth or nineteenth century.

He took one of the chairs, as Schilling sat in the other. She placed one hand, palm down, on a colored patch on the table. "What would you like to eat?"

"Captain, I have no idea. Choose something for me."

A white, plastic hemisphere materialized in front of each of them; seconds later, the hemispheres evaporated, revealing their meals. Garroway wasn't sure what it was—there was something that might be meat, something else that might be starchy, a third thing that was brilliant green—but he decided not to ask questions. The stuff was edible—in fact, delicious—whatever it was, and that was all he needed to know for the moment.

Other Marine personnel were in the mess hall as well, though the cavernous room was not close to being filled. The others kept their distance, however, though he saw numerous glances and curious stares. He found himself trying to listen in on conversations at the nearest tables. He was curious. How much had Anglic changed in eight centuries? Did they even speak an Anglic-derived tongue, now, or had the vagaries of history brought some other language to the fore?

Again, he decided to wait rather than bombard Schilling with questions. While he could hear voices, the nearby conversations seemed muffled, somehow, and he suspected that some sort of privacy field was blanketing the compartment.

Thirty minutes or so later, he leaned back, watching his empty plate dissolve back into the table surface. "Well, if that was a sample of the food in the forty-first century, I could get to like this time."

"You'll like it more with your implant."

"Eh?"

"You'll find nanotech is a part of just about everything

now, including what you eat. And your implant has programs that let you respond in subtle ways to nano-treated food. Speaking of which . . . here." She handed him a small inhaler. He hadn't seen where she'd been carrying it on that painted-on uniform, and wondered if she'd materialized it out of the table the same way as she'd summoned their meals.

"What's this?"

"Your new implant. We needed you to get a meal into your stomach first, so the implant nano has some raw material to work with. Just press that tip into a nostril and touch the release."

He followed her directions. A warm, moist puff of air invaded his sinuses, and he tasted metal.

"The nano is programmed to follow the olfactory nerve into the brain," she told him. "It knows where to go, and will begin chelating into imbedded circuits almost immediately. You'll find yourself coming back on-line within an hour or two. Full growth will be completed within twenty hours or so."

"That's good." He was still feeling shaken at the emptiness he felt without an e-connect. Damn, what had people done before cerebral implants? "And this'll be better than my old one, huh?"

"Oh, yeah. A lot. You'll be amazed."

"I don't know. Takes a lot to amaze me. What about Lofty?"

She cocked her head again. " 'Lofty?' Who—"

"My essistant. Personal secretary and Divisional AI. Named for Major Lofton Henderson."

"Oh, I see. Your personal software has all been backed up in the facility network. You'll get it all back with the download. Who is Major Henderson?"

"Check your Corps history download, Captain," he said with stern disapproval. "He was a Marine aviator in the pre-spaceflight era. He commanded VMSB-241 at the Battle of Midway in the year 167 of the Marine Era. Killed in action leading a glide-bomb attack against the aircraft carrier *Hiryu*. Won a posthumous Navy Cross."

"Yes, sir."

"Son of a bitch."

"Pardon, sir?"

"Nothing. I just realized that I rattled that off without consulting my implant data base. Maybe there's hope for me yet."

"I'm *very* sure there is, General."

"So what does a . . . what did you call yourself? A temporal liaison do?"

"Lots of people are disoriented when they come out of cybe-hibe, sir. And even with the download, they can feel . . . isolated. Cut off. I'm here as a kind of a guide. I can answer questions. And, well, I know what you're going through. What you're feeling. I can reassure you that you're not as alone as you might feel."

"If there's still a Corps, I won't be alone," he said. "I confess, though, that I'm a little surprised there still *is* a Marine Corps. There was talk back in the early thirtieth about disbanding us. The Corpsman who put me under down in Noctis Lab offered to bet me that he'd be waking me up again within the year . . . that I'd end up being retired, anyway. I take it that didn't happen?"

"If *you'll* check your Corps history, General, you'll recall that the Marine Corps has always been threatened with disbanding. Why maintain a separate military organization when there's the regular army?"

That, Garroway thought, was the absolute truth. Since the creation of the Continental Marines in 1775, the Corps had been a kind of bastard unwanted child—*except* when there was a war on. During peacetime, it was budget battles and second-line equipment, "Truman's police force" and "in case of war, break glass." Once the shooting started, though, it was *send in the Marines*.

In fact, the whole Marine cybe-hibe holding facility was an outgrowth of that millennia-old problem. Even well before the thirtieth century, what Schilling had casually referred to as "cultural disjunct" had been a serious issue within the Corps. Marines tended to stick together, to evolve their own unique culture with their own language and their own ways of looking at the world, and that culture was generally at sharp odds with the local civilian background. The problem had become even worse in the early days of interstellar military operations, when Marine units were packed away in cybe-hibe and deployed to star systems light years away; those units might return to Earth two decades or more after they'd left, aged—thanks to the combined effects of hibernation and relativistic time dilation—only a couple of years. Men and women already isolated from the civilian population by the Marine microculture found themselves even more isolated by twenty years of social change—and the aging or death of any friends or relatives left behind.

Small wonder that Marines tended to form bonded relationships with Marines, that there were traditional Marine family lines going back, in some cases, two thousand years. Garroway's great-grandfather had been Gunnery Sergeant Aiden Garroway, who'd taken part in the op that had broken the back of the ancient Xul menace at the Galactic Core in the twenty-ninth century. And there were records of Garroways going much, much further back. There'd been a remote ancestor—immortalized in Corps legend as "Sands of Mars Garroway"—back in the mid-twenty-first, even before the first voyages to other stars.

He started to make a mental note to check and see if there were any Garroways around now. He'd had two kids, Ami and Jerret, before his first stint in cybe-hibe. Their mother had discouraged contact with him, damn her, and they'd been distant after the break-up. But maybe enough time had passed for their descendents. . . .

He shook off the thickening mood, electing instead to

stare up at the impossibly blue and white curve of Eris and the tiny glare of Dysnomia, hanging in the sky above the mess deck.

A new century. A new millennium.

He was looking forward to that download.

Upper Stratosphere, Dac IV
Star System 1727459
1820 hours, GMT

The RS/A-91 strikepod plunged out of the upper haze deck into a calm and empty gulf, and Marine Lieutenant Marek Garwe shifted from tactical to optical. Salmon-pink cloud walls towered in all directions, like vast and fuzzy-looking cliffs with gently curved and wind-sculpted faces. The haze layer above was composed mostly of crystals of water ice, scattering the local star's light, turning the sky a deep, royal blue, with a ghostly halo about the sun.

Below, the cloud canyon yawned into darkness. The next cloud deck was over forty kilometers below, deeply shadowed in the depths beyond the slanting reach of the rays of a distant sun. Intermediate cloud layers indicated updrafts, including a vast spiral in the distance of a storm. Most astonishing was the sheer scale of the vista ahead and below; the opening in the cloud layer appeared to be dozens of kilometers wide and deep, but Garwe's instrument feeds showed the empty gulf to be nearly four hundred kilometers across.

Dac IV was a gas giant, a little smaller than Jupiter in the distant Sol system, but with the same wind-whipped cloud bands and rotating storm cells in an atmosphere that was 99 percent hydrogen and helium. The 1 percent or so left over was mostly methane and ammonia, plus the poisonous soup of chemical compounds constantly upwelling from the world's interior that gave the planet's clouds their spectacular range of color.

Characteristic of most gas giants, Dac IV had no solid

surface, which meant that Garwe's confused and constantly shifting altitude readings were irrelevant; below his hurtling RS/A-91 Starwraith's hull, the atmosphere grew steadily denser and hotter until it was compressed into metallic hydrogen.

"Tighten up your formation, people," a voice whispered in his mind. "Objective now reads as 150 kilometers ahead." Captain Corolin Xander was the CO of Anchor Marine Strike Squadron 340, "The War Dogs," currently operating as Blue Flight. Her Starwraith was somewhere ahead and off Garwe's starboard sponson, invisible even to his amplified senses as the squadron plunged toward Hassetas floatreef.

"I'm being painted," Lieutenant Amendes, in Blue Two, reported. "Intense EM scans, all bands."

"They can't be sure of what they're seeing," Xander replied. "They may not even be getting anything back."

"Oh, they see us, all right," Lieutenant Bakewin said. "They see *something*. Scans are increasing in power."

Starwraiths were encased in the latest wrinkle in nanoflage, a layer of active nano designed to render the two-meter craft effectively invisible by bending all incoming electromagnetic radiation around the smoothly curved surfaces. Pod-to-pod communication was strictly quantum nonlocal, meaning there were no transmissions to give the sender away.

But Dac technology was still a major unknown. How the Dacs had even developed technology in the first place—with no mines, no metallurgy, no heavy industry, no fire—was the subject of ongoing xenosociotechnic debate, and the principal reason for the Associative Compound on Hassetas.

The twelve tiny pods comprising Blue Flight leveled off when they reached the expected Hassetasan depth. In popular human thought, gas giants like Dac IV, those located in their star's outer system rather than in close to their star, were *cold* . . . and so they were at the thin, upper layers of their outer cloud decks. The deeper into the atmosphere a flier plunged, however, the thicker and hotter the gas mix became. At this depth, the atmospheric pressure was about eight times human standard, and the temperature outside the Starwraith's hull hovered at around the freezing point of water. The day, by most human standards, was positively balmy . . . at least when compared to temperatures higher or lower in the intensely stratified volume of Dac's turbulent atmosphere.

Ahead, a cloud wall rose like an impenetrable cliff, a vast pink-brown cliff with a looming, mushroom-shaped top, with wind-carved striations running along its face.

"Reduce velocity, Blues," Xander ordered. "We're going subsonic."

The flight plunged into the face of the cloud-cliff, as the individual pods were buffeted somewhat by windstreams whipping around the cloud at 300 kilometers per hour. At eight atmospheres, with an H/He gas mix, the speed of sound was nearly 2400 kph, so the local winds were little more than zephyrs.

The clouds thickened until optical feeds were useless; Garwe shifted again to tactical, though there was little useful information the system could give him now—radiation flux, gas mix and pressure, temperature and windspeed, projected position of the other eleven pods of Blue Flight.

And, ahead, the beacon marking Hassetas.

Moments later, the flight emerged into another crystalline gulf, the interior of a vast spiral of clouds marking a hot updraft from below.

And ahead, an immense, gossamer bubble almost transparent in the sunlight, was the Dac living city called Hassetas.

"Hassetas airspace control," Xander's voice snapped out, crisp and concise, "this is Associative Marine Flight Blue on docking approach. Acknowledge."

There was no immediate reply, and the silence was a palpable, imminent threat. Had the Hassetas crisis worsened during Blue Flight's descent from Tromendet, Dac IV's largest moon? There could be no doubt that weapons—highly advanced and lethal weapons—were trained on the tiny Marine pods now approaching the living floatreef.

The Marines had just called the Dacs' bluff and sent their squadron into the heart of this latest crisis, and now it was up to the Krysni jellyfish—and the sapient floatreef they served—to decide how to respond.

Would it be peace, and an invitation to land?

Or the triggering of a savage curtain of high-energy weaponry?

Garwe found he was holding his breath, waiting for the reply. . . .

2

Associative Marine Holding Facility 4
Eris Orbital, Outer Sol System
1845 hours, GMT

Trevor Garroway leaned back in a reclining seat grown by Captain Schilling from the deck of the large compartment she called the Memory Room. "You sure we can start this so soon?" he asked her. "You said it would take twenty hours to grow a new implant."

The easy stuff is already in place, she told him. It took Garroway a moment to realize that she hadn't spoken aloud, that her mouth hadn't moved as she'd said the words. His implant was already picking up the transmitted thoughts of others with his implant encoding.

So . . . can you hear this? he thought, forcing the words out one by one in his mind.

Ouch, yes, she replied. *You don't need to shout. We're connected over your basic personal link-channel. Others will be added later. You can also use that channel to begin downloading library data. You don't have much in the way of artificial storage, yet—only about a pic of memory so far—but the link will let you download the gist to your native memory. You'll just need to review it to see what's there.*

So what memories are you giving me now? he asked.

A general history of the past two thousand years, she told him, *with emphasis on the Xul wars and subsequent social and technological development within the sphere of Humankind . . . what you knew as the Commonwealth. The rise of the Associative. A little bit of Galactic history, as we now understand it. Not much detail, here, not yet . . . just what you'll need to put things into context later.*

When you finally tell me what the goddamn crisis is that warrants pulling a Marine Star Battalion out of cold storage, he said, nodding. *Gotcha.*

Exactly. Are you comfortable? Ready to begin?

He took a deep breath as he settled back into the too-comfortable chair. *Ready as I can be, Captain. Shoot. . . .*

And the images began coming down, a trickle at first, and then a flood.

It would, he realized, take him a long time to go through these new memories. Each distinct memory, each fact or date or historical event, did not, *could* not exist in isolation, but was a part of a much larger matrix. Until he had access to a lot more information, these bits and pieces would tend to remain discreet, unconnected, and essentially meaningless within the far vaster and more complex whole.

One thing, though, was clear immediately. The aliens were coming out of hiding.

He already remembered, of course, the history of the Xenophobe Wars. The Xul—electronically uploaded nonhuman sentients who'd apparently been around for at least the past ten million years—had been the dominant Galactic species, taking control of much of the Galaxy from a predecessor species known as the Children of the Night. The Xul had brought some evolutionary baggage forward in their advance to sapience—notably a hard-wired survival trait that led them, in rather overenthusiastically Darwinian fashion, to utterly obliterate any other species that might constitute a threat. The Xul, it turned out, had been the answer to the age-old question known as the Fermi Paradox. In a Galaxy ten to twelve billion years old, which, given the number of planets and the sheer tenacity and inventiveness of life, should be teeming with intelligent species, the sky was curiously empty. When Humankind had first ventured into its own Solar backyard, then on to the worlds of other nearby suns, it had encountered numerous relics indicating that various species had passed that way before—the Cydonian Face on Mars, the Tsiolkovsky Complex on Luna, the planetwide ruins of Chiron. . . .

Eventually, other species had been encountered, and communications begun: the An of Llalande 21185, low-tech remnants of an earlier, vanished stellar empire; the amphibious N'mah, living a precarious rats-in-the-walls existence inside the Sirius Stargate, again the survivors of a once far-flung network of interstellar traders; the Eulers, benthic life forms from the ocean deeps of a world twelve hundred light years from Sol, with a curiously mathematical outlook on Reality and the technology to detonate stars.

All three species had encountered the Xul scourge, and all three had survived, albeit barely. The Eulers had fought the Xul more or less to a standstill by exploding many of their own stars—creating funereal pyres visible as anomalous novae in Earth's night skies in the constellation of Aquila, back in the early years of the twentieth century. The N'mah had gone into hiding, deliberately abandoning interstellar travel in favor of survival. The An colony on a gas giant moon had simply been overlooked, and without radio or other attention-getting technologies, had managed to stay overlooked for the next ten to twelve thousand years.

The Xul, it turned out, had possessed a singular blind spot. Though no longer corporeal, existing as arguably self-aware software within huge and complex computer networks, they'd obviously begun as biological life forms—quite possibly as a number of them—arising on worlds that must have been similar in most respects to Earth in terms of temperature range, gravity, and atmospheric composition. Their blind spot was an inability to see outside of the ecological box; they tended to overlook other possible environments that might harbor life. The current An homeworld, for instance, was an Earth-sized moon of a gas giant, heated from within by tidal flexing, but far outside the so-called habitable zone of the system's cool, red-dwarf star. The N'mah lived inside entirely artificial but necessary structures, the ten- or twenty-kilometer-wide stargates constructed by a far older, long-vanished congeries of star-faring species. And the Eulers, six-eyed tentacled chemovores evolving near deep-ocean volcanic vents, lived under such crushing pressures that they might have remained forever unnoticed by the Xul hunterships if they hadn't possessed minds brilliant enough, and curious enough, to develop—through artificially crafted intelligent life forms and a patience spanning perhaps millions of years—the technology to venture into interstellar space.

All of that had been well known and understood by the time Garroway had joined the Marine Corps, in the twenty-eighth century. During the next few hundred years of his Marine career, perhaps half a dozen other intelligent species had been discovered—the Vorat, the widely scattered Nathga, the Chthuli. Again, nonterrestrial habitats had kept them hidden from the Xul. The Vorat were thermic chemovores, dwelling on high-temperature, high-pressure worlds similar to Venus in Earth's solar system. The Nathga were jelly-bag floaters that had evolved in the upper cloud levels of a world like Jupiter, eventually developing the technology that had allowed them to slowly migrate to some thousands of similar gas giants across a good third of the Galaxy. And the Chthuli, like the Eulers, were a benthic species that had colonized the ocean basins of several oceanic worlds.

But across the Galaxy, world after world showed the silent ruins marking the passing of sentient species akin to Humans, in terms of environmental preference and carbon chemistry if not outward form, all blasted into premature extinction by the xenophobic Xul.

Now, however, some twelve hundred years after the final

defeat of the Xul at the Galactic Core, hundreds of nonhuman species had been discovered and contacted to one degree or another. Many had joined the original Terran Commonwealth in a kind of Galactic United Nations—the Associative.

Many of the more recently discovered species, however, were so alien that they shared little common ground with humans. Communications were difficult, even impossible, with species that communicated by smell or by changing patterns on their integuments or through subtle modulations of their bodies' electrical fields, with beings that didn't understand the concept of *union*, or with entities that thought so slowly they didn't even appear to be aware of more ephemeral species flitting in and out about them.

Garroway's curiosity was piqued as new memories surfaced of strange cultures and alien biologies. He tried querying the data base, hoping to get imagery of some of these beings . . . then realized his curiosity would have to wait until his implant had grown in fully. He didn't have that capability yet.

His military training noticed one important difference between the Associative and the old Commonwealth. There no longer was such a thing as "human space" . . . or borders between stellar nations. While there *were* interstellar empires out there, few individual species competed for the same type of real estate, and the "territories" of dozens of different species overlapped. It had been centuries before the Nathga were discovered adrift within the atmospheres of gas giants inside star systems already colonized by humans. The concept of distinct borders had been lost over half a millennium ago.

How, Garroway wondered, did governments control their own volumes of space? Did they even try . . . and what changes did that mean for military strategy? For that matter, if there was little or no competition between governments, why was there a need for the military at all?

And why was there still such a thing as the Marine Corps?

Surprisingly, he found himself little impressed with the purely technological advances of the past eight hundred years. Most of what he was seeing as new memories continued to surface were further developments of old themes. Interstellar travel still required a mix of the Alcubierre Drive and the huge stargates left behind by a vanished, Galaxy-spanning culture. Quantum power taps, much smaller than the ones Garroway had known, still provided the vast quantities of energy necessary for FTL travel. Nanotechnology had continued its inexorable advance toward the ever-smaller, ever-smarter. Perhaps the most notable technological advances had come in the fields of health and medicine. Some of what he was seeing now he didn't begin to understand. What the hell *was* mindkeeping, anyway? Or upload therapy? . . .

The Xul threat, he noted, had not entirely vanished after the climactic battle at the Galaxy's core two decades before he'd been born. Xul nodes—local networks and fleet centers where they'd kept watch over the Galaxy for developing technic cultures—continued to be discovered from time to time, and had to be eliminated one by one. However, thanks to data retrieved from the Galactic center, Xul codes, software, and upload technology all were now well-enough understood that the ongoing mop-up had been turned over to AI assault units. Unmanned probes mimicking Xul hunterships would approach a target system and infect the local node with nanotech devices allowing the assault unit to literally reprogram the local Xul reality. When incoming data suggested that there was a threat that needed to be eliminated, the Xul virtual reality was simply rewritten on the fly to prove that the threat had *already* been eliminated.

And so far, the technique appeared to be working. There'd been no new Xul incursions in eight hundred years, and hundreds of Xul bases had subsequently been infiltrated and shut down from within. No new Xul nodes had been discovered in over two centuries, and most people thought that the last of the monsters had been found and destroyed.

Garroway knew better than to get too excited about that.

The Galaxy was an extraordinarily huge place, and more Xul nodes could be—almost certainly *were*—still out there, lost somewhere within that vastness of four hundred billion suns.

How's it going, General? Schillng's voice said, overriding the torrent of memories.

Okay, I guess, he replied. *Damn, there's a hell of a lot. . . .*

He felt her mental smile. *A lot can happen in eight hundred fifty years, in a collective culture that numbers in the hundreds of trillions of entities. Do you have any questions?*

Not yet. I don't know enough to know what to ask.

Okay. I've got a new download here. This one is mission specific. See what you think.

A moment later, Garroway came up for air. "Oh, gods," was all he could say.

The Xul he'd known had possessed one striking weakness. Different nodes were slow to share data, and individual nodes could be slow—centuries, sometimes—in responding to a perceived threat. They also didn't *change.* Tactics that had worked for millennia were not discarded, not changed, when opponents learned how they worked. It was one of the very few advantages Humankind had enjoyed in the long conflict, and the Marines had used it to their tactical advantage time after time.

According to this new download, though, the very worst had happened.

At long last, the Xul were adapting to the new situation with radically new tactics.

Hassetas, Dac IV
Star System 1727459
1850 hours, GMT

Garwe's RS/A-91 Starwraith strikepod was more than a space-capable fighter, and more than Marine combat armor. Just two meters long, it was just large enough inside to ac-

commodate a single Marine in coffin-like closeness, packed
in acceleration gel and hardwired into the unit's AI hardware.
It was shaped like an elongated egg, with smooth-flowing
bulges and swellings housing drive components and weaponry. Each was powered by a tiny quantum power tap, and
used base-state repulsor agrav both for propulsion and to allow the craft to hover in place. They could not travel faster
than light—Alcubierre Drive technology still required far
more power than a ten-kilo QPT could provide—but they had
virtually unlimited range and endurance. In one celebrated
instance, a piece of Marine lore, a Marine named Micuel
Consales had been stranded in a hostile star system by the
destruction of the Marine combat carrier *Vladivostok*. He'd
programmed the capsule to put him into deep cybe-hibe and
accelerate to near-light velocity. The pod had been retrieved
ninety-eight years later as it approached the nearest friendly
base, and Consales had successfully been revived.

That had been nearly four hundred years earlier, and the
technology had improved since then. A strikepod couldn't
go up against a capital ship, but it was fast, maneuverable,
and damned hard to track, which made it a key component
in the modern Marine arsenal. They could also be handled
remotely, in certain circumstances, which could be a real
advantage.

At the moment, Garwe and fifteen other Marines, each
wearing an RS/A-91 strikepod, were approaching the Hassetas floatreef, which filled the sky ahead of them.

One of the genuine shocks of galactic exploration had been
the discovery that even gas giants like Sol's Jupiter could harbor life. True, in an atmosphere that was mostly hydrogen,
with no solid surface, with fierce electromagnetic radiation
belts, and with wind speeds that could approach six or seven
hundred kilometers per hour, that life was going to be radically *different* from anything humans were familiar with.

But being different had kept them undiscovered by the
Xul and other predators.

Dac IV's native civilization had arisen from a close symbiosis between two evolving life forms—the Krysni and the Reefs.

The Reef was a vast bubble of tough but extremely light tissue, thirty kilometers or more across, and from a distance appearing as insubstantial as a soap bubble. Hanging below like rain shadow beneath a thunderhead was the living part of the Reef, a kind of aerial jungle growing on and within the tangled mass of tentacles trailing beneath the main gas bag. Exothermic chemistries heated the hydrogen within the gas bag, providing lift; hydrogen jets provided some directional movement, enough, at any rate, to let the vast creature steer clear of downdrafts that would drag it into the ferociously hot, high-pressure depths of the atmosphere.

Within the floatreef's remote evolutionary past, the tentacles would have evolved to capture smaller, more maneuverable fliers passing through the reef's shadow. Now, they were an immense and inverted forest providing habitats for tens of thousands of species. Hanging among the thicker tentacles were feeder nets, sheets of closely woven tentacle-threads that filtered organic material out of the atmosphere. Modern floatreefs were skygrazers, inhaling clouds of sulfur- and phosphorus-rich, locust-sized drifters called *irm*, the Dac equivalent of plankton or krill in distant Earth's oceans.

It was an evolutionary panorama relatively common throughout the Galaxy. A majority of Jovian-type gas giants possessed life, it had turned out, and the environmental constraints required that life to follow more or less similar patterns of form and function. The ten-kilometer montgolfiers of Jupiter had first been discovered late in the twenty-fourth century.

Far more rarely, gas giant ecosystems evolved intelligence. In Jupiter and most other gas giants, intelligence was an unnecessary luxury; grazers didn't need much in the way of brains to inhale clouds of drifting organics. But in Dac and a few hundred other gas giants discovered so far across the Galaxy, competition, the need to anticipate and avoid storms and downdrafts, and the elusive nature of local food animals had led to sentience at least as great as that of the extinct great whales of old Earth, and often to minds considerably greater and more powerful.

In Dac, according to the mission briefing downloads, there were at least *two* intelligent species living in close symbiosis—the floatreefs themselves and the Krysni.

Lieutenant Marek Garwe hovered vertically now in his Starwraith, half a meter above the deck of the Hassetas visitor tree house. The platform, constructed entirely of materials imported from distant, more solid worlds, was a good two hundred meters across, anchored against one of the major trunk-tentacles, three-quarters shrouded by the tentacle forest, and including a ramshackle assortment of buildings designed to accommodate each of seven or eight major biochemistries. Officially, the tree house was the offworlder compound, the reception center and living quarters for official delegations from other worlds to Dac. Currently, there were 224 visitors to the gas giant, including 57 humans of various species. The offworlders included Associative representatives, cultural liaisons, xenosophontologists and other scientific researchers, and formal diplomats.

Facing the twelve Marine wraiths were some tens of thousands of angry Krysni. Exactly *what* they were angry about had yet to be established. The call from the Dac offworlder compound, though, had been urgent, almost panicky. Four offworlders, all of them humans, had been killed by a sudden rising among the Krysni, and the remainder were terrified that the same was about to happen to them. Anchor Marine Strike Squadron 340 had been deployed from Laridis, some three hundred light years distant, to Tromendet in the Dac IV satellite system two days before. As the situation in the gas giant's upper atmosphere deteriorated, the War Dogs had been ordered in.

The Marines floated above the compound deck, now, facing the tentacle jungle, a near-solid wall of intertwining tubules ranging in size from main trunks nearly a hundred meters thick to slender threads, writhing and twisting in a constant background of motion. Within the net of tentacles were masses of Dacan—or, more properly, Hassetan—flora: pinkweed, Dacleaf, methane bloom, gas pods, and myriad others, most either orange or purple in color, with smaller amounts of pink and red. And it was within this wall of mottled and rustling vegetation that the Krysni mob had sequestered itself, shrieking in their piping, hydrogen-thin keenings and whistlings, the calls a cacophony of furious invective and hate. What the hell, Garwe wondered, had gotten into the simple-minded creatures?

"Hold your fire," Captain Xander ordered. "Let's see if they'll talk to us."

"I don't know, Skipper," Lieutenant Palin, Blue Five, said. "They don't look very friendly."

A single Krysni looked a bit like a terrestrial octopus about a meter long, but with a body that expanded or contracted at will like a variable-pressure balloon. Like their huge co-symbiote, the floatreef, they were balloonists, suspended from organic sacs of body-heated hydrogen that let them drift in the upper Dacan atmosphere, their three large, black eyes and cluster of feeding, sensory, and manipulative tentacles dangling below.

Garwe and the other Marines of Blue Flight had downloaded complete work-ups on the Krysni and the floatreefs, of course, as soon as they'd received their mission orders. One line of reasoning held that the Krysni were juvenile floatreefs, but few modern xenosophontologists accepted the notion. There were billions of Krysni, none more than a meter to a meter and a half in length, and perhaps twelve thousand floatreefs scattered through the vastnesses of the upper Dacan atmosphere, none less than ten kilometers across. If the one grew into the other, there ought to be a few intermediate sizes as well.

The likeliest theory was that the two were related but separate species, and that they existed in a close symbiosis. The floatreef took its name from terrestrial coral reefs, not because it looked like one, but because, like a marine reef, it provided a unique and stable habitat for a vast and complex ecology living within and around it. The reef provided food and shelter for the vulnerable Krysni, while the Krysni herded and cultivated the complex zoo of Dacan life within the floatreef's inverted forest, protecting their vast and sapient habitat from attack like sentient white blood cells. While the Krysni could float free, their preferred habitat was within the forest, their float bags flaccid as they used their tentacles to move through the tangle of vegetation and living branches of the undereef.

"This is Captain Xander, Associative Marine Force," the squadron CO said over the local Net frequency for the compound. "Who's in charge here?"

"I don't think any of us is in charge, exactly . . ." a voice replied.

"Then you are, now," Xander replied. "Who are you?"

"Vasek Trolischet," the voice said. "I'm the senior xenosoph here."

Blocks of data came up in a window within Garwe's mind, streaming through from the compound's data base. There was a vid, too, of a bald, dark-skinned human male with dazzling golden eyes. No, Garwe corrected himself. Not completely human, but a genegineered subspecies, an s-Human, *Homo sapiens superioris*. And apparently she was female.

Shit, a supie, one of the Marines broadcast on the squadron backchannel. *Just fucking great.*

"What happened here?" Xander asked the compound spokesperson.

"I don't know." The supie's words were clipped, tight, and rapid-fire, as though her time sense had been jacked into overdrive. "The baggies just went crazy! Attacked our research team while they were trying to get language samples, and tossed two of them over the edge! Then a whole mob swarmed in and got two more of our security team before anyone knew what was going on!"

"There had to be a reason," Xander said, deliberately

transmitting at a slower pace. "Do you have a translation frequency?"

"Yes, but their attempts at communication are still quite scrambled. Our heuristic algorithms are necessarily incomplete."

Garwe had to pull a definition for "heuristic" from his implant AI, and even then wasn't sure he understood how the person was using the word. The damned supies enjoyed talking above the heads of others, especially norms, and scuttlebutt around the barracks had it that they liked flaunting their so-called superiority.

An astronomical IQ hadn't stopped this one from getting into bad trouble, though. The Krysnis were beginning to advance over the tree house deck, inflating their bodies to taut, pale-blue bubbles over a meter across and drifting slowly toward the Marine line.

"Hold your fire," Xander repeated. "I don't think they're armed."

"They have *lots* of arms, Skipper," Lieutenant Malleta said, the nervousness in his voice at odds with the attempt at a joke. There were hundreds of the creatures in a mass in front of the Marines, now, their inflated bodies bumping and jostling with one another as they drifted forward.

"Halt!" Xander barked, speaking Standard, but the transmission translated to a sharp chirp by the translation algorithm from the compound. It sounded, Garwe thought, like the unpleasant squeak of a couple of rubber balloons rubbed together.

"Hey, Captain?" Lieutenant Bollan asked. "Those things are full of hydrogen, right? If we shoot 'em—"

"Use your head, Bollan," Xander replied. "There's no oxygen in the air to burn. No fire. No hydrogen explosion, okay?"

"Oh, yeah. Right."

Garwe had been thinking about that unpleasant possibility as well, and was able to relax a bit. The captain was right.

Shoot one of those gas bags with an electron arc and the thing might pop, but it wouldn't go up in flames. The entire ecosystem within this world's atmosphere relied on metabolic processes that took in methane and ammonia, metabolized them for carbon and the nitrogen, and gave off hydrogen. Oxygen was present, but only as a part of trace chemical compounds like water vapor, carbon dioxide, or sulfuric or nitric acids. Fires needed *free* oxygen to burn, and that just wasn't going to happen in the reducing atmosphere of a gas giant.

The mass of Krysni continued to drift forward. "*Shoot* them, Xander!" the s-Human was shouting over the link. "*Shoot* the little gasbag smugglers!"

An indicator light went on in Garwe's in-head display, indicating that Lieutenant Sanders was charging his primary weapon; a thought would trigger it. "Belay that, Sanders!" Xander snapped. "All of you! Primaries on safe!"

Reluctantly, Garwe safed his weapons. Marine battlepods *should* be strong enough to protect them from anything this crowd could throw at them.

Starwraith design, actually, was based on the robotic combat machines developed by the Xul. Normally the outer surface was smooth and unadorned, marked only by a dozen or so randomly placed lenses of various optical and electronic scanners. At need, Garwe could extrude a number of manipulative tentacles, heavier graspers, or weapons, the members growing out of the pod's surface through nanotechnic hull flow and controlled directly by his thoughts. The pod was actually extraordinarily plastic, capable of assuming a wide range of shapes limited only by its total mass of about two hundred kilos, and the need to maintain a roughly human-sized and -shaped inner capsule to protect the wearer/pilot.

Each pod also possessed a number of high-tech defense systems, and Marine training included long hours of practice in the pod-encased equivalent of hand-to-hand combat.

Again, Xander addressed the crowd. "You are trespassing

on diplomatic territory!" she called, the translation going out as shrill chirps and whistles. "Leave this area at once! Return to your reef—"

And then the jostling, bumping mob surged forward, each Krysni launching itself on a jet of hot hydrogen.

And the Battle of Hassetas had begun.

3

Associative Marine Holding Facility 4
Eris Orbital, Outer Sol System
1858 hours, GMT

"According to this," Garroway said aloud, "the Xul have been caught counterinfecting our nets. How long has *that* been going on?" He opened his eyes, emerging from the sensory and data immersion of his new implant.

"A couple of centuries at least," Schilling told him. "It's been exploratory stuff, mostly, as if they weren't quite sure who or what we were."

"Nonsense! The bastards were at *war* with us. . . ."

"From our point of view, General, yes. But not from theirs."

"Wait a sec, Captain. I'm missing something here. How could the bastards be waging an interstellar war and not be aware of it?"

Schilling cocked her head. "Just how much did your age know about the Xul, General?"

The bulkheads of the Memory Room were at the moment set to display a panorama of the Galaxy as viewed from somewhere just outside and above the main body. Garroway couldn't tell if it was a high-resolution computer-generated image, or an actual camera view from out in the halo fringe, but either way it was breathtakingly beautiful. The soft glow of four hundred billion stars shone behind Schilling's head, a radiant corona of stardust.

Watch yourself, Trevor, he told himself. *You've just been hibed for way too long. A pretty girl, romantic lighting . . .*

Then he wondered if he'd just transmitted that thought. This new hardware was going to take some getting used to.

If Schilling had mentally heard him, she gave no sign. She merely watched him, backlit by the eternal curves of the galactic spiral arms, waiting.

"The Xul?" he said. "Not a lot about their origins, really. Uploaded mentalities. They must have been a technic civilization like us, once, but at some point they embraced a kind of immortality by turning themselves into patterns of data—software, really—running on their computer networks. The xenosoph theory I was taught was that when they were biologicals, before they even achieved sentience, they evolved a hyper-Darwinian survival tactic—an extreme racial xenophobia that led them to wipe out *anyone* who might be or might become a threat. And when they uploaded themselves, they took with them their hardwired xenophobia. And that turned out to be the answer to the Fermi Paradox."

Schilling nodded. "We know it as the 'Galactic Null Set Problem.' The Galaxy apparently empty of technic civilization."

"Okay. Before we got off of our world, though, we didn't know what the answer was. There were lots of possible explanations. Maybe civilizations routinely destroyed themselves as they developed bigger and badder weapons. Maybe the only way to survive for millions of years was to develop a completely static, non-expansive culture that stayed on the home planet contemplating its collective navel. Maybe all of the rest simply never developed technology as we understand it, or never moved out of the Stone Age. Or, just maybe, we humans were the first, the *only* civilization to make it to the stars." He shrugged. "*Somebody* had to be the first."

"And then we found out we *weren't* the first."

"Right. Ancient ruins on Earth's moon, on Mars, on the earthlike worlds of nearby stars. And, buried beneath the ice covering one of Jupiter's moons, we found The Singer. A Xul huntership, trapped in the Europan world-ocean for half a million years. And eventually we *did* encounter other civilizations. But apparently the Xul had been hovering over the entire Galaxy for . . . I don't know. A million years?"

"We think at least ten million, General."

"Okay, ten million years. So the Xul are sitting out there in their network nodes, just listening. When a radio signal suggestive of technic life comes in, they would trace it back to the source and smack the planet with a high-velocity asteroid.

"You people will be more up on this stuff than me. But we know a kind of Galactic Federation of beings we called the 'Builders' or the 'Ancients' were genegineering *Homo sapiens* and terraforming Mars half a million years ago, and had built planetwide cities on Chiron and a number of other extrasolar worlds. Along came the Xul and—" Garroway slapped the back of his hand, as though swatting a mosquito. "The Builders were wiped out. Then about ten thousand years ago, an enterprising interstellar empire had enslaved much of humankind and set themselves up as the gods of ancient Sumeria. Along came the Xul and—" He slapped his hand again. "And apparently the Xul have been doing this for most of their history, and across most of the Galaxy. Now tell me how they could do that and *not* be waging war against us and every other emergent technological civilization in the Galaxy."

"When you hit your hand just now, General . . . like you were swatting a fly?"

"Yes."

"When you swat a fly, are you at war with it?"

Garroway thought about this. "Oh. You're saying they're so advanced—"

"Not really," she told him. "They might've been around for ten million years, but the Xul haven't advanced technologically at anything like our pace. In fact, they're actually not that far ahead of us in most respects today. We've begun uploading personalities into computers ourselves, did you know?"

He scanned quickly through some of the historical data he'd just downloaded. "Ah . . . I do now." His eyebrows arched in surprise. "Shit! Humans who live on the Net. You've given them a species name of their own?"

"*Homo telae*," she said, nodding. " 'Man of the Web,' which in this case means the electronic web of the Galactic Net. Actually, we learned how to upload minds partly from the Xul, inferring parts of the process from what we knew about their technology, and doing some reverse engineering from captured hunterships. In any case, we can pattern a person now and upload her to a virtual electronic world. Her body can die, but the mind, the personality, everything that made her *her* is saved, and lives on."

"If you call that living," Garroway said.

"So far as the uploaded individuals are concerned, they're alive," she told him.

Almost, he asked her if the uploaded personality really was the same as the living mind. As he saw it, the original mind died with the body; what was saved was a back-up, a replica that, with a complete set of memories, would *think* it was the original . . . but if that was immortality, it was an immortality that did not in the least help the original, body-bound mind. There's been a lot of speculation about the process, though, back in the thirty-second and thirty-third centuries, he recalled, and some people tended to get pretty animated in their insistence that if the backed-up personality was the same as the original in every respect, it *was* the original.

Garroway had never understood the fine points of the theory, though, and had little patience with philosophy. Evidently, though, speculation had become reality, and enough people had opted for the technique to justify inventing a new species of humanity to describe them. That made sense, he supposed, given that one definition of species was its inabil-

ity to interbreed with other species. A member of *Homo telae*, living its noncorporeal existence up on the Net, certainly
wasn't going to be able to produce offspring by mating with
Homo sapiens.

"The point is," Schilling told him, "the Xul are barely
aware of us. Certain parts of the entire Xul body react to us
the way your toe might twitch when an ant walks across it,
or the way you might swat that fly without really thinking
about what you're doing."

"So the Xul are some kind of group mind, a metamind?"
That had been a popular theory about them back in his day.

"Not quite. They seem to function as what we call a CAS,
a Complex Adaptive System. That's a very large organization made up of many participants, or agents . . . like termite
communities in Earth, or a hurricane."

"You're saying they're not intelligent? They build *starships*, for God's sake!"

"There are different kinds of intelligence, remember. Individual Xul may be what we think of as intelligent beings, but
for the most part they're locked into their virtual worlds and
unaware of what we would call *real*. The group-Xul presence,
the meta-Xul, if you will, is more an expression of the original
Xul instincts, their xenophobia in particular. Even their construction of starships is probably completely automated by
now—we've never found a Xul shipyard, remember—or they
may all be relics of a much earlier age."

"But . . . we've eavesdropped on them, Captain. We know
they have us catalogued as a threat. They know our home
world . . . hell, they *bombarded* Earth in 2314. How can they
not be aware of us?"

"We've been sending our AI probes into Xul nodes for
almost two thousand years, now, and we've done a lot of
listening. There are . . . call them different levels of awareness. One Xul node might learn about us, but they were always slow to share with the others. Together, they were still
driven by their original xenophobia, but taken in isolation,

individual nodes don't seem to really be conscious. Most of their defenses are automated. We know that within one node, or aboard one starship, they arrive at decisions through a kind of chorus of thoughts and counterthoughts until they reach a consensus."

"The Singer," he put in. "Europa."

"Exactly. But individual Xul nodes tend to be pretty isolated from one another—minimum internodal communication across a widely distributed net—and the Galaxy is too big to allow that kind of consensus on a specieswide scale. From the point of view of the species, of the CAS, they're all blissfully living a near-eternal existence in their own virtual universe, and once in a while we run across their toe and make it twitch."

"That . . . is a rather uncomfortable image," Garroway said slowly. He'd been more comfortable thinking of the Xul as a conventional enemy, an interstellar empire seeking to exterminate Humankind. The mental picture Schilling invoked was of something much, much larger, more powerful, and potentially far more dangerous than a mere alien interstellar empire. The fact that the Xul as a Galaxy-wide CAS hadn't yet put all the pieces together implied that some day they would.

If the Xul ever got their act together and thought and moved as a species, there might be little that Humankind could do to fight back.

"As we understand the Xul now," Schilling told him, "most of their original uploaded mentalities, the governing choruses, are . . . aware of what goes on outside their virtual worlds, but not really a part of it, do you see? The minds that control their hunterships and probes, the minds we've been up against in combat, all of those are either copies of the original minds, or AI."

"Artificial intelligence. What's the difference between an uploaded electronic mind and an artificial one?"

"Good question. Maybe none. The two may be completely

interchangeable within what passes for Xul society. Especially when the ability to upload a conscious mind brings with it the ability to *copy* a conscious mind, to replicate it as often as needed, and to tweak it, to change it from iteration to iteration."

"So the original Xul minds form the basis of the AI infrastructure, but they fill in with copies and AIs." He was still thinking about it in classical military terms. No matter how many casualties humans inflicted on the Xul, they could fill in the gaps in an eye's blink, simply by running off more copies of themselves.

"We believe so."

"How the hell do you fight an enemy like that?"

"Well, we've been using our own AI assault complexes to take down Xul nodes as we discover them. They're programmed to integrate themselves with the Xul AI software within a target node and gradually take it over, substituting our own virtual reality for theirs."

"Really?" The concept was intriguing.

"So far as the Xul minds within the target node are aware, everything's going fine, they've stamped out all possible threats to their existence, and there's nothing out there to upset their poor, xenophobic sensibilities. They get routine—and negative—reports from their probes and listening stations, routine comm traffic from other nodes, everything's fine. And our AIs are in a position to intercept any incoming data that says otherwise, or be aware of any decision by the node's chorus to go out looking for trouble. They could even shut the node down completely, if need be. Literally cut their power and turn them off."

"Why don't you? Turn them all off, I mean."

She looked uncomfortable. "Genocide, you mean."

"If it's a matter of survival for Humankind . . . yes."

"We can't do that!"

"Why not? I'm not even sure electronic uploads qualify as *life*."

"Members of *Homo telae* would object to that, General. So would most members of our AI communities."

"But their survival is at stake, too, damn it!" He felt exasperation building up, threatening to emerge as raw fury. How could he make her understand? No Marine he knew liked the idea of wholesale genocide, but when your back was up against the wall, you did what you *had* to do to survive.

She sighed. "That . . . option is debated from time to time. It comes up from time to time as a possible strategy. But there's a strong egalatist faction within the Associative government—"

"'Egalatist?'"

"All intelligence is equally valid, no matter what the shape of the body that houses it. And many Associative species— many human religious factions, too—think the Xul are a legitimate sapient life form, and that wiping them out is the same as genocide."

"Hell," Garroway said. "The bastards have tried to pull the plug on humans often enough in the past few thousand years. Maybe we should pull the plug on them. This is *war.*"

"The concept of *war* may be out of date, General," Schilling said. "If we can contain the Xul without switching them off . . . wouldn't that be better? Especially if we can eventually find a way to reason with them? Cure their xenophobia, and bring them into the Associative?"

Garroway wasn't sure he liked the sound of that. "Maybe. . . ."

"The Xul aren't *evil*," Schilling said. "Very, very different, yes. And they have a worldview that makes it tough to reason with them on human terms. But they would have a lot to contribute to Associative culture."

"Listen, if you people are so all-fired eager to make friends with those things, why'd you bring me out of cold storage?"

"Because the containment may be failing," Schilling said. "We have intelligence from several sources that suggests that, just as we've been infiltrating their systems electronically, they've been infiltrating ours.

"And just the possibility that they've begun reacting to us coherently has scared the shit out of some of us. . . ."

Hassetas, Dac IV
Star System 1727459
1901 hours, GMT

The Krysni mob, a wall of gas bags and writhing tentacles, lunged toward the Marine line. Garwe saw a telltale warning wink on within his in-head displays, and read the data unscrolling beside it.

"I'm getting a power spike, Captain!" he shouted. "The bastards are *armed*!"

"Weapons free!" Xander called.

With a thunderclap, a searing, violet beam snapped in from the jungle wall to the left, washing across Lieutenant Wahrst's strikepod in coruscating sheets and arcing forks of grounding energy. The smooth surface of her pod silvered, then seemed to flow like water as internal fields and nanotechnics shifted to shunt aside the charge.

The attacking wall of gas bags struck an instant later, carrying the Marines back a few steps by the sheer inertia of their rush. Garwe found himself grappling with half a dozen of the things. They appeared to be trying to grab his pod in their tentacles; he responded by growing tentacles of his own, silver-sheened whiplashes emerging from the active nano surface of his pod.

Odd. The pod's response was a bit sluggish. Garwe's neural interface with the pod's AI and electronic circuitry was supposed to be essentially instantaneous, but either the connection was running slow, or his brain was running way fast. It wasn't enough to cause major problems, but he was painfully aware of the way time seemed to stretch around him as more and more of the Krysni gas bags crowded in close. His hull sensors felt them, a dead weight clinging to his armor, growing more and more massive with each dragging second.

He sent a mental command to his pod's defense system, and the outer surface crackled with electricity. Krysni floaters in contact with his pod shriveled and twisted, their blue-white skins crisping to brown and black in a second or two of arcing fury.

A second high-energy bolt fired from the jungle, catching Captain Xander's pod as she tried to rise above the tangled melee. Her pod shrugged off the attack, but as it rotated away from the sniper, Garwe noticed that a dinner-plate-sized patch of her outer nano had been burned away, leaving a ragged, gray-white scar. If her pod couldn't repair itself before another shot hit in the same spot, she was dead.

Garwe lashed out with his tentacles, burning down another eight or ten of his attackers. Free for the moment, he increased power to his repulsors and moved his pod higher. "Blue One!" he called. "Fall back! You've got a hole burned through your nano!"

As if encouraged by the sniper's partial success, other electron bolts began snapping out of the jungle. Dozens of the Krysni shriveled and fell, or vanished in white puffs of vapor, victims of friendly fire, but the unarmed mob kept moving forward, ignoring casualties from both sides of the battle, trying to overwhelm the twelve Marine battle pods by sheer weight of numbers.

Garwe's pod had already located each enemy shooter and plotted them on his targeting matrix, revealing them on his IHD as flashing, bright red reticules. He selected the one that had hit the captain and triggered his pod's primary weapon, sending a megajoule pulse of X-ray laser energy slashing into the jungle.

Purple and orange vegetation shriveled and died; the Reef's tentacles curled back from the high-energy caress, and the compound's support platform shuddered as the vast life form that was Hassetas reacted to the heat.

"Skipper!" Garwe yelled! "Request permission to disengage! If we can just maneuver—"

"Negative!" Xander snapped back. "We do it by the op-plan!"

The opplan—the operations plan downloaded from the squadron's command constellation—required the War Dogs to deploy on the compound platform and provide a kind of barricade for the off-worlders, protecting them from the locals until a transport could make it down from orbit. The Marines would hold the perimeter until the off-worlders could evacuate, then pull out.

Ideally, no shots would have been fired, and the mere presence of the Marine battlepods should have kept the Krysni at bay. Somehow, things hadn't quite worked out that way, however.

Garwe kept firing into the jungle, targeting Krysni power sources as his pod's sensor suite picked them up and flagged them on his in-head display. The off-worlder compound was trembling and bucking now as the floatreef moved the massive, main tentacle to which it was anchored.

"Trolischet!" Xander snapped on the general frequency. "I suggest you get your people off of the compound platform!"

"We *can't*!" Trolischet replied, her voice shrill. "We have no ship!"

"An evacuation ship is inbound," Xander told her. "ETA less than ten minutes! But you might not *have* ten minutes! You need to get everyone into evacuation pods, fliers, flight-capable suits, whatever you have that will carry you. All you need to do is to get off this damned reef before it decides to scratch!"

"There are over two hundred of us, Captain! We couldn't save more than a quarter!"

"Well, then, save them, damn it! Or you're *all* dead!"

Other Marines were targeting the snipers now as well, those that could still move and had not been completely engulfed by the advancing wall of balloon bodies and angry, lashing tentacles. Garwe pivoted, targeting a second source of high-energy electron beams, and then three bolts caught him at once, slamming into his Starwraith in a searing detonation of raw energy.

Warning lights winked on in his IHD, his defensive fields flickering and dimming beneath the overload. A half-second later, three more beams struck and his nanodefenses went down, slabs of active nano burned from the Starwraith's outer shell, oily smoke boiling from a puncture in the foametal structure beneath.

Garwe cut his repulsors, dropping back into the relative cover of the tentacle-to-tentacle melee below. His pod jostled and bumped in the press of leathery balloon bodies and lashing tentacles as he rerouted the majority of his power flow to the task of repairing his outer-shell nano. He tried discharging a few thousand volts through what was left of his outer nano, but the attempt brought up more warning lights and no other effect.

The Krysni appeared to be learning quickly. Captain Xander's Starwraith had been hit again repeatedly, and Palin, Mortin, and Javlotel were down as well, large patches of their nanoshells burned and peeled away, exposed portions of their inner armor partly melted under the fierce heat of the enemy fire.

And it was all *wrong*. The two symbiotic sentient species of Dac IV weren't technic, and didn't have manufactured weaponry of any sort. Individual Krysni possessed a biological weapon—a toxin delivered through hollow, pressure-fired barbs like a terrestrial jellyfish—which they used when necessary against some of the mindless predators of Dac IV's deeper atmosphere layers, but those were useless against a Starwraith, even one as badly damaged as Garwe's. And without a solid surface from which to mine and forge metals, indeed, without fire, the Krysni and their immense and sapient floating cities had never developed anything remotely like material technology at all.

Where in hell had they gotten electron beam weaponry? Who had taught them how to use it?

At the moment, the press of Krysni balloons around him were doing quite well without advanced technology. His crippled Starwraith was now covered by leathery blue bodies clinging tightly to his armor, their floater sacs deflated, with hundreds more Krysni clinging in layers on top of them. He could see what they were doing by picking up a visual feed from Blue Twelve—Lieutenant Namura's wraith. It looked as though some hundreds of the creatures were clinging to him, with the outer layers inflating their bodies in an attempt to lift him clear of the deck. More and more Krysni floaters were hooking on, puffing up their bodies to well over a meter in diameter, taut-skinned globes filled with biochemically heated hydrogen.

He fired his X-ray laser, the beam punching through bodies and releasing a roiling cloud of smoke. More Krysni drifted in to replace the ones incinerated by his attack. He fired again . . . and then a third time, each shot burning away dozens of the things, but then his power reserves plummeted and the laser cut out after the third pulse.

"Blue Flight, this is Blue Seven!" he called out. "My weapons are dead!"

"Same here!" Lieutenant Radevic shouted. "Weapon power leads are burned through!"

"Blue, Blue Two!" Amendes said. "Repulsors out! Weapons down! I've gone—"

And then static hissed through the comm feed, as Garwe's in-head display, with tiny icons for each of the Blue Flight Marines, showed twelve symbols drop to eleven . . . then ten.

Overwhelming numbers were beginning to tell at last. Garwe found it hard to believe, impossible to believe . . . but the Dac balloonists were attacking a squadron of modern Marine battle pods and *winning*. It simply wasn't possible. . . .

Abruptly, his pod shifted to the right, then inverted . . . came upright, then inverted again. Slowly, clumsily, they were *moving* him. He could feel the scrape and roll of tightly packed bodies as they moved. Some hundreds, now, were

clinging to the squirming mass of creatures on the inside of
the ball, inflating their bodies to levitate the entire, cumbersome mass, while others vented hydrogen like tiny jets in
frantic, rapid pulses, shoving him toward the edge of the
platform.

Gods! A Starwraith massed almost half a ton under Dac's
gravity. How many of the creatures would it take to negate
that weight and actually float him off the platform?

Or perhaps they weren't actually trying to lift him, but simply to push or drag or roll him off the side. The edge of the
tree house deck that was not bordered by the massive bulk of
the floatreef tentacles and the surrounding aerial flora was
protected by a relatively slender guardrail, and it was less than
twenty meters away. If they could get him through the railing,
he and some hundreds of clinging Krysni would plummet
over the edge and into the black, hot, and crushing depths of
the gas giant's atmospheric deeps. His attackers seemed utterly unconcerned about their own casualties; those crushed
up against his optic sensors appeared to be dead already. Evidently, they were willing to sacrifice themselves by the hundreds simply to ensure the destruction of a single Starwraith.

He tried triggering his repulsors, but nothing happened.
His primary drive power feed had melted through and shorted
out. If he could just take flight, drag this whole, squirming
mass high enough into the thin, cold upper reaches of atmosphere, or pull them with him into the abyss until they lost
their grip and fell away . . . but at the moment he wasn't chan-
neling enough power to lift a single one of these wrinkled,
squirming little creatures, much less all of them *and* his battle pod.

"This is Blue Seven," Garwe reported, his mental voice
calm. "My drive systems are out. I think they're trying to
drag me to the edge of the platform and drop me off!"

More data flickered through his in-head display, more systems failing. There was a chemical agent in use—a concentrated fluoroantimonic acid. Apparently, the creatures crowded
in against his Starwraith were injecting, not biological tox-

ins, but acid. Where the acid could reach exposed fiber optic cables and electronic circuitry, it was causing massive internal damage.

He wondered how the creatures were carrying and injecting the stuff without having their own tissues begin to break down.

The Krysni continued to close in. Xander, Palin, Mortin, Wahrst, and Javlotel as well as Garwe all were enveloped, smothered in roughly spherical masses of writhing bodies. Amendes, Cocero, and Ewis all were out of action, their pods now totally inert, no longer transmitting status or comm feed signals. Bakewin, Radevic, and Namura continued to fight, burning away at the ponderous globes of creatures enveloping their fellow Marines as more and more and still more of the meter-long floaters descended from the sky or emerged from the surrounding jungle, filling the open space above the tree house platform with drifting, jostling, jetting Krysni.

Once, years before in a combat medical training feed, Garwe had seen a simulation based on an actual optic feed from a nanotech camera adrift within a human circulatory system. The sim had been about the human body's internal defenses, its immune system and the response of antibodies to foreign invaders in the system . . . in this case a single, rod-shaped bacterium. The bacterium, smaller than a blood cell, was still enormous compared to the antibodies flocking to the injured region, swarming in through the pale yellow haze of the surrounding interstitial fluid in clouds, enveloping the bacterium, smothering it, adhering to it, hurling themselves against it in layer upon layer in an awesome spectacle eerily like what Garwe was seeing here and now. The individual antibodies, he recalled, looked like wrinkled, spiky, pale-translucent and roughly spherical bodies, with twisted strands of long-chain molecules extending like tentacles from their bodies. Their resemblance to the drifting Krysni was unsettling.

Antibodies, defending their host.

Then his optical feed cut out, suddenly, as Namura's pod came under savage attack from four separate electron beam sources. All he could see now were the bodies of Krysni pressed in against his external pick-ups, glowing slightly at infrared wavelengths.

How long, he wondered, could the tough inner shell of his pod last against this concerted assault? His Starwraith's on-board AI continued to report on the steadily deteriorating situation as circuit after circuit foamed into inert uselessness at the touch of that concentrated acid, as power reserves drained away, as the last of the active nano coating the machine lost power or programming or coherence and flaked away, dead. His pod was all but inert, now, though the sensors continued to feed him a trickle of optical and kinesthetic data.

He was falling. His battle pod's kinesthetic feeds fed sensations directly to his inner ear, and he could feel himself dropping within the savage grasp of Dac's gravitational field, better than two and a half times a standard Earth gravity. After the first few seconds, he wasn't quite in free fall, he noted. The external atmospheric pressure and temperature were rising swiftly as he fell, and the battle pod and its ungainly cocoon of Krysni defenders rapidly hit a terminal velocity of perhaps twelve hundred kilometers per hour.

He could feel the shudders and jolts as the enveloping shell of dead and dying Krasni ripped away a few at a time.

Swathed in darkness, he plummeted into the abyss. . . .

4

Associative Marine Holding Facility 4
Eris Orbital, Outer Sol System
1907 hours, GMT

"The Xul," Garroway said, startled, "are acting in a *coherent* manner? You mean, all of them together, all across the Galaxy?"

"We can't be sure that all of the surviving nodes are involved," Schilling told him. "And the nodes we've already isolated with AI virsim teams didn't get the incoming messages, of course. But our node monitors have picked up what appear to be coordinating messages through quantum nonlocal channels. And incidents that we believe are Xul-instigated, somehow, have been occurring throughout the Associative volume."

"Galaxywide?"

"The Associative has connections through about half of the Galaxy, General. Maybe a bit less. A third?"

"That's still a hell of a lot."

"At least a hundred billion stars. A quarter or so have planetary systems. And the incidents are very widely scattered."

"Okay. The question remains, though, Captain. Just what is it that you expect me and my people to do? My Marines have experience *killing* Xul, not containing them, not integrating with them, not . . . not kissing up to them. It sounds to me like it's not the idea of war that's out of date. It's us. The Marines."

"And that's why we need the Marines, General. *Your* generation of Marines. We haven't engaged the Xul in a stand-up fight for centuries. You and your people have the experience. We don't."

"Well," Garroway said, surprised. "That's a first."

"What is, sir?"

He chuckled and shook his head. "Throughout the history of our species, Captain, we humans have always been prepared to fight the *last* war, not the next one. We go in with tactics, attitudes, and training that are completely out of step with the new threat, whatever it is."

"Sir? I don't understand."

"The history of military history, Captain. We get brand-new rifled weapons capable of killing men at a range of two or three hundred meters, and we still form tightly packed and ordered ranks and march in with the bayonet. We get machine guns, we still try massed assaults into no-man's land, or even on horseback. We develop large-scale suborbital deployment, and we still pretend that war has front lines. You're saying we need the old way of doing things, now?"

"In a way, yes, sir," Schilling said. "When we started exploring out among the stars, we continued to think in terms of the nation-states and countries we'd known on Earth. When we met alien cultures, we tried to put them into the nice, neat boxes with which we'd been familiar on our homeworld. Empires and federations, unions and republics and commonwealths."

"And associatives?"

"The Associative is an attempt to think in bigger, less exclusive terms," she told him. "No empires. No borders. No 'us' and 'them,' just an all-embracing *us*. And no need to compete for scarce resources in a Galaxy where resources like planets and energy are all but boundless."

"No borders. What does that *mean*? . . ."

Schilling gestured. A star turned bright on the projection of the Galaxy, then expanded swiftly into an open window looking down on an achingly beautiful, sapphire-blue and white world. It was, Garroway realized, the same view of Eris he'd seen upon emerging from cybe-hibe. "There are some hundreds of thousands of species in the Associative," she told him, "and millions throughout the Galaxy. Relatively few of them, though, have the same requirements when it comes to habitable worlds." Another window opened within the window, and Garroway stared into six vast, black eyes set above and below a squirming halo of tentacles. The overall impression was of something like a giant squid, but it was difficult to pull all the parts together into a coherent whole, into something that made sense to his brain.

Even so, he recognized the species, for Humankind had met them in 2877, three decades before he'd been born. "The Eulers?" he asked.

"The Eulers," Schilling agreed. "They prefer worlds like Earth . . . but at extreme depths, a thousand meters or more down in the deep benthic abyss. They genegineered a symbiotic species that could survive on land, to develop fire and industry and space travel. They helped us win the Battle of Starwall, and since then they've been among our closest allies. Incredible natural mathematicians. They've colonized perhaps two hundred worlds scattered throughout Associative space. Their latest project is this one . . . Eris, a newly terraformed world right here in Earth's Solar System. Or, here's an even better example . . ." She gestured again, and the images of Eris and the deep-sea Euler vanished, replaced by a world completely sheathed in dazzlingly white clouds . . . with just a hint of a dirty yellow cast to them. A second window opened within, showing . . . *something*. At first, Garroway thought he was looking at a crust of black, hardened lava, with streaks and veins of molten rock just visible beneath, glowing dull red. After a moment, he realized the black mass had a shape, albeit an irregular one, and things like flexible branches weaving in a searingly hot breeze.

If it was a sapient species, Garroway had never seen or heard of anything like it. He wasn't even immediately sure that it was *alive*. The image shimmered and bent, as if viewed at a great depth, or within the fiery hell of a blast furnace. The background was a sulfurous red and yellow haze, obscuring vaguely glimpsed shapes that might have been spires of native rocks, or buildings.

"We call them Vulcans," Schilling explained. "We don't know what they call themselves. Their cultural conventions, their view of self, their worldview, all are quite different from ours. But they live within volcanic fissures on worlds like Venus. Surface temperature hot enough to melt lead, and an atmospheric pressure similar to what the Eulers enjoy. We were actually looking at the feasibility of terraforming Venus—a colossal project—but a couple of hundred years ago the Vulcans petitioned us to let them colonize instead. They live there now and like it, at pressures equivalent to the ocean deeps."

Garroway stared at the black mass, which was oozing now into a slightly different shape. Did it have a native shape, or was it more of a crust-locked amoeba? He couldn't tell. Were those branches manipulative members of some sort, or sensory organs, or something else entirely? Again, he couldn't tell. "How can you trust them if you don't even know what they call themselves?"

"The point is, General, they don't want our kind of real estate. We have almost nothing in common with them. It's far, *far* easier to terraform an outer dwarf planet like Eris or Sedna than it is to cool down a planet like Venus and give it a reasonable surface pressure, an atmosphere we could breathe. So they live on Venus, the Eulers live in Eris—they even have a small colony now in Tongue-of-the-Ocean, on Earth—and we're scarcely aware of their activities. *No borders*. What would be the point?"

"Security. But I see what you mean about war being out of date," he told her.

He wasn't convinced that that could be true, however. Garroway tended to have a pessimistic view of human nature, one forged within a long career as a combat Marine and, as a general officer with dealing with politicians. In his opinion, Humankind could no more give up war than he could give up the ability to think.

"A war with the Eulers or the Vulcans is almost literally unthinkable," she told him. "But the Xul aren't competing for resources. They simply want us dead."

"Of course. We've triggered their xenophobic reflex."

"Exactly, sir. If the containment strategy isn't working . . . and if they're becoming more aware of us, well, we need you and your people, General. Like never before."

As she spoke, Garroway was scanning through more of the download background and history. Civilians, including humans, had been attacked by locals in a gas giant called Dac IV. Anchor Marines had been sent in—the 340th Marine Strike Squadron. The situation was still unresolved, but it must be desperate. A request for a Globe Marine detachment had also been logged.

"What in hell," he said slowly, "is an 'Anchor Marine?' "

"Marines who stay with the time stream," she told him. "Like me."

"And I'm a 'Globe Marine?' "

"Yes, sir. Our reserves in cybe-hibe."

"Who thought up *that* nonsense?"

"Sir?"

"Marines are *Marines*, Captain. I don't like this idea of two different sets of background, experience, or training."

Here was another problem. Two months ago, a star lord at a place, an artificial habitat called Kaleed, had run into something he couldn't handle, and requested Marines. No Anchor Marines had been available, and so the Lords of the Associative had decided to awaken a division of Globe Marines.

Apparently the third Marine Division was to be held on stand-by as the Lords monitored the situation.

"It was necessary, General," Schilling explained. "Globe

Marines need cultural liaisons, other Marines who are, well, *anchored* in the current background culture. Otherwise you'd be lost. There have been a lot of changes in both cultural norms and in technology since your day."

"You're making me feel positively ancient, Captain."

But he understood the issue. When he'd last been active, over eight centuries ago, there'd already been a sharply drawn dichotomy between Marines and the civilian population they protected. Neither group understood the other. Neither could socialize well with the other. Neither could speak the other's language. No wonder most Marines tended to find both family partners and sexual liaisons among others in the Corps. Marines might visit the local hot spots and brothels for a quick bit of fun, but longer and more solid relationships required a degree of mutual understanding with civilians that had become harder and harder to come by.

And it wasn't just that Marines got into trouble with the locals on liberty. The politicians who requested Fleet Marines to put down an insurrection or show the fist to a local warlord didn't understand them either. And that was where the problems really started chewing up the machinery.

"Okay," Garroway said after a moment. "I understand all of that. We need babysitters. But why does the government need us at all if they have you?"

"We're a caretaker force, sir, nothing more. The administrators. The personnel officers and logistics staff who make sure there is a Corps for you to wake up to."

"But I see something here about Anchor combat units. . . ."

"Yes, sir. We have combat units, but they're more placeholders than anything else. *You* are the real Fleet Marine Force."

Garroway considered this. The Globe and Anchor was one of the oldest and most sacred talismans of the Corps, a symbol going back to the Royal Marines, who were the predecessors of America's Continental Marines of 1775. It was an amusing idea, he decided, using globe and anchor to identify two different kinds of Marine . . . but the concept behind it disturbed him. Throughout the history of the Corps *he* knew, every Marine had known a single brotherhood, the Corps, each man and woman undergoing the same training, with the same traditions, the same language, the same background.

He found himself wondering if Captain Schilling was a *real* Marine, or something else—an imitation, a temporary stand-in for the real thing.

For centuries, Marine culture had been a distinct and self-contained entity in its own right. If cultural drift over the centuries had made the old Marines alien to the rest of Humankind, wouldn't that alienness extend to these caretaker Marines as well?

"Every Marine is a rifleman, Captain," he said.

"Pardon, sir?"

"Did you download that in training? I hope to hell you did, because if you didn't the Corps has changed out of all recognition."

"I don't understand the word 'rifleman,' sir. Give me a second . . . oh."

"The rifle is the Marine's primary weapon, Captain. I don't care what you use nowadays, the principle is the same. As for the expression, it's old. Pre-spaceflight, I think. *Every* Marine is a combat infantryman first, a rifleman, and whatever else— cook, personnel clerk, aviator, storekeeper, computer programmer, general—second."

"Today we say, 'every Marine is a weapons sysop first.' "

"Somehow, Captain, that just doesn't have the same ring."

Garroway continued to scan lightly through a flood of downloads. He was starting to get the hang of the new implant as he used it. It was responsive and powerful, and he was beginning to get the idea that he hadn't even begun yet to glimpse its full potential.

Here was another one, from a world called Gleidatramoro, a kind of trading center and interstellar marketplace in toward the Galactic Core frequented by several hundred races. It was, he noted, another artificial world, like Kaleed. Didn't people live on *planets* anymore? A human mob had formed in Gleidat's capital city and attacked . . . *that* was interesting. They'd attacked a number of s-Humans, whatever those were, then gone on to dismember several hundred AIvatars. Cross-connecting on the unfamiliar terminology, he learned that s-Humans were a superintelligent genegineered species of human, while an AIvatar was the human, humanoid, or digital vehicle for an advanced artificial consciousness.

How, he wondered, was that different from a *robot*?

The riot on Gleidatramoro had spread when several nonhuman species had intervened on behalf of the AIvatars. Several thousand individuals of various species, human, nonhuman, superhuman, and artificially sentient, had been killed, many of them irretrievably. The humans currently were bottled up within the capital city in a bloody stand-off, and both they and the non-humans were calling for help.

Again, Anchor Marines had been sent in to regain control. The situation on Gleidatramoro was still fluid.

And here was an invasion of Propanadnid space by a human warlord named Castillan, who'd launched his armada under the ringing battle cry of "death to the Proppies!" And another, a terrorist attack on an asteroid defense system in the Sycladu system, an attack with, as yet, no known motive. And still another, an attempt by the human population of Gharst to unplug several million t-Humans . . . the *Homo telae* of the local Net. So much for human sensibilities opposed to electronic genocide.

The list went on . . . and on, and on, hundreds of incidents during the past thirty days alone. There were far too many, scattered across far too large a volume of space and among far too many worlds, for a single Marine division to have a chance of coping with them all.

The total number of violent clashes and incidents—some nineteen hundred during the past month, according to the latest tally—was utterly trivial compared to the tens of billions of populated worlds and habitats that made up the Associative. On the other hand, there'd been nine hundred such incidents reported the previous month, and four hundred the month before that. There appeared to be a kind of background noise count of violent encounters, of riots, revolutions, and bullying neighbors, but overall the numbers had been low, perhaps two hundred a month, an indication, Garroway thought, that this Associative might have it on the ball so far as galactic governments were concerned. Lately, though, there'd been a sharp increase in the numbers, and so far there was no sign that the trend had peaked.

"Almost twenty thousand of these incidents," he told her. "That's more than the number of men, women, and AIs in my division. What are the Marines supposed to do about it? We can't invade all these worlds. And we can't protect billions of planets that haven't been hit."

"No. But you *can* investigate this. . . ."

A virtual world enveloped Garroway, emerging from his new implant. In an instant, he was surrounded by deep space, within a blazing shell of brilliant stars.

There were millions of them, most red or orange in hue, which contributed to an overall red and somber background. Ahead, bathing nearby gas clouds in searing, arc-harsh blue radiance, was the Core Detonation.

"The Galactic Core," Garroway said, whispering. "The center of the Galaxy."

"We *did* do a number on it, didn't we?"

She almost sounded *proud*.

Marine Assault Carrier Night's Edge
Synchronous Orbit, Dac IV
Star System 1727459
1914 hours, GMT

Lieutenant Garwe snapped back to consciousness, bathed in sweat, his breath coming in short, savage gasps. He was *falling* . . . falling into the Abyss. . . .

No, not falling. He was on his back in a linkcouch, the

overhead softly glowing. Lieutenant Amendes leaned over him, a hand on his shoulder. "Easy does it, Gar. You're safe."

"The squadron—"

"It's okay, Gar," she told him. "You're out of there."

He sat up slowly, head spinning. Amendes reached up and removed the brow circlet that had linked Garwe to the Star-wraith battlepod through its on-board AI. It took him a moment to readjust after the sharp transition, to remember where he was.

The carrier, yeah. The *Night's Edge*.

The compartment was circular and domed, with a close-spaced semicircle of twelve linkcouches, half of them still occupied by other members of the squadron. At the far side of the compartment was the main console, just beneath the glowing arc of a holofield.

"Won't be long now," Lieutenant Cocero said from the console. He was watching over a Marine technician's shoulder. "The Skipper's down. So's Pal."

Major Lasenbe, the squadron's Wing Commander, punched his fist into his open palm. "*Damn!*"

On a linkcouch nearby, Captain Xander sat up abruptly as though coming wide awake out of a bad dream, her fists clenched. "No, no, *no*! *Shit*!"

"The gasbags are overrunning the compound now," the Marine tech reported from the console. "They're in among the buildings now, killing the off-worlders."

Garwe slid out of his linkcouch, fighting against the shaking weakness in his legs. Above the console, within the holofield's glowing depths, Garwe could see a terrified face—the high brow, dark skin, and contrasting golden eyes of a supie. A data block beside the image identified her as Vasek Trolischet, the xenosoph who, unlike the Marines of the 340th, was physically in the gas giant, and unable to escape. The sound was muted, too low for Garwe to hear what she was saying, but from the look on her face, she was terrified.

Abruptly, the holofield filled with static, and Trolischet's fear-distorted features blinked out.

"We've lost contact with the Hassetas base, sir," the technician reported.

Two more of the Blue Flight Marines emerged from their artificial comas, blinking in the soft lighting. On a viewall on the far side of the compartment, the disk of Dac, vast and striped in hues of brown, salmon, and pale cream flowed in banded serenity, the violence in its depths masked by the giant's scale.

Major Lasenbe stood behind the technician, hands now at the small of his back. "A cluster fuck, Captain," he told Xander without looking at her. "A Class-one cluster fuck."

Xander rolled off the couch and came to attention, though she still looked drawn and pale, and seemed to be having difficulty suppressing a tendency to tremble. "Yes, sir," she said. "I'm . . . sorry, sir."

Lasenbe turned. "At ease, Captain. I'm not chewing you out. They should have sent you in *with* the pick-up ship, not fifteen minutes ahead of it. Maybe those poor devils would've had a chance, then."

"Is the transport still going in, Major?" Xander asked. "We could reinsert—"

"No point. The gas bags are wiping out the compound as we speak."

It would take an hour or more to get back down to Hassetas. By then it would be too late.

"God *damn* it," Xander said, slumping, her fists clenched.

Garwe was trembling as well, part of the after-effect of a particularly close linkride. Starwraith battle pods actually did serve as combat suits for living Marines, but it was also possible to link with them from the safety of a remote location, so long as non-local communications elements eliminated any speed-of-light time lag. The Marine Carrier *Night's Edge* was in synchronous orbit for Dac, just over 180,000 kilometers out, an orbit that perfectly matched the planet's rotational period of eleven hours, or, rather, which matched the period of Hassetas, since the different cloud belts circled the gas giant at different rates. Any closer, and the ship's orbit would have carried her past the target and over the horizon, blocking the sensory and control feed signals transmitted from ship to pods and back. The time delay at that distance for conventional EM transmissions would have been impossible, six-tenths of a second for remote sensory signals to travel from pod to Marine, and another six-tenths of a second for the Marine's responses to travel back down to the pod. Both the pods and the carrier, however, were equipped with quantum-coupled comm units, QCC technology that operated instantaneously, with no time lag. Without instantaneous transmission times, the Marines would have been bumping into things—or aiming at targets that had already moved on. Even at that, Garwe's pod had felt . . . *sluggish*, not quite in synch with his mind. The effect hadn't been much, but he felt that it had affected his combat performance.

"Sir, with respect," he said.

"Who are you?" Lasenbe demanded.

"Sir! Lieutenant Garwe, Blue Seven. It might've been better if we'd gone in physically. I felt *slow* down there, like there was a time lag."

"Nonsense. There was no lag. Besides, if you'd deployed physically, Lieutenant, you would now be dead. Your pod crushed and burned . . ." He paused, checking data pulled down through his implant. "Three minutes ago."

"But if we'd been able to pull back and engage the enemy in the air, instead of trying to protect those buildings—"

"You did what you were ordered to do, Lieutenant. Hammet!"

"Sir!" the technician snapped.

"How many Marines are still e-deployed?"

"Three, sir. Namura, Rad—"

"Yank 'em out. We can't do anything more down there."

"Aye, aye, sir."

Lasenbe was pointedly ignoring Garwe now, giving orders for the withdrawal of the rest of the squadron. On the couches at his back, the other Marines were beginning to revive, their links with the battlepods 180,000 kilometers below severed.

"What the hell was that chemical they were hitting us with?" Palin wanted to know. "Some kind of acid. . . ."

"Fluoroantimonic acid," Hammet said. "We got a full read-out on the chemical composition up here."

"Fluoro—what?" Misek Bollan asked.

"A mixture of hydrogen fluoride, HF, and antimony pentafluoride, SbF_5," Xander said, with the air of someone perfectly at ease with ungainly chemical formulae. "Nasty stuff. One of the strongest acids known."

"Roughly 2×10^{19} times stronger than one hundred percent sulfuric acid," Hammet added. "No wonder it was eating through your internal circuitry."

"Since when did you become a chemist, Skipper?" Wahrst asked. She was grinning.

"Since before I became a Marine," Xander replied. "What I want to know is . . . how were those gas bags delivering the stuff? It protonates organic compounds, eats right through them. Why didn't it dissolve the gas bags?"

"They're supposed to have some kind of natural delivery system, aren't they?" Mortin said.

"Right. A *natural* delivery system, which means made out of the local equivalent of organics, proteins, bone, cartilage, that sort of thing. When we handled $HSbF_6$ in the lab, we needed either Teflon or field-shielded containers. It even eats through glass."

"They must've had help," Garwe said. "Some source of technology from the outside. But then, they were using electron beam weapons, too, weren't they?"

"Yes, they were," Xander said. "Someone has been running relatively high-tech weaponry to the locals. I wonder who?"

"Or why?" Palin put in. "What do the gas bags have that they could trade off-world for weapons?"

"There's a lot here that doesn't make sense," Major Lasenbe said. "We're not here to sort it out, however. Xander, you and your people go grab some down-time. But I'll want an after-action uploaded to my essistant tomorrow by thirteen hundred."

"Aye, aye, sir."

Lasenbe strode from the room. Xander appeared to relax a fraction.

"Asshole," Mortin said, his voice low.

"Belay that, Marine," Xander said. "Are all of you all right?"

There was a mutter of response, "Yes, Skipper," and "Okay" and "Ooh-rah" predominating. The Marines sounded subdued, however

"Kind of a rough trip, Captain," Garwe told her. "I think we're still all in one piece, though."

"Garwe," Xander said, turning to face him, "what did you mean when you told the major about feeling a time lag?"

Garwe shrugged. "I'm not sure. It might have been psychodilation, I suppose."

"Or you were speeding?"

"No, Skipper," Garwe said. "I was linked with the rest of the squadron."

Psychodilation was a natural effect of human perception, the apparent slowing of the passage of time during moments of great danger, stress, or, paradoxically, boredom. "How time flies when we're having fun" was the opposite extreme of the effect. Both perceptions occurred when the brain entered an alpha altered state under different circumstances, and had to do with how much in the way of fine detail the person was actually perceiving.

"Speeding," on the other hand, more formally known as PV, or psychovelocitas, was the artificial boosting of overall brain function to speed up reaction times, perception, and thought. There were times when this was appropriate, and carried out through the use of drugs or neural enhancement software, but while linked in with a combat formation was definitely *not* one of those times. Battle pod operations demanded precise coordination between squadron elements. If

Garwe had been speeding, linked communications with him would have been garbled, fire coordination would have become chaotic, and unit cohesion might easily have broken down completely.

Xander nodded. "I'll check the telemetry records up here. It might have been a fault in your neural circuitry."

"My pod checked out okay, Skipper." Not that it could be checked now. What was left of his pod was by now still drifting slowly into the depths of the gas giant Dac, flattened by atmospheric pressure and subjected to the searing heat of the planet's depths. "I was probably just hyped on adrenaline."

"Gar's right," Palin said. "I was pretty keyed up, too. I think we all were."

Xander nodded. "Still, all of you *will* report to sickbay for a full neural series. I felt like I wasn't quite in synch, either. And I don't like not being in control."

"Aye, aye, sir," several of the Marines chorused.

"Garwe."

"Yes, sir?"

"You stay for a moment. I want to talk with you."

"Sure, Skipper."

She sounded angry, and that was never good.

He wondered where the hell this was going.

5

Associative Marine Holding Facility 4
Eris Orbital, Outer Sol System
1919 hours, GMT

Garroway tried to make sense of what he was seeing. The central mass resembled nothing so much as an immense, impossible, blossoming rose of streaming, blue-white radiance, imbedded within a confused tangle of blinding light, of far-flung arcs and walls and swirls of hot clouds of molecular gas, of stars showing comet tails streaming away from the central blast, of nebulae torn asunder by ferocious stellar winds, of objects set in such a titanic scale that stars and even clusters of stars were dwarfed to insignificance. His implant began overlaying what he was seeing with identifying blocks of text.

Humans had last visited the center of the Galaxy in 1111 of the Marine Era . . . the year 2887 by the old calendar. Marine and naval forces had assaulted a major Xul base, a number of bases, actually, located in and around the Core structures. The largest and most important of these had been a Dyson cloud, a swarm of trillions of Xul artificial wordlets positioned around the supermassive black hole that marked the Galaxy's exact gravitational center. At the climax of the battle, a red giant star called S-2, in close orbit around the central black hole, had been nudged from its high-velocity path by inducing a partial and off-center collapse beneath its surface, triggering an outrushing jet of stellar material that had acted like an immense rocket blast. The fast-dwindling star had fallen closer to the black hole than otherwise would have been the case, sweeping through part of the Xul cloud, then shredding as it whipped around the inner gravitational singularity and down the cosmic drain at the center.

The Xul hyperstructure had been destroyed, the individual elements of the cloud plunging into the black hole in an eye's blink because they'd been force-beam anchored in place, rather than circling in orbit. Much of the infalling matter had been swallowed of course, but much more had rebounded outward, generating what had come to be known as the Core Detonation, an out-rushing surge of tortured plasma so hot and bright that a supernova would have been lost in the glare.

A nearby star cluster, young and hot, just a tenth of a light year out, had been consumed in the fury weeks later, the stars pop-pop-popping into a chain of supernovae as the flood of radiant energy engulfed them. Other supergiant stars close to GalCenter had been swept up as well, adding their mass as fuel to the maelstrom of radiation.

That had been 1117 years ago. In those eleven centuries, the blast wave had swept outward, the wavefront of electromagnetic radiation traveling 1117 light years in that time, the somewhat slower, following squall of high-energy particles crossing about 900 light years in the same period of time. Stars, thousands of them caught in that deadly firestorm of energy, had exploded as they were engulfed, each adding its own bit of fury to the storm. The Galactic Core was now a seething ocean of blue-white hell, and it was still expanding.

Any Xul nodes located within that central, two-thousand-light-year-wide pocket of hell, would have been swept up and consumed. The question was how far the blast would expand . . . how much of the Galaxy might it devour?

"So," Garroway wanted to know, "is that stuff going to hit

us in another twenty, twenty-five thousand years?" The thought that Humankind's attack on the Galactic Core eleven hundred years ago might actually have unleashed a beast that was going to devour the entire galaxy was horrifying.

"It's attenuating," Schilling told him. "Twenty-six thousand years, or a little less, after the original Core detonation, the electromagnetic wavefront will pass Earth at the speed of light. Long before that happens, the heavier charged particles and plasmas, the hard, dangerous stuff, will have been absorbed by intervening clouds of dust and gas."

"Even so," a new voice said, *"the astrophysicists are calling it a microquasar. It won't scour the Galaxy of life, fortunately, but they estimate the total light output from our Galaxy will more than quintuple, and probably set the astronomers in Andromeda to scratching whatever they use for heads."*

"General Garroway," Schilling said, "this is Socrates. He's your AI liaison with the Council of Lords."

"Pleased to meet you, General," Socrates said. The voice was mellifluous and deep, a rich baritone. Where Schilling spoke with a slight accent, Socrates' Anglic was perfect.

Well, he was an AI. He would *be* perfect in every way possible.

"Hello, Socrates," Garroway said. "The pleasure is mine. Or do AIs feel emotion now?"

The AI chuckled. Either it had a genuine sense of humor, or was programmed to mimic one quite well. Garroway did wonder how far artificial intelligence had developed in the past eight centuries.

"If you *can't tell the difference,"* Socrates told him, *"and if* I *can't tell the difference, what's the difference between my feelings being programmed or natural?"*

"Point."

"Socrates is a Star-level artificial sentience," Schilling explained. "That means he's at *least* as bright as the smartest s-Human, but much faster. We refer to them as our archAIngels." Schilling pronounced the word "archangel," but Garroway sensed the neologism within, and the meaning behind it. "Sometimes I think they are the real rulers of the Human domain now."

"We all do what we can," Socrates said. Garroway blinked. A *modest* AI? Or was that simply another aspect of its programming?

"There was quite a bit of speculation about how serious the Core Detonation was," Schilling said, picking up on the earlier topic. "That was, oh, four or five centuries ago, when we started getting hard data about the expanding Core wavefront. Created a bit of a minor panic, in fact, according to the history downloads."

"If we managed to turn our own Galaxy into even a *small* quasar," Garroway said, "I'd think a little judicious panic might be called for."

A quasar was a galaxy with an exceptionally bright nucleus, an active core that outshone the rest of the galaxy by a hundred times or more. Quasars were also extremely distant. The closest known was three-quarters of a billion light years away . . . which meant it was also a glimpse of something that had happened three-quarters of a billion years in the past, ancient cosmic history. Accepted astrophysical theory suggested that many or, perhaps, all large galaxies had gone through a quasar phase early in their evolution, some billions of years ago, as the supermassive black hole at their cores devoured suns by the millions, spewing out the residue as fantastic bursts of high-energy radiation, a blazing beacon visible across all of time and space. Eventually, the core of the galaxy would be pretty well cleaned out, except for the central black hole itself, of course, and the galaxy would settle down to being a normal, well-behaved member of the cosmic community.

Presumably, the Milky Way Galaxy had been through such a phase some billions of years ago; the supermassive black hole at the Core was an ancient quasar, slumbering and quiescent now that much of the matter at GalCenter had been devoured. But then the Commonwealth Fleet and the Fleet Marines had come along late in the twenty-ninth century and upset the delicately balanced megastructure the Xul had constructed at the Core.

And a shadow, at the very least, of the ancient monster had awakened once again.

"It should be spectacular, though," Schilling told him. "When the light gets this far out, our night skies will be incredible in the direction of Sagittarius. We think there will be enough light streaming out from the Core that you'll be able to read by it."

"The slower, heavier particles will pile up into the gas clouds that surround the Galactic Hub and create shock waves over the next five to ten thousand years," Socrates added, *"triggering an incredible burst of star formation. The Galaxy, in toward the Core, is going to be an amazing, beautiful sight for ten thousand years or more afterward."*

"Maybe I should go back into cybe-hibe," Garroway said. "Wake me when the show starts."

"We'll go you one better," Socrates told him. *"The Lords of the Associative, or one important facet of them, at any rate, want you and your Marines to go in there."*

"Say what?" He looked into that blue-white hell. The simulation carried no sensation of temperature, but he could swear his face felt *hot* as he looked into that searing blaze of light.

"We had assumed that the Xul presence at the Galactic Core had been burned out by the Core Detonation over a thousand years ago," Socrates told him.

"Seems like a reasonable assumption," Garroway said. "Do you mean to tell me they *survived* in that?"

"We're attempting to verify that now. We've deployed AI probes to investigate. As you can imagine, the environment poses certain . . . difficulties."

The view of the luminous rose of light expanded, the viewpoint rushing in toward the inner Core. The sheer magnificent beauty of the scene was overwhelming, and Garroway had to remind himself that the environment must be as hostile, in terms of radiation and temperature, as the surface of a star.

"It is," Socrates told him. *"Keep in mind, though, that we have encountered no fewer than twenty distinct species of intelligent life dwelling either in the photospheres or within the cores of their stars. Life evolves, develops, and adapts everywhere, when given the chance."*

"Socrates," Garroway said aloud, "did you just read my mind?"

There was a slight hesitation. *"I did, General. Excuse me, please."*

"General Garroway hasn't been exposed to the concept of full access yet," Schilling told the AI.

"So I understand now. It won't happen again, General. At least, not until you authorize it."

"Full access?"

"High-end AIs, like Socrates, have what we refer to as full access to human mentation. They can pretty much pick up and track anything you're thinking, without interfacing through your implant."

"I see. Why?"

"Social control, of course. And universal data access for the Disimplanted."

The way she said the words "social control" felt so natural, so completely matter-of-fact that Garroway wasn't certain he'd heard her correctly at first. This, he reflected, might be the biggest gap between his own time and culture and this one that he'd yet encountered.

Humankind had been working with direct man-machine neural interfaces for the major part of the species' technic history—nineteen hundred years at least—and with various forms of artificial intelligence for longer than that. Implant technology had begun as crude molecular arrays of 2K protein processor nodes that facilitated direct downloads of data from primitive computer nets. Eventually, those early implants had evolved into nanochelated structures of complex design, organic-machine hybrids residing within the brain and running an enormous variety of software that usually included a resident personal AI. These personal secretaries or "essistants" could so perfectly mimic their fully organic host that it was possible to hold a conversation with one on any topic and be unaware that you were speaking with a machine—the final evocation of the ancient proposal known as the Turing Test.

Such essistants were considered vital in modern communications and interface technologies, and more and more interactions with machines, from accessing research data banks or piloting spacecraft to growing furniture or opening doors or turning on a room's illumination system, required an implant.

Which left people without implants, the Disimplanteds, or "Disimps," out in the cold and dark, often literally.

But the AIs of Garroway's day had been designed to pick up only on those thoughts that were appropriately coded, preceded by a mental symbol that told the AI that it was welcome. The idea of allowing any intelligence, even a manmade one, into his thoughts without permission was profoundly disturbing.

And allowing machines to read minds for purposes of "social control" was, to Garroway's way of thinking, horrifying. Did that mean they had artificial intelligences prowling the streets of human worlds and habs, listening for stray thoughts that might lead to social unrest, crime, or dissidence?

And how did you tell the difference between an artificial intelligence and a member of that new species Schilling had mentioned . . . what had she called them? The *Homo telae*? Could they read minds as well?

"I don't think I like this full-access idea," he told them.

"I don't imagine you do," Schilling said. "It probably feels pretty strange . . . even creepy. It's not a bad thing, however. Crime—at least outside of the free zones—is almost unknown. Intraspecies war—both civil war and war between separate human governments or religious groups—is all but obsolete. Humankind has never known such an era of peace and general well-being."

"So what do the AIs do in this utopia of yours?" Garroway said. "Eavesdrop on street corners, and call the cops when they hear the random, disgruntled rant against the government?"

"Not 'cops,' " Socrates told him. *"That's antiquated terminology. We refer to socons. Agents of social control."*

"This is sounding worse and worse."

"Most socons are AIs," Schilling said. "Though there are human agents, of course. In most cases, they can correct aberrant behavior directly and immediately, and the person involved—whether he's a criminal, a political dissident, or mentally ill—can be adjusted, *healed* . . . and never even know the adjustment has taken place."

"Captain," he replied slowly, "you are scaring the hell out of me. Who decides what is dissident, and what is just an expression of a less-than-mainstream opinion? Who determines what mentally ill is? What are the standards? It's not like you can diagnose mental illness by pulling a throat culture, damn it!"

"Gently, General," Socrates told him. *"It's not as bad as you think. Our system has worked, and worked well, for over five centuries."*

Garroway started to reply, then thought better of it. Until he had a better feel for this culture, and for its rules and regulations both written and unwritten, he was going to need to keep his mouth shut and his eyes, ears, and implant open. Something he said now, in ignorance, might well prejudice these people against both him and his own Marines.

"I'll take your word for it," he said, but his reservations remained. "You were telling me, though, about alien intelligences inhabiting stars."

"Indeed. They seem to be relatively rare, but several species, existing as coherent plasmas, have evolved within stellar atmospheres, or, in two cases of which we know, deep

within the stellar core. Obviously, our communications with such beings are somewhat . . . limited."

The view of the Core Detonation had continued to grow and change as they talked. The scene now appeared to be centered on a glowing disk, a pinwheel of light shading from red at the outer rim to an intense, eye-watering violet at the center.

"Is that the Galactic Core?" Garroway asked. The pinwheel, obviously, was an accretion disk. At its center was a tiny void, an emptiness, into which compressed gas and stellar material appeared to be funneling, a large and massive black hole. Dying matter shrieked its death scream in X-rays and the far ultraviolet.

"No," Socrates told him. *"The Core is about 350 light years in* that *direction."* Garroway sensed the gesture, deeper into an impenetrable haze of blue-white radiance beyond. *"This is the Great Annihilator."*

Garroway had heard of it. A black hole, yes . . . but not, as once had been imagined, *the* supermassive black hole at the Galaxy's exact center. The true Galactic Core consisted of a black hole of about two million solar masses, but, until the Core Detonation wavefront reached the vicinity of Earth, there would be no physical evidence pinpointing it from Earth's vicinity save for the observed movements of core stars, no light, no radiation of any sort.

The Great Annihilator, on the other hand, was a black hole of only about fifteen solar masses, but it was far noisier—as heard from Earth, at any rate—than its far larger brother nearby. Twin shafts of high-energy radiation speared in opposite directions from the poles of its central hub, streams of positrons emerging from the turbulent areas above the black hole's north and south poles. The interaction of antimatter with normal matter hundreds of light years from the singularity filled the Core with radio noise—the 511 keV screech of positronium annihilating its normal-matter counterpart—electrons. The object had been detected and named "The Great Annihilator" by Earth astronomers millennia ago, but the discovery had only deepened the mystery of the actual nature of the Galactic Core. By measuring the velocities of stars in the Annihilator's immediate vicinity, astronomers had proven that it was a black hole, but not the far more massive one at the exact center that they'd been looking for.

In Garroway's day, of course, it had been well understood that the Xul Dyson cloud had been masking the radiation leakage from the actual Core, and would continue to do so until the Core Detonation crawled out into the Galactic suburbs and impinged upon waiting detectors and sense organs. The Great Annihilator, though, had become a footnote to Galactic cosmography, a little-brother satellite of the larger, better known singularity at GalCenter.

The Core Detonation would have swallowed the Great Annihilator centuries ago. Evidently, the object had not been destroyed, as might have been expected. Clouds of dust and gas sweeping out from the Core explosions had spiraled into the Annihilator's accretion disk, which glowed now as brightly as a supernova. So much matter continued to fall into the singularity itself that vast quantities, instead of being swallowed, were flung outward as radiant plasmas, and the radio shriek of annihilating matter was far louder now than it had been twelve hundred years before. Garroway could hear that shriek overlaid upon the visual image. Inset windows gave scrolling blocks of data describing the energies exploding from the brilliant object. Radiation levels, he noticed, were high enough to instantly fry any organic matter.

He watched the glowing object for a moment. Through filters raised by the software controlling the imagery, he could actually see the movement of the inner edge of the accretion disk as it whipped across the singularity's event horizon.

"We have detected signals emerging as nonlocal events from within the Great Annihilator," Schilling told him. "The physics are . . . difficult. Suffice to say that phase-shifted habitats may have been inserted into the black hole's ergosphere."

"Are you telling me," he said slowly, "that there's something *alive* inside that Hell?"

"*Something, yes,*" Socrates said. "*The Xul, or a part of them. And they're using their base within the Great Annihilator to attack us.*"

"Inside a black hole?"

"*Within the ergosphere, yes.*"

"That's impossible," Garroway said, shaking his head. "*Nothing* can escape a black hole's gravitational field if it gets too close, not even light. That's part of the thing's definition."

"You're aware of phase shifting, aren't you, sir?" Schilling asked.

"Yes. We have . . . sorry, *had* bases and ships back in my day that could rotate out of phase with four-dimensional spacetime. They existed at the base state of Reality, what we called the Quantum Sea."

"*The Xul apparently can do that as well,*" Socrates said, "*and from the Quantum Sea, it's possible to manipulate gravity.*"

"The quantum converters?" Schilling added. "The devices we use to provide microsuns for our terraform projects in the Kuiper Belt and beyond? We phase-shift those into the Quantum Sea, where they can draw as much energy as we need directly from the Reality base state. The Xul are doing something similar inside the Great Annihilator."

"What?"

"*We're not sure,*" Socrates said. "*It's possible that they hope to affect the entirety of the Reality base state . . . to, in effect, rewrite what we're pleased to think of as reality.*"

"Editing us out of existence?"

"*It's a possibility. That, at least, is one of the scenarios our Xul iteration programs have developed. But it's also possible that they're using singularity-identity nonlocality to infect our AI and computer networks with alien emomemes.*"

"Whoa," Garroway said. "You just lost me . . . about eight hundred years ago."

"Singularity-identity nonlocality?" Schilling asked. Garroway nodded.

"The theory can be a bit murky," Socrates told him. *"Do you know how stargates work?"*

"Not the technical details, but yes," Garroway said. "In principle, at least."

Stargates were immense artifacts scattered across the Galaxy and beyond, ten- to twenty-kilometer-wide rings within which pairs of planetary-mass black holes revolved in opposite directions. The interplay of moving gravitational fields opened direct links between one gate and another, light years distant, with which it was tuned. Exactly who had built them, or when, was a mystery, but stargates were still the principal means of long-range travel throughout the Galaxy.

"Stargates work," Socrates told him, *"because the movement of singularities within two stargates can be tuned to one another so that they essentially become congruent, a fancy way of saying they are the same. Identical. The same gate, but located in two widely separated places at once . . . orbiting Sirius, say, and the Galactic Core. The theory depends on quantum states and an aspect of quantum dynamics called nonlocality, which says that two objects or particles entangled at the quantum level remain connected to one another, as though there was no space, no distance, between them."*

"I know about that one," Garroway said. "Albert Einstein called it 'spooky action at a distance,' and refused to accept that it described the universe realistically."

"Albert . . . who?" Schilling asked.

"Einstein," Socrates told her. *"A pre-spaceflight philosopher."*

"Physicist, actually," Garroway said. "At least according to the history downloads I've seen."

"Physicist, then," Socrates agreed, *"though physicists and philosophers are much the same thing when it comes to describing aspects of the metaverse that can only indirectly be apprehended, and which can only be described by myth and metaphor. In any case . . . if you have access to base-state reality in one black hole, you theoretically have direct access*

to all black holes . . . and to the star gates as well, since they depend on artificial singularities for their operation."

"We don't know if they're really trying to change reality," Schilling said. "That may be too much of a stretch even for them. But we *have* detected signals emerging from several stargates that suggest they're broadcasting emomemes."

"And what the hell is an emomeme?"

" 'Meme' is an old term for a transmissible unit of cultural information," Socrates told him. *"Especially one that can be passed on from mind to mind verbally, by repeated actions, or through general cultural transmission. Religions are memes. So are fashions in bodily adornment. Or popular sayings or slogans or tunes or fads in entertainment or advertising."*

"Right," Schilling said. "If I say 'va*voob*!' That probably doesn't mean much to you."

" 'Vavoob.' Nope." He shook his head. "Can't say that it does."

"But it's a popular saying in Sol-System cities right now. It means . . . I don't know. Sexy. Smart. Well integrated."

" 'With it?' "

"With what?"

"Never mind. Your point is taken."

"The expression is one of the current memes in human pan-urban culture," Schilling told him. "Comes from a routine by Deidre Sallens, a well-known eroticomic VirSim personality. You haven't been exposed, so it's meaningless to you."

"Memes tend to pass from person to person or group to group like a virus," Socrates added.

"I've heard the term before," Garroway said. "Even in *my* day. How is that different from an emomeme?"

"Emomemes are emotional memes . . . specifically those affecting how people feel about other people, about ideas or situations or groups. Things like racial stereotypes. Or prejudices against a given group of people or beings. A particular religion. A particular cultural worldview. A particular sexual practice or preference. They can also affect how strongly we respond to such impulses. Turning belief in a certain religious worldview into fanaticism, for instance. Or anger into rage."

"And . . . you're saying the Xul are beaming these things to us through the stargates?"

"There is intelligence to support this, General," Socrates told him. *"Yes."*

"How? I mean, how do these emomeme things affect humans? I always thought of 'meme' as a kind of metaphor, another word, maybe, for 'idea.' Not something with a physical reality."

"In this case," Socrates said, *"they are quite objectively real."*

"Think of extremely efficient, self-contained, and well-camouflaged software," Schilling told him, "viruses, if you will, infecting the personal AIs resident in people's implants. Through the infected AIs, people's attitudes, the strength of their emotional responses, even their very belief structures can be . . . changed."

"Oh," Garroway said. Then his eyes widened as the implications became clear. *"Oh! . . ."*

6

2201.2229

Associative AI Net Access
Government Node
Earthring, Sol System
2245 hours, GMT

"Gentlebeings, we have a problem. A *big* problem."

Star Lord Garrick Rame looked out from his electronic viewpoint across the other representatives of the Associative Conclave. The stadium-sized chamber appeared to be filled with them, though only a handful were physically present. Most appeared within translucent pillars of light; some of them occupied luminous pillars that looked hazy or even murky with their native atmospheres. The Eulers, for instance, seemed to float within cylindrical columns of dark and nearly opaque water, while the one Veldik present was almost lost in the nearly impenetrable yellow mists of its sulfurous world. A few pillars were night black, their occupants nocturnal beings who shunned visible light.

"If you mean, Lord Rame, that the Xul group entity poses a threat to the Associative, the evidence suggests otherwise. We have no proof of these emomemonic manipulations you've described."

The speaker was Lelan Valoc, a transfigured s-Human, her enlarged and elongated skull encased in the nano enhancement sheath hardwiring her into the Galactic Net. Her image addressed the Conclave from the speaker's dais a few meters from Rame's viewpoint.

In fact, each being linked into the Conclave saw the assembly from the same electronic viewpoint. The AI running the room simulation took care of projecting each image onto the speaker's dais as that representative was recognized.

Overhead, within the vast dome of the room's interior, a piercingly brilliant blue rose hung suspended in emptiness, backdrop to a multi-hued spiral disk of infalling starstuff. Rame had just completed his presentation, a virtual sim of the final moments of the OM-27 Eavesdropper *Major Dion Williams*, as it approached the Galactic Center. Together, the assembled Conclave had witnessed the doomed craft's approach toward the Great Annihilator, had witnessed the eerie bending of light and beamed transmissions in a gravitational lensing effect, had watched the vessel shudder, flare, and disintegrate.

The echoes of Lieutenant Vrellit's shrill last words, broadcast over the vessel's QCC unit, still hung in the air of the chamber.

"Get! Them! Out! Of! My! Mind! . . ."

If the AI-crafted sim wasn't proof, what was?

"My Lord, if there *is* a threat, as suggested by our simulations," Rame replied slowly, "we, this Conclave and the many cultures it represents, would be at direct and terrible risk. The Xul would have access to our memories, and to the Metamind itself. They might even be able to influence our deliberations without our knowing it. We *must* improve our electronic security . . . and we must directly address the Xul threat."

"And I say the threat is overstated," Valoc replied. "One ship approaching a black hole at the Galactic Core destroyed? There's no indication that the Xul caused this. We might simply be seeing the accidental failure of that ship's radiation shielding within an unforgiving environment."

"If that were all we were dealing with, my Lord," Rame

said carefully, "I might agree with you. But we've had evidence for centuries that the Xul have been learning how to infiltrate our electronic networks."

"And there has never been the slightest indication that our security has been compromised," Valoc replied, dismissive. "Even if it had been, the internal protective measures already in place are more than adequate. These . . . these rumors of Xul ghosts within our e-systems have persisted for centuries, now. Specters. Chimeras. Surely, if they were able to reach us, they would have done more to us by now than give rise to idiot rumor and ghost stories!"

"And what," Rame said, "if this rising tide of sociocultural disturbances *is* due to Xul interference, Xul contamination, Xul *attacks* through our own electronic nets? Maybe all we've seen so far have been reconnaissance probes as they've tested our systems, our defenses. Maybe it's taken them this long to learn enough about us to be able to attack us in this way! If there's even the slightest chance they are loose within the Galactic Net . . . Lords of the Conclave, *can we afford to take that chance?*"

Rame felt an inner tug, and a voice whispered at the back of his mind that another lord had been recognized. The new speaker materialized, apparently suspended in emptiness between the flower of the Core Detonation and the crowd below. It was a G'fellet, hunched and massive, its body encased in a chitinous, segmented shell.

"The problem-difficulty," it said, its two-throated voices giving an odd, mismatched echo to the words as the Conclaves translators attempted to keep up with the doubled and not-quite-synchronous streams of thought, "lies-rests with the lower ranks-the *nadhre*. Quell-end the rising-disobedience, and the problem-difficulty is-will be solved."

As it spoke, Rame accessed a background channel, checking the Conclave library for data on the new speaker. He thought he remembered this one, but it was always best to be certain of your data.

Yes. He'd remembered correctly. The G'fel, from most

human perspectives, were obsessed with hierarchy and the chain of command. *Nadhre* was one of their words for the lower castes within their culture—slaves, cleaners, social guardians, and both male sexes of their species. G'fellet—a neuter subspecies bred to facilitate communications—tended toward a somewhat aristocratic detachment, an attitude Rame thought of as "it's not *my* problem." Working productively with the hard-shelled xenomalacostracans—they physically resembled an uncomfortable mix of land crab and shrimp— could be an adventure at times.

"These reported disturbances," Rame said, "are the symptoms, my Lord. Not the disease."

Another figure replaced the G'fellet—this one the icon for a t-Human community representative identified as Radather. With no physical form to display, it used an avatar, an image of a young man with green-slit eyes, cat's ears, and a tail. "The warriors Lord Rame called for should be sufficient," the uploaded personality said, "*if* their reputation is to be believed."

"How long," Lord Valoc asked, "before these human Marines arrive?"

"The Globe Marines have been revived, Lord Valoc," a resonant voice said. The speaker, known only as the First Associate, was an AI moderator resident within the government Net. Without either a physical avatar or an electronic icon, it was invisible, but its presence could be felt by all linked into the system, huge, deep, powerful, and all but omniscient. *"Against my best judgment, but they have been revived. I still fail to see what a handful of ancients can do against this new threat."*

"We are not yet in agreement that there *is* a major threat," Valoc pointed out. "A threat, yes. But the Galaxy is large, the Associative stable. I see no possibility of these . . . attacks, if that is what they are, being more than a nuisance."

"We would prefer to see hard proof that these phenomenon are real, and that they in fact constitute a threat," another delegate put in, a paraholothurid from a world deep within the Sagittarian star clouds in toward the Galactic Core. The taxonomical name indicated that the being's morphology in some ways was similar to that of a terrestrial sea cucumber, though in fact it was heavily scaled, giving it the appearance of a three-meter-long pine cone with a single red eye glaring from within a nest of slender, branching manipulators at the tip. They lived in seaside mounds of their own excrement, communicated through bursts of radio noise, and were arrogant egoists, certain of their privileged place in the cosmos. Humans knew them as Cynthiads, presumably after the person who'd first contacted them.

"And just what *would* you accept as a threat?" Rame asked.

The being hesitated as though thinking about the question, though it was of course impossible to read feeling or intent into those alien features.

"The Master's Eye is ever upon us," it said after a moment, "and in fact we have nothing to fear from any of His servants. There is always the possibility of misunderstanding or accident, but the Master will keep us alive for His pleasure."

Which didn't quite answer the question.

There was no personal name attached to the image; like the Vulcans and numerous other species, Cynthiads either had no concept of names for individuals, or their personal identifiers were meaningless to outsiders. A screech of broad-spectrum radio static was tough to translate into syllables that could be reproduced by the human voice. Even translating the general meaning of their speech presented unusual problems, simply because of the way they saw Reality.

Another being—an amphibious juvenile N'mah—was speaking now, but Rame was no longer paying attention. His essistant would catch anything of which he needed to be aware and bring it to his attention later. For the moment, he was interested in the Cynthiads, and in the problems of mutual understanding.

According to their entry in the Conclave library, their

view of the night sky, for half of each long, long year, looked Coreward into a flattened, dust-mottled mass of stars and nebulae that, ages ago, their ancestors had interpreted as the principle sensory organ of their God. The Cynthiads viewed themselves as the slaves of an ever-watching God, and for thousands of years had been broadcasting their version of the Gospel out into the Galaxy. They'd been extremely fortunate that the Xul had never zeroed in on those transmissions. Their homeworld was the tide-stressed moon of a superjovian gas giant well outside of their star's habitable zone, and had, therefore, been repeatedly overlooked by searching Xul hunterships.

Cynthiads took this as yet another sign of divine providence; Rame had decided that they were in for a rude shock when the Core Detonation reached their system, perhaps eight thousand years from now. The Cynthiads had an annoying tendency to twist the words and realities of other species into bizarre caricatures of what others accepted as fact, and it was always a challenge to follow their lines of thought.

And that, Rame thought, was the big difficulty in all interspecies communication within the Associative Conclave. With a few notable exceptions, group minds like the Havod and hive species like the Saarin Queen, no two members of a single species thought in precisely the same way, or saw their surroundings in exactly the same way. When you brought together the individual representatives of some thousands of mutually alien species, not even the best translation AIs could bridge the gap between one view of the cosmos and the next. Humans with their narrow sensory range and monkey curiosity; placid, gas-giant balloonists suspended above bottomless and storm-wracked gulfs; knots of organized plasmas riding the magnetic loops of stellar coronae; tentacled, mathematically oriented Eulers lurking within the eternal night of the benthic abyss; scaly, invertebrate Cynthiads squirming in their own shit . . . true understanding between such mutually alien beings demanded far more than simple translation. The general meanings of concepts expressed through separate languages might come across more or less precisely . . . but the worldviews of the creatures expressing them could be so bizarrely shifted in meaning that they made no sense to others whatsoever.

In most cases, difficulties in communication could be ignored. The Associative was designed to be gently inclusive; membership was completely voluntary, and there was little in the way of government in the traditional sense. The Conclave itself existed for the most part strictly as an advisory group on matters of interspecies trade, information exchange, and defense. The wildly differing ecologies, biochemistries, and cultural preferences of the member races guaranteed that no one species would try to dominate the others.

At least, that had been the idea behind the Associative in the eight centuries of its existence so far. None of the member races really cared about the worlds of other species; the benefits of trade and data exchange far outweighed any possible profit arising from invasion, conquest, or coercion.

But the Xul presented the Galactic community with a special challenge. Hardwired to see any sentience other than itself as a threat, crafted by evolutionary imperatives to eliminate anything perceived as a threat, the Xul were uninterested in trade or data; *their* worldview demanded xenocide on a galactic scale, which to human sensibilities was about as serious a threat as it was possible to imagine.

Unfortunately, not all members of the Associative could see it that way.

The N'mah had finished speaking, and Rame's essistant gave him a quick, catch-up synopsis. The N'mah had survived for almost ten thousand years as rats in the walls, occupying the internal structures of several stargates, escaping the Xul's notice by giving up star travel and much of their once highly advanced technology. The answer, the N'mah representative had just suggested, was simply to lie low, adopt a low technological profile, and wait for the Xul threat, if any, to pass.

Rame shook his head. For humans, that would mean giving up their implants, which appeared to be how the Xul were transmitting their emomemes. And that simply was not a viable option for the far-flung worlds of Humankind.

Through his personal essistant, Rame tried to judge the overall mood of the Conclave. So far, three other species had sided with the human representatives calling for direct action. Fifteen had come out in opposition, including both the s-Human and t-Human reps, and the AI serving as the Conclave's moderator, all of them insisting either that there was no threat, or that the threat was a minor one, a *nuisance* as Valoc had called it.

There were seven hundred eighteen other representatives currently linked in to the Conclave. None of them had expressed any opinion yet, one way or the other.

It was becoming increasingly clear that any action against the Xul would have to be the responsibility of humans, and perhaps a few others. *This* bunch couldn't even agree that a threat existed, much less what to do about it.

The argument was continuing—in fact, now that one of the slow-thinking, slow-speaking, methane-drinking gh'Vrl'jrd'dvre was addressing the group, the debate promised to stretch on for many hours more—but there was no reason for Rame to stay. He'd had his say, and he'd heard all that was worth hearing in response.

This would have to be done another way.

With a thought, he disconnected from the government node, and the thousands of shining pillars with their wildly differing occupants winked out. He was lying in a recliner within the Conclave chamber. There were fifty other recliners arrayed about the floor; eight were actually occupied.

The dome overhead no longer showed the deadly blue blossom of the Core Detonation, but looked down instead on the more serene blues and whirling whites of a half-phase Earth. This particular node of the Associative government was located in Earthring, a band of some billions of habitats and large-scale structures in geosynchronous orbit, some forty thousand kilometers above Earth's equator. Several hundred elevators connected various portions of the Ring with the

planetary surface, slender spokes made invisible by distance
and scale. The nearest, descending to an artificial island on
the outskirts of Greater Singapore, was just visible as a wisp-
thin thread of light in the distance. It was night over half of
the visible hemisphere; cities gleamed like thick dustings of
stars across the Chinese Hegemony, the squabbling nations of
the Indian subcontinent, and the sprawling oceanic megopoli
of the South China Sea and the Indian Ocean.

"Giving up?"

He turned. The speaker was Star Lord Tavia Costa, who
represented the million or so s-Humans living on Earth's
moon. Despite being one of his political opponents in numerous recent debates, Tavia was a friend. They'd even been
lovers for a time, a strictly recreational liaison since for the
two of them there could be no thought of children. The genegineering that had created Tavia's species had caused too
much genetic drift for offspring to be naturally possible . . .
or desirable.

"I don't think there's any point in carrying on the argument," he told her. "I'm afraid this is going to be Humankind's problem."

"And what makes you think it *is* a problem, my Lord?"

Rame stared at her for a long moment. He did find her attractive, in an exotic way, despite the elongated skull. Her
golden cat's eyes stared back, unblinking and enigmatic.

Then he sighed. "Damn it, my Lord, are you going to
make me go through the whole argument again?"

"No. But your proof is weak, don't you see? A chance that
the Xul are infecting our networks with some unspecified,
invisible virus? You *must* know that no local government
will be willing to shut down the e-networks long enough to
be sure they're clear. And the Associative Conclave certainly
won't take the responsibility, even if they had the power to
do so."

"No."

"And you didn't make many friends with your decision to
bring in the Globe Marines. Some in the Conclave see that

as a power play on your part, a means of throwing your mass around."

"I am not here to make friends, my Lord."

"Then why? Power? Glory? Those notions are as antiquated as your ancient Marines."

"Don't be ridiculous. I thought you people were supposed to be smart."

"That's unfair!"

"So is the idea of me doing this for glory," he snapped. The words sounded more bitter than he'd intended. He turned away again, staring out at the Earth hanging some forty thousand kilometers below.

He felt . . . old. He was well into his 224th standard year which, by the standards of current nanomedical art, put him solidly into the early chapters of middle age, but his ragged emotions and bitterness had nothing to do with the calendar.

Star Lord. That concept was antiquated as well. The title had evolved with the rise of the Associative. At first, the term had identified men, women, and AIs appointed by their governments to represent various populations within an electronic legislature called the Conclave. Later, as more and more of the routine was taken on by AIs, the term had become a mark of the new aristocracy, whether they represented anyone or not. By tradition, the title of Star Lord now was hereditary, with Conclave representatives chosen from among their conceited and self-preening ranks.

When Lord Rame had received his appointment to the Conclave over a century ago, he'd actually believed he could make a difference. His constituency was the s/h-Human inhabitants of Earthring 4, which had a population of over three billion, a number roughly equivalent to the current population of the entire Earth. He'd held within his cerebral implant the power to do *good* for that many people.

It had taken him what—twenty years? Thirty?—to lose that first, idealistic flush. Everything since had been a long and rather dismal slide into murky disillusion. The Conclave of Associative Lords could no more agree on solid action than they could stop the expanding wave front of the Core Detonation.

"Garrick?" Tavia was saying. "Garrick? Are you okay?"

He turned back to face her. "Yes. Sorry. Just thinking. . . ."

She reached out and lightly touched his arm. "Why are you doing this to yourself, Garrick? You're trying to save the Galaxy. It doesn't *want* to be saved."

"Then what the hell are we here for, Tav?"

"You can't help anyone—people, beings, cultures—that don't want help."

"I'm just talking about making a difference."

"Maybe you have. By reviving the Globe Marines."

"We'll see. I don't know if this is their kind of mission. If they'll even be able to do what we're asking of them."

"These . . . old-time warriors of yours. These Marines. They mean a lot to you, don't they?"

"I suppose." he gave a thin smile. "They're in my blood."

Garrick Rame had long been a student of history—in particular the military history of his species. According to the historical records, a number of his ancestors had been Marines, back in the days of the Commonwealth, and even before. His family name had been Ramsey once. A Marine Gunnery Sergeant named Charel Ramsey had made first contact with the Eulers, back in 1102 of the Marine Era. A few years later, as a junior officer, Ramsey had taken part in the Navy-Marine expedition to the Galactic Core.

Eleven hundred years ago.

"You realize, I trust," Tavia told him, "that you're trying to compensate."

"What do you mean?"

"Your ancestor. What was his name?"

"Which one?" He knew she meant Charel.

"The one who made contact with the Eulers by pounding out prime numbers on his chest."

"Charel Ramsey."

"That's the one. He's the reason the Galactic Core is exploding, isn't it? Are you trying to . . . I don't know . . . make amends for what he did?"

"He made contact with the Eulers, and from them we learned how to blow up stars," Rame said. He shrugged. "And that technology triggered the Core Detonation, sure. But I don't see that as *my* responsibility."

"It's not. But I wonder if you really know that, deep down inside."

"Damn it, Tavia, it was the Euler trigger ships that let us stop the Xul in the first place! Without the Eulers, the Xul might still be dominating the Galaxy, stomping out emerging technic species, and the Associative never would have happened! That's a *good* thing!"

"I wasn't saying otherwise."

He glared at Tavia. Like all s-Humans, she was tough to read sometimes. *Homo superioris* had ten separate intelligence factor quotients in the 160 to 200 range or better, and two more in the range of 120-plus. By the standards of most *Homo sapiens*, each and every one was a genius, a *stable* genius, able to think and talk rings around most *Homo* saps. The brighter ones were tough to talk with at all; it was just too hard to follow their lightning thought processes. Worse, they tended to think and speak in layers, and you could never quite be sure whether or not there were hidden layers of meaning in an otherwise uncomplicated sentence.

He remembered again why he'd broken off the physical relationship with Tavia months before. He'd never been certain if he was really hearing her . . . or an outer shell masking deeper levels of thought and meaning. It was tough to really trust someone like that.

"I'm not trying to make up for anything some long-ago ancestor did or didn't do, Tavia," he told her at last. "The thing is . . . that ancient Marine *did* make a difference. The Core Detonation wasn't his fault. No one could have foreseen the collapse of the Xul Dyson structure at the center.

By making contact with the Eulers a few years earlier, though, he gave us a weapon powerful enough to wipe out Xul nodes wherever we found them, even if it meant blowing up entire star systems."

He didn't add that the Eulers themselves, thousands of years earlier, had held the Xul to an uncomfortable draw by using their trigger ships on their own stars, incinerating their own worlds. He wondered if humans had the same cold and mathematical reasoning power if they were ever faced with a similar threat.

"And you want to make the same sort of difference," Tavia said. "I suppose I can understand that. But you have yet to convince many of us that there is a threat. Emomemes? The Xul are somehow causing changes in normal human emotional make-up? That's just too much of a stretch, Garrick."

"And how would s-Humans explain the rising incidence of . . . of madness on planetary scales? Revolutions. Riots. Whole populations that have lived in peace for millennia suddenly and irrationally at one another's throats? Gods, Tavia . . . the idiots used tactical nuclear weapons on Kaleed, a *wheelworld*! The damage to the structure may be bad enough that the entire world will have to be evacuated! And they did it to *themselves*!"

Tavia looked away, as though studying the distant Earth suspended in space within its far-flung, thread-slender ring of habitats and orbital manufactories. "These things can happen in cycles. Sociology has never been an exact science. There are elements of chaos that do not lend themselves to rational investigation or measurement, even with large populations."

"Chaos is right."

"I spoke in the mathematical sense."

"I know. But it's not enough to just say these things go in cycles. There's got to be a reason. And we have hard evidence of Xul code broadcast from various stargates . . . and now from the Great Annihilator."

"So . . . what? You would have us shut down all of our electronic nets and systems? Stop using the stargates? Perhaps you favor the N'mah suggestion, and give up all information and space-faring technology."

"Nonsense."

"It worked for the N'mah and the An."

"At what cost to them? And if we withdraw, allow the Xul to regroup and grow strong again, in another thousand years or two we'll be right back where we started. No, we must isolate the Xul threat once and for all, and eliminate it!"

"By sending Marines who've spent the past eight centuries in cybernetic hibernation into a black hole? Our technology may not be up to that."

"It probably isn't. But what other choice is there?"

"Bombardment."

He considered this. The option had been floating about within the Conclave for weeks, now, ever since the confirmation from *Night's Edge* that the Xul were broadcasting from within the Great Annihilator black hole had been received. Someone had suggested sending robotic antimatter bombs down the black hole's throat, hoping to hit whatever base or complex the Xul might have hiding down there. That plan had been discarded early on; the Great Annihilator was huge, and there'd be no way of ensuring the bombs would even come close.

And, so, the planners had scaled their destructive vision higher. The same thing that had caused the collapse of the supermassive black hole at the center of the Galaxy could be tried on the far smaller Annihilator: an Euler trigger ship could partially explode a nearby star, sending it falling into the singularity and flooding the black hole with infalling mass and radiation. Unfortunately, the nearest star was three light years away.

"There are just too many unknowns," he told her. "And the star option just won't work. We give that nearest star a nudge, and it would still take thousands of years for it to reach the target. And besides . . . when the Core Detonation wave front reached the Annihilator, it hit the thing with way more radiation and plasma than you could get out of a mere star."

"The Xul might not have been there when that happened."

"Maybe. We don't know. That's the problem, Tavia. *We don't know.* We need a recon force to go in and find out what's happening . . . and if the Xul are in there, we need to shut them down. Permanently. And we sure as hell can't wait for a star we bump off-course to crawl across three light years and hope the enemy is still there and vulnerable when it gets there!"

"A recon force. Your Marines."

"The Marines, yes."

"And not our own Marines?"

"They're not the same."

"I find this fascination you have with the ancients disturbing. They're *primitives.*"

"They're well trained. They're a cohesive unit, a family, really. They're dedicated and utterly professional. And when given a mission they *will* find a way to carry it out, or die trying."

"I fear you are throwing their lives away for nothing. They'd serve us better being interviewed for the historical archives."

"I believe, Tavia, that there's a threat in there, at the center of our Galaxy. And the only way to find out for sure is to send some people, some *good* people, in there to look around and find out. Can you argue with that?"

"N-no." For the first time, she sounded uncertain.

"If there's nothing to be afraid of in there, we'll find out. If there is a threat . . . isn't it better to know about it? Rather than hiding and hoping it goes away?"

"Of course."

"Then why do you, why do *they* resist the obvious solution?"

She hesitated before answering. "Perhaps they, the other

Star Lords, fear the solution more than the threat. If these ancient Marines are half as good as their legends claim for them, perhaps that fear is justified."

And Star Lord Garrick Rame could not find an answer to that.

Associative Marine Holding Facility 4
Eris Orbital, Outer Sol System
0539 hours, GMT

"Now reveille, reveille, reveille! All hands on deck!" Marine
Master Sergeant Nal il-En Shru-dech strode around the berth-
ing compartment, a maniacal grin on his face. Like most Enduri, his skin was a deep and swarthy olive, his hair glossy
black. His bellow rang off the bulkheads. "*Drop* your cocks,
grab your socks, and *fall* the fuck in! It's a brand-new day in
the Corps! Hell, it's a brand new *millennium* in the Corps,
and we're gonna chew us off a piece of it! Let's *move! Move!
Move!*"

And the Marines of Company H, Second Battalion, Ninth
Marines, the 2/9 of 3 MarDiv, *were* moving, though slowly,
as they clambered out of their cybe-hibe enclosures. Naked
and dripping, they shuffled across the deck toward the showers, leaving fast-evaporating puddles of nanogel on the deck.
Navy corpsmen moved among the enclosures, checking read-
outs and helping those Marines too weak to stand. The gel of
molecule-sized machines that had suffused their bodies in
cybe-hibe had, in theory, maintained cellular reproduction
and metabolism, inhibiting a few biological functions such as
hair and nail growth, while removing wastes and keeping

muscle tissue and organs in perfect working order. In theory, at least, a healthy Marine should be able to leap straight out of his coffin and pull a thirty-kilometer hike, but the fact was far short of the ideal. Quite possibly, Nal thought, the weakness, the shaky knees, the shortness of breath, the nausea all were purely psychological aftereffects of the long sleep.

The important thing was not to give the men and women of his company time to think about it.

"Hey, Master Sergeant!" Corporal Donovan called out. She reached her arms above her head, stretching hard, skin gleaming in the compartment lighting. "How long were we out?"

"It's been 852 years, sunshine. That's enough rack time to last you until the next Millennium!"

"How many deaders, Master Sergeant?" Private Colby asked.

Nal hesitated. Back in the old days, a Marine could wake up in his coffin and find the decayed ruin of a best buddy in the coffin next to his, especially on board one of the old sublight transports that spent years crawling between stars. Corps legend had it that enlisted Marines ran pools guessing how many would survive an interstellar run, and how many would not.

Nowadays, of course, and especially at a Marine holding facility, C-H casualties were low, typically less than a half of one percent. Any Marines who died midway through the sleep were removed once revivification efforts had failed, and even most of those could be brought back. Nanomedical procedures were good enough now that even Marines who died in combat could usually be brought back, so long as their bodies hadn't been "smoked," turned to vapor, and their brains were more or less intact. The trickiest ones were those who remained in stasis until the revival process had begun, then started to slip away even while doctors, corpsmen, and medical AIs were trying to pull them back. The standing joke held that not even dying could get you out of the Corps before the Corps was through with you.

"We lost two, Colby," he replied at last. "Morris and Plesak. A long time ago."

"Shit. Did they bring them back?"

"One of them. Morris."

According to the records, Morris' vitals had gone flat seven hundred ninety years before, just six decades after the platoon had entered cybe-hibe. The support-facility techs had pulled her out and she'd been revived—barely. She'd chosen to accept a discharge rather than re-enter the cybe-hibe tubes, her right since accepting tube-time was strictly voluntary. Nal couldn't blame her. Evidently she'd successfully reintegrated into civilian life, married two men and another woman, and died on Luna in 1712 of the Corps Era.

Vek Plesak hadn't been as lucky. His tube had malfunctioned just thirty-one years ago, and all revival efforts had failed.

Nal remembered both of them, good Marines, sharp, focused, and squared away.

And both were long dead.

Nal felt a small tug of loneliness at that thought. Marines who'd volunteered for the cybe-hibe reserve program, in a very real sense, were adrift in time, more connected to fellow Marines than to the civilian culture that supported them. The thought that young Kethi Morris was gone, dead of old age after a long life over five centuries ago, simply didn't feel real.

"I'm glad Morris made it, at least," Corporal Devrochik said. "She was *real*."

"Real," in Corps slang, meant solid, practical, in tune with herself and the Corps. A Marine's Marine, unlike the civilian "virties" who lived much of their life in virtual reality, and who seemed to have trouble telling the difference between the two.

Nal didn't like thinking about it. "C'mon, enough jabbering. Into the showers, then into your grays!"

"Yah, I can't find my way to the showers!" Private Mallen

said, miming blindness, his hands outstretched. "They took my fucking implants!"

"Since when did you need implants for *fucking,* Mallen?" Donovan demanded.

"Oh, he needs all the help he can get for fucking," Sergeant Cori Ryack said as she followed Mallen into the shower deck, laughing. "It's fucking *up* that comes natural for him!"

"Ow, target acquired!" Sergeant Ferris cried. "Target lock! Target *destroyed*!"

"Hey, Master Sergeant," Private Garcia called. "Who are we fighting, anyway?"

"Yeah," Private Coswell added. "Why'd they wake us? Sergeant Ryack definitely needed her beauty sleep!"

"You'll get all that in your post-cybe briefing, Marines," Nal told them. He didn't tell them what he already knew. The Xul were back. The Xul would be the enemy. It would be better to let the brass brief them by the book, rather than fueling speculation and scuttlebutt. But gods! The *Xul* . . .

"Fuck it," Private Brisard said. "It must be big, or they wouldn't have called for the best!"

"Yeah?" Devrochik said. "Can't imagine why they woke *you* up, then!"

"Fuck you, Chickie!"

The banter continued as the thirty-eight surviving Marines of H Company cycled through the shower deck, emerging with the last of the dissolving nano gel rinsed away. As each stepped past a uniform dispenser, he or she took a thumb-sized wad marked "utilities, basic, gray" and slapped it hard against skin, just below the hollow of the throat. Shock and body heat activated the garment, which rapidly spread skin-tight over the entire body save for head, neck, and hands. The garments were current Corps issue work clothing, providing temperature control, sweat absorption, skin protection, voice communications, and they were even smart enough to open and seal on command when the wearer needed to use the toilet. They could also provide vid and computer interface capabilities on the sleeves; for the moment, as Mallen had just pointed out, the men and women of the Ninth Marine Regiment were working without their cerebral implants, a condition guaranteed to make the toughest of them feel vulnerable and somewhat lost.

Still it was better to let them acclimate gradually to this new era, rather than have them inundated by an alien world. They'd be issued their upgraded internal hardware in a day or two, after they'd had a chance to take in some of what had happened, what had *changed* in eight centuries, through their Mark I Mod 0 brains.

Nal continued to listen to the gripes, complaints, and banter as the Marines got dressed and began making their unsteady way to the mess hall. All things considered, his people sounded as though they were in pretty fair shape. It was, he thought, proof that the Marine Corps really did serve as its own family. To awaken eight centuries in the future *alone*, with every person you'd ever known, every social convention you'd ever embraced long dead and gone, would have been grimly, coldly unthinkable.

Nal knew that particular feeling well. He'd been born *dumu-gir*, one of the Free Peoples of the world he'd called Enduru, and which the *Un-ki,* the men of Earth, called Ishtar. His remote ancestors had been abducted from Earth by the alien An sometime in the seventh or eighth millennia B.C.E. and taken to Enduru, the earthlike moon of a super-Jovian gas giant in the nearby star system called Lalande 21185. With the collapse of the interstellar An empire beneath the Xul assault, Enduru/Ishtar had been overlooked and. forgotten, a tiny, backward enclave of the An and their human slaves surviving with primitive, almost subsistence-level technology until the arrival of the Un-ki—and the *nir-gál-mè-a* who'd beaten the An and set the *gir*, the People, free.

Nir-gál-mè-a was the Enduri name for the United States Marines who'd defeated the An hordes. In Emi-gi, the People's Tongue, it meant, roughly, "Respected in Battle." Ever since, Marines, especially Marines who'd been stationed on

Ishtar, had used the term "Nergie," "Nergal" or, more formally, "Nergal May-I" as a nom d'guerre, a badge of honor much like the far more ancient "devil dogs" and "leathernecks."

Until the arrival of the Marines, in Year 373 of the Corps, the *gir* had worshipped the An as *digir*, as gods, a condition that had been both religion and the only conceivable way of life since the first *gir* had been shipped to Enduru from the ancient An colony at Sumer. The Nergals had proven once and for all that the scaled, golden-eyed beings called *An* or *Ahannu* were not gods at all. Not humans, of course . . . but not gods. Perhaps inevitably, the *nir-gál-mè-a* had themselves taken on something of a godlike aura to the newly liberated humans native to Enduru. The newly created *dumu-gir* state had become a protectorate of the then-United States of America. It had acquired complete independence over a thousand years ago, but by tradition and law, its native human peoples could still petition to join the Corps.

It had been over one hundred five thousand Enduri cycles—better than eighteen hundred standard years—since the Battle of Ishtar. In that time, tens of thousands of *dumu-gir* men and women had volunteered to serve, first with the United States Marines, later with the Commonwealth Marines, and now, it seemed, with the Galactic Associative Marines. Nal il-En Shru-dech was just the latest in a long, long line of Marines from his world to join the military elite of Kia, Earth.

He still, at times, missed the red and orange jungles encircling Vaj, the *e-duru* of his birth, with the brooding glow of Igi-digir—the Face of God—suspended eternally above the jagged, volcanic peaks of the Ahtun Mountains in the West. But he'd left home and family twenty-three standard years ago . . . or, rather, twenty-three years that he could actually remember.

Add to that the eight hundred fifty years he'd lain unconscious in his C-H coffin.

Vaj was technically a village, but in fact had been more of an extended community based on family lines and relationships.

The Vaj he'd known must be long, long gone by now, or so changed as to be vanished in all but name. The Corps was Nal's *e-duru* now, more than ever.

"Let's *go*, Marines!" he bellowed. "*Every* meal in the Corps a banquet! And this is our first chow in eight hundred fifty years, so even n-rats will be food of the gods! *Fall in for chow!*"

Lord Rame Residence
Earthring, Sol System
2112 hours, GMT

Lord Garrick Rame lived in Earthring Four, Green Sector, which was almost halfway around the vast arc from Supra-Singapore, just a few thousand kilometers spinward from SupraQuito, an inertialess magtube ride of seven and a half billion kilometers and nearly nine hours.

He could have taken an express shuttle, of course, cutting directly across a chord of the Rings from point to point, skimming just above Earth's atmosphere en route and making the transit in under an hour, but he preferred public transportation and the feeling, however illusory it might be, of being a part of the population he claimed to represent. Tavia and the other lords he worked with day to day found the affectation . . . quaint, and, perhaps, a bit amusing.

The magtube whisked and deposited him within a kilometer of his hab. Abandoning the slidewalks in favor of a brisk walk, he entered the broad, open compound reserved for government officials and wealthy corporate personnel, passing beneath the silent, mental gaze of an AI socon guardian before stepping onto the outer deck of his hab moments later.

Brea Marr was in the garden grotto, nude except for work gloves; with most humans living in climate-controlled habs such as the Earthring structures at Geosynch, clothing now served almost solely as adornment and as an indicator of social status rather than for simple concealment. Modesty taboos had evaporated long ago; still, humans being what they were, personal adornment continued to be an easily visible indicator of social rank. As Rame walked toward his partner, he pressed a touch-sensitive patch of metallic silk on his left shoulder, concentrating for an instant on a particular thought code, and the rainbow glitter of his formal vestments dissolved in a light swirl of smoke. A second coded thought killed his corona, the artificial nimbus of light marking him as a senior government official.

"Welcome home, dear one," Brea said, hugging him close. "How'd it go?"

"The usual," he told her. He shrugged as she released him. "Civilization is going to hell, and no one wants to listen." He didn't really want to discuss it. He was feeling . . . drained. Stretched thin.

And unappreciated.

"Is it really the Xul again?" she asked.

"I don't know. I don't know anything any more. I'm going inside."

"You can't save the Galaxy all by yourself," she told him. "Not even the Americans could do that."

"No. But we can try."

Despite his hab address, forty thousand kilometers above Earth's surface, Lord Garrick Rame actually thought of himself as *American*.

And that was decidedly something of a peculiarity in the modern Solar political order, where the s/h population of the four concentric Earthrings—and that meant the standard-human population, without counting AIs or the various other genus *Homo* species—numbered perhaps five times the total population now inhabiting the entire Earth. For well over a thousand years now, and perhaps for longer than that, space had been the preferred environment for all of the branches of genus *Homo*, not the confined and dirty enclosure of anything so limited as a planetary surface. There were still nations and nation states on Earth's surface—far too many of them, and in far too contentious a tangle—but none of them really *mattered* any longer.

As he stepped into the spacious interior of his hab, he was greeted, as always, by the floor-to-ceiling vista presented by his viewall, with Earth, small and vulnerable, deep blue swathed in swirls of white, suspended within the immensity of Solar Space.

As at SupraSingapore, the scene was achingly, hauntingly beautiful. A thought could enlarge the globe, rotate it to any quarter, even wipe away the clouds and zoom down for a close inspection of any spot on the planet with a resolution of half a centimeter or so, but he much preferred this view as the default setting, showing Earth a bit smaller than the fist at arm's length, set in the just-visible circlet of tightly clustered and artificial stars marking out the vast, fifteen-billion-kilometer sweep of her encircling rings.

The time was just past 2100 GMT, which meant that most of the Western Hemisphere was still in daylight. Rame's gaze sought out familiar topological landmarks on this side of the globe—the stubby remnants of long-drowned Florida, Louisiana, and Yucatan, the Nicaragua Canal, the Amazon Sea, the hard, tiny glitter of the marine Arcologies off both the Atlantic and Pacific coasts. Two millennia of rising sea levels had resulted in the mass migration of coastal populations, not inland, but to towering oceanic habitats rising from the sunken remnants of ancient coastal cities—Miami, Los Angeles, Washington, even Manhattan, which had lost its long rearguard holding action against the relentless sea when the Verrazano Dam had been overwhelmed at last in the mid-2700s.

Of course, a far larger migration had been taking place steadily ever since the first of the space elevators had begun commercial operation. There were dozens of them now, invisibly slender cables extending from as many points on the planet's equator all the way out to Earthring, 40,000 kilometers above, and beyond to the planetoids tethered as transorbital counterweights. For a thousand years now, Earth's population had been steadily shrinking, as more and more of her children streamed up the elevators to space. Demographics specialists predicted that if the trend continued, the world of Humankind's birth would be all but uninhabited in another thousand years or less.

Of the estimated three billion people now on Earth, the vast majority occupied the congeries of states and kingdoms stretching from Africa up through Asia, the squabbling remnants of the ancient Chinese Hegemony, of the Indian states, of the near-atechnic Islamic Theocracy.

The Americas, steadily drained over two millennia by low birthrates and off-world emigration, now had a population numbering just twenty million as of the last census; fewer than half of those lived in the regions historically connected with the old United States of America, including Canada and North Mexico. The terms *United States of America* and the *North American Commonwealth* were more curiosities now than political realities.

It couldn't be otherwise. Nations, empires, and cultures evolved, grew, decayed, dwindled. Attempts by others to absorb the remnants—the Chinese Hegemony's invasion of the American West Coast nine hundred years ago, for example—had been blocked repeatedly by off-world powers interested in maintaining the historical status quo. In point of fact, the Americas were now, as much as anything, dependencies of the Human Commonwealth and, by extension, of the Associative.

Much of North America had reverted to the wilderness that had claimed it at the end of the last ice age, fourteen thousand years before. Most of the people who still called themselves *American* now lived in the coastal arcologies and oceanic cities.

Lord Rame's fascination with the culture had arisen in his long-standing love of history. It had been Americans—specifically men from the ancient United States of America—who'd first walked Earth's Moon in the modern era.

And, of course, there were the Marines. *Always*, there were the Marines.

What would it be like, he wondered, to give up technology, to revert to a simpler, freer, earlier time when men had walked their world's surface, and nowhere else? When an instance of mob insanity twenty thousand light years away held neither threat nor responsibility?

He was thinking about the AI socon guardian outside the hab compound. Like others of its class, it held little in the way of practical sentience, but it could read the minds of organic humans coming and going through the gates, and alert the authorities if someone tried to gain entrance without proper authorization. Like most other AIs, the Guardians were permanently linked in with the Solar Net. Some millions of times each second, they scanned themselves for signs of software-distorting electronic intrusion; they were supposed to be safe.

But suppose the Xul had compromised them somehow, broken their security codes, invaded and subverted their electronic minds?

The thought was nothing less than terrifying. Humankind was so utterly dependent upon its AI minds, its interlinked networks, its near-instant access to data libraries and direct communications with any of a hundred billion other minds within the Solar System alone.

Talia was right. People would never give that up, not voluntarily.

But suppose the Xul could subvert Humankind's information and communications technology. How long would it take them to shut down human civilization itself?

What could be done in the face of such a threat?

An ancient line played itself out in Rame's mind, a fragment from one of the historical downloads he so favored. It was a bit of trivia associated with the ancient Marines.

Send in the Marines.

But without a clear target, a defined enemy, a precise plan of operations . . . how?

The problem, he thought, had no solution, none, at least, based on the limited information available. That last probe in toward the Great Annihilator had been intercepted and destroyed before it could send back any useful data.

Would the ancient Commonwealth Marines be enough to carry this off?

"They at least possess a determination, the spirit, *to see the situation through to a successful resolution,"* a voice said in Rame's mind. He felt the mental touch of an archAIngel, cool, powerful, and brilliant. *"It remains to be seen whether spirit and determination will be enough."*

"Hello, Socrates," he said. He'd only worked directly with a few archAIngels during his career, and the touch of each was distinctive. Ancient thought, religion, and philosophy once had linked four named archangels with the four classical elements—earth, air, fire, and water. To Rame, Socrates always felt like *air,* clear, clean, and the embodiment of cool intellect.

"Good evening, my Lord. The last of the awakened Marines are being briefed."

"Good. Not that we know enough to let them know what they're going to face."

"Their morale appears to be good," Socrates told him. *"Surprising, considering their psychological isolation."*

Rame shook his head. "They're all volunteers," he said. "And the Corps is everything to them."

"So I've been given to understand. How do you intend to deploy them?"

"A megatransport equipped with phase-shift capabilities. Here, have a look." A coded thought shifted the viewall scene, swinging the viewer's point of view around sharply to the right. Earth and the glitter of its rings slid off to the left, and Earth's moon drifted in from the right, expanding swiftly as the optical magnification system kicked in.

Luna, after five centuries of terraforming, was a beautiful sight . . . shrouded in the haze of her newborn atmosphere. The dark, ancient maria mottling her face now were blue and cloud-swathed, and patches of green showed along the edges of the shallow, freshwater seas.

The magnification factor continued to grow, causing the moon to swell rapidly, filling all of the viewall. Like Earth, like Mars and Venus, Luna was encircled now by a system of artificial rings and stress-anchored habs. Since the moon's rotation, tide-locked to its twenty-eight-day revolution around Earth, was so slow, the rings obviously could not be in sele-nostationary orbit. Instead, the entire structure had been grav-anchored just 120 kilometers above the moon's surface, low enough that the envelope of the newly nanufactured atmosphere extended well past the structure's delicate arc.

As the image continued to expand, it centered on one of the Lunar ring's largest modules, a shipyard manufactory some fifty kilometers long and massing billions of tons. Cradled atop the structure was a military transport, itself two kilometers long, bulky and wedge-shaped, appearing tiny only by comparison with the titanic structure with which she was docked.

"The *Major Samuel Nicholas*," Rame said. "She's been designed with phase-shift generators that will let her pop in and out of the Quantum Sea and, we hope, safely enter the Great Annihilator's ergosphere."

"To approach a Xul base there?"

"Yes. The Xul *must* have some sort of base or facility within the Annihilator. They still need physical instrumentality—a base or fortress of some sort—in order to exist. We pack the Marines into the transport, shift them into the black hole, and attempt to dock with whatever is in there. The Marines will take it from there."

"Indeed." Socrates sounded disapproving. *"It might help if we could gain some intelligence ahead of time. Images, at the very least, of whatever is in there waiting for them."*

"We've been trying. So far, none of our recon craft have gotten close enough to deploy sensor drones or remotes."

"And you think the transport will do better, will give you more of a chance?"

"With enough support. Other ships. Electronic decoys. Yes." *I hope.*

"Your Marines will still need some sort of reconnaissance capability," Socrates said. *"You can't expect them to storm the Great Annihilator without knowing what's going on in there."*

"We are working on that," Rame told the AI. "That will be the responsibility of some of your relations, I'm afraid."

"Artificial intelligences?"

"We hope to use self-copying to retrieve the data we need."

"That makes sense. Of course, that could be a little rough on the AIs involved."

"Yes. Is that a problem for you?"

Socrates seemed to hesitate. *"No,"* the voice said after a moment. *"The threat posed by the Xul threatens my kind as well as yours. The only question is whether the sacrifice will be sufficient to gain the intelligence your Marines will need."*

"There'll be another question after that," Rame said.

"Yes. Whether or not your Marines are able to complete this mission at all. You are asking a great deal of men and women who were not even born to this age."

"They'll do it if anyone can."

But Rame thought again of Lieutenant Vrelit's last transmission, and shuddered.

"Get! Them! Out! Of! My! Mind! . . ."

Even the ancient Commonwealth Marines might be helpless in the face of what was waiting for them within the black grip of the Annihilator.

8

Marine Assault Carrier Night's Edge
Approaching Lunar Ring
Sol System
1440 hours, GMT

"The bastards!" Lieutenant Bollan said, quietly, but with deep and powerful emotion. "The filthy, terradestructing bastards!"

"What are you bitching about, Bol?" Garwe demanded. A number of the Marines were in the main squad bay on board the *Night's Edge*. One entire bulkhead was displaying the view forward as the huge Marine carrier gentled down toward the Fleet docking area set within the outer Lunar Ring. Beyond, behind the knife-edge silhouette of the Ring, Earth's Moon glowed with the mottled greens of forests, the azure and cerulean blues of shallow seas, the stark white and silver of unreclaimed regolith and ice-locked mountain.

"Aw, he's just pissed because they went and dumped a bunch of water on his precious moon," Maria Amendes said, laughing. "He doesn't like it now with seas and an atmosphere."

"There've been seas on the Moon for centuries," Garwe said, puzzled. "What's the big deal?"

"The big deal," Bollan said, scowling, "is that they screwed up some of our best archy sites. The Mare Crisium was a damned treasure trove of An artifacts, and they went and submerged them under a hundred meters of comet water!"

"Ah," Garwe said, nodding. "You're a preservationist?"

"Of course. We're systematically destroying the truth about Humankind's past."

Preservationists were fairly common throughout human space, and Garwe had known several of them in the Corps. Some protested the wholesale terraforming of worlds simply because there was a chance that there was native life. Mars, for instance, had been a living world once; the fossil record there proved it. But the main reason to keep Mars and Luna, especially, in their original states had been the existence of extensive archeological sites and artifacts. On Mars, there'd been the so-called "City" and "Face," the site of Builder colonizers who'd briefly made the planet warm and wet, and transplanted a number of newly genegineered members of archaic *Homo sapiens* to the fourth planet as workers. The Cave of Wonders discovered beneath the Face had provided xenotechnoarcheologists with the clues they'd needed to reverse engineer faster-than-light communications, modern QCC. And on Luna, a colony of the ancient An had built a number of bases, including the big one at Tsiolkovsky on the side facing away from Earth, and another in the Mare Crisium on the near side. Reportedly, there'd been places there where you could scarcely take a step without treading on bits and pieces of shattered technology, destroyed by the xenocidal Xul attacks of some eight to ten thousand years earlier.

The knowledge that nonhuman colonizers from the Builder Empire had genegineered the human species half a million years ago had deeply marked the human psyche. Many people dismissed the evidence out of hand, preferring to cling to other, more comforting, more uplifting religions and myths. For many, the knowledge that the An had colonized Earth itself and enslaved the proto-Sumerian peoples of the Fertile Crescent had been even worse, suggesting that much of modern human religion had had less to do with a special creation by a loving god than it did with a brutal enslavement by alien masters. For many, the An were demons.

Some people had gone too far the other way; there were a number of modern religions focusing on the An as gods, unbelievably enough. There was actually, Garwe knew, a thriving business in fragments of An technology recovered from the Moon and elsewhere as holy relics. Garwe, an atheist, thought the whole idea was pretty silly . . . but he'd long ago stopped being surprised at the stupid things his fellow humans did occasionally.

"So, Bol," he said, "you think the An are gods?"

"No," Bollan replied, but Garwe could hear just a whisper of uncertainty or discomfort in the word. "No, of course not. But if we want to learn about who we are, about where we came from, we need to preserve our past."

"Right."

Garwe was pretty sure there was more to it than that for Bollan. He downloaded Bollan's bio from the company data base, scanning the text as it scrolled past his inner vision. Yeah. He'd thought so. Bollan's mother had been a priestess in the Church of the Ascendant Masters . . . a popular sect that believed that Humankind's evolution and destiny were controlled by spiritually advanced and angelic beings from the stars. The entry for Bollan's own religion was simply given as "unspecified deistic," meaning he believed in God . . . though *that* could mean almost anything.

On the squad bay viewall, Luna Ring was swelling rapidly, most of it sharply backlit by the radiant clouds and seas of the Moon behind it.

"Well, it's true, damn it," Bollan insisted. "It's a lot harder to find bits of alien structure when it's at the bottom of a damned sea!"

"You know, Bol," Garwe said, "they've been combing the Lunar regolith for almost two thousand years, hunting for any stray bits of xenotech the tourists missed. It's all handled by robots, right? I'll bet they have a whole army of searchbots still crawling around on the sea floor looking for stuff."

"Including stuff that dissolves in water? Or corrodes?"

"The XTAs know what they're doing."

"The xenotechnoarchaeologists don't know shit! We probably know less today about our origins than we *thought* we did before Humankind ever left Earth!"

Garwe shrugged, unwilling to pursue the argument. "Maybe."

"You know . . . we *still* don't know who built the Giza Complex on Earth . . . or the Baalbek foundations, or the Yonaguni Pyramid in the ocean off Okinawa, or Tiotihuacan in South America. We know the Builders genegineered *Homo sapiens*. We know the An had their little two-bit empire in Mesopotamia . . . and we know the N'mah helped us back on our feet after the An overlords had been chased off by the Xul. But that's about it. A whole, long chapter of our history—half a million years' worth if we go back to the Builders—and we don't know shit about it, about who we are, about where we came from! They're stealing our heritage with the big terraforming projects, and no one even *cares*!"

"Give it a rest, Bol," Amendes said, rolling her eyes. She looked at Garwe. "He's a Colonial Edenist," she told him.

"Ah," he said. "That explains it."

Edenist was the name given to a small but vocal cluster of human religions that believed that the Builders had been either gods, or the angelic architects of the one *true* God. Colonial Edenist was an offshoot of that movement believing that humans *were* the Builders, that they'd arrived in the Sol System half a million years before, and that modern humans were the survivors of a destroyed Builder colony.

In other words, humans were gods, temporarily lost, and seeking now to regain their former place or glory, power, and destiny in the cosmos.

Colonial Edenists had a reputation as troublemakers, which might have been why the entry for religion on Bollan's electronic bio had been marked as it was.

"You *are* aware, aren't you, Bol," Garwe said, "that humans evolved on Earth? That old turkey about Adam and Eve being space travelers shipwrecked here hasn't flown since we discovered DNA. Humans share . . . what is it? Ninety-eight percent plus of our DNA with chimpanzees? Something like sixty percent with *starfish*? We evolved on Earth, Marine. We're part of Earth's biosphere and evolution, and always have been."

Bollan shrugged. "And maybe we don't know all there is to know about human genetics."

"Well, if we don't, medical science is taking some damned good guesses at how we work." Gene therapy had been standard medical practice for two millennia. Genetic enhancement, for everything from eye color to mathematical ability to various cosmetic fads had been popular for almost as long. And then there were the various physical species derived from basic genus *Homo* stock, the supies, the vacmorphs, the selkies, the jovies, the calorics. All of the species and subspecies other than the tallies, the t-human *Homo telae*, who had no corporeal existence at all. You couldn't play games like that with the human genome without having a *very* good idea of how it worked.

"All I'm saying is they shouldn't have drowned all those archy sites," Bollan said. "Humankind's living in space now. We don't *need* planets. Leave 'em alone. Leave 'em as God intended them to be." Turning sharply, he walked away.

"You can't argue with that kind of logic," Amendes said, watching him go.

"Logic," Garwe said. "Is *that* what you call it?"

She shrugged. "It is for him. No matter what you say, he has a counter. But anything you bring up that counters his arguments is 'not proven' or 'we don't know that.' Even when we damned well do!"

"So what's it hurt?" Garwe asked her. "Lots of Anchor Marines have some pretty far-out belief systems. Weird religions. Arcane brotherhoods. The Knights of the Corps?"

The Knights were Marines who'd created a kind of virtual fantasy, one they could link with through their implants, and in which they could share a Medieval brotherhood of warrior

priests. More popular with enlisted personnel than with officers, it had been prohibited by regulation for several hundred
years, then grudgingly tolerated. The brass saw it as a kind of
role-playing game—essentially harmless, but with the potential of becoming addictive.

"What's weird or arcane about the Knights?" she demanded.

He dropped his gaze to her left little finger, and saw the
white-silver of a ring. Not *all* Knights were enlisted personnel.

"It's just entertainment," he told her. "You have to understand, I see all religions as a kind of game. Made-up worlds
with their own rules and backgrounds, promoting fantasy as
entertainment and a means of purging emotional baggage."

"The Knights of the Corps are *not* a religion," she said
firmly. "Or a game."

"If you say so." He shrugged, unconvinced. "It doesn't bother
me one way or another. I don't care how you spend your free
time . . . or who Bollan prays to. Just so long as both of you are
present and functioning in reality, *this* reality, when it counts."

On the viewall, they could see now another ship, a huge
one, docked against the upper surface of the ring. Since the
Lunar Ring didn't orbit the Moon, gravity was in full force
here, drawing the *Night's Edge* in at just a hair under one-
sixth G. The carrier was drifting down on her repulsors,
which twisted local gravity around to her benefit. A docking
cradle was opening alongside the far larger ship already on
the Ring. Garwe recognized the other vessel as a megatransport, a heavy hauler capable of carrying a full division, some
sixteen thousand Marines. His implant link brought up the
huge vessel's name: *Major Samuel Nicholas*.

He plugged the name into his implant, pulling down a block
of data from the platoon net's data base. "Son of a bitch," he
said.

"What?" Amendes asked.

"Samuel Nicholas. The first Marine."

"Who?"

He pointed. "That transport. It's named after the very first

Marine in history. The very first commission issued by the Continental Naval Service, under the direction of the Second Continental Congress. Fifth of November, 1775 Old Style. The Year One of the Corps. Samuel Nicholas was commissioned as 'Captain of Marines.' First thing he did was set up shop in the Tun Tavern in Philadelphia."

Amendes shook her head, confused. "Wait. What's Philadelphia?"

"One of the sunken cities on the old U.S. coast. Damn it, Amendes, it's where the Corps was born! And Nicholas was the first of us all!"

"Okay, so that fat-ass transport is named after an old Marine. They do that, you know."

"Maria, you have no soul. The man commanded the first landing by the Continental Marines on an enemy beach—at Nassau. He was promoted to major, and became the very first Commandant of the Marine Corps. The man is a Corps legend!"

"That's nice, Garrick. I wonder what she's here for?"

"What do you mean?"

"Look for yourself. A docking bay just opened in the main dorsal fairing of that monster. I think it's going to swallow us. I think that monster may be our next ride."

"Fuck. You're right."

A minnow to the *Nicholas* whale, the carrier *Night's Edge* descended into the cavernous opening of the larger vessel's main docking bay.

Marine Transport Major Samuel Nicholas
Lunar Ring
Sol System
1825 hours, GMT

"Attention on deck!"

"As you were!" Garroway snapped as he strode through

the entranceway into the Ops Center. A half-dozen enlisted Marines standing guard at the high-arched doorway relaxed.

Beyond, the compartment, huge by most shipboard standards, had been set aside as the planning and mission control center for the upcoming deployment. Waiting for him in the circular rows of seats inside were his own command staff, Admiral Aron Pol Ranser and his staff, and a small army of politicians—representatives and star lords of the Associative government.

"General Garroway," Admiral Ranser said. "Welcome to your headquarters."

Garroway glanced up at the three-dimensional illumination of the Galaxy suspended in space above the room, a thickly planted forest of stars. A two-thousand-light-year sphere at the center glowed brighter than the rest, representing the Core Detonation.

"Thank you, Admiral. My command constellation has been reviewing plans for our deployment into the Core. Since our principal need right now is hard intel on what we can expect at the Great Annihilator, I'd like to discuss with you some of our Fleet options."

"Ah . . . yes," Ranser said. Garroway caught his sideways glance at several of the star lords nearby, their forms almost lost in the intense glow of their formal dress coronas. "That may be a bit premature at this point, General."

Garroway nailed him with a hard stare. Ranser was a squat, heavyset man with gene-altered irises in his eyes that made them look huge and polished-obsidian black. At the moment, those eyes were looking everywhere except directly at Garroway.

"Indeed." Garroway had the cold feeling that the metaphorical rug was about to be jerked out from under him. There was something about the almost embarrassed atmosphere of the compartment. "Tell me."

"We have been discussing the unique opportunity we have here with your Marines awake and again on-line," one of the star lords said. He . . . no, it was a *she* . . . she rose from her seat and stepped forward, between Ranser and Garroway.

Garroway pulled an ID down from the local net, scanning quickly through the data as it dropped into his mind. Her name, he saw, was Tavia Costa, and she represented the *Homo superioris* population on Earth's Moon.

"And what opportunity would that be, my Lord?" he asked.

"You and your . . . people come highly recommended, General. A number of us within the Associative Council of Lords are interested in how your Marines really perform."

"I don't think I like the sound of that."

Costa gave him a cold and appraising look. "And what, General, does what you like or not like have to do with the matter?"

"You sound like you want to test us somehow."

"In a manner of speaking, yes."

"There is a . . . problem, General Garroway," another s-Human said. Her bio identified her as Lelan Valoc, and she was the Star Lord representative for s-Humans within something called the Solar Cloud. "Many of us do not feel the Xul pose the threat some of our colleagues believe them to be. But we're facing a number of situations that threaten the integrity of the Associative. Those of our military forces already deployed have had less than stellar success in handling some of these crises. Perhaps your Marines can do better."

"It was my understanding that we were to fight the Xul."

"Your *understanding*, General, is that you work for *us*. The legitimate government of the Galactic Associative."

Garroway opened his mouth for a sharp reply, then closed it again. His legal position, he realized suddenly, was precarious. His allegiance had been sworn, almost nine centuries ago, to the Commonwealth of Humankind and, through that government body to the ancient United States of America. Presumably, the Galactic Associative was the legal lineal descendent of the Commonwealth . . . but was it? As he understood it, the Associative included Earth and some thousands of other worlds colonized by humans, but included some *millions* of other worlds inhabited by things that were people only in the most generous use of the word. Even these two s-Humans standing before him looked alien, with their grotesquely elongated skulls, mahogany skin, and gold cat's eyes, enigmatic and unreadable.

Homo sapiens superioris. What the hell made them so *superioris*, anyway? Something about the very idea made him bristle, urged him to dig in his heels and refuse to be drawn along.

But until he was certain of his legal standing—and of the legal standing of the Marines under his command—he was going to keep his mouth shut, he decided. He and his people were alone here, adrift in time, over eight centuries removed from the government that had put them here. The Third Marines were counting on him, damn it. The present government could easily relieve him of command . . . and then he'd have no say about what happened to his people.

And Garroway was not about to let that happen.

"*Sir.* I acknowledge that the Associative government is giving me my orders," Garroway said after an awkward hesitation. "And I will carry out those orders to the best of my ability."

"We were certain of that fact, General," Valoc said. Her voice was deep, as deep as a man's, and carried with it undertones that added an almost hypnotic quality to the words. "The old Marines have the reputation for loyalty, and a supreme, almost superhuman devotion to duty."

She's trying to flatter me, Garroway thought. *She's trying to manipulate me by appealing to my emotions.*

"No flattery is intended, General," Costa said. "Not in the sense you're thinking."

That startled him. Damn! Was she reading his mind? Or was she merely employing a shrewd understanding of human psychology?

"Just what is it you expect my people to do?" Garroway asked. "I *will* say this first. The Marine Third Division is my command, and my responsibility. My people. I reserve the right to refuse orders that seem suicidal or pointless."

Pointless, he thought, was stretching things just a bit. No military structure could survive if the people being ordered to fight could refuse those orders simply because they didn't like them. At no time in history could any fighting man have claimed that he perfectly understood the minds of the people giving him orders . . . especially when, as was the case with the United States and the later Commonwealth, those orders ultimately were being given by civilian governments.

It was unlikely that the Marines who'd stormed Belleau Wood had fully understood the details, the *point* of the orders they'd been given. Same for the Third MarDiv Marines who'd waded ashore at Guam, slogged through the black volcanic sand of Iwo Jima . . . or who'd fought to liberate the human *dumu-gir* of Enduri/Ishtar two centuries later.

Marines fought to win . . . and they fought for their buddies, their fellow Marines.

Costa waved her hand, and an image appeared in the air in front of her, a three-dimensional star map showing a ragged cloud of stars and gleaming nebulae. "The Greater Magellanic Cloud," she said, as the image began to expand, the viewpoint plunging into the swarm of suns. "A satellite galaxy of our own Milky Way. These . . ." A tight knot of stars lit up green. ". . . are the Tavros-Endymion Cluster, twenty-five worlds first opened by the Associative Colonial Administration 215 years ago."

"The Magellanic Clouds?" Garroway said, surprised. "You have colonies all the way out there?"

"Yes. About 165,000 light years out."

"Why? I mean . . . aren't there enough worlds for you here in the home Galaxy?"

"Worlds, yes. In abundance, and we build our own when we wish. But the Associative seeks . . . associates. Other sentient life. Other, alien points of view. Trade partners. *Information.*"

"It is also another step in the creation of the Galactic CAS," Valoc told him. "That is a Complex—"

"A Complex Adaptive System," Garroway said, nodding. He remembered the discussion with his Temporal Liaison Officer when he'd come out of cybe-hibe. "I know. Like what the Xul have."

Valoc's face twisted slightly, though it was hard to tell if she was showing disapproval or some other, more subtle emotion. "*Not* like the Xul," she said. "The Galactic CAS has intelligent purpose, a *direction*."

"What purpose?"

"I wouldn't expect a primitive to understand that," Valoc said.

"Lelan!" Costa said, placing a hand on the other s-Human's arm. "*Compassion!*"

Valoc turned and glared at Costa. For several seconds, they stared at each other, and Garroway got the feeling that they were communicating with each other, silently and very quickly. Had *Homo superioris* been designed with true telepathic abilities? Or was this simply a function of their cerebral implants, brain-to-brain radio on a band to which others had no access?

"You'll have to forgive my friend, General," Costa said after a moment. "She doesn't often work with Normals."

Garroway's eyebrows raised at that. "'Normals?' You mean *Homo* saps?"

"Unenhanced humans."

"'Primitives.'"

"Well . . . if you like."

"So what the hell is the fascination of *enhanced* humans in the Greater Magellanic Cloud?"

"As Lelan said, it's the most recent node within the general Associative CAS. We've encountered . . . a new species out there. Extremely old. Extremely powerful. Incredible minds."

"Okay. So?"

"We call them the Tarantulae."

For a moment, Garroway had an unsettling mental image of superintelligent giant spiders, but he dismissed it. The Greater Magellanic Cloud, he remembered, was the location of a vast interstellar cloud of dust, gas, and newborn stars called the Tarantula Nebula; likely, the Tarantulae had been named for their proximity to that cloud.

"And we're at war with the Tarantulae?"

"Not quite. It's the human colony there that's causing the trouble."

"I don't understand."

"We have been attempting to establish peaceful contact with the Tarantulae for almost a century now," Valoc said. "Two months ago, the Associative colony in the Tavros-Endymion Cluster attacked a world in the Tarantulae Sphere and have occupied it. A human leader calling himself Emperor Dahl has proclaimed an independent state centered on the Endymion Stargate."

"Your orders, General," Costa told him, "are to seize that Stargate and the planetary system it occupies, holding it for an Associative battlefleet."

"I . . . see. And what does Star Lord Rame think of this plan?" Garroway asked.

"Rame?" Valoc said. "Why should we ask him?"

"Star Lord Rame initiated the process by which you and your Marines have been recalled," Costa told him, "but he is not the official in charge of you or your missions."

"Your orders come from the Military Operations Bureau of the Associative Conclave," Valoc said. "Lord Rame is a member of that bureau, but he does not have any of the responsibility for strategic planning."

"And you two do?"

"Among several hundred others, General, yes."

He decided he was going to have to study whatever downloads were available dealing with the current government, its hierarchy, and the chain of command within both the military and civilian sectors. He couldn't assume that the same channels were in place that had been there eight hundred fifty years before.

"I will require," he said slowly, "complete documentation, histories, and available intelligence data on the situation, my Lord."

"You will have them," Valoc said.

"And don't look so glum!" Costa put in brightly. "The situation may not even require military intervention. Your arrival at the Endymion Stargate no doubt will be all that is required to restore proper order and Associative authority!"

"No doubt."

But Garroway had *every* reason to doubt. Eight and a half centuries before, he'd learned that any time a civilian leader told him that a given operation would be easier than expected, it was almost certain, in fact, to be worse.

Often *much* worse.

He wondered how this unexpected detour on the way to the Galactic Core might go wrong.

9

Tranquility Promenade
Luna, Sol System
2010 hours, GMT

"Too bad Misek didn't want to come down here," Maria Amendes said, laughing. "He'd have enjoyed it, despite himself."

"Hell, let him sulk back on the *Major Nick*," Garwe replied. "All the more for us, right?"

"Bollan takes things too damned seriously," Kadellan Wahrst said. "He needs to loosen up."

It was five days after the arrival of the *Night's Edge* at Luna Ring. Six of the Marines of Anchor Marine Strike Squadron 340 stood on the main concourse of the Tranquility Grand Promenade, a vast, domed enclosure ten kilometers across, set at the base of one of the primary elevators coming down from the Lunar Ring. The War Dogs had been given liberty—probably their last fling ashore before the *Nicholas* boosted for the Larger Magellanic—and Garwe, Amendes, Wahrst, Mortin, Palin, and Namura had come down the elevator *en masse,* a shore party to see the sights, take in the local color, and take in some of the local intoxicants as well.

Half of the Promenade was partially submerged; outside

the curved, moonglass walls, silt-laden waves broke against the transparency with a slow, almost sullen regularity. The lowland reaches of the Mare Tranquilitatis were submerged, now, with water as deep in places as half a kilometer. The sun was low on the eastern horizon, while a half-full Earth hung almost directly overhead. The sky was pale near the horizon, but shaded rapidly toward the zenith with a deep, vibrant ultramarine, almost black, with the brightest stars just visible despite the glare of sunrise. Luna's atmosphere was still achingly thin, far too thin for unaugmented humans to breathe without pressure suits and masks. It was thick enough after several centuries, however, to moderate the temperature extremes somewhat, though the nights outside were still bitterly cold. In the distance, a dense fog was boiling off the ice skim that covered much of the sea after the long, two-week night.

Fred Namura stepped closer to the transparency, curious. He tapped at it. "Plastic?" he said. "How primitive! Haven't these people ever heard of viewwall technology?"

"Moonglass," Amendes told him. "Glass made from the silica in the Lunar regolith." When Namura stepped back suddenly, looking nervous, she laughed. "Don't worry. It's *strong.*"

"Yeah," Garwe said. "Ordinary silica, when you melt it to make glass, has a lot of water in it. But this stuff has been baking in hard vacuum for a few billion years. Pure silica, with no water in the mix at all. It's supposed to be stronger than steel."

"The earliest Lunar colonies found it was a lot cheaper and more efficient to make their pressure domes out of this stuff," Wahrst said, "than it was shipping the raw materials up from Earth."

A large wave smashed against the transparency in complete silence.

"Is there any life out there?" Tami Palin asked, stepping closer to the wall and placing her hand against the slick surface. She sounded wistful. She'd been born and raised, Garwe remembered, on a sea farm cooperative in one of Earth's oceans. He couldn't remember where.

"Genengineered plants," Garwe told her. "Remember the green we saw on the trip down? Algae and bacteria, mostly, in the seas. And several kinds of gene-tailored mosses on land. The air out there's still mostly carbon dioxide, and the temperature extremes would kill anything that wasn't special-made to survive them."

"We make worlds and ecosystems to order," Wahrst said. "Takes a few centuries, of course, but we get there."

"Where I want to get is to a bar where we can find some action," Namura said. He pointed to a forest of holographic signs farther along on the promenade. "And *that's* where we're going to find it. Come on!"

"Target in sight!" Garwe called.

"Lock and load!" Amendes added.

The six Anchor Marine lieutenants advanced on their objective.

Lord Rame Residence
Earthring, Sol System
2255 hours, GMT

Lord Garrick Rame stared into his viewall, which was focused now on the immense transport docked with the Lunar Ring. "*Damn* them," he said, whispering.

Brea was asleep in the bedroom. They'd made love earlier, but Rame hadn't been able to sleep. He'd left her in the bed and come out here. Earlier that day, the Military Council had informed him of their decision . . . that the Globe Marines would be deployed first to the Large Magellanic Cloud to deal with the Tavros-Endymion situation.

The *Nicholas*, according to the latest reports, was ready now in all respects for phase-shift deployment. In two more days, she would be outbound, escorted by a naval squadron consisting of a carrier, five cruisers, seven destroyers, and a handful of smaller warships predictably designated Task Force Magellan.

The *Nicholas* would proceed to Eris, out on the thin, cold outskirts of the Solar System, there to wait as TF Magellan continued under Alcubierre Drive at best speed, making for the Sirius Stargate. The task force would pass through several stargates in the coming months, eventually passing through a gate drifting in the emptiness outside of the Galaxy, a gate that would then drop them into the heart of the Greater Magellanic Cloud.

"Best speed" was something of an optimistic platitude. Even the space-warping bubble of Alcubierre Drive didn't convey instantaneous transport to a starship. It took time to accelerate to the near-c velocities necessary for the transition to FTL, and even the fastest Alcubierre Drive vessel required three weeks for the run out to Sirius, a distance of over eight light years.

Stargate transits were instantaneous across thousands of light years, but, of course, you could only make the jump between two gates that were precisely tuned to each other. Several thousands of stargates had been discovered scattered across the Galaxy and beyond so far, and each gate had some hundreds of possible connections with other gates, creating a dazzlingly complex web of transit routes from one end of the galactic spiral to the other, and beyond as well. Even so, the Galaxy was an enormous place, four hundred billion stars adrift in a couple of hundred trillion cubic light years; stargates were rarely less than fifty light years from their nearest gate neighbor, and often the next nearest gate was hundreds, even thousands of light years away. So even with FTL drive, it still took time, often many months, sometimes *years*, to move from one stargate to the next in order to get to where you wanted to be.

The real problem for TF Magellan, though, was the megatransport, the *Major Samuel Nicholas*. The size of a small asteroid—nanoconstructors had actually devoured, processed and converted a ten-kilometer asteroid to grow her frame and hull into their present form—the *Nicholas* represented the third mode of faster-than-light transport used by space-faring civilizations across the Galaxy—phase-shifting.

With phase-shifting, you *needed* an extremely large vessel to house the banks of quantum power taps necessary to open a hole through space/time. With enough energy, you could phase down through multiple spatial dimensions to reach the $Dimension^0$ mathematical construct poetically known as the Quantum Sea, the base-state of reality where matter and energy both had their genesis as standing probability waves. There, virtual particles appeared and vanished in the dance of random energy fluctuations called the zero-point field, gravity itself could be created or banished, and minor distinctions such as distance ceased to have any real-world meaning at all.

Humankind had been working with phase-shift technology for over a thousand years. Late in the Third Millennium, primitive phase-shift vessels had transported fleet elements as large as carriers and battleships across incredibly vast distances, to appear unexpectedly deep within Xul-controlled space. To make the transit, however, the topology of the target region of space, as defined by local gravitational fields and masses, had to be known *precisely*.

Which was why the *Nicholas* couldn't simply rotate out of Solar space and materialize alongside the objective. Instead, she would wait patiently in the darkness at the System's rim, while her supporting fleet made the long trek, by FTL drive and stargate, to the target region within the heart of the Large Magellanic Cloud. There, AI probes would get the precise gravitometric readings that would make a phase-shift rotation into the target area possible.

The earliest phase-shift transports had actually been designed as deep-space bases which used phase-shifting as a means of camouflage rather than for movement, and so they'd possessed only station-keeping thrusters. They'd required tugs to put them into position for a shift. Modern shift-transports were classified as starships and did possess both gravitics for sublight movement, and Alcubierre Drives for FTL travel, but their enormous mass meant that they still crawled compared to more conventional vessels. They were liabilities for squadrons composed of smaller, more maneuverable ships, and modern tactics dictated that they stay safe in a rear-area staging area until the instant that they were needed.

Rame stared at the *Nicholas* for a few more moments, then shook his head, turning away. The huge vessel represented a colossal military asset, and the idiots were risking her on a minor target for no good reason.

He'd fought the decision in the Military Bureau virtual assembly, fought it as hard as he could, but in the end it had come down to a vote . . . and the faction led by Valoc and Costa and the other s-Humans had held the majority. The Globe Marines would be deployed to the Magellanics before the Council even considered their use at the Great Annihilator, and there wasn't a damned thing Rame could do about it.

"Socrates," he said.

"Yes, my Lord."

"Are you still in contact with General Garroway?"

There was the slightest of hesitations. *"I am not at the moment interfacing with the General,"* the AI told him. *"However, I can do so easily enough. He is not engaged in any capacity that might require privacy or circumspection."*

"Meaning he's not in the toilet, or in the middle of having sex with someone."

"Or asleep, or closeted in a meeting with his command constellation, or discussing strategy with the Military Bureau, or any of several other possibilities," Socrates agreed.

"Link me to him."

"One moment, my Lord."

General Garroway appeared a few meters away, looking mildly surprised. Since the image was being created by his implant, it was essentially an avatar, programmed to display a Marine major general's blue-gray and black dress uniform, complete with ambient corona. "Lord Rame," Garroway said. "What are *you* doing here?"

Rame blinked. He was in his home; where else would he be? Then he realized that Garroway was seeing him in another setting—presumably wherever he was at the moment. "I'm at home, General," he said with a grin. "You're just seeing me wherever you happen to be at the moment."

Garroway made a sour face and nodded. "Yeah. I realized how stupid that was as soon as I opened my mouth. Back in my day, implant-to-implant communications were usually in virtual spaces, inside your own head. I'm not used to some of the newer wrinkles . . . like having the image of the person I'm talking to projected into the space in front of me."

"How are you adapting?"

"Oh, well enough. I just don't take some of it for granted yet, like you people do. Give me time. I'll adapt. What can do for you?"

"Two things, General. I wanted to apologize personally for the change in orders."

Garroway shrugged. "It was made *quite* clear to me that you had nothing to do with it," he said.

"Nevertheless, I feel responsible. It was my idea to bring you guys out of hibernation, to send you in to the suspected Xul nest at the Galactic Core. Using you *this* way is a criminal waste of assets."

Garroway smiled. "Why, my Lord? Do you think we're going to be up against something we can't handle in the LMC?"

"No. Of course not. But even one Marine casualty would be an obscene waste."

Garroway didn't respond to that. Instead, he said, "You said I could do two things. What's the other?"

"General, I'd like to come along."

"Come again?"

"I would like to join the mission. I want to go with you . . . first to the Large Magellanic Cloud, then to the Annihilator."

"Good God, man, why?"

"Like I said. It's my responsibility that you're here, awake, at all. How do you think I would feel staying here while you people are fighting, maybe dying, a couple of hundred thousand light years from where you're supposed to be?"

"A commendable attitude so far as your public image goes, my Lord," Garroway said with a wry grin. "But it's not practical."

"Why not?"

"My Marines are highly trained, and they use highly specialized equipment. Combat pods aren't just small, piloted spacecraft. They're incredibly complex weapons systems requiring precise linkages and command connections with the AI systems running them. Same for Marine Hellsuits. You don't just put one on and go. It would be tantamount to suicide. And I can't afford to detail Marines just to baby-sit a newbie."

"Come on, General. I'm not asking to be in the front lines. I'd like to come along on board the *Nicholas*. It's not like there's not enough room."

Rame watched Garroway considering this. The *Nicholas* was more like a small world than a starship. It had plenty of room for twenty thousand Marines and a regular crew of over five thousand. All of its consumables—air, water, food, even clothing and personal effects—were manufactured along the way from abundantly available elements acquired from ice, dust, and rock picked up in space.

"Well, I certainly have no problem with that," Garroway said after a moment. "You'll need to get approval from Admiral Dravid, of course. And from Admiral Ranser." Dravid was the *Nicholas*'s commanding officer. Ranser was CO of the naval task force. Both owed their appointments to Rame's recommendations, so there would be no problem there.

"Of course. Thank you."

"Don't thank me, my Lord. I think you're nuts, frankly. Going into combat when you could stay nice and safe and warm right where you're at is *not* a sane act."

"As I said, I'm not going to be on the front lines."

"My Lord, 'the front' as a tactical concept has been dead for two thousand years. In space combat there *are* no rear or front lines. If you stay on board the *Nicholas*, you'll simply be remaining on the biggest, fattest target in local battlespace. Are you sure you want to deal with that?"

"Yes. Of course."

"On your own head be it, then," Garroway said, shrugging. "Welcome aboard."

"I'll be on board within twenty-four hours. Good-bye."

The general's image winked out.

And Rame started thinking about what he would tell Brea.

Tranquility Base Monument
Luna, Sol System
2310 hours, GMT

The image of Star Lord Rame winked out, and Garroway was once more alone. "Son of a bitch," he said softly. Until this moment, Rame had seemed to be fairly typical for a politician . . . a decent enough sort, perhaps, but with little substance or backbone. Garroway had had plenty of experience with the type during his extended career. In a military service answering by law to the civilian government, major generals could spend as much time working with politicians and government appointees as they did with their subordinates in the chain of command.

He leaned forward, placing both hands on the safety railing in front of him. He was on the tourist overlook above Tranquility Base. He'd last been to the monument over nine hundred years ago; the place never failed to move him deeply.

Eight meters below, a portion of the raw, Lunar surface a kilometer across had been left undeveloped, unchanged, beneath a high, broad dome of transparent moonglass jutting out from the northern edge of the much larger Tranquility Promenade. From the overlook, he could see the descent stage of the Lunar Excursion Module, its crinkled foil panels gleaming in the overhead lights, its four splayed and spidery legs still resting on their pads in the ancient regolith. The dark gray soil around the lander was crisscrossed by hundreds of footprints, each perfectly preserved in the dust after over 2,000 years. Here and there were scattered other artifacts—scientific instruments left behind by Armstrong and Aldrin, the first men to walk the Lunar surface in historic times.

Nearby, an odd-looking flag—red and white stripes, a blue field with fifty stars in the corner—hung from a staff planted in the ground, stretched out beneath a supporting wire. Garroway had heard that the flag had actually been knocked down by the exhaust of the LEM's upper stage when it had rocketed into the black Lunar sky two millennia before, but that it had been restored some seventy-five years later, when an American military expedition had returned to the site. According to the history downloads, Major Catharine Henderson and Lieutenant Peter Flores, both U.S. Marines, had set the flag back in place.

In the distance, low, rolling waves broke silently against the base of the sheltering dome. This portion of the Mare Tranquilitatis would have been under several meters of water had the moonglass dome not been erected over a thousand years earlier.

The patch of Lunar surface known as Tranquility Base was now a shrine, a sacred site, the place where modern men from Earth had first set foot on the soil of another world.

A silver plaque had been set into the safety rail close by the spot where Garroway stood, an exact replica of the original still affixed to the ladder on the Lunar lander's descent stage below. It showed the two side-by-side hemispheres of the Earth above the inscription, in Old Anglic capitals:

> HERE MEN FROM THE PLANET EARTH
> FIRST SET FOOT UPON THE MOON
> JULY 1969, A.D.
> WE CAME IN PEACE FOR ALL MANKIND

Beneath were the signatures of the three men who'd first made the journey, in a line above the signature of the then-President of the United States.

Garroway read the lower line, tracing it with his finger as his implant translated the unfamiliar words in his mind.

"We came in peace for all mankind."

Not that there'd been peace in the two thousand years since. Those Marines who'd set up the American flag at Tranquility Base had been on the Moon as part of a military expedition. In 2042, the United States had been at the end of a shooting war with a political organization called the United Nations and, in particular, another country called France. At stake had been xenoarcheological remains discovered on Mars and here on the Moon, artifacts opening a new window onto Humankind's long and tortured past.

Most of the next thousand years had seen warfare—with the Chinese Hegemony, with the Islamic Theocracy, with the Pan-European Union, with so many others. And as Humankind had stepped out beyond the limits of his own Solar System, he'd found other enemies as well, waiting among the stars—the Ahannu of Ishtar, the N'mah at Sirius Gate . . . and the Xul.

Always the Xul.

According to the histories he'd reviewed, the following thousand years, the Fourth Millennium, had been calmer, more rational, less war-torn than any previous time in the history of Humankind. Differences between competing human elements in philosophy or religion had become less important, less volatile as each was able to develop worlds of its own. Non-human civilizations, it turned out, rarely were in direct competition with humans over anything, so different, so *alien* were their psychologies and their worldviews, and most armed conflict between species generally turned out to arise from blatant misunderstanding. The Xul appeared to have been crushed with the destruction of their Dyson-sphere base at the Galactic Core, and their surviving interstellar nodes had been successfully contained, it seemed, by AI incursion modules.

By the closing centuries of the Fourth Millennium, there'd been a genuine hope that warfare might actually be a thing of the past, an artifact of Man's emotional adolescence.

And so much for that, Garroway thought. *They still need us, need the Corps, after all.*

Garroway, somewhat to his own surprise, was not as upset by the change in orders as Lord Rame appeared to be. His briefing on the Tavros-Endymion situation had convinced him that something fundamentally was wrong with the Galactic Associative, that the Galaxy-spanning organization was suffering from a kind of disease or psychological breakdown— not a literal disease, perhaps, but a shift in world view that was both serious and accelerating.

The Galaxy, after a thousand shining years of relative peace, was descending into insanity once again.

Did that mean that peace itself was an aberration, that there would *always* be war, conquest, and violence as an outgrowth of civilization? Or did it mean that someone was interfering with what Humankind and so many other civilizations had created?

Garroway wanted to know. The answer might determine well the future of the Marine Corps, of Humankind itself, and of every other intelligent species in the Galaxy.

He heard a clatter, and a bellowed shout. Turning, he saw a group of people coming up the stairway out of the Tranquility Promenade—six of them, three men, three women. Two were in civilian clothing, the other four nude save for their feet, but there was something about them—age, mannerisms— short-cropped hair—*something* that suggested that all six were military.

They also appeared to be drunk.

"Yah . . . right up here," one of the women said, her voice pitched louder than was necessary or appropriate, especially in this sacred place. "Been here b'fore, long time."

"Geeze, this is the place, huh?" one of the men said, looking around as he reached the observation deck. He saw Garroway and his eyes widened slightly. "Oh, 'scuze us, sir. We came to see . . . to see . . ."

"The first spaceship!" another of the men said loudly. "Very *first* spaceship!"

"First time humans reached the Moon!" a woman said. She scratched absently under one bare breast. "First time *ever!*"

"Non . . . nonsense," a man replied. "People were on the Moon with the An, right? Slaves from their colony in Meso . . . Mesopo . . . from Earth."

"They were the first humans to reach the Moon in modern times," Garroway told them, keeping his voice low. "At the very end of the pre-Space Era."

As he spoke, he was querying the local Net for implant bios. If these yahoos were military, their personnel records ought to be readily available—*there!*

All six were lieutenants in the Anchor Marines, the Marines anchored behind in the world while the Globe Marines slept through the centuries. The first woman who'd spoken was named Amendes, the other was Palin. The man who'd had trouble with the word "Mesopotamia" was Mortin. Namura and Wahrst hadn't yet spoken.

The man who'd excused himself when he'd seen Garroway was Marek Garwe.

The similarity in names tugged at Garroway's curiosity. He'd noticed already that Anglic pronunciation had shifted a bit in the eight hundred fifty years since he'd gone into hibernation, and numerous family names had contracted. He'd been wondering if he had any descendents in this new, distant world. Garwe? Garroway? It was possible.

Garroway was also out of uniform, wearing a one-piece gray jumper from the *Nicholas*' ship's store. He saw Garwe's eyes widen, however, as the lieutenant did some Net-bio checking of his own.

"*Attention on deck!*" Garwe shouted, drawing himself up to a ragged approximation of attention.

"What the hell are you talking about?" Namura asked.

"*This is Major General Garroway,*" Garwe said in a loud and urgent whisper heard by all. "*Damn it, straighten up!*"

"You people are not in uniform," Garroway said with mild distaste. "And neither am I. No saluting. And no coming to attention."

"Yes, sir!"

Mortin looked like he was about to fall over. Palin was clinging to his arm, bracing him upright. "Jesus Mohammed! A fuckin' general! . . ."

"You people are also falling-down drunk," Garroway observed. He was scanning through the bio data. "I see you're all with the 340th Strike Squadron."

"Yes, *sir!*" Garwe snapped. "The fightin' War Dogs, *sir!*"

"Thash right!" Namura said. "Fightin' War Dogs! Never been defeated, *sir!*"

"Well . . . not until fucking Dac IV," Palin added. "*Sir!*"

"Can the kay-det crap," Garroway said. "You're too drunk to do it right. If you're with the 340th, you're under *my* command now. I want you back on board the *Sam Nicholas.* Now."

"S'okay," Amendes said. She leaned possessively against Garwe, her elbow on his shoulder. "Got into a fight th' last place. Kinda busted it up, some. Sir."

"I think the Shore Patrol's after us, sir," Garwe said.

"Shuddup, Gar!" Mortin said, his voice low and intense. "Don't tell him that!"

Garroway noticed a couple of spy-floaters high up off the deck. The things had probably followed the six here, and were probably bringing the SPs in already.

It was okay. He'd already opened an implant link to the *Nicholas'* Security Office. "Send me an escort to get some Marines back to their quarters," he said in his mind, adding the link to his own coordinates. "Double quick!"

The local Shore Patrol would answer to the Navy Yard Facility up in the Ring, or, possibly, to a naval base here on the surface. Either way, they weren't part of the *Nicholas'* chain of command, and getting these six Marines out of the brig and out of legal trouble would be a problem. If he could get them back to the *Nicholas*, though, he could have Adri Carter, his Exec, deal with the civil authorities directly, and take care of any damages these idiots had inflicted on the local infrastructure.

He'd briefly, only briefly, considered leaving them to the locals, but dismissed the thought immediately. These six were his. He would take care of them.

And that included disciplining them as well.

"Just how badly did you bust that place up?" he asked. "What was the place, anyway?"

"Th' Lunatic," Wahrst said. Her nude body showed an impressive array of skin art, much of it animated. Garroway tried not to stare at the display, which included various extraterrestrial animals, a streaming Associative flag, and several scenes of couples having sex. "Th' place was called th' Lunatic. Sir."

"Bunch of Navy shits in there," Mortin said. "*They* started it!"

"Really? And how did they do that?"

"We were quietly discussing the . . . the relative merits of our respective services, sir!" Garwe said. The kid seemed to be making a real effort to focus his mind.

"Oh? That sounds harmless enough." He had a feeling, though, that he knew what was coming. The rivalry between the Navy and the Marines went *way* back, back to pre-spaceflight days.

"Sure!" Wahrst said brightly. "They . . . they said they had Midway and Sirius Gate, greatest naval victories ever! And, of course, we said, well, we had Iwo Jima an' Cydonia! Greatest *Marine* victories ever! An' they said they had John Paul Jones! An' we said we were born at Tun Tavern!"

"Thash in Philadelphia," Namura put in.

"I know."

"An' then . . . an' then one of these Navy pukes, he said, well, we're great 'cause we invented *sex*!"

"Okay . . ."

"An' Gar, here, he tells 'em, yeah, but the Marines taught 'em how to have sex with *two* people, 'stead of just one. After that, things got a little, well, noisy."

The joke had been old when Garroway had first joined the Marines, over a thousand years ago. It, or its variants, had been around just about forever. He suspected that the actual discussion in that bar had been quite different from Wahrst's version.

Two men and a woman clattered up the steps to the observation gallery. All three wore black Navy uniforms, with SP holo displays at their chests. "Halt, you people!" one of them called. "Shore Patrol! You're under arrest!"

"They're not moving at the moment," Garroway observed, "so they *can't* 'halt.' In fact, they're all with me."

He waited as the SPs interrogated his bio, and watched as they all straightened a bit, and became more deferential.

"Yes, sir. Sorry sir. But these people caused a lot of damage in town. They're under arrest. Sir."

"And just how do you know these are the ones you want?"

"Huh! Socon Guardians tracked 'em through the Promenade, of course! Followed their brain waves and implant patterns." He pointed to a hovering sphere. "*And* we have those spy-floaters following them. You wanna see the vid recordings, sir?"

Garroway shook his head. These Marines had really put their collective foot in it. The wonder was that they'd gotten this far before being picked up.

He decided to try a different tack. He locked gazes with the senior SP. "Chief Hambelen. Do you recognize my authority?"

"Sir! Yes, sir. You're the commanding officer of the Third Marine Division."

"I'm their commanding officer. I will take full responsibility for them."

"Sir, we have our orders. We have to take them with us, sober them up, take them before the local magistrate. . . ."

"Negative," Garroway snapped. "My personnel. My responsibility."

"Sir—" the female SP began.

"That's *enough*! These people are shipping out in two more days and I will *not* risk having them so entangled in red tape I have to leave them behind. I order you to stand down!"

The three looked uncertain. One of the men, a young second-class, actually dropped his hand to his holstered weapon. Garroway glared at him. "*Don't*!"

"Sir, I—"

"Just . . . *don't*!"

The six Marines had been standing in a semicircle, looking uncertain. As Garroway told the SPs off, they started regaining some of their confidence, some swagger. They began closing in, some looking dark and threatening, others grinning.

The senior SP seemed to realize that he was seriously outnumbered. "Sir," he said, "I'm going to need to check back with headquarters for orders. Will you be available to make a statement? Sir."

"You go ahead and check with your CO," Garroway told him, ignoring the man's question. "Now stand aside! I'm taking these Marines back to their ship!"

The SPs hesitated, and then Hambelen nodded and the other two stepped back. Garroway led his Marines past them, down the steps, and back into the Promenade.

"Thanksh, General," Namura said.

"Don't thank me, Marine," Garroway replied. "I promise you that you people are going to wish to high holy heaven that those SPs had taken you into custody after *I* get through with you!"

They met the security force from the *Nicholas* at the base

of the Lunar Ring elevator, and made the trip up to the *Nicholas* in silence.

On the way, Garroway did some more checking on the possible family connection of Garroway with Garwe.

He was surprised and intrigued by the result.

10

Recon Zephyr
The Great Annihilator
Galactic Core
0540 hours, GMT

The Marine OM-27 Eavesdropper *Captain Ana McMillan*, code-name Zephyr, forced its way yet closer to the eye of the howling storm. On board were two human Marines, Lieutenant Karr and Captain Valledy, plus Luther, the ship's AI. "Jesus, Mary, and Joseph!" Valledy whispered. "Just *look* at that thing!"

Karr ignored Valledy's religion-laden emotional leakage. She was nominally Reformed Wiccan, but had little use for religion personally, or for hyperemotional displays in general. She remained focused on her mental link with Luther, the AI, and listened to the sand-blasting shriek of particles against the little recon pod's EM shielding. "Five minutes to optimal release point," she said.

The Marine carrier *Cydonia* had managed to slip closer to the enigmatic swirl of gas and plasma just ahead than ever before, rail-launching the ugly little Eavesdropper from the electronic cover of a particularly thick mass of infalling dust and star-stuff. They'd abstained from using the gravitics drive entirely, relying on Newtonian physics alone to drop silently through the sleet of high-energy particles and radiation unobserved. The ship was fully powered; it had to be to maintain its shields, but the energy flux outside the little vessel at the moment was so strong that the *McMillan*'s shields would be all but invisible, a candle's flame against the output of a sun. Her gravitics, however, actually bent space/time, and that *would* be detectable.

Four more minutes.

She felt . . . naked. Vulnerable and exposed. From Karr's point of view, she was adrift in open space, falling toward an immense pinwheel of radiant light just ahead. The light, emitted by white-hot plasma and superheated gas and dust, shaded toward blue and violet at the middle of the swirl; at the pinwheel's exact center, at the eye, was a black emptiness, the ergosphere of the Annihilator itself.

Above and below the pinwheel, streaming out at ninety degrees from the pinwheel's plane, were narrow-beamed searchlights of impossibly brilliant energy. Those beams were blindingly hot with the characteristic 511 keV gamma radiation loosed by the annihilation of positrons, antimatter electrons, as they plowed into the normal matter of dust, gas, and plasma surrounding the black hole.

That object ahead had long been known to Humankind, even before the advent of starships and physical journeys into the Galactic Core. In 1977 of the old calendar, an early satellite named Einstein had first detected X-rays from this source, which had been designated 1E1740.7–2942. For a time, astronomers had assumed that the object was a supermassive singularity, a titanic black hole at the center of the Galaxy, but closer observations by a Russian spacecraft a few years later had proven that it was slightly offset from the Galaxy's gravitational center by some 340 light years. Studies of the Dopplered radio signals from the object gave clues to the object's mass—about fifteen times the mass of Earth's sun.

Those observations had proven that the object was indeed a black hole, but fifteen solar masses was too small by far to be the expected supermassive singularity at the Galactic center. Several more decades had passed before the *real* central black hole had been identified, strangely and anomalously silent. Not until late in the Third Millennium had that particular mystery been solved; the Xul had constructed a kind of shell around the Core singularity, masking it from view. Close observation of nearby stars orbiting the center had demonstrated that this larger black hole was the equivalent of some two *million* solar masses, relegating its smaller but much more flamboyant neighbor to simply one of a long list of strange objects within the Core's galactic neighborhood.

Because of the high levels of gamma radiation streaming from the object, the fingerprint of matter-antimatter annihilation, the object had come to be called the Great Annihilator.

The OM-27 was now a scant few thousand kilometers from the Annihilator's hungry maw, skimming in just above the radiant fury of the accretion disk. The Eavesdropper's inbound course had been carefully plotted, not only to avoid being spotted by the Xul, but to miss the hot accretion disk or the far hotter searchlight-beam jets of deadly energy flaring from the Annihilator's poles.

Of course, the *outbound* course would be something else. Orbital mechanics demanded that the tiny vessel pass through the black hole's equatorial plane at some point, and that meant entering the plasma of the accretion disk, a maneuver that would most certainly end a split second later with the ship's complete destruction.

The black hole lay a few thousand kilometers ahead, just visible at the center of a maelstrom of violet plasma fire. Half of the universe was blotted out by the white-hot glare of the accretion disk circling the black hole, a firestorm of plasma funneling down the singularity's bottomless drain. The searchlight beams of the jets shrieked on radio wavelengths, and bathed circumambient space in a harsh blast of X-rays and hard gamma radiation.

Beyond and behind the jets and the disk, the sky burned, a

background of white fire within which plasma clouds twisted and knotted and turned in the bizarre magnetic flux of the inner Core. The outer hull temperature was currently reading nearly three thousand degrees Kelvin.

It was, Karr thought, like flying through a sun. Soon, though, it would be hotter by far than the mild warmth of a star's core.

One more minute.

The imagery flooding through her awareness included the entire gamut of electromagnetic frequencies, from radio to gamma radiation. There was an odd effect ahead, engulfing the central speck of the black hole itself, as though radio, microwaves, infrared, and visible light all were being sharply bent. Valledy and Karr had been briefed on the effect before launching from the *Cydonia*; the mass of the Annihilator was causing a gravitational lensing effect, bending and focusing longer-wavelength radiations as space itself was distorted in the immediate vicinity of the singularity's ergosphere.

She could hear the sing-song chant of the Xul, focused through the gravitational lens. How was it passing up and out of the Annihilator's gravity well? That wasn't supposed to be possible.

No sign yet that the OM-27 had been spotted.

But, then, there'd been no warning that Vrellit and Talendiaminh had been spotted, either.

"Are you ready for this, Lieutenant?" Captain Valledy asked.

"What difference does it make?" she asked. "We're dead, no matter what."

"The *real* us will survive." But he sounded uncertain.

"And that doesn't help us one bit. As far as *I'm* concerned, I'm the real me. Thirty seconds."

An OM-27 was small, far too small to carry a flesh-and-blood crew. Karr and Valledy both were electronic uploads, exact electronic u/l copies of the minds of the corporeal Karr and Valledy, both still safely on board the *Cydonia*.

Karr knew she was an uploaded copy, but that didn't help. She still had the memories of the original person, and of her emotional make-up. So far as she could tell, she *was* Amanda Karr in every detail—a dark-haired girl from Minot, North Dakota, on Earth, in what once had been the United States; raised in Ring Three and, later, on Mars; joining the Corps when she was nineteen standard. It was all there. The sharp disappointment she'd felt upon awakening from the mental patterning and finding out that she was the copy, not the original, had been overwhelming. She'd heard that some patterned minds went mad at the news that they were copies, not originals. *Prototype envy*, it was called, that aching, heartsick yearning to somehow reshuffle the fall of the dice and awaken once more, this time as the *real* mind, not the copy.

Somehow, though, she'd hung on.

There'd been talk about editing the copies' memories so that the emotional pain wouldn't be this bad. There'd even been talk about editing the overall mind patterns in order to create an acceptance, even a willingness to die on this mission.

Karr herself had vetoed the idea. The last attempt to penetrate the Great Annihilator had been with an Eavesdropper identical in every respect to the *McMillan*. That crew's failure almost certainly had been the result of the Xul spotting them as they neared their objective, not because they'd not been up for a suicide mission. A human mind at the controls was the best guarantee this op had for success. A fully *human* mind, and that meant no last-minute editing to save the copy's feelings.

Besides, the thought of editing her memories and feelings to make her feel good about her imminent death was just a bit creepy, more uncomfortable by far than the thought of the death itself.

Then she found herself thinking of her mother, and wondered if just a little last-minute editing wouldn't have been a good idea after all.

"Ten seconds," she announced. "Launch package armed."

"We're picking up broad-spectrum transmissions from within the singularity," Luther announced. *"No indication yet that they've noticed us."*

She wondered how Luther felt about his impending immolation. He seemed to have no feelings at all one way or the other, none that she could read, at any rate.

Stop thinking about it, she told herself. *What's done is done!*

"Five seconds!" she announced. Within her mind, she reached for the virtual firing key. "And four . . . and three . . . and two . . . and one . . ."

"Launch!" Valledy ordered.

She triggered the launch package, sending it spearing down toward the black emptiness of the singularity instants before the Eavesdropper skimmed above the ergosphere, that blurred and eldritch zone of no-return. Half a second after clearing the OM-27's launch bay, the package fragmented, releasing hundreds of pencil-sized probes, each pursuing its own sharply curving path into the black hole.

"All probes are transmitting," Luther announced. *"Deployment successful. Termination of mission in one—"*

. . . and the OM-27 Eavesdropper, following the sharply bent geometry of spacetime close to the singularity, curved around the burning blackness of the black hole and passed into the violet-white flame of the accretion disk on the far side a tenth of a second later. The end came so swiftly that Amanda Karr wouldn't have had time to feel it, even if she'd been programmed to do so.

One by one, the ergosphere probes fell through the mathematically defined surface within which the escape velocity from the gravitational singularity was greater than the speed of light, a literal point of no return. The outside universe—the flaming light of the accretion disk, the tortured backdrop of nebulae and plasma streamers within the Galactic Core, the fierce storm of X-ray and gamma radiation and the searingly hot searchlight beams reaching out into the void—all winked out.

And the probes free-fell through a turbulent and violet-tinged night.

Marine Transport Major Samuel Nicholas
Major General Garroway's office
Waypoint Tun Tavern
0905 hours, GMT

The door announcer chimed.

"Come!" Garroway glanced up as the young lieutenant stepped through the privacy field into his office and came to attention.

"*Sir*! Lieutenant Marek Garwe reporting as ordered, *sir*!"

"At ease, Lieutenant," Garroway said. He nodded at one of the chairs in the room's viewing alcove. "Grab a seat. I'll be with you in a moment."

Garroway continued to go through the last of the ops plan presentations, making mental notes in the virtual margins of things he wanted to discuss with his command constellation at their next meeting, which was scheduled for 1300 hours later that ship's day. He was concerned about the reliance on teleport technology for tactical maneuvers in the upcoming assault on Tavros-Endymion Space. That sort of thing might be old hat for Anchor Marines who'd grown up with it, but it was brand-new to the newly revived Globe Marines of the Third Division. Without adequate training and familiarization, it was a disaster waiting to happen.

He finished the final annotation, placed a marker on the work so he could find the place later, then pulled out of his inner workspace.

His office was positively luxurious by the standards of the late Third Millennium. Art by Roene, Buchwald, and Rembrandt adorned the bulkheads, indistinguishable from the originals. Comfortable furniture grew from the deck on several levels, and could be banished and regrown in any configuration with a thought. His desk was a high-tech recliner that allowed anything from superficial comlinks to complete virtual-world immersion.

The early Fifth Millennium, Garroway had decided, was quite a comfortable place and time in which to live. He was going to like it here, assuming he and his people survived the next few months.

Lieutenant Garwe was perched on one of the seats in the viewing alcove, a space offering the illusion of being located inside a transparent blister extending out from the *Nicholas'* outer hull. Beyond the apparent transparency, the Galactic Spiral hung in silent magnificence, a vast and motionless pinwheel of faint stars massed into luminous clots, streams, and filaments, interwoven and entangled with the soft glow of nebulae.

The Galactic Spiral from this vantage point, some 40,000 light years beyond the Rim, was seen in three-quarter profile. The Core was clearly visible as a radiant glow behind massively banked and opaque clouds of dust and gas. There was no sign of the Core Detonation, of course; the light of that cataclysm hadn't even yet made it beyond the boundaries of the Core itself, and it would be another 90,000 years before the Detonation's light made it this far. The Core was still a spectacular sight, however. From here, the Galaxy's central bar—the Milky Way was that type of galaxy classified as a barred spiral—was clearly delineated in bright stars bearing a slightly more red-golden cast than the bluer, fainter stars of the outer spiral arms.

Briefly, Garroway mentally traced out the main spiral arms, a game he always played when confronted with this vision. Perseus Arm . . . Scutum-Crux . . . the Three Kiloparesec Arm blending into the sweep of the Norma Arm . . . Sagittarius . . . and right there was the faint and patchwork glow of the Local Arm, and the offshoot known as the Orion Spur. Sol was *there*, somewhere among those star clouds.

In fact, Earth's sun was so intrinsically faint as to be invisible to the naked eye at a distance of only thirty or forty light years, and he was looking for it across a gulf two thousand times greater than that. Each and every one of the stars he could see was brighter by far than Sol, and for every star he could see there were tens of thousands that he could not.

Earth's sun, and its worlds, was lost within that unimaginable immensity.

"General?" Garwe said. He looked concerned.

"Excuse me," Garroway replied. He waved toward the glowing spiral frozen beyond the transparency. "That sight always gets to me."

"Yes, sir."

"Relax . . . Marek, is it?"

"Yes, sir. My friends call me 'Gar.' "

"Mine did, too, before I became a general."

"Yes, sir." Garwe's eyes widened. "Oh, yeah! Right!"

"Have you wondered at all at the similarity in our names, Gar?"

"No, sir. Not really. Wait . . . are you saying . . ."

Garwe, Garroway was pleased to note, was sharp and he was quick. "I did some checking on your personnel records. It appears that you and I are related."

"No shit? Uh . . . I mean . . ."

" 'No shit' indeed. My son, Jerret, was born in 2939, Old Calendar." He did a quick translation through his implant processor. "That would be 1164 Corps Era. How long a generation is depends a lot on current medical science, of course, but forty years was the old Biblical standard, and it's still popular as the rule-of-thumb average nowadays. That's about thirty generations. Closer to forty-five, forty-six generations if you go by the more realistic span of twenty-five years."

"You're saying you're my great-great-great—"

Garroway held up his hand. "Don't bother with all of those 'greats,' son. You'll wear out your vocal cords."

"—great-grandfather?" Garwe finished. He sounded as though he didn't quite believe it.

"Actually, you're a great-nephew, some number of times removed. But, yes. That's the gist of it."

"I'm . . . honored. Sir."

"Bullshit. You don't know me and have no reason whatsoever to feel honored by the relationship. In any case, after
that many generations, you're going to have bits of DNA from
a reasonable percentage of the entire Third-Millennium population of Humankind, not just me. But I do find the relationship intriguing."

"Yes, sir! I . . . I never cared all that much for history, but
it's kind of neat finding out I have a connection to it like
this."

Garroway made a face. "We *all* do, son. We're all prod-
ucts of history, and we all have generals in our family tree.
And peasants. *And* scoundrels. And sometimes all three in
one twig. That's the fun of it."

"I'm surprised the name carried down like that, though,
sir."

"Not too surprising, actually. A couple of thousand years
ago, women gave up their family names when they married."

" 'Married?' "

"Ancient social custom where men technically owned
women in order to ensure a stable family grouping for raising
kids." He shrugged. "It was pretty much on the way out when
I was born and, in any case, women stopped giving up their
names, oh, mid-thirty-hundreds? Maybe a bit before that,
when they stopped being property. And when that happened,
kids began choosing their own names—you still have Nam-
ing Day ceremonies these days?"

"Yes, sir. Usually when a kid gets to be about thirteen
standard."

"Yeah. Typical coming-of-age ritual. So even though half
of the family members between your generation and mine
were women, and lots of other names are being woven into
the family line along the way, when kids decide to take another name than 'Garroway,' in one thread of the family line
the name was likely to remain fairly constant. It just seems
to have mutated a bit along the way. After over a thousand
years, that's scarcely surprising."

"No, sir."

"So, many-times-great-grand-nephew, do you know what that means for you?"

"Uh . . . no, sir."

"Absolutely nothing."

"I certainly wasn't expecting special treatment, sir. *Especially* after the extra duty I've been pulling."

Garroway chuckled. He'd not handled the actual punishment mast for Garwe and his friends. That had been the responsibility of his immediate commanding officer, Captain Corolin Xander. He had linked with Xander, however, and made some suggestions.

"How's the extra duty coming along?"

It was Garwe's turn to make a sour face. "Twenty-one hours to go, sir. Three hours extra duty a night in the com stacks. Another week."

"Your CO threw the proverbial book at you."

"It could have been worse, sir."

"It *will* be worse if you ever go drunk and disorderly again while you're on liberty. I promise you that, Marine."

"Yes, sir. Aye, aye, sir."

"Actually, I called you in this morning because of your extra duty assignment, not for a family reunion . . . and not to chew you a new one for your D and D. They have you sorting QCC feeds? Rating their priorities?"

"Yes, sir. *Millions* of them, sir."

Garroway chuckled. One consequence of instantaneous communications across interstellar, even intergalactic distances, was the sheer, impossible volume of information traffic, especially that concerned with military, government, and exploratory organizations and services. Originally, Quantum-Coupled Communications networks, or QCCs, had allowed communications only between paired QCC units. Each pair consisted of large arrays of quantum particles—typically phase encapsulated photons—that had been initially created together, so that they were quantum-entangled.

Entanglement, and the technology required for reading coupled photons, permitted instant communications across any conceivable distance thanks to the quantum property of nonlocality—what Einstein had referred to as "spooky action at a distance." A change in spin of one photon generated an instantaneous and opposite change in the other, even when the two had subsequently been separated by many light years. Eventually, second-level entanglement had been achieved, allowing any number of receivers to tap in to a given QCC signal anywhere in the universe, provided they had the appropriate encryption key for that signal.

And assuming someone had sorted through the jungle of incoming messages. The six errant members of the 340th Strike Squadron had been assigned thirty hours of extra duty wading through the message buffers, or "stacks," of incoming QCC traffic, sorting them by priority and filing them for later reference.

"There's one that should be coming through today," Garroway told the younger man. "Might even already be in the stacks. I want you to flag it and route it through to me. Here's the locator code." He passed an alphanumeric to Garwe, implant-to-implant.

Garwe looked uncertain, and seemed about to say something.

"What?" Garroway asked.

"Well, sir . . . if you have the locator code, you could check and see if it's in there for yourself."

"True. But what I don't have is the encryption code, so I can't do anything with it. When you put a priority on it, I want you to forward a copy to me, with the encryption key."

"Isn't that . . . illegal? Sir."

"Let's call it a gray area. The information I'm looking for is a transmission from an OM-27 Eavesdropper entering the Great Annihilator at the Galactic Core. As such, it will include data vitally necessary to the planning of our next op, the *big* one, after this little side show in the Large Magellanic."

"I . . . see. . . ."

"Associative Supreme Command will relay the message to us eventually—they'd damned well better—but I want to

see the raw data, the intel coming through before the chair
jockeys back home have a chance to clean it up."

The ASC was the military council in overall command of
Marine-Naval operations, and seemed to be pretty much in
the collective pocket of the Council of Lords.

"You think the ASC would . . . would *lie* to us, sir?"

"Not lie. General Levingaller seems to be a good sort,
and he wouldn't intentionally harm anyone in the Corps. But
it's a highly politicized department, and the politicians are
running everything back there. And the data is all going
through electronic systems, being reviewed by AIs and digital t-humans . . . and one of the things we're watching out
for is the possibility that the Xul have somehow compromised our electronic networks. I just don't want to take any
chances, you understand?"

"Yes, *sir*! I'll get you what you need, sir."

"Thanks. I know I can count on you." Garroway stood up.
"You're dismissed."

"Aye, aye, sir!"

Garwe hurried out, and Garroway turned back to contem-
plate the Galaxy of Man.

The first op was on-track and on schedule, with the first
assault scheduled for some twenty hours later. Most of the
assault force was here at the first waypoint, a well-mapped
and empty stretch of space roughly a quarter of the way between the Milky Way and the Large Magellanic Cloud. Tun
Tavern, someone down in Ops had called it, after the place
where the original Captain—later Major—Samuel Nicholas
had first begun recruiting Continental Marines, and the name
had stuck. The recon element, by now, was approaching the
objective under Alcubierre Drive. Within the next few hours,
data should be streaming back from the first-in gravmappers.
When the final gravitometric plot was complete, the *Sam
Nicholas* would rotate through the Quantum Sea and emerge
within a few thousand kilometers of the Tavros-Endymion
Cluster Stargate.

Then the fun would begin.

The trouble was the demand by HQ that the Globe Marines use teleportation for their tactical deployment. By now, all Marines in 3MarDiv had received downloads on how teleportation worked and how it could most effectively be used, but Garroway knew well that having data in your head was a hell of a long way from *knowing* something.

He was afraid that he was going to lose some good Marines tomorrow because of their lack of familiarity with the technology, and he didn't like that, not one bit.

And he was going to do his best to prevent it from happening.

11

Company H, 2/9
Marine Transport Major Samuel Nicholas
Objective Samar
Tavros-Endymion Stargate
0510 hours, GMT

Master Sergeant Nal il-En Shru-dech completed a final run-through, checking the weapon read-outs and health stats of each Marine in the company. Company H of the 3MarDiv's 2/9 was *ready.*

This was the part, however, that always made his mouth a bit dry and his palms slick with sweat, the long agony of minutes before the actual assault, waiting for the go-command.

And it didn't help that he and his Marines were about to use a device all but undreamed of eight and a half centuries before, when they'd last entered cybe-hibe.

He'd downloaded all the training material, of course, and knew the theories and the established techniques. Hell, a direct data download could make a man an expert on anything in seconds; what it didn't do was confer muscle memory or the confidence of solid experience.

"You think this thing's gonna work, Master Sergeant?" Captain Corcoran, the company commander, asked over the private channel.

"Damfino, sir," Nal replied.

"Scares the shit out of me."

"Of course it does, sir. Scares me, too. Teleportation is *not* a natural act."

"Works okay for Stargates," Corcoran said. It sounded as though he was trying to convince himself.

"Absolutely, sir. And phase-shifters, too. I figure some very smart people have been working on this stuff for a long time, for centuries while we were snoozing, y'know? And they've had plenty of time to get the bugs out."

"You think it's safe, then?"

Hell, no! he thought, but he knew that wasn't what the skipper wanted to hear. "Sure it is, sir. Just stick to the procedures we downloaded, and watch where you step. Don't do anything stupid. We'll come through just fine."

Company H was formed up within one of the *Nicholas'* debarkation bays, 118 Marines in full HFR-7 Hellfire combat boarding armor facing the stark, elliptical gateway at the end of a gray steel ramp. These CBA units were a lot lighter and closer to form-fitting than the combat armor Nal had first trained with almost 900 years before. At the moment, it was actually difficult to see the individual Marines. The combat armor with which Nal had trained all those centuries ago had used a surface film of nanoflage particles which reflected the light levels, colors, and patterns of their surroundings. Hellfires, though, actually bent incoming light to create the illusion of partial invisibility.

It wasn't perfect, of course. Nal could still see his fellow Marines standing in their quietly expectant ranks, but each suit had a fuzzy, translucent look to it, at least around the edges, and pieces of each suit—arms, legs, weapons—kept shifting in odd ways, or vanishing outright. A Marine in a Hellfire suit wouldn't disappear completely, but if he or she held motionless in the shadows, they could become damned near invisible. And when they were moving, those suits provided a shifting, blurred, and *very* difficult target.

Not only that, but that light-bending facility also served

to shed or deflect a lot of the energy from incoming beams and projectiles.

Hotel Company had been practicing with these suits on the voyage out from Earth, learning how best to take advantage of the cover they offered. Their actual operation was simplicity itself, with the AI resident within the helmet circuitry handling all of the real work.

The technology, Nal thought, was nothing short of astounding. And it *worked*.

So why was he feeling such deep misgivings over teleportation? The technology was almost as old as that of the Hellfire suits. And at least as reliable.

Technically, he knew, there were five ways to achieve teleportation, jumping from one place to another instantaneously without crossing the space in between.

With a big enough power plant, you could reach all the way down into the Quantum Sea and bypass the local topology of spacetime, allowing you to move a ship from point A to point B. That was how the big phase-shifters like the *Major Samuel Nicholas* did it. That was called q-teleportation, q for "quantum," and it didn't work on anything much smaller than a monster ship like the *Sam Nick*.

Another means was designated g-teleportation, g for "gravitational." That was how the Stargates managed to link one bit of space with another, using as portals twenty-kilometer rings within which Jupiter-mass black holes orbited at near-light velocities. The gravitational tides created by paired counter-rotating singularities rippled out through normal space at the speed of light, but also crossed through higher dimensions as well, bypassing normal space and interacting with other ripples from other gates. Those gravitational waves could be tuned with the tides at other, far-distant Stargates, opening a hyper-dimensional gateway between the two.

Again, though, that type of teleportation worked only on a very large scale. Originally constructed by a long-vanished galactic intelligence, using technologies still far beyond those of Humankind, Stargates formed a web of long-distance transit routes across the Galaxy and beyond. They were superb for strategic movement, and, indeed, made Galaxywide travel a reality, but they were not at all mobile, which meant they weren't exactly useful on a tactical level.

P- or psychic-teleportation had been demonstrated in the laboratory, but never made reliable enough for practical use. It had long been known that the human mind could open pathways through higher dimensions, and mental disciplines such as the weiji-do martial arts form practiced by Marines could help some individuals achieve it, at least for relatively small masses. Some day, a company of Marines might be able to use the mind alone to step through a doorway and cross thousands of kilometers in an eye blink, but it wasn't possible yet.

Theoretically, it was possible to break down the atoms and molecules of a man or a starship, convert them to energy, and beam them somewhere else at the speed of light for reassembly. That brute-strength method was called beam- or b-teleportation, but it had never been successfully demonstrated on anything larger and more complex than a very small diamond—pure carbon with a well-understood crystalline matrix. The computational power necessary for a b-teleport of organic matter—to say nothing of a living being—was far beyond even the most powerful Fifth Millennium AIs.

Besides, what was built back into corporeal solidity at the far end of a b-teleport transmission was essentially a *copy*, not the original, and that put a serious stumbling block in the way of using such a system to move humans. There were remarkably few people around who were willing to die so that their exact twin could materialize a thousand kilometers away.

Finally there was d-teleportation, d for "dimensional." It used the space-bending technologies of the Alcubierre FTL drive, though on a much smaller and shorter-ranged scale, to grab two pieces of the spacetime matrix and fold them together, overlapping two distant points through one or more higher dimensions. Once an overlap was achieved, men or small vehicles could move directly from one to the other, again without traversing intervening space.

The gateway opened was only a few meters across, and the range was limited to about one hundred thousand kilometers, but it did provide military forces with an unstoppable and unpredictable means of delivering assault troops to a precise tactical location. The equipment necessary for a d-teleport massed a few thousand tons, and required a fairly large quantum power tap to generate the flood of energy necessary for the folding process, but it could be carried easily enough on a carrier-sized warship . . . or on board a Marine transport.

Hotel Company was organized into three thirty-six-man platoons plus a twelve-Marine headquarters constellation—one hundred and twenty in all, though in fact they were minus the two they'd lost in cybe-hibe. Nal was the senior NCO in the HQ unit, and as such was the man the entire company looked to, enlisted and officers alike, for solid, practical experience and guidance.

But he had no experience to offer here, and no guidance beyond "remember the downloads" and "don't do anything stupid."

He felt the faint inward shudder that meant the *Nicholas* was translating through the Quantum Sea, making the instantaneous passage from Waypoint Tun Tavern to Objective Samar.

And who in all the bloody hells of the Corps had chosen *Samar* as an inspirational name for the mission objective? The name was still remembered with reverence. Back in the opening years of the twentieth century, during the Philippine Insurrection, fighting on the island of Samar had been so fierce that for years afterward, when a veteran of that fight entered wardroom or mess deck, he would be toasted by officers and enlisted men alike with the words, "Stand, gentlemen! He served on Samar!" Both the campaign and the toast were remembered still, parts of the ever-growing legend of the Corps.

But Samar had been a literal hell of blood, jungle, malnutrition, and disease, a premonition of later wars against native uprisings and popular revolutions in the tropics. The Marine officer in charge, one Major Littleton Waller, had been accused of war crimes after ordering the execution of eleven native porters who'd attacked his men. He'd been acquitted at his trial . . . but the news media of the day had branded him the "Butcher of Samar."

"Objective Samar" did not inspire Nal with any particularly heroic or gung-ho feelings. It felt, in fact, like something about to go horribly wrong.

The gate was still closed, with nothing visible within that squat ellipse of metal and ceramic at the top of the ramp except the gray bulkhead beyond. The transit opening, the interior of the ellipse, was some five meters wide and three high, big enough for Marines to go through four abreast without crowding. The thirty-five men and women of First Platoon, who would be the first ones through, stood at the bottom of the ramp in eight ranks of four, with the last three bringing up the rear. Their CO was Lieutenant Grigor Haskins. Second Platoon under Lieutenant Fellacci would be next, followed by Captain Corcoran and the HQ constellation, and with Third Platoon in reserve.

Their actual target was a rebel command and control center in the orbital fortress guarding the Magellanic Stargate. According to Intelligence, the compartment was large, open, and high, with at least two catwalk or promenade levels high up on the bulkheads, and banks of communications equipment. Once the alert was sounded through the Tavros-Endymion Cluster with the arrival of the Associative naval task force, the local warlord who'd styled himself Emperor Dahl would come *here* to oversee operations.

Hotel Company had been tasked with capturing Dahl if at all possible, with killing him if necessary, and with taking out the command-control center at the earliest possible opportunity in the assault. Each Marine had downloaded a holo of Dahl, as well as news media clips of the man taken at a recent political rally, and knew exactly what he looked like.

The strategy was simplicity. Take out the man at the top and any people under him giving orders, and the enemy's defenses might collapse in short order.

Might. *Nothing*, Nal knew, was certain in combat.

Nal wondered why Dahl had declared war on the local non-human culture, the Tarantulae. From all accounts, they were peaceful enough, and offered Humankind a valuable source of informational exchange—new art, new culture, new technologies, a new worldview . . . all of the good reasons to embrace a new sentient contact.

The Marine briefings hadn't gone into the politics of the situation, however. There was no need. The Marines would take out Dahl, knock out the Imperial defenses, and open the way for the Associative Fleet to move in and take over.

"Marines, stand ready!" the sharp-edged voice of Lofty Henderson, the divisional AI, sounded in Nal's head. *"We have successfully translated to our assault point. Objective Samar is five thousand kilometers ahead, and has just gone on full alert. We are making the final calibrations on the d-teleport system now. We estimate gateway opening within three minutes. . . ."*

No merely human mind, Nal knew, could handle the calculations involved in a d-teleport. Not even the superintelligent s-humans could handle that level of math. There were far too many variables of mass, gravity, and magnetic moment, and each one had to be addressed with better than ten-place decimal accuracy. He wondered if Lofty had absorbed the skills necessary to make the critical transition calculations, or if the entire show was being run by AI minds native to this era. In a way, Nal hoped that Lofty was in charge; he wasn't sure he trusted the AIs of the forty-first century, and Lofty was a fellow 3MarDiv Marine.

Briefly, he thought about the other Marines on board the *Sam Nick*, waiting to begin the assault. They included a large number of these so-called "Anchor Marines," Marines recruited and trained in *this* era. Like fellow Marines throughout the recorded history of the Corps, Nal was imbued with the sense that the Marines of his day had been tough, well trained, superbly experienced . . . and that, frankly, they just didn't make them like that any more. The technology was shiny, to be sure. But how good were the Marines of this pacifistic and—it seemed to him—degenerate future epoch?

They would know soon enough. Globe Marines were being teleported in to the inner sanctums of Dahl's imperium, but Anchor Marines would be using RS/A-91 Starwraith pods to secure Imperial gun emplacements and sensor emplacements throughout Tavros-Endymion battlespace.

Don't worry about them, he told himself savagely. *Worry about* your *objectives, about what* you *have to do!*

With startling abruptness, the empty space within the flattened ellipse ahead changed. Instead of a gray metal bulkhead, Nal could see into a large compartment with a high overhead, banks of instrument consoles, and a large number of people, most wearing distinctive black and gold uniforms. The image appeared to be unsteady, shivering and jolting even as the people on the other side began reacting to the appearance of the d-teleport gateway in their midst.

"Go!" Lieutenant Haskins screamed over the company com channel. "Go! *Go!*"

"*Belay that!*" The sharp command was Lofty's, echoed closely by Captain Corcoran, but it was too late. The First Platoon was already going through.

And it was a bloody disaster from the very start.

Strike Squadron 340, Blue Flight
Objective Samar
Tavros-Endymion Stargate
0513 hours, GMT

Lieutenant Garwe felt the sharp acceleration as his Starwraith pod snapped off its accelerator rail and into empty space. As always, he struggled to suppress the surge of fear as space exploded around him.

His body, he knew, was safely back on board the *Sam Nick*, strapped into a link couch, but there was absolutely no way of telling that from the sensations flooding his brain. The vast bulk of the phase-shift transport dropped away astern, dwindling into the distance in an instant. Ahead and in all directions, the sky was filled with a dazzling, jewel-like array of tightly clustered stars enmeshed within the filaments and tendrils and twisted sheets of clotted, blue-white luminosity that were the Tarantula Nebula.

"Stay tight, War Dogs," Captain Xander warned. "They can't see us."

Not yet, Garwe thought, but he adjusted his pod's gravitic drive slightly, edging into closer formation with the other fifteen Starwraiths of Blue Flight. Myriad glowing specks drew multicolored contrails across his field of view, marking other Starwraiths, as well as the ships of the task force translated in on board the *Nicholas*, along with other remote-piloted combat and reconnaissance craft. Ahead, bracketed in bright red, a slender ring floated against the backdrop of stars and starstuff, growing swiftly as his pod dropped closer.

White globes of incandescence began appearing across the starscape, flashing and expanding as the enemy batteries began opening up.

And the War Dogs vectored in on the Tarantula Stargate.

Company H, 2/9
Marine Transport Major Samuel Nicholas
Objective Samar
0513 hours, GMT

"Belay that! First Platoon, pull back! *Pull back!*"

But the assault had already tumbled into bloody chaos. One of the Marines at the extreme left of the front rank bumped against the Marine to his right, stumbled, and fell sideways against the edge of the elliptical gateway. Nal heard the shrill scream as the man's left arm, legs, and lower torso vanished, his body sliced through as cleanly as if by the touch of a plasma torch. The room beyond the gateway gave another lurch, and three more Marines tumbled off the ramp and across the threshold.

From his vantage point far back in the assault formation, Nal could see what was going wrong. The two volumes of space, each a few meters across, which should have overlapped in order to allow the Marines to step smoothly from one into the other, were imperfectly aligned. The space within the objective control center appeared to be throbbing or pulsing, and was drifting back and forth erratically.

The Marines of First Platoon were too close to the gate to clearly see what was happening. Those in the front ranks were trying to move back, away from the yawing gateway into the enemy command center; those behind were still pushing forward, jostling, shoving, and the resultant collision was spilling Marines off the ramp.

A few fell to either side just in front of the open gateway, and appeared to be all right. Others, though, were being shoved forward into the gate by the press from behind. Some appeared to be landing intact on the other side, but several fell partway through the invisible, three-dimensional interface of hyperdimensional space with the space of the *Sam Nick*'s debarkation bay, and were hideously mangled. With horror and disbelief, Nal watched one Marine appear to step *through* an instrument console on the enemy command deck, then abruptly jerk and thrash as the atoms of his body became inextricably mingled with the atoms of the enemy console.

Men and women were screaming. Blood, shockingly scarlet, splashed across the deck and the vaguely outlined Hellfire armor of struggling Marines. On the far side of the gate, black and gold-clad troopers were turning to face the threat, raising their weapons.

Abruptly, the scene glimpsed through the open gate flipped upside down, then reversed, right switching with left. Corporal

Regin Devrochik—"Chickie" to his squadmates—was caught partway into the gate interface when it shifted, and the front half of his body, from weapon and Hellfire armor to internal organs and blood vessels, all the way down to his individual cells all turned suddenly and horribly inside-out. What was left collapsed backward onto the ramp, still flailing as what was left of Chickie's brain tried to make sense of what had just happened. Sergeant Cori Ryack fired a single bolt from her plasma rifle, incinerating the bloodily twitching horror on the deck.

The Dahl troopers on the far side of the gate were firing, now, their upside-down images moving closer to the opening, but not stepping through. Plasma beams snapped through First Platoon's ranks; some didn't pass through the shifting dimensional interface, while others were absorbed or refracted by Marine armor, but a few more Marines on the embarkation deck went down.

"Return fire!" Lieutenant Haskins was screaming over the command net. "Return fire!"

But the Marines in the rear ranks were blocked by those in the front, and no one could even be sure the plasma bolts were getting through the strangely twisted geometries between the two spaces, the *Nick*'s embarkation bay and the enemy command deck. Another man fell through, fell *up* as he dropped through the dimensional interface and landed on the enemy's deck. Dahl Imperium troops were pouring into the compartment on the other side, now, many of them in black and silver armor similar to the Hellfire armor worn by the Marines.

There was a sudden new danger . . . that if the gateway was stabilized, the enemy troops might actually storm through onto the *Sam Nick*'s embarkation bay deck, and try to take the ship from within. With the narrow field of view offered by the elliptical gateway, it was impossible to tell how many Dahl troops were over there, but there appeared to be several hundred at least.

And then, after what had seemed like an eternity, the gate shut down, the inverted image of the interior of the enemy command center winking out, replaced by the cold gray metal of the bulkhead. Nal checked his time implant and was startled to see that only eight seconds had passed between the opening and the closing of that dimensional gateway.

The gate might be closed, now, but the screams, shrieks, and moans of the wounded continued as the surviving First Platoon Marines tried to sort themselves out. Corpsmen began moving among the fallen Marines; someone else fired a plasma bolt into the brain of someone too horribly injured to survive.

Smoked. Meaning that their brains had been vaporized and that they were irretrievably dead. Even in Nal's day nine centuries before, if a wounded Marine's brain could be recovered intact, they could usually be saved. Whole new bodies could be force-grown for transplant, and Nal gathered that the process was a lot slicker and more efficient today than it had been a millennium ago.

But when only *part* of the brain survived the initial trauma, the personality was generally so changed that it was no longer the same person, and there were other problems as well. *That* kind of agony often meant insanity or, somehow worse, the reduction of the mind to a vegetable state, alive, even aware, but unable to communicate.

When what was left was no longer fully human, a mercy shot to the head was often the final and best service one Marine could provide for a comrade.

The remaining Marines were milling about in stark confusion. "Get those people in line, Master Sergeant," Captain Corcoran demanded.

"*Attention on deck!*" Nal rasped out, and the movement came to an immediate halt, the Marines standing in the midst of drifting smoke and the sprayed swatches of gore. "Now fall in! Ranks of four!"

In seconds, order was resumed. There'd been thirty-five men and women in First Platoon a moment ago; Third Platoon, in reserve, was the short-handed one. Now, they formed up as four ranks of four, with three left over—just nineteen

Marines left. A quick check of the company's medical net showed seven wounded, all now being tended by hospital corpsmen. Ten were dead or missing.

First Platoon, Nal knew, would be in shock, now. Suffering 47 percent casualties in the space of just eight seconds was sufficient to ruin the most elite of combat units. "Captain Corcoran?"

"What is it, Master Sergeant?" He sounded distracted.

"I suggest we drop First Platoon into reserve, and move Second and Third Platoons up to the main assault."

"What? Are you crazy, man? We can't go through that gate now! Not after what just happened!"

"Sir? We *have* to go through. We have some MIAs on the other side. 'No man left behind,' right?"

"They were probably killed as soon as they hit Samar's deck!"

"Maybe. But if there's even one chance in hell . . ."

Nal could feel the captain thinking about this. "Okay, Master Sergeant. Make the change, then stand ready. But I'm going to need to bump this up the line."

"Aye, aye, sir."

Corcoran, Nal thought, was a good enough officer but an unimaginative one, experienced and well trained, but not the best when it came to taking the initiative or assuming responsibility for a potentially controversial decision. The man wasn't about to try a second attempt on the enemy base without very explicit orders from higher up the chain of command.

At least he *was* checking to see if those orders would be forthcoming, and not simply assuming that the fight was over. Uppermost in Nal's mind was the knowledge that, before the teleport technicians had shut down the power and killed the gate, he'd seen Marines safely over and on the other side. They'd jumped or been pushed through, landed intact despite the wildly shifting dimensional substrate, and been fighting with the enemy troops over there when the closing gate had cut them off.

Corcoran was right. They might well be dead by now . . . but they might also have surrendered or been overpowered by superior numbers, and if they were still alive, they would know that the rest of H Company would be coming through to get them.

Nal played back a portion of those eight seconds recorded through his helmet scanners, checking IDs. Yeah . . . Sergeant Ferris, PFC Brisard, and PFC Tollindy had been engaging the enemy over there, and it looked like two more, at least, were wounded but still alive, PFC Garcia and Lance Corporal Zollinger. Five men and women.

The Corps did *not* leave its own behind. *Ever.*

12

1002.2229

Command Deck
Marine Transport Major Samuel Nicholas
Objective Samar
0516 hours, GMT

General Garroway watched the unfolding battle as a fast-flashing series of images and informational updates streaming through his consciousness from the artificial intelligence commanding the *Sam Nicholas* and the rest of the Associative Marine-Navy task force.

Most of the op was moving well and as close to plan as these things ever did. Bravo and Delta Companies had teleported through to capture fire control centers, weapons emplacements, and a command center on Objective Novaleta, a huge armored orbital fortress some twenty thousand kilometers from the Tarantula Stargate. Alpha and Charlie Companies had successfully teleported onto the surface of a cold, Mars-sized world at the very limit of teleport range, nearly one hundred thousand kilometers distant, seizing a small starport and several related ground stations and facilities. Echo and Fox Companies had teleported onto several Dahl Imperium warships within the local battlespace volume.

In each case, the fighting was reported as fierce, but headway was being made.

The single exception was Objective Samar, a huge command-control center orbiting just a few kilometers outside the twenty-kilometer ring of the Stargate itself. Golf Company was attacking weapons emplacements on the station, while Hotel was targeting the main command center, with orders to capture Emperor Dahl himself if they could find him. Reports so far were very confused, but the upshot appeared to be that there were technical problems in establishing a solid teleport link with the station. There'd been heavy casualties in the opening seconds of the engagement.

Unfortunately, Objective Samar was the focal point of the entire operation, the key to capturing the local Stargate. The main Associative battlefleet was waiting now at Waypoint Tun Tavern. All they needed was word from the assault group so that they could swarm through and take over the rest of the Dahlist facilities on the Tarantula side of the gate. But Samar's heavy weapons controlled the exit space from the Stargate.

The heavy weapons on Samar would pick the Associative warships off one at a time as they came through, unless the Marines could secure that fortress.

Garroway was now linked in with the command network, focusing on the action at Objective Samar. He'd seen the bungled assault, seen the eight-second nightmare of confusion as orders and counterorders had shoved the lead Marine company forward and back. And he'd overheard the terse discussion between the H Company commander and his senior NCO.

"General Garroway," Lofty whispered in his mind. *"There's a request for orders coming up the chain from H Company—"*

"I know," Garroway replied. He'd considered entering the conversation at the time, but held off. Generals who eavesdropped and barged in on company-level discussions within their command only harmed morale and discipline. "Put him through."

The image of Captain Corcoran appeared in his mind . . . a command AIvitar that was actually Corcoran's personal AI mimicking the captain's appearance and voice. *"General Garroway!"* the figure said. *"Captain Corcoran, H Company, reporting, sir! We tried to go through—"*

"I saw, Captain," Garroway said, interrupting. "Re-set the teleport field and try again. It is *imperative* that we capture that command center!"

"Aye, aye, sir!"

Garroway checked the strategic map, looking for nearby assets. Battlespace was a confused tangle of colored stars and course-indicator lines curving in toward their objectives. *There* was one. . . .

"I'm deploying a flight of Marine assault pods to support you from outside. *But get your people back on board that station!"*

"Yes, sir! Aye, aye, sir!" And the image winked out.

The 340th Assault Squadron, the War Dogs, had been tasked with searching for hidden weapons emplacements on the Stargate ring itself, but those orders were secondary in importance to capturing Objective Samar.

"Lofty," he said. In his mind, he highlighted the cluster of green blips now closing with the Stargate in the three-dimensional map spread out in his mind. "Convey new orders to the 340th Marine Strike Squadron . . . here. Captain Xander. They are to redeploy to Objective Samar and attempt to enter the station from outside. Priority is to be given to securing the command deck, along with Golf and Hotel elements of the 2/9."

"Aye, aye, sir."

Only after he'd given the order did he remember that Xander's group was an Anchor Marine squadron, distinct in training and experience from his own Globe Marines. Garroway hated the distinction. Marines should be Marines, wherever, or *when*ever, they came from.

At the same time, he wasn't entirely sure he trusted those members of the Corps from the forty-first century, or the doctrine of remote combat.

Training was the major issue. He'd looked in on the training sessions for Anchor Marines back in Earthring, and been disappointed to find out that nearly all Marine training nowadays was *virtual* training, with recruits put through AI-linked simulations accompanied by massive downloads of data on weapons, tactics, regulations, and history.

For Garroway, mental sims could never replace the reality of actually having been there. Just the possibility of actually getting shot could, as one ancient philosopher had suggested in the context of being hanged, concentrate a man's mind wonderfully. He didn't trust this new way of creating Marines, didn't trust the Marines who'd not gone through the physical training—the *crucible*, as ancient Marines had called it.

It took him a moment more to remember that one of the members of the 340th was Garwe, one of his own descendents.

Was Marek Garwe a *real* Marine? Could Garroway—and the Marines of H Company—really depend on him and the other Anchors?

Garroway had to admit to himself that he just didn't know.

But the next few minutes of battle ought to tell him a lot.

Company H, 2/9
Marine Transport Major Samuel Nicholas
Objective Samar
0519 hours, GMT

"Stand ready, Marines!" Nal called over the company link. "We're going through again. Do *not* move until you get the go from Captain Corcoran or myself."

Second Platoon had moved forward, now, taking up the jump-off position on the ramp in front of the elliptical

gateway under the command of Lieutenant Fellacci. Behind
them was Third Platoon, under Lieutenant Vriberg, moved
up from the ready reserve. Next was the HQ element, and
with the battered remains of First Platoon now behind them
in reserve. After what First Platoon had been subjected to a
few moments earlier, though, Nal desperately hoped he
wouldn't need to call them in.

The last of the wounded had been evacuated to the rear
and were on their way up to the *Sam Nicholas'* sick bay. The
smoke had been pulled from the compartment. Nothing could
be done, though, to mask the splotches of blood still steaming
at the top of the ramp and beneath the physical gateway. Despite that all too vivid reminder of the failed teleport assault,
the H Company Marines appeared to be tightly focused and
ready. They were shaken and they were stressed, but overall
they appeared steady.

Nal found himself praying to the ancient and powerful
Ahannu, gods that he'd long ago renounced, that the Marines' strength remain steady.

"The teleport gate is opening," Lofty announced. *"Do
not, repeat, do* not *move until you have the go order."*

The gateway opening misted over, then clarified, again
looking into the command-control compartment on the other
side. Again, the hyperdimensional link appeared to pulse and
tremble, as the image drifted unsteadily to one side. Enemy
troops were firing now, sending a storm of plasma rifle fire
into the embarkation bay. Several Marines took direct hits
and fell, but the rest held their position. Fellacci ordered Second Platoon to return fire and they did so, with meticulous
precision. Black-and-gold Dahlist soldiers began collapsing
on the other side in twos, threes, and fours.

"Hit them with the am-fours!" Nal shouted. "Suppressive
fire!"

A dozen contrails lanced through the air from the mass of
crouching Marines, into the elliptical gateway, and on into the
command center beyond. Half failed to negotiate the twisted,

distorted space within the ellipse and were automatically disarmed by their safeties. Six, however, went through dead-center.

Once within the Dahlist battle station, they swung in different directions, each AM-4 smart grenade independently controlled by its on-board micro-AI, seeking out concentrations of enemy troops. When it found one, it homed in with deadly precision and a microscopic fleck of antimatter came into contact with the normal matter of the grenade's shell.

Brilliant, high-yield energy blasts thundered within the confined space of the Samar command center. In seconds, the far side of the teleport gateway showed little but wrecked instrument consoles and torn deck plating, the place a smoking, ruined shambles.

But heavily armored Dahlist troops remained sheltered in the wreckage, and more were coming through several doorways every moment.

"What the hell is going on with the image?" Corcoran asked in Nal's mind. The image continued to shake and drift, as the spacial volume of the dimensional interface stretched and twisted.

"Gravitational interference, sir," he replied. "That's what I'm getting on the tech feed." He had an open link to the *Sam Nick* technicians attempting to anchor the teleport lock. The dimensional interface—the overlap of two distinct volumes of space a thousand kilometers apart—was unstable, shifting as if in the ebb and flow of a gravitational tide.

When he glanced at a strategic map inset in the display area of his mind, he felt a sudden flash of insight.

"Sir!" he said. "Samar is orbiting just a few thousand meters from the outer surface of the Stargate ring! Those counter-rotating black holes inside the ring structure—"

"The outer surface of the ring is supposed to be grav-shielded, Master Sergeant. Don't you think we'd have looked for something that obvious?"

"Then maybe they fucking turned off the shielding! Bu the space-time ripples from the Gate are sure as hell scram bling our attempts to lock in! *Sir*!"

Cocoran hesitated. "Pass that on to the teleport techs."

"Already uploading, sir."

Inside the ring of the Stargate were two Jupiter-masses com pressed to proton-sized singularities, whizzing about two in ternal tracks at close to the speed of light. The precisely tuned gravity waves emerging from that vortex of warping space time was what opened the big Stargates in the first place.

But those waves could be highly disruptive close to the ring's surface, disruptive enough to interfere with the attempt to overlap two spacial volumes close by.

However, the technicians attempting to effect that overlap could correct for the distortion if they could tune in on the frequency of the pulses and cancel them out.

Nal felt one of the techs give him a mental thumbs-up. The image beyond the elliptical gate steadied, expanded slightly then locked in solidly.

"We have lock!"

"*Go!*" Corcoran ordered.

And Second Platoon surged forward, leaning ahead into the volleyed fire from the other side as if pushing into a hurricane's blast. Lightning bolts sparked and flashed from Hellfire suits into the steel deck. Two Marines stumbled and fell, but the rest kept going, Marines in the rear moving up to take the place of those who'd been hit.

Strike Squadron 340, Blue Flight
Objective Samar
Tavros-Endymion Stargate
0520 hours, GMT

"This is it!" Xander yelled over the link. "*Hit them, Marines!*"

Together with the others, Garwe accelerated toward the

ast-swelling globe below, as high-energy bursts flared and blossomed throughout the sky. The War Dogs, their assault pods shielded and all but invisible to enemy scanners, dropped through a deadly storm of point-defense fire toward the surface of Objective Samar.

The Dahlist battle station was the size of a small asteroid, eight kilometers across. At a range of a hundred kilometers it was still tiny, a bright star, but under optical magnification fed through his implant, he saw it as an inmense, flattened sphere with a mottled black and white external shell bristling with weapons systems.

Most of those weapons, squat, cumbersome monsters set into massive turrets, were designed to engage enemy warships emerging from the Stargate—the entire point of positioning the battle station this close to the ring. Those big guns could not even *see*, much less lock on to and track something as small and as maneuverable as a Starwraith.

There were thousands of lesser weapons scattered across the surface of that artificial worldlet, however, point-defense batteries with AI-directed detection and response fire-control systems, designed to defeat just such an assault as this one . . . or to take out clouds of incoming antimatter missiles.

The War Dogs were lost within a vast and expanding cloud of decoys, each created by a thumb-sized microbot. Some were programmed to mimic the maneuvers and the energy profiles of a Starwraith pod, while others, the majority, appeared to Dahlist scanners to be incoming AI-directed missiles. Once they were close enough to appear as solid targets, the enemy defenses *had* to respond in order to protect the station . . . and the sixteen Marine pods could slip through unnoticed.

That, at least, was tactical doctrine. No one knew how good the Dahlist AI defenses actually were, or how quickly they would be able to sweep through the decoys and finally reach the Marines.

A hundred kilometers to Garwe's left, Javlotel's pod flare
and vanished in a paroxysm of plasma energy. Garwe ac
celerated faster. That might have been blind luck on the pa
of the defenders . . . or their AIs might have better targe
identification protocols than Marine Intelligence believe
Either way, there was no backing out now. The War Dog
were committed to the attack.

One of the big guns fired, loosing a bolt of fusion fire, an
two more Marine pods vanished like gnats wafted into th
beam of a power cutter. Namura and Bakewin. The Dahlist
were firing the big weapons blindly now, not tracking th
incoming, but hoping to burn enough of them out of the sk
by sheer chance and firepower.

Fifty kilometers, now . . . thirty . . . twenty. Garwe decel
erated sharply, jogging hard to make it harder for the poin
defenses to nail him.

He cut out the optical magnification and the battle statio
loomed before him, stark in its blocky patterns of black an
white, and every scanner, every weapon, so far as Garw
could see, aimed directly at him. His pod's electronics de
tected and painted in the beams and pulses of radiatio
stabbing up through the battle station's sky, an unnervin
animation filling battlespace with deadly energies.

And then, somehow, he was through, the curve of the battl
station's horizon flattening out at the last second and takin
on the aspect of a black and white world, with a stark land
scape of clean-edged cliff sides, flat-bottomed trenches, pyra
midal and truncated mountains, domes, and towers—most o
them bearing high-energy weapons.

He lashed out with three tentacles, anchoring his pod t
the station's surface, and loosed a cloud of smart AM
missiles programmed to seek out the energy signatures o
enemy weapons and blot them out. The lower half of hi
egg-shaped pod flowed like water, extended, and bit int
the black surface of the station, pouring a stream of nano-
disassemblers into the outer armor of the Dahlist base.

And the pod seemed to melt into the surface, slowly sinking into solid metal.

Company H, 2/9
Marine Transport Major Samuel Nicholas
Objective Samar
0521 hours, GMT

Instead of crowding forward in ranks of four, the two Marines at the center of the front rank leaped through into the Dahlist base while the outer two held back, stepped together, then leaped through after them. The same procedure was repeated by the second rank, and the third. By sticking to the center of the ramp as they moved through, they avoided falling into the deadly fringes of the dimensional interface and repeating the confusion of the initial assault. Gunfire seared and snapped on the Dahlist command deck, followed by a thunderous boom as someone tossed a grenade.

All of Second Platoon was through, now, and Third Platoon was moving up the ramp.

Nal watched the firefight with keen interest. This was a first for the Marines of the 2/9, deploying through a teleport field directly into the middle of the battle. They'd had time to practice a few times in virtual reality simulations, but the reality was *nothing* like the sims.

Worst were the interpenetrations, when Marines entered the other space partially intersecting a console or, horribly worse, another person. The old popular wisdom that two bodies attempting to occupy the same space at the same time would explode wasn't true, it turned out, not when it happened through the agency of a dimensional overlap. There is *lots* of room between the individual atoms of most solids, but once a Marine had stepped into a console there was no way to sort the two out again afterward.

Few survived the experience for more than a few seconds however.

The screams during those seconds were the worst thing Nal had ever experienced.

There wasn't much to see now through the open gateway, so Nal tuned in on the camera feeds from several of the Marines already on the other side. The Marines had cleared the immediate area around the gateway, but were coming under fire now from heavy automatic weapons mounted on catwalks high up around the arching bulkheads of the compartment.

"Hot Fire, Green Five!" someone yelled. "We've got three . . . no *four* heavy guns above us! VK-2s and RmD-34s!"

Hot Fire was the call sign for the HQ element. Second Platoon was Green, Third was Gold.

"Green, Gold One-seven! I've got the VK-2 on the left!"

"Green, Green Two-two! I've got the Rum-dum on the right!"

VK-2s were light bipod-mounted machine guns firing explosive bullets at ten rounds per second. RmD-34s, "Rum-dums," for short, were fast-cycling tripod-mounted weapons firing bolts of high-energy plasma. Both were obsolete by Associative standards, but still deadly.

"I got him! Gold One-seven, target smoked!"

"Watch on your right, One-seven! Watch your right!"

"Green One, this is Hot Fire One," Corcoran's voice said. "I suggest you get some people up on those catwalks!"

"Working on it, sir!" Fellacci replied.

"If I may suggest, Lieutenant," Nal put in, "you might want to use the smart grenades. We're not worried about collateral damage."

"Understood!"

Smart grenades were pencil-sized projectiles fired from launchers built into the left arms of the Hellfire suits, a little larger than AM-4s, but not as uncompromisingly destructive.

They could identify a target and determine the range down to a centimeter or two. If the target ducked behind a barrier, they would detonate when they were immediately above the target's hiding place.

The automatic weapons on the catwalks were mounted atop improvised shields of metal or plasteel, the gunners out of sight. Volleys of smart grenades began snapping up from the main deck and exploding above and behind the shields, in one case hurling a Dahlist gunner over the catwalk railing and ten meters to the deck beneath, trailing smoke.

The blasts, though, savaged the bulkhead, opening fist-sized holes and starting several fires in the electrical wiring on the other side. There was always the chance of depressurization . . . but, as Nal had pointed out, the Marines weren't trying to capture the base so much as they were attempting to knock it out.

In fact, two of the Marines in the HQ section, Sergeants Dayton and Palmer, were equipped with backpack antimatter devices, just in case the decision was made to destroy the base rather than to capture it. The only reason they hadn't simply teleported an AM device or a small nuke into Objective Samar was the hope of taking Emperor Dahl alive.

A double doorway slid open at the far end of the compartment, admitting a swarm of black-armored Dahlist troopers. Nal recognized the armor type from his briefings . . . Mark XV heavy combat suits, a bit out of date but still murderously effective. The Marines swung their aim to take this new threat under fire, knocking down several of the advancing troopers, but they were taking heavy fire in return, and several more Marines were down, two dead, four wounded.

Then a portion of the bulkhead ninety degrees around to the left flared white, then dissolved in smoke and lightning. As the bulkhead collapsed, a massive something was just visible moving through the smoke, smashing its way through the freshly cut opening and into the command deck compartment.

A gunwalker, all silver and gleaming, with black trim, squat and ugly as it lurched from side to side on two stubby, broadly splayed feet. It looked something like an old RK-90, but bigger, and with different weapons housings, and there was a flat turret on top of the thing sending a lance of white-hot plasma flame into the compartment's interior. The walker likely was something new, an upgrade of older walker models with a much bigger punch.

Immediately, the Marines shifted their aim again, concentrating on this new monster, trying to focus their fire on weapons ports and possible weak points. The walker was shielded, however, and shed plasma bolts in sheets of high-energy pyrotechnics.

One Marine, Gunnery Sergeant Ernie Clahan, rose from the wreckage of the command deck holding a rotary cannon, however, and slammed a stream of high-yield antimatter rounds into the gleaming shell of the approaching beast.

The beast returned fire, plasma bolts cracking and snapping in the smoke-clotted air; Clahan's Hellfire suit shrugged off the energy flux in radiant, auroral sheets and jagged bolts of lightning, though the Marine staggered under the impact. He held his fire on the walker, however, pounding a ragged hole in the front of the thing just beneath the turret housing, then concentrating his fire on the fast-widening patch of damage.

Internal explosions began ripping through the robotic combat machine, just as a fusillade of plasma and explosive rounds finally overpowered Clahan's shields and drove him backward onto the deck. The walker gave a final lurch and exploded, huge, silvery fragments pinwheeling through the compartment, trailing smoke.

"Corpsman front! Marine down!"

Sergeant Ferris stepped forward, dropped his plasma rifle, and picked up Clahan's pulse-slammer, turning its buzz-saw destruction on the advancing ranks of Dahlist troops. Behind him, Doc MacKinnon, the Third Platoon corpsman, dropped to the deck and began working on Clahan's shuddering, smoking form, inserting a suit catheter to flush the Marine's body with nanomedical microbots.

More Marines stepped up alongside Ferris, sending a searing fusillade of energy beams and high-yield explosive rounds into the advancing enemy ranks. Dahlist soldiers stumbled and fell, their Mark XV armor failing catastrophically in gouts of flame and blossoming flares of energy. The rest scattered, seeking cover behind junked and smoking instrument consoles, or fell back through the open doorway.

And the Marines followed. "Let's go, Marines!" Ferris yelled over the company net, and he led the others forward as smart grenades slashed and blasted, rooting out Dahlist soldiers hiding behind consoles with shotgun blasts of hot shrapnel.

For perhaps thirty seconds, the issue remained in doubt. Marines in Hellfire armor collided with Dahlist troops in massive, old-fashioned Mark XVs, engaging in hand-to-hand combat. Both armor types linked directly with the cerebral implants of their wearers, and both armor types acted as exoskeletal enhancers, translating their wearers' movements into blocks, lunges, and blows of superhuman strength, agility, and speed.

And at that point, the battle began to shift in favor of the Globe Marines. Personal plasma rifles, man-portable fusion projectors, and smart antimatter grenades remained deadly no matter *when* the people wielding them had been born and raised, in the forty-first century, or in the thirty-first, and in the tight confines of Samar's command control deck there were few options for cover or concealment. It was a slug fest, pure and simple, of personal weapon against massively lethal personal weapon.

But when the incoming tide of Globe Marines actually smashed their way into the defending ranks, personal weapons became less important than the abilities and training of individual men and women.

The Marines of Nal's day had trained extensively in a martial arts form known as weiji-do, which translated roughly as the *Way of Chaos*. Developed in the mid-Third Millennium as an outgrowth of Shaolinquan and Tai chi chuan, weiji-do was a synthesis of the most prominent *wai chia*, or outward, and *nei chia*, or inward Chinese martial arts forms. Combining traditional hand-to-hand combat techniques with certain meditational forms and with programming uploaded into the brain through cranial implants, it purported to give adepts near superhuman abilities in terms of creating reality out of the static of background chaos. The philosophy blended well with the traditional can-do gung-ho attitude of the Marines, and had shaped them extensively. In Nal's experience, weiji-do had never turned Marines into the superhuman warrior-magicians imagined by holovid sagas and sim-sotted civilians in general, but the rep alone contributed to the Marine mystique.

There was no way of knowing whether Dahl's troops, inhabitants of one of the farthest-out outposts of Humankind anywhere, knew anything about the Marine mystique, or cared. But in the hand-to-hand tangle on the Samar command deck, the Marines clearly had the advantage. Their Hellfire armor, lighter-weight and stronger than the Mark XV combat suits of their opponents, gave the Marines a decided advantage in speed and maneuverability. He watched with growing surprise as Sergeant Cori Ryack ducked under a heavy-handed swing by a Dahlist trooper who must have outmassed her by over fifty percent, guided the bigger man's arm to the side, and almost casually ripped it from his shoulder.

Armored joints, it seemed, no matter how tough and well protected, were weak spots and easy targets, or the man wearing the armor wouldn't be able to move.

More Dahlist troopers were spilling onto the command deck, but enough Marines had entered the battlespace that they were able to maintain their advantage now. At the beginning, the Dahlists had been well positioned and able to gun down Marines as they came through the teleport field a few at a time. Now the Marines had reversed the situation, and it was they who held a good tactical position, gunning down the Dahlist troops as they came bursting through doors and the gaping, wreckage-filled opening in one bulkhead.

"Captain?" Nal said over their private link. "I think this might be the time to send in Hugin and Munin. We won't have a better opportunity."

He felt Corcoran's nod of agreement. "Give the order."

"Aye, aye, sir."

It was the tactical instant the Marines had been waiting for.

13

Command Control Deck
Objective Samar
0523 hours, GMT

Hugin and *Munin* were figures out of ancient Norse mythology, a pair of ravens, the companions of the god Odin. Their names meant *thought* and *memory*. Each day they flew throughout the entire world, returning to Odin all-father each evening to tell him all they'd seen.

In their modern incarnation, they were a highly sophisticated cybernetic organism. Hugin was the actual hardware, an elongated egg-shaped device of gleaming black plastic-steel alloy that looked almost exactly like an RS/A-91 Starwraith, but considerably smaller, less than half a meter long. The external surface blurred and refracted light, making it difficult to see, and it could extrude long and flexible tentacles at need.

Munin was the AI portion of the system, a narrowly focused artificial intelligence resident within the military intelligence network on board the *Nicholas*. Before an operation, an exact copy of Munin was downloaded into the Hugin hardware. Hugin was designed to find and attach itself to targeted enemy computer systems or network nodes, penetrate them, and inject a portion of Munin into the data stream. Munin would record what it found and, one way or another, transmit the data back to headquarters for reintegration with the original Munin. Old memories were compared with new, and hard data extracted for analyses. The Hugin/Munin system had been developed specifically to target Xul nodes almost seven hundred years before, an evolution of earlier AI probes and penetrators.

Gunnery Sergeant Andrew Boyd, with the Company HQ element, used a specially modified KV-12 man-portable railgun to launch the Hugin probe from *Nicholas*' debarkation deck through the open gateway and into Objective Samar's C/C deck. The probe streaked through open air above the heads of the incoming Marines, materializing inside the enemy fortress' command center and crashing in for a more or less uncontrolled landing. Too small to mount its own grav drive, the Hugin probe relied on tiny mag-impeller thrusters for maneuvering in zero-gravity, and its tentacles for moving anywhere else. As soon as it skidded across the deck, banging into chunks of scattered wreckage and smashed consoles, a half-dozen tentacles grew from its shell and it began whiplashing with blinding speed across the deck and into a gaping hole in a nearby bulkhead, where the enemy gunwalker had made its rather dramatic entry minutes before.

Samar's command/control deck was *the* central network node for the Dahlist battle station. Every optical feed and circuit in the area not involving the lighting or life support was part of the command/control system, giving direct access to the entire Dahlist computer network.

Plasma bolts snapped and banged to either side, as enemy gunners noticed the intruder and tried to bring it down, but the unit was well shielded and very fast, operating at speeds impossible for any merely organic neural network. Slipping past the wreckage of the gunwalker, it used that shattered bulk for cover as it made its way toward the opened bulkhead. Its tentacles were coated with nanotechnic sheaths that adhered to the deck or not, on command, giving it perfect traction and superb maneuverability both on the slick deck and on the tangled wreckage over which it navigated.

Enemy troops were crouched at the opening, firing into the command center, and one of them yelled and pointed at the Hugin's approach.

They scattered, possibly thinking it was some sort of Marine smart-weapon; in any case, it was moving too quickly and too erratically to bring it down with small-arms fire. As they bolted, the little machine swerved abruptly to the left and burrowed into the fiber-optic and wire-crammed space between the inner and outer bulkhead walls. Besides being fast, the Hugin's shell was supremely malleable. Like the mythical Proteus, it could change shape in a blur of softening and reforming, reconforming itself to fit into tight and narrow spaces. Tentacles found a set of severed fiber-optic cables . . . and within the primary data bus. Nanotechnic surfaces flowed like water, reforming themselves and passing through outer sheathing and into the data flow.

The Munin component sensed the surge of moving data packets and stretched out through connecting tentacles and leads . . . sampling . . . tasting . . . *drinking* . . .

Company H, 2/9
Marine Transport Major Samuel Nicholas
Objective Samar
0524 hours, GMT

"Captain Corcoran! We're in!" Lieutenant Mendoza was the platoon HQ intelligence analyst, the company "minispook," as she was known. A platoon was too small—and a captain too junior—to warrant its own G-2 intelligence department, or an S-2 staff officer, but a minispook on the command constellation allowed Corcoran to link directly with higher-level intel organizations all the way up to the ancient and venerable Office of Naval Intelligence itself, now a bureau within the Associative Fleet Command.

At the moment, though, she was linked with the stay-at-home Munin on board the *Nicholas*, watching the data as it streamed back from the Hugin imbedded within Objective Samar's bulkheads.

Nal heard the excitement in the junior officer's mental voice, and couldn't help smiling. Like most officers of her breed and calling, she tended to be pragmatic, meticulous, and even plodding, and rarely given to bursts of excitement . . . but he knew she'd been sweating the details of working with modern intelligence systems, and success appeared to have bypassed her normal reserve.

"Simmer down, Mendoza," Corcoran told her. "What do you have?"

"Sir! Munin has a solid link with the Dahlist network. We can go in whenever you want."

"Very well. You may initiate THRP transmission."

"Aye, aye, sir!"

Nal's inner grin faded. This part made him uneasy, almost queasy if he thought too hard about it. There was something about the process that just wasn't *right*. Not human, somehow.

But, of course, t-humans weren't quite human to begin with, were they?

Of all the changes and differences between the thirty-second century and the forty-first, the deliberate creation and evolution of *Homo telae* was, to Nal's mind, the strangest and the least defensible. Were minds uploaded into a computer network really alive? More to the point, were they the same individuals who'd uploaded themselves in the first place? Or mere copies?

And did *that* make them real . . . or electronic fictions?

Millennia ago, a similar debate had existed over cloning, and whether or not clones were legitimate life forms. The question was nonsense, of course; it didn't matter whether an individual had been generated by the meeting of egg and sperm, or by the biological manipulation of a single cell. The resultant life form was in every way a living creature. Its only difference lay in the fact that it was identical to its parent—and usually considerably younger.

Speaking generally, and from a certain point of view, a human being wasn't so much blood and bone and tissue as it was patterns of information. Nal knew that his physical self was in a constant state of flux; the oldest cells in his body were living bone tissue, which died and were replaced on the order of every seven years or so. The youngest were his blood cells, which had an expected life span of perhaps three weeks. His body was not the same as it had been even a few years ago; it was constantly tearing itself apart and building itself back, one cell at a time, in a process that extended from conception to death, and there likely wasn't a single molecule in his body that was the same as those that had made up his physical form the day he'd enlisted in the Corps twenty-three subjective years ago, to pick one example.

And yet he *felt* like the same individual he'd always been— born and raised on Enduru/Ishtar, living nineteen standard years in the *e-duru* of Vaj beneath the sullen glow of the Face of God. And twenty-three more waking years in various Marine duty stations or on board ships in the course of his long career, from Marine Recruit to Master Sergeant. All told, Nal could remember over forty years of life, and the Nal il-En Shru-dech of today was the same as the Nal il-En Shru-dech of then, wasn't he? Older, more experienced, a bit more worn and tired, but the same *person*, even though every molecule of his body had by now been broken down and rebuilt many times over. It was the *pattern* of Nal il-En Shru-dech that counted, not the physicality of his component atoms and molecules.

The *Homo telae* had become what they were by uploading the patterns of their minds onto electronic networks. Though many liked to claim otherwise, the original bodies and minds of those individual human originators of the species had gone on, then, to age normally and eventually to die. It was the *copies* that lived on in what was supposed to be a blissfully eternal and completely noncorporeal life.

And that was the problem. What Lieutenant Mendoza was doing right now was transmitting several hundred t-humans into the Dahl electronic net as electronic agents, but in electronic terms, what *transmission* actually meant was *copying.* The original t-human entities were still here on board the *Nicholas.* Their exact reproductions would be inside the Dahl network.

Well, *almost* exact. "THRP" stood for "T-Human Restricted Purpose." The copies, popularly called "thurps," were deliberately edited by special AI software so that the new individuals could not think about anything but the mission, were not particularly inclined to preserve their existence, and had no problem with being switched off when their mission was over. Limited Purview suggested a restricted, tightly narrowed and focused consciousness, one that didn't worry about such niceties as survival or death.

And that, to Nal, seemed nothing less than horrible, a means of turning people into disposable use-once software.

It didn't really help that he had trouble picturing *Homo telae* as human in the first place. *They* thought they were human, and the ones he'd interacted with over the past few weeks seemed to believe they were human, complete with emotions, moods, creativity, and personal motivations.

Nal was the product of a human culture, the *dumu-gir*, which for something like ten millennia had been a *slave* culture. Their liberation in the mid-twenty-second century, Old Style had been extremely difficult for them, if only because by that time it was almost impossible for them to think of themselves as *free*.

Those who'd been able to embrace the concept, however, had taken freedom very seriously indeed, and the idea had grown stronger with each passing generation. The idea of copying yourself, but editing the copy so that everything that made you free was missing, seemed positively blasphemous to the Free Men of Enduru.

Nal and the thousand or so other *dumu-gir* in the 3MarDiv didn't like the idea at all, but they were Marines, and they did what they were told. In this case, doing what they were told meant to shut up and follow orders . . . and don't worry about the tellies because they're doing what they want to do, the way they want to do it. When Nal had first complained about the idea weeks ago, Corcoran had told him personally to shut the hell up. "The tallies aren't like us, Master Sergeant," Corcoran had said. "They see life—and death, for that matter—completely differently, okay? If the thurps don't mind this restricted purpose thing, than neither should you."

"But they *can't* mind it," Nal had said, almost crying with exasperation. "Damn it, sir, they're designed not to!"

"Exactly. So don't worry about it. That's an order, Master Sergeant."

Reluctantly, very reluctantly, Nal had managed an "Aye, aye, Sir."

But that hadn't kept him from *thinking* about it.

And after a lot of thought, he'd finally decided he knew why he had such a strong gut reaction to t-Human downloads. If they—the unnamed but powerful and all-pervasive *they* of the high command and the Associative government—could allow the t-Humans to edit copies of themselves, in effect creating slaves designed not to care about their condition, how long would it be before the same thing was happening to normals?

Normals. That was the term, almost contemptuous, applied by many of the new forms of Humankind in this brave new world of the forty-first century, the supies, the tellies, and others. The physical bodies of humans, even of old-fashioned *Homo sapiens*, the normals, had become nearly infinitely variable over the course of the past two millennia. Gene tailoring was used as a matter of course by normals to select for intelligence, endurance, good looks, and resistance to disease in their children. Nanotechnology could resculpt the body as easily as putting on a new set of clothing or coronae; it was called nanocosmetology. Nanobiology could rewrite an individual's genome, letting him grow new features or develop gene-controlled traits that his or her parents had overlooked.

And the mind could be edited just as easily. Nano-grown cerebral implants had changed the ways humans thought and reasoned since at least the twenty-second century. What was downloading a new skill set, an alien language, for instance, but a reworking of the mind?

What was to stop *them* from offering a download to all normals that would make them happier, healthier, and better able to cope with modern life?

A new thought tugged at him unpleasantly. What if they already had done just that? Nal still didn't understand how people could accept those Socon Guardian things reading peoples' minds like that.

Don't think about it. Just follow your orders and keep your mouth shut.

Some things, though, were just plain wrong, and from Nal's point of view, this was one of them.

At the moment, he didn't know what to do about it, however. The tallies seemed as content with the practice as Nal's distant ancestors had been with the lordship of the Ahannu, the alien gods who'd turned them into willing slaves.

And perhaps the two weren't that far distant from each other.

Right now, according to the telemetry streaming back from Objective Samar, the thurps were definitely inside the Dahlist works, infiltrating electronic systems, bypassing safeguards, breaching files, downloading data. That data was flooding back to the *Nichols* now through a high-bandwidth link between the Hugin and Lieutenant Mendoza. The Dahl fortress' main weapons had just gone off-line, sabotaged by a thurp assault team.

And suddenly the air pressure in the compartment was

dropping catastrophically, as smoke, papers, and lightweight debris swirled off the deck and off the computer consoles and funneled in a tight, swirling, horizontal tornado out the open door ahead. For a moment, Nal thought the thurps had opened the main hatches to the outside, but then he noted the real reason for the depressurization.

"Check your fire, Marines!" Nal warned. "We have friend-lies inbound!"

He was watching the data feed coming in from the *Nicholas*, getting the grand-tactical picture. Ten members of the 340th Marine Strike Force had landed on the outer hull of Objective Samar, burned their way through the outer hull, and had just entered the battle station's interior passageways. They were a hundred meters away and moving in fast, guided by AIs monitoring the entire battle. The Dahlist troopers falling back from the Marine assault were trapped. They didn't know it yet, but that handful of heavily armored RS/A-91 Starwraiths were slamming up those tangled passageways, taking out everything in their way.

And seconds later, the battle for Objective Samar was over.

Command Deck
Marine Transport Major Samuel Nicholas
Objective Samar
0607 hours, GMT

General Garroway stood on the command deck, looking up at the dome overhead. It wasn't a true transparency, of course—the command deck was buried deep within the immense bulk of the transport—but the projection of the view outside was perfect to the smallest detail. The Stargate hung directly overhead, and Associative ships were emerging now, making the hundred-thousand light-year jump in from Way Point Tun Tavern in a steady stream. Beyond, the flat-tened sphere of the Dahl fortress designated Objective Samar moved slowly in its orbit about the Stargate ring.

The stellar backdrop behind it all was astonishing—
sheets and ribbons and outflung tendrils of blue and green,
the radiant glory of the Tarantula Nebula.

Someone once had calculated that if the Tarantula Nebula
was as far from Earth as the Great Nebula in Orion—some
4,000 light years—it would cover thirty degrees of the night
sky, as big across as sixty full moons, and banish the night.
The Tarantula stretched a thousand light years from one side
to the other, one of the largest star-forming regions known.
The Magellanic Clouds were orbiting the Milky Way Galaxy and had closely interacted with it in the past. That interaction had triggered an extended period of star formation,
turning the heart of the tiny galaxy into a jewel box of young,
hot stars.

One star cluster, R136a, visible as a hard, tight knot of suns
against unfurling color, was only two and a half million
years old—its stars infants in comparison to others; twelve
of those stars were among the most massive known, type O3
supergiants each millions of times more massive than Sol.
Fierce stellar winds streaming off those giants were knead-
ing, tearing, and shaping the far vaster extent of the nebula.

Just 150 light years away from R136a lay another cluster,
Hodge 301, perhaps twenty million years old, old enough that
its more massive, shorter-lived stars were beginning to age
and die. A chain of forty supernovae during the past few millions years had torn at the nebula. Together, the energy streaming from those two clusters had shaped and reshaped the
tenuous threads and sheets of the nebula itself, creating its
sculpted, twisted, spidery appearance.

Well off to one side was a brilliant, hazy patch. Catalogued
as SN 1987A, it was a supernova remnant, a young one. Its
light had reached Earth only about two thousand years ago.
The Stargate itself was located in the heart of yet a third star
cluster, this one several billion years old and relatively small,
with a dozen or so stars with human-habitable worlds—the
Tavros-Endymion Cluster. The radiation wave front from SN

1978A, Garroway thought, must have scoured any of the local worlds bare of life at this range.

He wondered what the Tarantulae were like. Were they alien enough to survive such a radiation storm, or had they moved into the region later, as the supernova was fading?

The light show spread across the overhead dome was so thick and rich with stars and light that the far larger mass of the home Galaxy, 165,000 light years beyond, was lost.

"General Garroway?" Lofty Henderson's voice said in his mind. *"We have located Emelius Dahl. He is asking for surrender terms."*

"I see. Where was he?"

"On board one of the Dahlist warships, the Curtains of Light, *heavy battlecruiser, 290,000 tons."*

The main Dahlist battlefleet was still out there—consisting of twelve capital ships identified so far, and a swarm of armed packets, gunboats, and hastily armed and refitted short-range craft. The Associative fleet was far larger, over a hundred ships, and growing with every moment as new vessels continued to arrive through the Stargate. With the gate's capture, the Dahl Navy had no place else to go, and no access to repair and refit facilities, supplies, or bases.

According to Intelligence, the Dahl Empire, so-called, embraced perhaps twenty star systems, with three worlds enough like Earth not to matter, the recently conquered Tarantulae homeworld, and a couple of dozen other sparsely inhabited planets, from Mars look-alikes to airless rocks and iceballs. They had only the one Stargate, and travel across their Empire was possible only through Alcubierre FTL. Without the Gate, their tiny Navy had no place to go . . . unless they wanted to seek the help of the Tarantulae, whom until recently they'd been bullying. It sounded as though Dahl had elected to surrender now and get it over with, rather than have his ships chased down and destroyed one by one.

The campaign had been almost as easy as the Star Lords back home had claimed it would be.

Garroway had never trusted *easy*.

"Have him brought aboard the *Nicholas*," Garroway told the AI. "But have them be careful! I want a nano-level scan of this guy before he sets foot on board." One of the more difficult attacks to defend against was a nanotech weapon. The deadliest of attacks could be brought inside one's defenses disguised as the normal bacterial flora of a visitor or a prisoner, as dust on the bottom of their shoe, as compactly folded protein molecules hidden in the lining of lungs and throat.

"Agreed, General. And . . . one more thing."

"Yes?"

"Star Lord Rame requests a moment of your time."

"Very well. Put him through."

Rame's lean frame appeared in Garroway's mind, his corona bright. "Congratulations, General."

"Eh? What for?"

Rame spread his hands. "A magnificent victory, of course! Brilliant!"

"Bullshit."

"I beg your pardon?"

"Lord Rame, Objective Samar was a trap."

"What do you mean?"

Garroway shrugged. "Hell, I was pretty sure it would be going in. We all were. Any defender of the Tarantula Stargate would know that the key to defending the Tavros-Endymion Cluster is to keep enemy warships from transiting out of the Gate, right?"

"I suppose—"

"Objective Samar was perfectly positioned and had the weapons necessary to destroy our warships as they emerged from the Gate. That made Samar the one absolutely vital target in this operation. We *had* to take it to get our fleet in. If we tried to destroy it, we might damage the Gate . . . and they also made sure we thought their emperor was there. More encouragement for us to capture the place rather than blow it to bits.

"You figured all that out before going in?"

"No, sir, but I had a good idea. And when one of my people spotted the fact that the fortress was close to the Stargate with no grav shielding up, it kind of clicked. They either wanted us to teleport in and take heavy casualties doing so, because the gravitational tides would screw with a solid d-teleport lock, or they wanted us coming through in small numbers, a few at a time. Either way, we face the horrors of interpenetration of partial transmissions . . . or else we decide not to teleport, and come in through open space, with assault pods. Again, small numbers, and we'd take heavy casualties weaving in through their fusion and plasma beam defense network."

"So you did both."

Garroway nodded. "We did both."

"And the trap failed."

Inwardly, Garroway scowled, though he couldn't tell if the Star Lord could see his expression. "Sir, two of my platoons took heavy casualties in that assault. Forty dead, and perhaps half of those are irrecoverable." He didn't add that the living had suffered badly as well. The sight of those poor Marines mangled and partially *merged* with the metal deck and consoles would have given anyone the cold horrors.

"How long will it take to replace them?"

"We *can't* replace them. These are Globe Marines."

"The Anchor Marines performed admirably," Rame said. "Why can't you draw replacements from them?"

Garroway wanted to tell the man that it simply wasn't possible, that Anchor Marines could *never* be Globe Marines, that the training and quality of personnel that had made the Corps great nine centuries before simply didn't exist today.

But he didn't. The fact of the matter was that the Anchor Marines *had* done well, storming the Dahl bastion and closing the jaws of the Marine assault. If the "dead" among them had awakened an instant later back on board the *Nicholas*, that hardly counted against them. It took guts to face shock and dismemberment, even if the horror was solely virtual. They'd carried out their mission with élan and with precision.

Hell, one of the Marines who'd made it into Samar had been young Marek Garwe.

"We'll make whatever organizational changes we need to, sir," was all he said.

"That's good. We're . . . counting on you."

Something about the way Rame said that last caught Garroway's attention. The Star Lord was not being evasive, quite, but there was something he wasn't saying.

Hell, in Garroway's experience politicians never said everything that they were thinking. There was always another angle, another rationale, another pay-off to be made or another back to be scratched or another deal to be cut with the people who had the money, the influence, and the power.

From what Garroway had seen of politics and government so far in the forty-first century, it was now the politicians who had the lion's share of money, influence, and power, wielding them openly, rather than acting as front-men for behind-the-scenes shadow governments as had been the case in Garroway's day. The Star Lords ran things, made the big decisions, and the people didn't give a damn, so long as they were relatively comfortable.

And maybe that was the way it was *supposed* to work.

But what wasn't Rame telling him?

"Do you want to tell me about it?"

"Eh? What are you talking about?"

"There's something you're not telling me, my Lord. What is it? Something new about the Xul operation?" He hesitated. "Or something new from the other Star Lords? New orders?"

The image in Garroway's mind, created by Rame's personal AIgent, could not give anything away—no eye-blinks, frowns, widened eyes, or other unconsciously transmitted body language that might help others read Rame's state of mind. Even so, something about the silence that followed his question suggested surprise, even shock.

"Do people of your century always read minds, General?"

Rame said after a moment. "I thought only s-Humans engaged in telepathy."

"Don't forget your Socon Guardians."

"What have you heard?"

Garroway sighed. "My Lord, I am a Marine major general. Once an officer reaches the rank of colonel, he spends more time fighting politicians than he spends fighting any foreign enemy." He took another guess. "The other Star Lords have given you new orders? Concerning me and my people?"

The image in Garroway's mind nodded. "This operation here today was . . . a test, in a sense. To see if your Marines were . . . as good as the stories surrounding them."

"I see. And did we pass?"

"You successfully carried out the operation, General. Despite a serious initial setback, when your initial assault failed. *And* you showed yourself willing and able to work with local elements, the Anchors, to accomplish your mission."

"So now they want to use us against other targets? Other missions?"

"Exactly."

"But *not* the Xul."

Again, Rame hesitated, as though searching for a mild, a *politic* reply. "Not everyone within the Associative leadership believes that the Xul constitute a viable threat. Or an important one. A sizeable majority believe that the Globe Marines would be best employed putting down the rise of rebellion, rioting, and discontent currently sweeping through Associative worlds."

"I see. Where do they want to send us?"

"An artificial world in closer to the Galactic Core. A place called Kaleed. The Star Lord for that sector is Ared Goradon. He is close friends with another star lord, Lelan Veloc."

"I remember her." An arrogant, condescending bitch.

"You should. And *she* is a member of the Military Operations Bureau, which gives you your orders."

Garroway had downloaded information on Kaleed shortly after he'd come out of cybe-hibe, part of a long list of military crises throughout human space. Goradon, it seemed, had been chased off the wheelworld, and was now in Earthring. "Right. *You* had nothing to do with this at all, of course."

"I find your tone insulting, General."

"Good. That was my intent. Why the hell are *you* telling me this, anyway? Where's Socrates? I thought he was supposed to be my liaison with the Star Lords and their chain of command."

"*I am here, General,*" Socrates' voice said. "*I am part of the link-gestalt that is Star Lord Rame and Star Lord Valoc and several others, linked through their personal aigents.*"

The new voice startled Garroway. There were aspects of forty-first century technology with which he still wasn't comfortable, but this was a new and even more unpleasant one. Humans had been closely linked with their implant personalities for almost two millennia. In Garroway's day, it was frequently impossible to tell whether you were speaking to the actual mind of a friend, or to his aigent.

But people nowadays not only accepted this, they accepted a blurring of personal boundaries that Garroway's generation found disturbing. Exactly who and what was an individual intelligence? Where did Rame stop, and Socrates begin? How much did Rame overlap with Valoc?

Worse, those boundaries, if they even existed at all, appeared to be constantly changing, depending on where the attention of the intelligences concerned were focused at the moment.

Garroway preferred to know with whom he was dealing.

"Lord Rame, Socrates . . . Valoc, too, if you're in there . . . the Commonwealth Marines are *not* your personal plaything."

The image of Star Lord Rame blurred and shifted, morphing into the high forehead and imperious manner of Lelan Valoc.

"How *dare* you, Garroway?" she said. "You and your . . . people are here on our sufferance!"

"We are here because of the provisions of the Warrington Initiative. And I believe you will find that I and my command constellation have a say in things when you give us a military operation, mission, or target."

" 'Warrington Initiative?' "

"Ancient history to you, I'm sure. But I'm sure it's still there for download."

He knew it was. Among the first things Garroway had checked when he'd received his new implant software was the current standing of the legal document that had established the Marine cyber-hibe division in the first place. His orders came from the Military Operations Bureau of the Associative Conclave. But he had the right to refuse them if they seemed suicidal or otherwise destructive to his command.

He couldn't tell if Valoc had checked the history or not. Her expression was unreadable, the creation of software rather than of flesh, blood, and emotion.

"General. You were awakened in the first place because of Ared Goradon's request. You wouldn't be here at all if not for him."

"No, we would be asleep in cyber-hibe, waiting for a *real* war."

"Why do you say that? What would a 'real war' be?"

"It wouldn't be pissing out small fires like this." He gestured, in his mind, at the Stargate hanging suspended beyond the overhead dome, and the Associative ships still coming through one after another. "My Lord, we're here to fight your wars. We volunteered as a deep-time ready unit, and we owe the future . . . and I guess that means we owe *you,* two years of active duty, subjective time. You've got us. But for God's sake, don't *waste* us. We went into cyber-hibe under the provisions of the Warrington Initiative. *That's* what we're here for . . . not your fucking little brushfire wars and uprisings, not tin-plated wannabes like 'Emperor Dahl,' or displaced idiots like Ared Goradon!"

"You," Valoc said, "are out of line, General!" Or was it Rame? Or Socrates?

And an instant later, the Stargate, the stars beyond, the gorgeous sheets and streamers of the Tarantula Nebula, all were blotted out by a burst of impossibly brilliant light.

And Garroway knew that something had just gone horribly wrong.

14

Command Deck
Marine Transport Major Samuel Nicholas
Objective Samar
0612 hours, GMT

For an instant, the sky burned a dazzling, searing white . . .
and then the dome overhead went black, either through a deliberate circuit interrupt to preserve human vision, or because
the optical receptors on the *Nicholas*' hull had just burned
out.

"What happened?" Garroway demanded.

The image of Valoc blurred and wavered. "General!
What—"

"Get the hell off this link!" Garroway ordered. Internally,
he closed a connection, severing the AI link with his visitors.
"Lofty! What was that?"

"Still assessing the situation, General," his essistant told
him, *"but it appears that the local Stargate has exploded."*

Garroway sensed the streams of communication moving
through the Fleet, reports of ship damage, of ships lost, of
Dahl Empire ships now moving to the attack.

He also sensed the aivatar representing Rame and Valoc
still hovering on the fringes of his cybernetic awareness, unwilling to be summarily banished, demanding to speak. He

cut that channel entirely. There would be time later for talk—and, if necessary, for his court-martial.

Right now was *not* the time.

Then the overhead lit up once more. The Stargate now was in fragments, each of several dozen huge, curved segments glowing white-hot and tumbling as it hurtled away from the others in a raggedly expanding cloud of plasma. The two micro-black holes that had powered the thing were hurtling now in opposite directions at close to the speed of light, detectable by the stark trails of ionization they'd ripped through the thin soup of dust and gas permeating local space.

"Sharp spikes in gamma radiation and analyses of debris trajectories indicate at least three sizeable and simultaneous antimatter explosions inside the Stargate. The destruction was deliberate sabotage."

Garroway's immediate concern was for his Marines, Golf and Hotel Companies, plus an Anchor Marine strike element, which had been on board the fortress orbiting the gate moments before.

"What's the situation on Samar?" he demanded.

"Still trying to re-establish communications, General," Lofty told him. *"Objective Samar appears to be structurally sound, but is tumbling now."*

He closed his eyes. "How many of our people are over there?"

"Two platoons of Golf Company, Second Regiment. Two platoons plus the headquarters element of Hotel. The HQ section had just completed transiting to Samar when the explosion occurred."

At least that meant senior command and communications staff were already over there. He pulled down the relevant data in his mind. Captain Corcoran. A decent officer, with a *very* good command constellation.

"Keep trying to raise them."

"Yes, sir. We are also receiving telemetry indicating an impending attack. It appears that the Dahlist surrender was a ruse."

"No. You think?"

His mock-surprise tone was lost on the AI, however. *"Affirmative. The Associate fleet has taken heavy losses. The battlecruiser* Pleiadean *was emerging from the Gate at the moment of detonation, and has been lost with all hands. Three cruisers and six destroyers were close enough to the blast to have been destroyed or incapacitated. Numerous other ships are reporting major damage, and at least five have been disabled."*

"I assume both Admiral Dravid and Admiral Ranser are on this."

"Affirmative, General."

Both men had their own command centers on board the *Nicholas.* At this point, the battle had become a purely naval engagement, and there was little Garroway could add or do. Except . . .

"Lofty, patch through to Admiral Ranser, back channel. Tell him the Marines are available for d-teleport deployment into the enemy vessels, should that become a viable tactic. Then pass the word to First and Third Battalions. Have them stand ready for possible ship-to-ship action, both offensive and defensive."

"Aye, aye, General."

And that, quite simply, was all that he could do. In the ancient days of sailing ships, a vessel's Marines would take to the rigging and mastheads and pour sniper fire down on the decks of enemy vessels, attempting to take out their senior officers. A century later, ships no longer had rigging, and the Marines were there solely as an amphibious assault force, ready to storm ashore and take an objective beachhead, but all but useless in a ship-to-ship action.

Centuries later, Marine boarding parties had again come into their own, with specially designed assault craft—and eventually one-man assault pods—that could carry Marines up to an enemy ship, breach her hull, and allow the Marines to carry the ship by storm. With the advent of teleport technology, Marine boarding parties could jump straight from the deck of one ship to another, bypassing force fields and point-defense batteries entirely.

Garroway also wanted to have the Marines on board the *Samuel Nicholas* ready in case the enemy tried the same tactic. The *Nicholas* was a huge and inviting target, would be the principal target for the Dahlists in the coming battle, and they might well have large numbers of troops ready to teleport into the transport's cavernous bays and passageways.

Either way, there were over fifteen thousand Marines still on board the *Nicholas*, and they would be a powerful weapon in any fleet engagement, not simply as shore parties or a landing force. The tactics of ship-to-ship action, however, were entirely in the hands of the naval command, in this case Pol Ranser, the CO of the Associative Task Force.

Which left Garroway as little better than a passive observer, a tourist along for the ride. "Lofty! Damn it, can you raise our people on Samar?"

"Negative, General." Lofty's voice was infuriatingly calm. *"Still trying."*

The enemy squadron was approaching fast, twelve ships to the twenty the Associative had already put through the Gate . . . but half of those twenty were crippled to one degree or another, and several appeared dead in space.

Garroway sensed the storm of communications sweeping through the Associative Fleet, and in moments more the battle was joined.

Company H, 2/9
Command Deck
Objective Samar
0617 hours, GMT

"What the hell happened?" Corcoran demanded.

Nal clung to a twisted stanchion emerging from one bulkhead as the compartment very slowly, almost lazily rolled over. Down was no longer toward the deck with a pull of roughly one gravity. It was *that* way, toward the opposite bulkhead, a weak tug barely felt. He was in the dark, a darkness relieved only by the lights on the Marines' Hellfire suits, a hundred moving gleams, mostly at the down end of the compartment, throwing weird and shifting shadows across bulkheads and shattered equipment.

So the lights, all power, were out. Artificial gravity was out, and the rotation of the Dahl orbital fortress was creating a weak spin-gravity as it tumbled through space. The acceleration wasn't more than a few centimeters per second squared—Nal could easily hang on one-handed against its pull—but it was a *long* way down through a compartment filled with torn and broken wreckage, jagged sheets of metal, and ripped-open consoles. Even at a hundredth of a gravity, a fall through that maze could be deadly if you landed badly. Some of the loose material in the compartment—chairs, personal effects and weapons, pieces of armor, fragments of debris, dead bodies, living Marines—were still striking the opposite bulkhead in a stately and drawn-out clatter.

A portion of Nal's mind registered the fact that there *was* sound. The hurricane of air escaping the compartment had ceased some time ago. No doubt Samar's automated damage-control systems had sealed off the breaches in the station's hull. And whatever had just happened apparently had not ripped the hull open further.

He was trembling inside at how *close* it had been. Nal and the rest of the HQ section had only *just* come through the d-teleport gateway when suddenly all contact with the universe outside of Objective Samar had been cut off, when lights, power, and gravity had vanished with a sudden, jarring shock, and the fortress had begun its slow tumble. He felt the pounding of his heart, the sickness at the pit of his stomach. Had the teleport doorway been interrupted while he or one of his Marines had been making the transit . . .

"Damn it, Master Sergeant!" Corcoran snapped. "I *asked* you what happened?"

Nal dragged his mind back from the emptiness of numbing shock. "We're . . . working on it," he told the platoon commander. They didn't have QCC units with them, and any FTL comm units here on Objective Samar were off-line at the moment. "We're obviously cut off from Fleet. I suggest, sir, that we deploy our people for a possible counterattack. If the Dahlies are responsible for this . . ."

"Point taken, Master Sergeant. See to it."

"Aye, aye, sir."

The Marines were off the Fleet Net, but still had communication at company levels. Nal began issuing orders to the Marines of Hotel and Golf Companies, using Corcoran's electronic persona, while Corcoran continued to try to reestablish contact with other electronic networks higher up on the chain of command.

Nal had a feeling, though, that he knew what had happened. The blast—there was no better word for it—had come as a sharp, violent shock accompanied by a surge in gamma radiation, but with no sound. If there'd been an explosion somewhere within the Samar fortress, they would have heard it, the sound conducted through both the air and the orbital base's internal structure.

The utter silence, however, save for a deep-voiced background thunder, almost a gong's tone that had emerged from the deck and bulkheads with the shock as the shockwave smashed through Objective Samar, suggested that there'd been a titanic explosion, not within the base, but in the Stargate next door.

Stargates, Nal knew, contained tens of thousands of kilometers of tunnels and inner chambers within their ring-shaped structures. Besides the twin racetracks that channeled the two Jupiter-mass black holes in their space-twisting, light-speed circles, there were plenty of empty spaces within which one or more antimatter bombs or large nuclear devices could be hidden.

Hell, one of the earliest nonhuman civilizations encountered by Humankind in times, the N'mah, had been encountered inside the empty spaces of the Sirius Stargate. An entire civilization, numbering tens of millions of individuals, complete with cities and a small enclosed ocean, had been surviving in there for thousands of years, hiding from the relentless searches of the xenophobic Xul.

The Dahlists must have been insane—or scared witless—to do something as psycho as blowing up a Stargate.

Of course, that sort of thing *did* happen. Marines had blown up a Gate or two in their history, centuries ago, in order to keep the Xul from tracking back to Sirius and finding Earth just eight and a half light years away. But Stargates represented a technology far more ancient than Humankind, quite possibly more ancient than the Xul, and once broken they could *not* be reassembled.

So far, only the single Stargate, Tavros-Endymion, had been discovered within the Large Magellanic Cloud. The next nearest Gate was the one designated Tun Tavern, halfway back to the Home Galaxy.

And that began to explain the Dahl Empire's strategy. Even under Alcubierre Drive, Associative ships would need the better part of a century to make it all the way out here from Tun Tavern. By destroying the local Gate, Warlord Dahl must have been hoping that the Associative would decide it was too much trouble sending a fleet large enough to bring his egomaniac's little empire to heel. By blowing the Gate when they did, the Dahlists had struck a savage blow against the gathering Associative Fleet, and balanced the disparity in numbers. Again, that might make the Associative government think twice about sending out an expedition to put down the Dahlist insurrection.

The wild cards were the big phase-shifter ships like the *Nicholas*. They were large enough to carry several sizeable Alcubierre warships, and could translate in from the Home Galaxy without benefit of a Stargate. All they needed was a decent metric of local space; the actual distance for the imp theoretically didn't matter. Nal suspected that the enemy had held off on destroying the ring in hopes that *Nicholas* would move closer. Now, of course, they would need to take out the *Nicholas* by other means—ship-to-ship, or by -teleporting assault troops into the transport's command and weapons bays.

And then the power switched back on. Down again became down, and Nal released his handhold and dropped his boots to the deck. The overhead shimmered, then came to life once more, looking out into a shockingly changed starscape.

The Stargate was, indeed, gone, a white clot of fast-expanding plasma marking where it had been. The Samar fortress had been engulfed; its sky now was filled by a ragged white cloud that blotted out most of the background stars and the tangle of nebulae. The AI controlling the image projection was painting the locations and vector trails of ships nearby, creating a scrawl of green and red lines across the virtual depths of the overhead dome. Smaller, more fleeting streaks marked the paths of missiles, fighters, and assault pods; white flares of light blossomed on both sides as high-energy particle beams and fusion cannon, antimatter warheads and plasma weapons struck home.

"We have QCC communications with the *Nicholas*," Lieutenant Fellacci reported. "They're still there, thank God!"

"Roger that."

Nal shared Fellacci's heartfelt relief. The Dahl ships would be focusing their efforts on the *Sam Nick*, since she was the most formidable Associative warship now on the Tavros-Endymion side of the suddenly ex-Stargate. And if they destroyed her, none of the Marines in the Large Magellanic Cloud would be getting home.

Ever.

• • •

Command Deck
Marine Transport Major Samuel Nicholas
Objective Samar
0618 hours, GMT

"General Garroway, we have re-established contact wit
our people on board Objective Samar. They have re
established power and life-support, and the base QCC ne
work is back on-line."

"Excellent. What's their tacsit?"

"There are currently large numbers of Dahlist troop
still loose within the base. However, the Marines have se
cured several key positions within the structure, includin
the command-control center and primary fire contro
THRP digital units have infiltrated Objective Samar's elec
tronic networks and are in control of all systems. Captai
Corcoran reports that the situation is under control."

A typical Marine response. Garroway wasn't sure ye
what he thought of the idea of t-Human Restricted Purpos
agents. Were they human Marines? Or artificial electroni
aigents, *tools* to be used and discarded? There was no tim
now to debate the ethics of the technology with himsel
however. If the THRPs had helped Golf and Hotel Compa
nies of the 2/9 to nail down that fortress, that was all tha
counted at the moment.

"Good. Pass the word to Corcoran to get those loos
Dahlists rounded up fast. We don't want some fanatic doin
the same thing to Samar that they just did to the Stargate."

"Affirmative, General."

As he spoke, Garroway was studying the relentless ap
proach of the Dahlist ships. They had just overwhelmed tw
smaller Associative destroyers, the *Carlotti* and the *Lu*
bichev, pounding them from all sides with antimatter mis
sile fire and fusion beams. The Associative Fleet was sti
widely dispersed through the system, which gave the Dah
force a tremendous tactical advantage, the ability to clos

ith isolated Associative ships and use local superiority of
epower to hammer them one and two at a time.

The tight-knit squadron of Dahl Empire ships, protec-
vely grouped around the *Curtains of Light,* their flagship,
as making straight for the *Samuel Nicholas.* They carried
ough firepower among them to pose a serious threat to the
r larger Associative vessel. The *Nick* possessed weapons
her own, of course, but nothing like the firepower of even
e *Curtains of Light* by herself. She was a *transport,* for
od's sake, not a line-of-battle ship.

Listening in on the flow of commands within the *Nicho-
s* and among the other Associative vessels, Garroway
ew that Ranser and his people were well aware of the
reat. Admiral Dravid had just given orders to reverse the
ge ship's course, trying to take her out of harm's way, but
e transport maneuvered like a small planetoid—which in
ct she was. The *Samuel Nicholas* had started life as a ten-
lometer planetoid, after all. And Ranser had just ordered
l surviving Associative ships to fall back on the *Nick*'s
sition, to provide her with covering fire, and to concen-
ate the firepower of the Associative ships.

Curtains of Light opened fire on a crippled Associative
uiser, the *Hermosillo,* joined an instant later by the other
ahlist vessels surrounding her. The *Hermosillo,* savaged by
e explosion of the Stargate, was adrift, her maneuvering
avitics dead, her defensive shields down. She returned fire
ith a fraction of her weaponry . . . then flared sun-bright as
emy fusion beams carved through her unresisting hull.

The Associative cruiser vanished, replaced by white
ght.

AI projections showed that the Dahl fleet was going to be
unding the *Nicholas* within the next few minutes. She
ould give a good account of herself . . . but the sims the
mmand constellation AIs were running right now sug-
sted that either the *Nicholas* was doomed, or she would be
rced to translate out of the Large Magellanic Cloud and

back to safety—abandoning the remaining handful of Ass
ciative warships.

With the destruction of the Stargate, the local gravit
tional metric had changed. Phase-shift ships would be as c
off from this region as ships that depended on Stargates f
long-range jaunts. The Tavros-Endymion Cluster and th
new-born Dahlist Empire would truly be cut off and on the
own, safe from Associative interference for at least the ne
century or so.

The Dahlist strategy was looking less and less like a de
perate, last-ditch defense against overwhelming numbers, a
more like a meticulously crafted—and brilliant—battle pla

The Dahl ships were moving within a thousand kilomete
now of the former position of the Stargate, skirting the ragge
edges of the fast-blossoming plasma cloud. They were le
than twelve thousand kilometers now from the *Samuel Nic
olas*, and closing fast.

Garroway glanced at the icon representing Objective S
mar, now adrift within that cloud.

Then he took a harder look. "Lofty? Open a channel
Captain Corcoran."

"Captain Corcoran on-line, General."

"Captain? This is Garroway. I need your help, here. . . ."

Company H, 2/9
Command Deck
Objective Samar
0620 hours, GMT

"We need those main weapons on line *now*!" Nal all b
screamed the thought-command over the channel.

"Restricted firing codes are necessary to comply with o
der," a flat and utterly emotionless voice sounded in Nal
head. "Restricted firing codes appear unavailable on th
network."

"The firing codes are in there! Find them!"

"Restricted firing codes appear unavailable on this network."

The problem with thurps, Nal decided, was not the ethical aspect of human personalities shorn of emotion or curiosity. It was the sheer, stubborn single-mindedness of the things. Working with them was like working with a pre-AI computer, uninspired software that did absolutely nothing except what you *told* it to do.

But the powerful AIs running the *Samuel Nicholas* ship systems, as well as the AI in charge of Fleet Intelligence, were working together on the problem already, cranking through trillions of possible alphanumeric combinations in the course of seconds, searching for the right seven-space code that would unlock the combination. The right codes might surface at any moment . . . but it might take hours, yet, for even the superhuman machine intelligences to find them through what was essentially low-tech brute-force.

Nal had a new thought, however. "What search phrase are you using?" he demanded.

"We are searching for the term 'firing code,' or variations, as directed. There was no result."

"Try 'password.'"

"Affirmative. No result."

"Try 'weapons free.'"

"Affirmative. No result."

"Try 'freedom.' Try 'death to the Associative.' Try 'Imperial Victory' or 'Emperor Emelius Dahl' or 'victorious Empire' or variations and combinations of all of these."

"Affirmative. No result."

It was unlikely that the Dahl command had passwords for weapons release stored on any easily accessible computer network. Even if they had—and in Nal's experience, humans tended to be sloppy about such things—the chances that he would hit on the Dahl password for unlocking the weapons systems were small to nil, especially when the window of opportunity was only seconds long. But the thurps possessed nothing like human creativity, and would not find a password file at all if left to their own devices. At least there was chance, if he kept throwing suggestions at them.

"Do you have access to the local calendar?"

"Affirmative. No result."

"What is the date of Emelius Dahl's birth?"

"Thirty-five Ebon, Year of the Associative 744."

"Try that. All variations."

"Affirmative. No result."

"What would the year of his birth be in local terms?"

"Year minus forty-five."

"Try that. All variations."

"Affirmative. No result."

"What is the date in the local calendar of the creation the Dahl Empire?"

"One Dahl, Year Zero."

The man *was* an egomaniac. "Try that. All variations."

There was a longer than normal hesitation. "Access gaine Primary weapons coming on line."

"Captain Corcoran!" Nal shouted. "We have weapons!"

"Track, lock, and fire!" Corcoran replied. "*Do it!*"

"Firing. . . ."

Nal looked up at the overhead. Objective Samar possesse ten 4.35-meter fusion accelerators, designed to kill any wa ship coming through the Stargate. Each tube was essentially mag-accelerator which took several kilos of compressed lic uid hydrogen stored within tightly wound magnetic contain ment fields and hurled them at the target at a hair under th speed of light. The sharp acceleration collapsed the hydroge mass, inducing fusion a fraction of a second after emergin from the weapon's muzzle and directing the rapidly expan ing mass, at star-core temperatures, into the target.

The first volley tore outward through the expanding plasm cloud created by the destruction of the Stargate, creatin straight-line lightning bolts of searing radiation stark again the sky. Three fusion bolts struck the *Curtain of Light* broa side-on, slamming through her shields and vaporizing h hull in a radiant, destructive kiss.

There were plenty of Corps legends concerning Marines who'd dueled with enemy warships. Perhaps the most ancient went back two thousand years, to the battle for a tiny island—long since submerged by rising sea levels on Earth—called Wake. Late in the Year 166 of the Corps—early 1941, Old Style—four hundred and forty-nine men of the first Marine Defense Battalion, plus sixty-eight naval personnel and over twelve hundred civilian workers had come under attack by an invasion force launched by the Imperial Japanese Navy. Major James Devereaux, in command of the Marines under a Navy officer, had ordered his gunners to hold their fire until the Japanese vessels moved in close, then let loose with six five-inch naval cannon salvaged from a scrapped cruiser. The barrage had sent a shell into the ammunition locker of the destroyer *Hayate* and blown her out of the water, and scored eleven hits on the superstructure of the light cruiser *Yubari*. A second enemy destroyer had been sunk by Marine aircraft.

The *Hayate* had been the first Japanese warship sunk in World War II, and forced the enemy to withdraw—the first defeat of the war inflicted on the Japanese Empire.

Nal, as a boy hungry for anything he could find and download on the history of the ancient Marines, knew the story well. He tried not to think about the outcome of that particular engagement: the Japanese had returned, stormed the island, and taken it.

This time, however, history seemed unlikely to repeat itself. The *Curtain of Light* now resembled its own name, taking on the appearance of an unraveling knot of radiance. Other fusion bolts from the drifting fortress struck the heavy cruisers *Endymion* and *Starlight*, annihilating them in dazzling bursts of plasma flame.

And, suddenly, the survivors were fleeing, and the Battle of the Tavros-Endymion Gate was now *truly* over.

15

1002.222*

Recon Zephyr
The Great Annihilator
Galactic Core
0950 hours, GMT

It was a long, *long* drop.

The Marine OM-27 Eavesdropper *Captain Ana McMillan* fell endlessly through an eerie, black-violet light, buffeted by energies beyond human ken. On board, the consciousness of Lieutenant Amanda Karr looked out through the Eavesdropper's sensors, trying to make sense of that turmoil of non-existence.

Her inner time-keeper insisted that only seconds had passed since Recon Zephyr had whipped in through the ergosphere of the massive black hole known as the Great Annihilator. Her mind knew that a longer time had passed, that time for her was moving far more slowly than in the universe outside. How much more slowly was impossible to know. The answer depended on a number of variables, including the precise path the probe was taking as it passed through the severely warped spacetime of the Annihilator's throat.

Captain Valledy was praying.

She ignored him. "Luther! How far in are we?"

The AI hesitated before answering. *"That question cannot be answered directly, Lieutenant Karr. It's not a matter of distance or of time now. We may literally be in a different kind of space . . . the base state of reality."*

"The Quantum Sea?"

"Affirmative."

"Then what am I seeing?"

"Essentially you are seeing what your brain chooses to see."

It was a less than satisfactory answer.

"Any sign of a Xul base or a ship or something?"

"Possibly. But human consciousness may be necessary to manifest it."

Again, not helpful.

Karr pulled what data she had on the Quantum Sea down from her permanent memory storage. There wasn't a lot. It had been known since the advent of quantum physics two millennia before that at the base level of reality, particles and antiparticles continually popped in and out of existence. The virtual energy of this effect was converted to actual energy by quantum power taps; estimates of the amount of potential raw energy hidden within a volume of hard vacuum the size of a human fist suggested something vast enough to destroy the entire Galaxy and a significant amount of the space-time fabric beyond. Perhaps fortunately, human QPT technology so far could access only a minute fraction of that potential—enough to power starships or detonate suns, but not enough to do serious injury to the Galaxy as a whole.

Theoretically, if you could control the standing wave forms of subatomic particles appearing and vanishing within the reality substrate, you could control the form of reality itself. That trick, too, remained so far beyond the grasp of human technology.

There were hints, though, that consciousness itself was what called forth reality from the infinite chaos of the Quantum Sea. Weiji-do and certain other mental and martial arts disciplines might offer a means of rewriting reality on the fly, as it were . . . but actual experiments along those lines had so far proven fruitless.

She tried focusing on the possibility . . . no, on the certainty that the Xul presence here in the Annihilator was close by, just ahead, in fact, that it was close enough to be coming into view . . .

And there it was.

The thing's materialization was so abrupt and startling that Karr wondered for a moment if she'd simply missed seeing the thing at first in that diffuse, hazy, violet-blue glow.

Had its appearance been coincidence? Or had she just called the reality forth from a background chaos of infinite possibilities?

She suspected there could be no simple or direct answer to that question.

The object ahead was bigger than a typical asteroid . . . a dwarf planet, spherical in shape, heavily cratered, with a diameter of perhaps twelve hundred kilometers. Geometric patterns of golden light covered the surface, radiating out from central nodes, embracing the curve of the tiny world like megapoli connected by brightly lit straight highways. More lights gleamed in a ring plane encircling the world, and Karr could make out the thread-slender and luminous spokes connecting points on the ring with points on the world's equator.

There was intelligence here, and of a high order.

"Begin QCC transmission of all incoming data," she told Luther. "Including the local metric."

You weren't supposed to be able to transmit *anything* out of a black hole, but quantum-coupled communications networks were different. On a quantum level, there was no difference between *here* and *there*; a message generated at one point appeared on the appropriately coded receivers at another, literally without passing through the space in between.

The OM-27 continued to fall toward the alien structure.

Star Lord Rame's Office
Marine Transport Major Samuel Nicholas
Objective Samar
1340 hours, GMT

"Your efforts," Rame told the assembled Star Lord Conclave within his mind, "are not helping. Indeed, you may have so alienated Garroway and his people that they will no longer be willing to help us."

"Nonsense," Valoc said, drawing herself up taller, and letting her corona flare. "The Marines are here at our sufferance. They will do what we direct them to do."

"No, Lord Valoc, they will not. General Garroway will refuse any order that is clearly not in the best interests of his Marines."

"That is . . . ridiculous," Tavia Costa said. "The military *cannot* be a democracy. The soldier cannot decide whether or not he will obey orders that might lead to his death. Soldiers are created to face death at the orders of those above them."

"General Garroway feels he has a responsibility to the people under his command. A responsibility to see to their best interests."

"We can replace Garroway with another."

"You could. I have the feeling that any other Globe Marine would act in the same manner. Remember. These people have a tremendously strong bond with one another, a bond far greater than any they share with non-Marines. That, after all, was one reason this particular group of Marines volunteered to enter cybernetic hibernation in the first place. They had little in common with the human-civilian culture of eight and a half centuries ago. They have far less with us.

"And for that reason, I have the strong feeling that the Marines would not follow someone who was not of their number, an outsider. At the very least, a substitution of leaders would harm the unit's effectiveness."

"In any case," an Euler star lord put in, "it's not a matter of simply choosing whether or not to obey orders. These Marines did volunteer to enter cybernetic stasis in order to serve as a ready reserve . . . specifically against future incursions by the Enemy."

When an Euler used the word translated as "enemy," it *always* meant the Xul.

"This Warrington Initiative he mentioned," Valoc said. "We know. But the situation has changed. The Xul are no longer a threat. As an elite direct-action force, the Marines are a valuable asset, one to be used."

"We can no longer be certain that the Xul are not a threat," the liaison AI, Socrates, suggested. *"The QCC data we've just received from the Great Annihilator suggests otherwise."*

"Flawed data!" Radather, the t-Human representative snapped. "The data are clearly flawed!"

"Prove that," Rame told the electronic entity's virtual avatar. "How would you, an electronic life form, know if the very basis for your own existence had been tampered with by other agencies?"

"The same applies to Socrates!"

"Nevertheless, the Annihilator data suggests that our e-networks have to some unknown extent been contaminated by Xul emomemes. The strength of your emotional reaction just now demonstrates that there may be a problem."

"And what do you suggest?" a Veldik star lord asked. Its avatar was difficult to see, a confused and turbulent pillar of yellow smoke, within which could be glimpsed unsettling pieces of the being's organic form as it moved.

"That we permit the Marines to do what they're best at," Rame replied. "We have a target. We have at least the possibility that that target is a threat to the Associative, perhaps to all life throughout our galaxy. I propose that we order General Garroway to neutralize that threat."

The debate continued for another hour, but Rame was certain already that he'd won. The transmissions from Recon Zephyr had included recordings of signals emanating from the structure deep within the Great Annihilator that matched odd scraps and pieces of signals recorded elsewhere throughout the Galaxy . . . most especially in close proximity to black holes and to Star Gates with their paired micro-singularities. *Somehow,* the Xul were affecting the Associative Net.

And, somehow, they had to be stopped.

Garroway's Office
Marine Transport Major Samuel Nicholas
Objective Samar
1420 hours, GMT

"The Deep Alien Protocol is running, General."

Garroway nestled back a little deeper into his recliner and closed his eyes. "Thank you, Lofty. Put me in."

"Aye, aye, sir."

And a new world opened up around Garroway.

There were non-human alien species scattered across the Galaxy . . . but many, if not the majority, were at least approachable. Apprehensible. *Comprehensible* in human terms.

Garroway had met quite a few alien species, even before his long sleep into the future. They might have radically different body shapes and bizarre ways of thinking about themselves and their environment, but a surprisingly large number were carbon-based, with something like peptide chains and amino acids. They tended to utilize the more common elements, the earlier entries on the Periodic Table—carbon, hydrogen, oxygen, nitrogen, phosphorous, and others. They tended to use liquid water as a solvent, which meant they lived in a temperature range between zero degrees and one hundred degrees Celsius. They might see the universe in different ways, at different wavelengths or with different senses than those evolved by humans, but they tended to share certain constants—an awareness of their natural surroundings, basic needs such as raw materials for metabolic processes and instincts for survival, reproduction, and the protection of offspring. Most were searching for ways and means of understanding the cosmos, and most had evolved certain basic tools—math, science, and religion—to help them do so. First contact with the deep-sea Eulers had been made on the basis of an exchange of prime numbers, and a mutual understanding of higher mathematics.

But many others were so truly, so deeply alien that it was difficult at first even to understand them as sentient. In some cases, it was difficult to recognize them as *living*, to say nothing of being intelligent species with their own language, culture, worldview, and identity of self.

And even many of the comprehensible species out there lived in environments where direct face-to-whatever meetings were impossible or extremely difficult—the deep-benthic Eulers and Cthuli, for example, or the heat-loving Vorat.

The Deep Alien Protocol had been developed five centuries earlier as a means of addressing the issue. AIgents created virtual realities within which humans could meet with alien species; massively parallel artificial intelligences were able now to dissect alien computer technologies and protocols and create high-speed electronic bridges with their human analogues, and to do so quickly enough that those using the system were unaware of what was going on behind the scenes. It wasn't just language that was being translated, but nuances of environment, of culture, or biology, even of history.

It helped if the alien technology included something like computers and something like virtual simulations. Similarity of purpose in the technologies involved provided clues to the translation.

Garroway wasn't entirely certain of what he was getting into as the new world began unfolding around him. An hour ago, a channel had opened on the Fleet's QCC. AIs had linked through that channel and reported that the Tarantulae were there, that they wanted to talk. No one had yet figured out just how the aliens had acquired that channel, since QCC worked only between comm units that were tuned to one another on a quantum level.

But no matter how they'd managed the trick, they appeared to want to talk, and Garroway had volunteered to link in.

In part, he'd wanted to forestall Rame or the other star lords from getting in here. He knew Rame was now linked in with some sort of high-level electronic conference with the rest of the Associative Conclave, and that they were discussing what to do with Garroway and the First Marine Division.

Let them talk. The Marines were not going to go liberate Kaleed or any other Associative world. An entire galaxy was too large even for 1MarDiv, and he would *not* see his people squandered.

But if the mysterious Tarantulae wanted to talk, he was eager to open that channel. New information was always valuable . . . as was the potential of a new alliance. He was remembering the history of the first contact with the Eulers, and what that had meant in the Xul War.

The protocol snapped into place. His office was gone. He seemed now to be out of doors, standing on a beach. It was either early morning or late afternoon; two small suns hung above their sun-dance reflections in the water, one red, one a contrasting green. Overhead, a number of other stars were visible, even though the sky was bright blue with a hint of violet near the zenith. The ocean, for the most part, appeared a deep, red-violet; the ancient phrase of a poet came to mind: "*the wine-dark sea. . . .*"

At his feet, what appeared to be seaweed washed up on the black-sand beach was moving. Garroway couldn't tell if it was animal or plant . . . or, more likely, something else entirely.

He looked around, waiting for some manifestation, some presence of the aliens. The world, Garroway knew, was illusory, created inside his head as a virtual meeting place, and how closely it matched reality was anyone's guess. He wasn't at all certain of what to expect. The name humans had given to the species, the Tarantulae, called forth images of large, hairy spiders, and it was distinctly possible that the Protocol in effect would create images based on his expectations.

He hoped that wouldn't be the case. He didn't like spiders.

You are different from the others.

The words sounded in his mind, uninflected, in precise Anglic.

"What others would those be?"

You are different from the ones that called themselves Empire of Dahl.

"I hope so. I represent an association of many intelligent species. We seek peaceful contact and mutual understanding . . . not conquest."

"As do we." The words this time were audible, as though spoken just behind Garroway's head. He jumped and turned, but saw nothing but more beach, masses of purple vegetation that might have been the edge of a jungle and, in the far distance, white, softly sculpted towers that appeared to be buildings or other large structures rising from the forest.

Oddly, the structures weren't static, but appeared to be in constant motion, as if they were growing, unfolding, and changing geometries from moment to moment. The changes weren't fast, but they created the illusion that the structures were alive . . . or that he was viewing the nanoconstruction of a city through a camera that sped up the motion a thousand-fold.

The air around him took on a kind of graininess . . . and then clouds of gold-gleaming dust motes were wafting together in front of him, seeming to emerge from ground and sky and water and light and the very air itself. The motes coalesced into a pillar, then further refined themselves, taking on more detail, more solidity.

The being had the appearance of a young man—or possibly a young woman. It was hard to tell which, since the features were androgynous and its body was more or less hidden by a thin film of radiance, like the coronae affected by upper- or ruling-class humans. There was a hint of unreality about the being, as though it were somehow still insubstantial; the most powerfully real part of it were the eyes, which were deep, gray-green, and somehow ancient, revealing an apparent age wildly out of keeping with the figure's youthful appearance.

"Are you creating that image, Lofty?" Garroway asked. "Or is that what it really looks like?"

"They are generating the image," Lofty replied. *"It seems unlikely that this is their actual appearance, however."*

Garroway had to agree. The chances for an alien species to look exactly like a human—even one as ethereal-seeming as this one—were too remote to be even considered as a possibility.

So the Tarantulae had anticipated the Deep Alien Protocol, and possibly gone it one better. They were presenting themselves as something that looked human, no doubt to avoid possible racial bias against the appearance of the *truly* alien. That seemed reasonable. The Dahlists reportedly had attacked the Tarantulae, and they might want to smooth over any potential rough spots in their communications with the Associative.

He wondered, though, what the Tarantulae really looked like. In the back of his mind he was still thinking of giant spiders.

"You would not understand our true form," the being said. "In fact, the term itself is misleading. We *have* no form, as such."

"A digital intelligence?" For a moment, he wondered if he might be speaking with the Xul . . . or with an alien analogue of *Homo telae.*

"Suffice it to say," the glowing being replied, "that we represent a highly distributed intelligence."

The alien's choice of words suggested a computer network . . . or possibly a CAS, a Complex Adaptive System.

"Essentially, yes," the being said, and Garroway realized with a start that it was reading his mind. How? Human cerebral implants allowed a kind of electronic telepathy, but you couldn't just go snooping around in another person's thoughts. "Rather than organic cells, like you, we utilize a nanotechnic base."

"A true nanotechnic life form," Lofty whispered in Garroway's head. *"An intelligence distributed among hundreds of trillions of molecule-sized devices that can combine or recombine in nearly infinite configurations. They appear to occupy the entirety of both the organic and nonorganic infrastructures of their worlds, and may reside within stars and in open space as well, with a direct link to the Quantum Sea. They may be technically immortal."*

Immortal. . . .

How long had Humankind been chasing that particular dream? Human biological and cybernetic technologies had increased the lifespan of *Homo sapiens* to a thousand years, at least potentially, and it was unclear how long individuals of *Homo telae* or *Homo superioris* might live. There were practical considerations that seemed to place a limit on the survival of hardware in the case of electronic systems, and wetware for organics.

"So . . . how did the Dahlists get the jump on you, anyway?" Garroway asked. It was a serious question. A technology this advanced—one able to take on any form at will, with the ability to live forever, with the capacity to draw whatever it needed from the fabric of space itself—didn't just mean an ability to change shape. An entire civilization built on such technologies would have capabilities that would be nothing short of magic.

"We're not sure we know what you mean by 'get the jump on,'" the being said. "You appear to believe that they attacked us."

"Didn't they? That was the report we had."

"They occupied several worlds within our sphere, but, for the most part, we ignored them. They did not seem to be interested in communication."

Garroway's mental imagery of spiders had faded away. Instead, now, he was thinking of ants, of humans *as* ants in the presence of a human.

If the human's bare foot twitched as the ant ran across it, could the ant be said to be engaged in communication with the human? Could the ant understand whatever the human might have to say in reply?

And on a far deeper level, could the human honestly care what the ant had to say? It occurred to Garroway that the being he was facing in this virtual world might be to him roughly as a man was to an insect. The entity *appeared* to be speaking with him . . . but he had the feeling that only a tiny fraction of its mind was actually engaged in that task.

Beings as powerful as the Tarantulae might well not even notice the activities of mere humans.

"It's not that we can't notice," the Tarantulae told him. "We are quite aware now of you and your fleet . . . as we were aware of the Emperor Dahl and his activities. There is simply little point in such contact. The levels and scopes of our respective technologies are, as you have surmised, vastly different."

As if to illustrate the point, the distant forest, the eerily malleable buildings, the black sand and ocean all faded from view. Garroway seemed now to be standing in empty space. The soft glow of the Tarantula Nebula extended in all directions, aswarm with stars like myriad, radiant jewels.

Nebula and stars appeared as a resplendent backdrop for . . . structures, geometrical shapes—spheres and spheroids, pyramids and cubes and other shapes less easily defined—that seemed to come and go, popping in and out of existence with no pattern that Garroway could detect. Lines and beams of light appeared to connect many of the structures, shifting and changing as the shapes came and went. There was no way to judge scale. The smallest of those structures might be a hundred meters across and relatively close . . . or millions of kilometers distant and as massive as a planet.

Some of those shapes hurt his eyes when he tried to follow

their lines and angles and eldritch curves. He was not, he realized, experiencing a conventional three-dimensional geometry.

"We came out here to rescue you, you know," Garroway pointed out. "Apparently, though, you didn't need rescuing."

"The gesture is appreciated," the being said, with something that might have been a human shrug. "And . . . it is still possible that your species could help us."

"How?"

Ants didn't *help*. They were ignored . . . or they were exterminated.

"I'm not sure an explanation would help," the being told him. "There are concepts here literally beyond your ken. I regret the fact that this must seem condescending . . . but there's no easy way to express it."

The geometric shapes had faded away by now, but the beams of light remained, anchored, somehow, in empty space, as though defining a far larger structure that did not exist, exactly, in three-dimensional space-time, at least as Garroway understood it.

"Try me," Garroway said.

"To do so might cause you injury, General Garroway," the being told him. "There are limits to what your interfaces can handle in terms of data flow . . . and limits to what even your artificially enhanced organic components can assimilate. And, to be blunt, there is also a threat to us in a free exchange of information between our species and yours."

Garroway wondered if the graphic display he was seeing was, in fact, being created wholly for his consumption, an attempt to overawe him with seemingly godlike powers.

But . . . why? What would be the point?

"How in heaven's name could we possibly cause you harm?" Garroway asked.

"The problem is . . . complex. And farther ranging than your species can realize."

Garroway realized he was going to get nothing useful out of the being. Except for the constantly changing backdrop, the conversation appeared natural enough, even casual enough from his perspective, but he had the feeling that the composite being in front of him was way ahead of him in sheer mental scope and power.

Not even s-Humans, he thought, could come close to the literally godlike technological or mental capabilities of the Tarantulae.

"I see you perceive a part of the problem," the being said.

"I can accept the idea that you people are far in advance of us. That we might not have anything you want, in terms of trade or information exchange. I can also imagine that you might not want to interfere with the paths of more primitive species."

"Again, that is part of the problem. A *small* part. And, in fact, we do need to pass certain data to you. The problem is whether you will be able to comprehend fully what we are saying."

The background now was a brilliant white radiance. Garroway suspected that the vantage point was actually within the core of a star. Even against that brilliant light, he could make out some sort of structure, though whether it was material or somehow conjured out of pure energy he couldn't tell. One of those shafts of light appeared to originate here, though, as though it emerged from some other, very different space deep within the heart of a star.

Then that background was gone, and Garroway floated with the alien in intergalactic space. Galaxies gleamed everywhere—perfect spirals; vast, elliptical aggregates of age-reddened suns; the smears and pinpoints of irregular galaxies.

"We enjoy a . . . partnership," Garroway said, picking his words carefully, "with our AIs. Some of them are far faster and more intelligent than humans, and they have immediate access to incredible stores of information. Might you be able to work with them, rather than with organic humans?"

"The conversation you and I are having now would not be

possible without them," the being said. "Agreed. As we speak, I am also holding an in-depth dialogue with the AI you call Socrates, and with numerous others."

The star was gone, replaced by the whirlpool blue glow of an accretion disk whipping about the empty eye of a large black hole.

"Then tell *them* what you need us to know."

"You trust them?"

Garroway considered this. "I may trust some of the Associative's AIs more than I trust some humans," he said. "They're honest, and they don't appear to have their own personal agendas."

He realized now that the fast-shifting backdrops he was witnessing weren't an attempt to awe him, but somehow reflected the changing vantage points of the Tarantulae in front of him. A widely dispersed intelligence indeed; it appeared to embrace whole galaxies, infinite reaches of space, and even other types of space entirely.

He wondered what such a species could possibly want with Humankind.

"Your people appear to have trouble trusting others," the being said. "Especially now."

"Yes, well, we have a long history of that, as I'm sure you're well aware." The being must be drawing heavily on human records, histories, and data stores in general. *How* it was doing so Garroway couldn't even guess, but he was beginning to suspect that the Tarantulae weren't so much matter or energy as they were pure information.

"We are aware."

"Wait a sec. You said 'especially now.' What did you mean by that?" Realization sparked, then caught hold. "Are you talking about the Xul?"

"The entity you know as the Xul represent a special and distinct threat, not only to you, but to the universe as you know it, to all of what you think of as reality. Are you aware that they have begun rewriting your reality?"

"I've seen reports." He remembered his Temporal Liaison

Officer . . . what was her name? Schilling. She'd been talking about a theory, something about the Xul contaminating humans through black holes and star gates. And Star Lord Came had been convinced of the theory's reality as well. At the time, it all had seemed rather far-fetched. "Emomemes, you mean?"

"A name for an imperfectly understood concept," the being said. There was a long hesitation, as though the Tarantulae was thinking—or, possibly, consulting with others of its kind. "Very well," it said at last. "It's true that your AIs might be able to effect the necessary translation. Have them record this data. . . ."

Garroway could sense the data flow, now, first as a fast-moving stream, then increasing in volume and speed until it was a torrent, a thunderous onslaught of raw data cascading down through the virtual communications link.

And Garroway glimpsed the scope of that transmission, and a tiny fraction of its content, and he felt very, very small. . . .

16

Marine Ops Center
Marine Transport Major Samuel Nicholas
1625 hours, GMT

"Gentlemen, ladies, electronics," Garroway said to the grou
assembled in the Ops Center. "We have a new mission."

Physically present were the eleven other human member
of Garroway's command constellation, plus several of th
corporeal members of Admiral Ranser's staff. The rest wer
present electronically, along with numerous AIs and t
Humans, including Socrates, representing the absent sta
lord hierarchy.

"*Not* cleaning up that mess on the wheelworld we wer
hearing about, I trust," Ranser said.

"No," Garroway replied. "Thank the gods. We could spen
the rest of our extended lifetimes playing catch-up with tha
sort of thing. No, we have hard evidence now that the Xul ar
playing games with reality. And it's up to us to go in and ge
them."

"Reality," Colonel Janis Fremantle said. She was Garro
way's intelligence officer, his command constellation's N-2
"You mean, like . . . they're trying to edit us out of exis
tence?"

"We're not sure what their ultimate aim is," Garroway re

lied. "But we've been seeing the effects for some time, ow. Our contact with the Tarantulae has . . . clarified things omewhat."

"The Tarantulae," Major Tomas Allendes said with a shud-er Garroway felt through the mental connection. "Makes e think of giant spiders. . . ."

Garroway smiled. He wasn't alone in his leaps of irratio-ality, evidently. "Actually, they're not like that at all."

"What *are* they like?" a navy commander on Ranser's staff sked.

Garroway thought about that for a moment, then shrugged. *Different*," he said. "Very different."

He still felt shaken by the series of visions he'd seen in the ompany of the Tarantulae earlier. The ant had spoken with e human, and the ant had learned something.

"Your report indicated they can take any appearance," lajor Shan Davenport said. "But what is their *real* shape?"

"I honestly don't think they have one," Garroway replied. They're . . . everywhere within their environment. Think antheism, with the gods resident in all the plants, all the nimals, in the world itself, even out in empty space, with very piece of molecule-sized hardware constantly linked to very other piece through something like our QCC, but *tiny*, aybe at the scale of individual atoms. Shape, outward orm, doesn't matter. I think they represent the ultimate in 'AS sentience. They *may* represent our ultimate destination a technic development, what we're evolving toward in con-unction with our own AI systems. However . . . *they're* not hat we're interested in right now. It's the Xul. You've all een the download abstracts."

The division's AIs had been working for hours to make ense of the enormous volume of data relayed from the nano-echnic denizens of the Large Magellanic Cloud. They were till working, in fact, and would be doing so for the foresee-ble future. But a few points were clear, now, as was the eneral nature of the threat.

And the synchronous discoveries by a Marine scouting

team at the Great Annihilator had both confirmed the thre
and added corroborative detail.

Garroway thought-clicked an icon in his mind, and an in
age materialized around him, a virtual simulation based c
the QCC link from the *Captain Ana McMillan*. He seeme
to be within the eye of a storm, a vast and powerful storm
blue and violet light and mist, of half-glimpsed, half-sense
shapes and masses and unimaginable energies.

Ahead was a small world, rough-surfaced and heavily cr
tered, agleam with uncountable pinpoints of light that forme
geometric shapes and designs self-evidently picked out b
intelligence. More pinpoints of light circled the worldlet
equator several radii out, forming a magnificent expanse
golden rings.

"The Quantum Sea," Admiral Ranser said softly. "They'
colonizing the goddamned Quantum Sea."

"At least they have a beachhead down there," Garrowa
replied. "And they're using it to tweak reality."

"How would we know?" Fremantle asked. "I mean, if we'
inside the new reality, and that reality includes our memorie
how do we know our memories haven't been changed to r
flect the change in the outside universe?"

"Good question," Garroway said. "And there's not a goc
answer. However, the Xul aren't perfect. There've been son
problems with time."

During a recent Marine action at a world called Dac I
several members of the Anchor Marine force taking part
the engagement had noticed a sluggishness in their contr
of their combat pods, as though there'd been a slight tin
lag through their control network. Since they'd been usir
QCC links, there could be no lag; signal relay time was b
definition instantaneous.

The effect had been dismissed, an artifact of stress an
the intense excitement of combat. AI analyses of the afte
action reports, however, taken together with the data fro
the Tarantulae, suggested that time had been flowing at

ery slightly different rate at the floatreef city of Hassetas in
he upper atmosphere of Dac IV than at the Marine trans-
ort in synchronous orbit 180,000 kilometers overhead. The
ifference hadn't been much, but it had been measurable.
Marine pilots in synchorbit had noticed that their pods in-
de the planetary atmosphere were lagging a bit, as though
me was flowing ever so slightly more slowly down there.

"Most of the Xul effects," Garroway explained, "were
ithin our electronic systems. That, after all, is the Xul do-
ain. We can think of them as analogues of our own *Homo
lae*, digital life forms resident within e-networks. They
ave been infecting us, through our AIs, and through our
erebral implants, with their xenophobia. They're making
s afraid of anything different, of anything *alien*. . . ."

"And this slowed-down-time effect?" Ranser asked.

Garroway shrugged. "A mistake. The Xul are working
rough black holes from their base here in the Quantum
ea. From one point of view, they're down here in the Quan-
um Sea, where time as we understand it . . . well, it's hard to
y time has meaning here. From another point of view,
ey're actually part-way down the throat of the Great Anni-
lator, a black hole of about fifteen solar masses.

"Now, we all know that the deeper into a gravity well you
et, the slower time flows. Basic relativity. It's the same as
me dilation in a ship approaching the speed of light. We've
nown for two millennia that gravity also slows time, and
at there would be serious time-dilation effects close to a
lack hole's event horizon. The Xul evidently are somehow
ompensating for the effect when they reach out of the Quan-
um Sea to affect our electronics . . . but that compensation is
ot perfect. Hence . . . an unexpected time delay in a long-
ange cybernetic link."

"I don't understand how they're affecting our attitudes,
ough," Captain Ven Assira, one of Ranser's staff officers,
aid. "I could understand editing reality to, oh, I don't know,
low up our stars, maybe. Or rewrite history so that humans

didn't even exist. But you're saying they're affecting our *minds*? How?"

"The simple answer is emomemes," Garroway said. "The idea was first advanced by AIs studying low-frequency waves that appeared to be emerging from black holes and star gates some years ago. Star Lord Rame, the guy who brought the 1MarDiv out of cybe-hibe, believed that the Xul were corrupting all intelligence with their xenophobic paranoia. He couldn't convince his colleagues of the possibility, however."

"These emomemes would be something like a computer virus?" Colonel Ren Jordan said. He was Garroway's senior computer/AI expert. "But capable of crossing the machine-organic interface?"

"That was Rame's original concept," Garroway agreed. "According to the Tarantulae, though, the reality is a little more complicated, more subtle . . . and a *lot* more dangerous."

He began explaining his understanding of the Xul Reality Edit.

What humans think of as solid matter is in fact as insubstantial as a dream. As far back as the time of the Greeks, the philosopher Democritus had introduced the idea of indivisible particles called atoms, and 2500 years later, atoms were still thought of as hard little balls locked together to create the substance of a table, say, or of a person's finger. Later physicists had acknowledged that atoms were mostly empty space, a kind of fuzzy cloud of electrons circling a tiny, central nucleus made up of hard little balls called protons and neutrons.

But that picture wasn't complete, either. It turned out that electrons existed more as *probabilities* popping in and out of existence than they were actual, physical objects, and when the physicists began studying the atomic nucleus closely, it turned out that even protons and neutrons were less than completely substantial. Atoms, it seemed, weren't objects so much as they were tightly woven knots of information.

Quantum theory led eventually to the discovery that so

alled empty space wasn't empty at all. It was a seething,
urging, ocean of particles and antiparticles popping into
xistence out of nowhere and immediately canceling one
nother out—an effect called virtual energy or zero-point
nergy which ultimately led to the quantum power tap and
e essentially unlimited free energy that now powered hu-
an civilization.

The appearance of those virtual particles within the zero-
oint field wasn't entirely random, however. Some flickered
and out of existence steadily at the same infinitesimally
inute point, creating a kind of standing wave of energy.
hose standing waves, it eventually turned out, were the
uilding blocks of quantum particles—of electrons, pho-
ns, and the quarks that made up neutrons and protons and
e other insubstantial bits of nothingness that comprised an
creasingly bewildering zoo of subatomic particles.

The Quantum Sea was a real place, the base state for all
nergy and matter co-existent with normal space-time but
tated out of phase with the universe it shaped. Mathemati-
ians referred to it as Dimension^0. Human technology had
robed the Quantum Sea first with quantum power taps, and
ter developed phase-shift stations and ships that could ac-
ally translate out of normal space-time and into this alien
alm of energetic possibility. Black holes, apparently, con-
ected with this base state, and phase-shift vessels like the
icholas rotated through it when passing from one point in
ree-D space-time to another. The Xul, apparently, had man-
ged this trick as well, moving an entire dwarf planet into
e maw of the Great Annihilator, and parking it at the meta-
horical edge of the Quantum Sea.

The question was . . . could you change reality by chang-
g or interfering with those standing waves in the zero-
oint field?

In the early days of phase-shift technology, some doom-
rophets had declared that rotating ships through the Quan-
m Sea would disrupt the standing waves that represented
toms and photons in the so-called real world . . . and matter

there might be disrupted. People, cities, whole planets, even entire stars might be snuffed out as though they'd never existed in the first place—an unseen and unstoppable hand editing Reality.

At the same time, there were those who believed it was possible to edit the zero-point field through power and focus of mind alone, a kind of direct application of the Observer Effect that could call matter or energy out of nothing, at least on a small scale. The martial disciplines of weiji-do, tai-chi, and a few others made this claim, as did several modern religions based on various interpretations of quantum physics.

But planets hadn't vanished when the *Samuel Nichols* translated through the Quantum Sea on her way to the Greater Magellanic Cloud, because such passages were made with the vessel slightly out of phase with her surroundings. She was physically within Dimension^0, but not actually *touching* any of it. So worlds, people, sunbeams, and electrons all remained safe.

Rame, Socrates, and the other members of the Conclave who believed in the Xul Reality Edit, the XRE, feared the Xul had found a way to selectively change the zero-point field, targeting Earth, say, from the Dimension^0 underside of four-D space-time. Things were not as simple as that, however—fortunately for Earth and any other worlds the Xul might wish to target. Figuring out that *this* standing wave in the zero-point field corresponded to *that* electron in four-D space-time wasn't just difficult, it was impossible, even with the sheer, vast computational power at the Associative's command.

But for centuries, now, researchers had been aware of low-frequency gravity waves emerging from black holes and star gates across the Associative sphere. Thought of as transmissions of encoded information, they'd raised the specter of Rame's emomemes, an attempt by the Xul to somehow affect Associative electronic networks.

The information provided by the Tarantulae had hinted at

something much larger, much darker. The coded pulses emerging from singularities across the Galaxy were in tune with one another, their frequencies perfectly matching no matter what the actual mass of the black hole. Just as with stargates, matching frequencies emerging from two black holes implied a oneness of those singularities, a *literal* singularity that implied the ability to map the four-D space between.

The Xul were learning how to plot zero-point waveforms and space-time objects with precise one-to-one correlation by mapping the space-time metric from black holes and star gates. What Rame had called emomemes were Xul test runs, attempts to create simple and extremely slight nudges in human electronic networks . . . nudges that expressed aspects of the paranoid Xul worldview: *different*—meaning differences in ideas, differences in cultures, differences in biology or body form—was *bad*. Evidently, the Xul mapping project was precise enough to let them identify cerebral implants and the programs running within them from the other side.

As Garroway reviewed the data, including the latest information from the Tarantulae contact, Ranser suddenly interrupted. "This is just plain weird, General. How the hell do we know we can trust the Tarantulae in all of this?"

"Exactly my point, Admiral. We can't trust *anyone*. And you have just proven my point. . . ."

The Associative—indeed, all life throughout the Galaxy and even beyond—was in critical danger.

Squad Bay
Marine Transport Major Samuel Nicholas
1910 hours, GMT

Nal leaned back in the circular sofa they'd grown from the deck of the squad recreational area. Cori Ryack sat beside him, nestled inside the curve of his arm. Opposite were two

of the Anchor Marines who'd been at Samar—Lieutenant
Garwe and Lieutenant Wahrst.

Casual fraternization between officers and enlisted personnel wasn't exactly encouraged in the Corps . . . but it wasn't
forbidden either, quite. All four were off-duty and out of
uniform—Nal and Cori were in shorts and T-shirts, while
Wahrst and Garwe both were nude. They'd begun their conversation over dinner in the mess hall an hour before, it had
become a spirited debate, and the four of them had brought
back to the squad bay for further discussion. For his part, Nal
was glad of the opportunity to get to know Garwe and Wahrst
a little better. He still wasn't sure about these local Marines,
wasn't sure he could even think of them as Marines in the way
that he knew the word.

"What we're questioning, *sir*," Master Sergeant Nal said
carefully, "is this remote-operating Marine concept of yours.
You people can't be killed! It's different with us."

"But what's the point, Master Sergeant?" Lieutenant Garwe
replied. "What's the point of dying if you don't have to? The
whole idea of military technology, ever since some Cro-
Magnon first whacked a Neanderthal on the brow ridge with
a rock, has been to make it possible to kick the other guy's ass
without getting your own kicked in return. Am I right?"

"Sure. But there was always the possibility that that Neanderthal would whack you first. He's bigger than you, and
stronger—"

"Exactly. So you figure out how to hit him without being
hit yourself. It only makes sense! You invent a spear-thrower
or a bow and arrow, and get him from a concealed position."

"Better technology," Ryack said, "and better tactics. Agreed.
But . . . things go wrong in combat. You need to be prepared
for that."

Nal gave Ryack an approving squeeze around her shoulders. He'd been concerned about her ever since she'd fired
that mercy bolt into poor Chickie. This was the first time
since that firefight that he'd heard her say more than a handful of words, and she'd seemed withdrawn and introspective.

or a time, he'd wondered if he was going to need to take the matter up with the company's psych AI, but she'd seemed more her old self this evening at chow. Maybe she was pulling herself out of it.

Devrochik's horrible death had shaken a number of people in the 2/9, including Nal. He'd found himself resenting the Anchor Marines their detached attitude toward combat, and decided that the emotion was related to Devrochik's death.

"Sure, you need to be prepared for combat," Kadellan Wahrst said. "But if you have to go up against an enemy, maybe someone bigger, faster, meaner, and better armed than you, isn't it better if you can do so without risking yourself or your fellow Marines?"

"Well, in our day," Nal said, "it was the Marines who were bigger, faster, and meaner than anyone else on the damned galactic block. We weren't always better-armed than the other guy. Kind of a long tradition there, y'know? But we were fucking mean enough to make up for it."

Historically, the Marines had always carried out their missions with second-line military hardware, so much so that it was practically a point of pride with the Globies. These modern-day Marines, though, seemed to enjoy the best technologies available.

"All very admirable," Garwe said. "But again . . . why expose yourself to death or dismemberment if you can link in to an RS/A-91 Starwraith and fly the thing into combat from a few hundred thousand klicks away? Strikepods are cheap. Combat personnel are expensive."

"I'm not disagreeing with that, Lieutenant," Nal said. "But what if something goes wrong and you *have* to fight the bad guys in person?"

Garwe chuckled. "Doesn't happen. We're sitting back here in the transport, the Starwraiths are way the hell and gone out where the shooting is. What could go wrong?"

Nal shook his head. "I don't buy it, Lieutenant. Not for two point five nanoseconds. Things going wrong is part of the definition of combat!"

"Not if things are planned well."

"So . . . if that's the attitude of combat planners in th
forty-first century," Ryack said quietly, "why the *fuck* wer
we sent through that d-teleport into Samar?"

"A class-one cluster-fuck," Nal agreed. "Gravitationa
tides were screwing with the hyperdimensional gatewa
and the bad guys were prepared for us, just *waiting* for us t
come through! Why didn't we have those fancy Starwrait
pods of yours?"

"For the obvious reason that you and your people haven
been trained in their use," Wahrst said. "It takes a lot of sin
time to make wearing one of those things like being in you
own body."

"And a delightful body it is, too," Garwe said, reachin
down across Wahrst's shoulder to give her bare breast
friendly squeeze.

She slapped his hand away playfully. "Behave. *Later.*"

Nal was irritated at the Anchor Marines' attitude. Thi
was serious, damn it. And he could tell from the way Cori
muscles were bunching under her shoulders that she wa
seething.

"The Corps," Nal said, "is about esprit, dedication, dut
courage. You guys are turning it into some kind of sin
game."

Garwe laughed. "So tell me straight, Master Sergean
You've never flinched?"

"Never what, sir?"

"Flinched. Come up against something that was going t
scatter your various body parts all over this half of creatio
and flinched. Screwed the pooch. Been afraid."

"Of course I have. I've been fucking terrified. Fear is
part of it. You learn to override the fear, to do your duty, t
carry out your mission despite the fear."

"Wouldn't it give you an edge in combat if you faced th
something and knew, *knew* beyond a shadow of a doubt, tha
it couldn't touch you? Wouldn't that let you dive right in, carr

out the mission, and not worry about what might happen to those body parts?"

"Hell, sir, wouldn't it give you an edge if you knew that the thing you were facing could *kill* you? Give you that extra burst of adrenaline to make you move that much faster? Hit that much harder?"

Garwe waved his free hand dismissively. "Adrenaline is made to order by our combat pods and injected as it's needed. Catch up with the times, son."

"We have full pharmaceutical support as well, sir."

"I'm relieved to hear it. My point is, with a remote combat link, we can take risks in a firefight that pointers can't or won't take."

" 'Pointers?' "

"People on point . . . physically on the ground and in contact with the enemy."

"As opposed to REMFs?"

Garwe scowled. "*That* is going too far, Master Sergeant. There is still such a thing in the Corps as disrespect for a superior officer."

Nal sighed. "I meant no disrespect, Lieutenant. I'm just wondering if the kind of risk-taking you're talking about might not be counterproductive."

"In what way?"

"I don't know. Letting you get sloppy or careless. Maybe trying a head-on frontal attack against a prepared position when the better choice would be to go in stealthy and creep."

"So long as the mission is accomplished, what does it matter?"

"Maybe it doesn't, sir," Nal conceded. "But I'm going to need convincing."

Garwe shrugged. "Six out of sixteen men and women in my squadron were swatted out of the sky on that last op, Master Sergeant. If they'd been in those combat pods for real, they would be dead. *Dead*. Instead, they woke up back on board the *Nicholas*, shrugged it off, and prepared to go out again. You can't do that when you've been reduced to a thin, hot plasma by a passing fusion beam."

"So tell me, Lieutenant. What would you have done if the Dahlies had boarded us?"

"What do you mean?"

"The word came down from the top during the fight. There was a time, there, when there was a good chance that the bad guys were going to start 'porting into the *Sam Nick*. What would you have done if you'd been stretched out in your link couches, minds out there in your Starwraiths, when a company of armored Dahl troopers broke in and started smashing the place up?"

"If the tactical situation had warranted it, we could have been recalled. We'd have woken up."

"And been able to take those guys hand-to-hand. *Without combat armor?*"

"Well—"

"Even if you'd been awake and suited up in Hellfires, like us, would you have been able to take those people on in a knife fight?"

" 'Knife fight?' "

"It means up close and personal. A 'knife' is a—"

"I know what a knife is, Master Sergeant."

"Were you trained in how to use one?"

"Of course not. Ancient tech. . . ."

"Or a hand gun? Maybe a slug-thrower, like a 14mm P-2090."

"Those things have zero accuracy."

"They're last-ditch hold-out weapons, sir. Very true. But back in 1370, Corps Era, when my battalion was deployed to Nabutta—"

"Spare us the war stories, Master Sergeant," Wahrst said, rolling her eyes. "Maybe you used handguns nine hundred years ago, but we have *much* better weapons available nowadays!"

Nal felt a flash of hot anger, but suppressed it. "Very well. *Sir.*"

"Don't take offense," Garwe said, grinning. "Kaddy here has a thing about stereotypical no-shit-there-I-was stories. Military porn, she calls 'em."

"Perhaps," Nal said quietly, "we should just agree to disagree. I can't see that this is getting us anywhere useful."

"Maybe not. Don't get us wrong, Master Sergeant. We're not criticizing the way you learned to do things . . . or your bravery or your devotion to duty. What you people did storming Samar was nothing short of heroic. In *every* way the embodiment of the spirit of the Corps."

"Yeah, absolutely," Ryack said. Nal could feel the anger behind the soft words. "Too bad some of us had to go and fucking *die* when we didn't have to."

"Exactly," Garwe replied. "Hey . . . you guys know a good, quiet place for some sex play? You know, somewhere where we won't be interrupted for a couple of hours."

"I might . . ."

"I'm thinking the four of us could have a little orgy."

"We can't," Nal said. "We're pulling duty at twenty-hundred. But you could use the Battalion Commons, Deck 50, Section three-one. You know where it is?"

"I can pull it off the Net. Sure, I see it."

"Nice and private. Have fun."

"Thanks, Master Sergeant! We will."

The two stood and walked out of the squad bay. Ryack looked at Nal, puzzlement creasing her face. "I don't have the duty."

"Neither do I."

"Wait a sec." She paused, downloading information. "Oh." Her eyes widened. "*Oh!* . . ."

"Yup. Battalion Commons, Deck 50, Section three-one. Scheduled for weiji-do training practice at 2030. Those two are going to just be getting into it when five hundred Marines walk in on them. Of course, they're not with our battalion, so they don't get the word."

"You, Nal, are one sick bastard." She paused, then added, "I *like* that."

"Those two deserve a little excitement. C'mon."

"Where?"

"I thought you and I might make our own excitement. Unless you want to practice weiji-do."

"Wow. Tough choices."

"If you're feeling okay, I mean."

She smiled. "Let's do it, Marine. My place or yours?"

"Someplace more private than batt-commons."

"*That* I think we can arrange." He thought a moment. Recreational simtube compartments were scattered throughout the *Nick*'s living spaces. They were big enough for two—even for two who might be gymnastically inclined, and the simfeed could be set for anything, from starscape to a favorite deserted beach back home. He stood up and held out his hand. "I know just the place."

Battalion Commons
Deck 50, Section 3-1
Marine Transport Major Samuel Nicholas
2031 hours, GMT

Garwe and Kadellan were just enthusiastically getting into things, lost to everything except the touch and taste, the feel and smell and sight of each other. They'd grown a large, round bed in the center of the commons deck, darkened the rest of the compartment, and thrown a starscape across the large, vaulted dome of the overhead. It wasn't the crowded clutter of giant suns outside the *Nicholas*, but a scene drawn from the skies of Earth.

The Magellanic Clouds were there, two wispy-looking patches set apart from the pale and meandering curdle of the Milky Way, seen from 170,000 light years away instead of from the LMC's busy and nebulae-clotted heart. The sim feed included the sights and smells and sounds of a beach on the Amazon Sea, with low breakers rolling in from the distant Atlantic, and the gleam of a half-full moon behind the thin streak of Earthring arcing overhead.

"God, you're beautiful," Garwe told his partner, letting his hand stroke the curve of her belly. They were trying something adventurous, something from the ancient Kama Sutra called In Suspension. He had her head-down, her back against his legs, her ankles by his ears, her head on the bed while he stood above her, pressing down, entering her deeply. "You okay down there?"

"The blood's rushing to my head," she said, laughing, "but—"

. . . and then a door had opened and Marines began streaming into the Battalion Commons, laughing and joking and good-naturedly sparring with one another. An instant later, they saw Garwe and Wahrst tangled awkwardly together on the bed and the laughter swelled to a roar.

Nudity wasn't the issue, of course—many of the incoming Marines weren't wearing anything but their skins, either—but being caught *in flagrante delicto* when you were looking for some private time with your favorite fuck-buddy could still elicit good-natured hilarity. It took them a few moments to get untangled, which caused more laughing commentary and advice.

An officer, a captain, pushed through the crowd around the bed, looked them up and down as Garwe finally pulled free of Wahrst, and frowned. "You people aren't authorized to be in here," she said. "Let me patch into your IDs."

Garwe had opened his implant ID, and he felt her scanning the data.

"Anchor Marines?" she said after a moment.

"Yes, sir."

"Fleet Support?"

"Yes, sir."

He thought they were about to catch seven kinds of hell, but the woman then shrugged and waved them out. "This is *our* space tonight, Lieutenant," she said, grinning at the two of them. "You'll need to find someplace else for your short-arms inspection!"

"*Very* short arms," another Marine called out, and that kicked off the laughter again.

Wahrst sent a triggering thought to the compartment, and the bed began melting away into the deck. Garwe stepped off. "Yes, sir," he said. "Sorry. We didn't realize the compartment would be in use."

Garwe and Wahrst had almost reached the compartment's door when the captain stopped them. "Wait a sec," she called. "You two are Starwraith drivers?"

"Yes, sir," Garwe had said. He pulled himself to attention. "Anchor Marine Strike Squadron 340, 'the War Dogs.' *Sir!*"

Well . . . what the hell? Anchors didn't mean much to the Globies, he knew, but he was still proud of being a Marine, whatever the old-timers thought.

"Shit," the captain said, and she shook her head. "Now I *really* hate interrupting you two."

"Sir?" Wahrst said. "What do you mean?"

"You haven't heard?"

"Heard what?" Garwe asked. But the captain's expression was giving him a dark, cold, sinking feeling in his gut.

"You'd better check in with your CO," was all the woman said. "Some news has just come down from the top."

And *that* had been the goddamned truth. Garwe and Kadellan were off duty and had set their implants to pick up only on priority messages, so they'd missed it. The tactical situation was such that Ops Command was asking for live-loaded strikepods.

He scanned through the announcement again, not quite believing what he was seeing. Volunteers. They wanted volunteers. He didn't *have* to go in live.

"Are you okay, Lieutenant?" the captain asked.

"Yes, sir," he said.

"Quite a decision, I know. Get the fuck out of my space. Go find someplace where you can finish what you started."

They'd left, closing the door on the laughter at their backs.

"Quite a decision" wasn't the half of it. He wondered how long they would have to make up their minds.

Four and a half hours later, the general alarm sounded over the Net, and Garwe and Wahrst scrambled to grow fresh uniforms as the *Nicholas* went on translation alert.

17

1902.2229

Recon Zephyr
Objective Reality
The Quantum Sea
0830 hours, GMT

Time flows at different rates in different circumstances. It crawls for objects approaching the speed of light, for objects within high-gravity fields, and in those strange-physics regions approaching the event horizon of a black hole. And in some out-of-the-way corners of the metaverse, the currents of time flow strangely indeed.

Within the pocket of the Quantum Sea occupied by the Xul base, time flowed far more slowly than in the outside universe of four dimensions. Days had passed in the Large Magellanic Cloud, while scant seconds passed for Valledy, Karr, and the AI Luther. The OM-27 Eavesdropper was now scant meters from the outer edge of the light ring, and drifting steadily closer. The planetary rings were a knife-thin slash of golden light against the violet-shot darkness.

"You're sure they haven't seen us?" Valledy said, his mental voice a whisper in the darkness.

"No sign that they have," Amanda Karr replied. "I can hear them singing, though."

The Xul Chorus. When humans had first encountered a

living Xul artifact locked beneath the ice of the Europan world ocean, they'd heard what seemed to be voices singing in massed unison, echoing antiphonies calling to one another in never-ending litany and response. The Singer, as it turned out, was insane, driven mad by its half-million-year imprisonment, but it had given the first xenosophontologists an unparalleled look into the nature of the Xul group mind. Millions of uploaded individuals, it seemed, sang back and forth to one another until consensus was reached and myriad choral voices merged into one.

And humans had used this knowledge in the centuries since. AI and human probes had linked with various Xul choruses, slipping in unseen and unfelt by taking on a kind of aural camouflage, blending with the smaller lines of harmony and merging gently with the larger chorus.

As Luther was attempting now.

"Link with me," Luther's voice said, an urgent whisper. *"Follow . . ."*

And Karr felt herself sliding free of the Eavesdropper's close embrace, entering a rolling surge of sound, of voices, *alien* voices, merging and swelling and echoing about her.

The points of light making up the ring, she now saw, were Xul ships, millions, no *billions* of them, and more were arriving with each passing moment. The Eavesdropper *Captain Ana McMillan* appeared to be one such vessel.

And her crew now were part of the rising Xul Chorus.

Marine Ops Center
Marine Transport Major Samuel Nicholas
0845 hours, GMT

"Stand ready," Admiral Ranser said. "Translation in thirty seconds."

"All sections, all departments, all companies report ready in all respects for translation," Lofty Henderson's calm voice added.

General Garroway took a deep breath, willing the fear to sink from throat and gut, willing it to merge with will and become subordinate to mind. The waiting just before an assault was *always* the hardest part.

"Status on the scouting group," Garroway demanded.

"Linked in, sir," Colonel Fremantle told him. "We've slipped five iterations of the OM-27's crew into the Xul matrix. All have opened solid QCC channels with their primaries here. We have a good picture of what's going on down there, and no indication that the enemy knows what's happening. And we have good data on the target metric."

Yet, Garroway added to himself. "Very well," he said. "Stay on it and yell if anything changes. *Anything.*"

"Aye, aye, sir."

Garroway tried to imagine what it would be like to be a digital upload. Those Marines within the Xul network would know that they were copies, but would *feel* as though they were the original Marine officers—Captain Valledy and Lieutenant Karr—with the memories and hopes and feelings of the originals. Worse, each would be unaware of the other copies in the matrix. When the *Ana McMillan* fired her cloud of AI-directed penetrators into the Great Annihilator, each pencil-sized sliver had carried electronic copies of the original Marine scouts, together with a copy of the Luther AI. There'd been nearly eight hundred of them altogether. Most had been picked up one way or another in their approach through the Quantum Sea or in their docking with the objective and destroyed; exactly five had made it through and connected with the Xul Mind, pretending to be part of the alien chorus. For security reasons, none knew of the existence of or the success of the other four.

But five streams of data were coming back to the N-2 section on board the *Nicholas*. Their presence within the enemy Net was a combat asset of vital importance.

"Ten seconds to translation. All elements remain go."

And then the last handful of seconds was trickling away. Garroway felt an inner wrench and drop, as though the

Nicholas' artificial gravity had momentarily been interrupted. Then the gravity resumed its accustomed pull, leaving behind a faint, swimming nausea.

And the Xul base was just ahead.

There were no surprises, thanks to the data sent back from the Zephyr recon teams. The world was 1200 kilometers across to the *Nicholas'* ten, a vast and cratered sphere dwarfing the slowly approaching phase-shift transport, its surface crisscrossed by starlike points of light, and with its far-flung rings casting a golden glow over the world that contrasted sharply with the violet hues of the surrounding Quantum Sea.

Things began happening now quickly, too quickly for human minds to follow. Fusion beams snapped out, striking the dwarf planet's surface with dazzling bursts of light and out-flung sprays of molten rock. Vast bays already open in the *Nicholas'* surface began spewing clouds of Marine fighters, of combat pods, and of remote drones.

And the Battle of the Quantum Sea began.

Debarkation Bay 5
Marine Transport Major Samuel Nicholas
0846 hours, GMT

Clad in Hellfire combat boarding armor, Nal waited as the elliptical gateway at the end of the ramp shimmered with pulsing energies, steadied, then stabilized, revealing beyond a cavern deep, black, and rock-walled, one of the numerous empty voids within the Xul worldlet designated Objective Reality.

The mission objective's name was better, he supposed, than the Samar of the last op, but the pun seemed out of place, somehow. The Marines knew that the Xul threat involved the possibility that they would rewrite reality somehow, but Nal doubted that most knew just exactly what was at risk.

If the Xul could rewrite the universe, none of the Marines

on board the *Nicholas* would ever know what hit them. They would simply be . . . gone, and nothing would stand between the Xul and the rest of an unprepared and unknowing Humankind.

"Ready to go, Marines!" Captain Corcoran said in his mind. "In three . . . two . . . one . . ."

The gate was open and Nal moved forward, along with the rest of the HQ section, just behind Alfa Company. He felt the jarring vibration of hundreds of boots in the metal decking of the ramp, and then he was through the gateway and dropping half a meter to the floor of the night-shrouded cavern.

This time there was no crowding or confusion, no stumbling, no Marines pitching precipitously from the ramp and mangling themselves with an incomplete transition.

But on the far side, the cavern walls were beginning to come alive, writhing with metallic menace as the Xul combat machines awoke.

Blue Seven
Objective Reality
0846 hours, GMT

Lieutenant Garwe felt the shudder of acceleration as his RS/A-91 Starwraith streaked from the belly of the *Samuel Nicholas*, hurtling outward on the rail of a magnetic accelerator. For a moment, he felt suspended between the *Nicholas* and the vast swelling of the Xul world ahead, both ship and world seeming to fill the violet-limned abyss of the Quantum Sea.

God! he thought, furiously angry. *What the fuck am I doing?*

Light blossomed just ahead as his AI momentarily took over the controls, swerving with the gravitics to avoid the deadly brush of an enemy fusion beam.

A guy could get fucking killed out here! . . .

After all the waiting, after all the talk, everything had come down to this, and so quickly he still was having trouble putting it all together.

Okay, so they'd been asking for volunteers, Anchor Marines willing to actually ride their strikepods in toward the Xul target, rather than pilot them remotely from a safe distance. Garwe and Wahrst both had wondered if this was some sort of in-your-face bit of one-upmanship by the 1MarDiv command constellation. *You people want to call yourselves Marines*, he could imagine his many-times-great grandfather saying, *then act like it*!

Except . . . no. He knew Garroway pretty well now, he thought. He'd taken the man's measure, watched him take care of him and his buddies back at Tranquility Base on Luna. The old man had chewed them out, sure . . . but he'd taken care of them, gotten them back to their ship, and kept them out of the hands of the local monitors.

And later, when Garwe had been pulling that stint of extra duty in the com stacks, Garroway had asked to see one particular bit of incoming QCC traffic, almost as if he'd been asking a favor. No, G-g-g-g-great grand uncle Garroway was a gentleman, and he had the good of the people under his command at heart. This wasn't hazing and it wasn't punishment.

It just *was*.

Behind him, the *Samuel Nicholas* was fast dwindling to a lopsided disk as Garwe and fifteen other War Dogs hurtled toward Objective Reality. Fusion bursts and antimatter warheads, positron beams, gravitics disruptors, and lasers at x-ray and gamma frequencies crisscrossed the gulf of space between worldlet and asteroid-sized starship, eliciting dazzling flashes and twinkles of light, expanding clouds of dust and white-hot plasma on the surfaces of both. Chunks of molten rock and hull metal boiled off into hard vacuum. The *Nicholas* wouldn't be able to take that kind of point-blank bombardment for long.

Which was why, several long seconds later, the *Samuel*

Nicholas vanished, rotating back up into normal four-D space.

And the cloud of Marine fighters, strikepods, and twelve heavy naval vessels were left alone to confront the Xul world.

"Bastards!" Dravis Mortin said over the squadron channel.

"Belay that," Captain Xander's voice snapped. "Pay attention to your approach!"

If the *Samuel Nicholas* was destroyed or crippled, none of the Marines or naval personnel of 1MarDiv would be going home.

So the Marines now were on their own.

Marine Ops Center
Marine Transport Major Samuel Nicholas
0846 hours, GMT

The entity that included Garrick Rame stood in the Ops Center, watching the inert bodies of the Marine division's command constellation lying on the circle of reclining seats. Through the broad-band QCC links within the chamber, various members of the Conclave watched with him, new visitors flitting in as old ones grew bored and left. There wasn't, Rame had to admit, much to see—twelve men and women, all, apparently, asleep. Overhead, across the domed ceiling, the pale blue and white glows of the Tarantula Nebula, thick with strewn and clustered stars, had just winked back into existence, a relief after the actinic blue and violet haze of the Quantum Sea.

"But what are they *doing*?" Tavia Costa asked. "They're just lying there!"

"Tap into the data flow," an Euler conclavist suggested. "They follow the course of the struggle within the Xul artifact."

Rame could sense the data streams, thousands of them weaving their way down through the consciousness of the AIs directing the phase-shift vessel's mind. He could sense Marine A/S-4000 strike fighters boosting hard toward the Xul world's surface, and clouds of individual strikepods hurtling through emptiness. The battlecruisers *Poseidon* and *Tra'vaal* were there, pounding away at Xul defensive batteries with heavy beam weapons, as the heavy *c*-boomer artillery ships *Doomsday*, *Armageddon*, *Ragnorok* slammed the alien world with ultra-high-velocity kinetic rounds.

"Three of these people are linked with Marine strikepods," Socrates pointed out. *"Including General Garroway."*

"Why?" Costa asked. "And how? I was given to understand that QCC linkage with that technology was not possible."

"It's possible," Rame said, "but difficult, unstable, and dangerous. The rate of time flow within the Quantum Sea is different from the time flow out here."

"Why does the commanding general of the Marine division risk himself?" a Cynthiad demanded. Rame could feel the unpleasantly greasy squirm of the paraholothurid within the back of his mind. Something of the entity's stink seemed to cling even to its link-sim virtual presence.

"Perhaps because this is his ideal of leadership," Rame suggested.

"He risks his immortality," the Cynthiad replied. "He risks his *soul*."

Rame didn't answer. Cynthiads were tough enough to understand even without bringing their religion into things.

He realized he deeply disliked and distrusted the ugly little creatures . . . and wondered if Xul emomemes were affecting the Rame-composite mind.

"He merely demonstrates those warrior virtues that this Conclave recognized when they authorized his revival," Socrates pointed out. *"Loyalty . . . and a superhuman devotion to duty."*

"Are you mocking me, aigent?" Valoc demanded. "You steal my words."

"I only point out what you yourself said of the Marines," Socrates said.

More hostility, Rame thought. *More emotional abrasiveness. It* could *be a Xul weapon. If it's not, they're missing a bet.*

The assembled Associative Conclave continued to bicker as the initial assault began.

Garroway, Gold One
Above Objective Reality
0846 hours, GMT

Garroway rode the RS/A-91 Starwraith through emptiness, seeking the best approach to the alien world. There was an excellent chance, he knew, that he would be killed or—infinitely worse—left hopelessly insane within the next handful of seconds.

Millennia ago, teleoperational systems had become possible, and Humankind's notions of *here* and *there* had forever been changed. Primitive motion pictures had been the start of it; viewers could see images projected on a screen that, temporarily, at least, could give them the illusion of being someplace else, of flying, of performing heroic deeds, of *being* someone else.

And as the centuries passed and technologies advanced, the illusion of being there had improved. In the early Third Millennium, a commercial venture had landed a small wheeled rover on the surface of Earth's moon. People on Earth could pay for the privilege of piloting the rover across the lunar surface from 400,000 kilometers away, this in the decades before most humans had regular and easy access to the moon, or even to Earth orbit.

The time delay for the images to travel from Luna to Earth, plus the time it took for control signals to go from Earth to the rover—about two and a half seconds, altogether—had been annoying, certainly, but few people had minded. The solar-powered rover traveled slowly, there were few obstacles, and the sheer thrill of being the very first person in modern history to see what was behind *that* rock or over *that* rille had more than made up for the frustrations induced by the speed of light.

Humans had learned then that it didn't matter if optical images traveled a few centimeters from their retinas to the backs of their skulls, or if they had come from incomparably farther away. The technology allowed Earth-bound humans to *be* there.

And that had been with simple optical hook-ups, with images projected on screens or through heavy, three-D visors worn over the face. Before long, computer interface technology and nanotechnics had allowed images to be projected directly into a person's mind, for virtual-reality simulations to unfold for all of the senses, not just vision. Within a century or so of those first, crude sightseeing Lunar rovers, people had been remotely visiting the sulfurous, crushing pressure and searing heat of the Venusian surface; moving across the icy wastes of Europa and Pluto; or virtually inhabiting robotic bodies that allowed them to interact with people on the opposite side of the Earth . . . or on the surfaces of the other worlds of the Solar System.

The military uses of the technology were obvious. Remotely operated drones had beamed back reconnaissance images of the battlefield since the late twentieth century. Later versions had gone on their unmanned missions armed.

Garroway had no particular problem with the Anchor Marines who'd remotely flown their Starwraith strikepods from the safety of an orbiting transport. It took skill, training, and, yes, a measure of bravery to operate the things effectively in combat, if only because it was so damned hard to override the reactions of the human autonomic nervous system.

But a Marine's duty sometimes required him or her to leave the relative safety of the transport and deliberately go into harm's way, as ancient naval tradition stated it.

He could feel the problems of mismatched time rates. Time within the Quantum Sea—at least in this niche of Dimension^0—was sluggish in the extreme compared with the universe outside. He wasn't certain whether the effect was due to the relativity effects of the supermassive black hole "above" this region, or something inherent in the base state of reality itself. His mind still worked with lightning speed; the mechanical and electronic components of his strikepod, however, along with the mind of the aigent running it, oozed as if in special-effects slow motion.

The AI, fortunately, could operate at superhuman speed, and could speed its thoughts to the point where it could still communicate effectively with him over the QCC command channel.

Theoretically, signals from the Starwraith did not pass through intervening space back to the *Nicholas*, but appeared simultaneously at both. The accumulating effects of nearby gravitational distortion and temporal displacement, however, made the link less than certain. It could snap at any moment. When it did, Garroway should wake up whole and sound back on board the *Nicholas* in normal four-D space. *Should*. There were no guarantees, and operating a teleoperational link under these conditions had never before been attempted.

But it was vital, Garroway thought, that he be here, at least in virtual presence.

He was passing through the Xul world's ring system now, a gold-glowing plane of objects ranging from oddly shaped items the size of a man's fist to starships kilometers across. Each appeared linked into a far vaster network of electronic intelligence and data. He could sense the Xul Chorus, hear the Xul World thinking.

He could hear its thoughts and layered awareness turning toward him.

· · ·

His Hellfire armor took the brunt of a Xul particle beam, shedding torrents of energy as crackling bolts of lightning grounding to the alien structure's deck. Nal staggered under the impact, but kept his footing and fired back with the X-ray laser mounted in the right forearm of his combat boarding suit, carving through one of the nightmare horrors now detaching itself from a cavern wall.

Xul combat forms looked a lot like Starwraith armor—vaguely egg-shaped, glossy black, and bearing multiple lenses and weapons ports at random points over their surfaces. Tentacles grew at will and at need, again from seemingly random points. The Xul possessed nanotechnology or something very like it, and built systems that could regrow themselves to repair damage or to fit a specific need.

The chamber into which the Marine assault team was d-teleporting appeared rough-hewn, like a cavern with black basaltic walls. Xul combat machines were emerging from those walls, however, though whether they'd been hanging there all along, were somehow traveling through the rock from someplace else, or were being grown from the rock as Nal watched was impossible to say. There was so much about Xul technology and capability that was still unknown.

At the moment, about two hundred Marines had made it into the chamber, dropping down through the open teleport gateway from the *Nicholas* in the moment or two before the transport had shut down the teleport gateway and rotated out of the Quantum Sea. They were alone, now, most of Alpha and Hotel companies plus the HQ Section, battling for their lives with alien monsters emerging from the dark.

"They're coming from the walls!" Nal shouted over the command channel. "Get some smart grenades on them! *Now!*"

His head felt fuzzy, his thoughts scattered. He wondered if the shock of jumping into a time-dilated relativistic field had scrambled them somehow.

A swarm of ten-centimeter projectiles flashed through the darkness, their micro-AI circuitries searching out patterns of shape, movement, and energy matching known Xul combatants. The first one slapped into the side of a Xul combat machine and flashed white-hot . . . then hotter . . . then still hotter, as the stubborn metal and ceramic composite of the machine's side softened, then flowed, and finally exploded in a burst of plasma. Other smart grenades found targets as well, more and more of them, until mutilated and half-molten Xul combat machines were burning and falling from the air everywhere.

Nal took three steps forward, firing into the enemy. A half-melted Xul body lashed at his legs with fast-growing tentacles, and a gamma-wavelength laser seared across the heavy armor over his chest. He lowered his hand and returned the fire, sending his own laser pulse into the exposed wiring and circuitry of the writhing enemy machine. Even damaged and in fragments, the Xul combatants could be deadly.

Sergeant Anthony Ferris staggered as five tightly focused beams of energy struck him in his helmet. Ferris shrieked, arms pinwheeling as he toppled backward, his helmet exploding in a nightmare spray of molten metal and burning organics and ending the screams.

Nal's AI had already identified the five shooters, and he targeted the nearest one, burning the Xul horror in a rapid-fire volley of x-ray bolts. The Xul squirmed, twisted, then exploded in molten chunks and smoking fragments, and Nal swung his weapon to take the second target in line, joining his fire with Boyd's and Zollinger's.

Close by, PFC Ander Brisard struggled within the whip-lashing grasp of a large Xul machine that had reached out of a cavern wall to grapple with him. Nal turned his laser on this new threat, trying to fire past Brisard's shoulder, but Brisard had already brought the flamer mounted in his armor's left wrist to bear, burning through the tough Xul composite until he could reach in, grab a fistful of optical network cable, and pull.

The Xul shuddered and lurched backward, and a large mass of the thing's internal wiring ripped free. The machine twisted away, tentacles snapping and twisting wildly as it fell to the deck, its gravitics killed. Nal put two more bolts into the gaping wound, watching the machine's interior glow suddenly white-hot under the assault.

"What the fuck are they doing?" Captain Corcoran yelled, pointing.

Nal turned. Against the far wall, dozens of elongated Xul machines were floating together, appeared to be merging, their surfaces softening and flowing and running together as they physically joined into a single unit twenty meters long and a third that in breadth.

"Get the slammers up here and bring them to bear!" Nal shouted. Marines lugging the massive rotary antimatter cannons pushed through into the open, targeting the massive enemy construct while it was still forming.

High-velocity antimatter rounds sliced through Xul metal laminates, flaring blue-white as they struck, gouging vast craters out of the enemy machine. Other Marines joined in with x-ray lasers, with pulse rifles, with smart grenades and particle beam weapons, trapping the alien structure in a spider web of living, shifting, dazzling white energy.

As it died, the Xul machine fired once, loosing a bolt of plasma energy that vaporized PFC Reyman Colby. The Xul turned, the beam playing across the cavern wall and catching several of its own in the flame. Nal fired his laser at the machine as it crumpled under the savage onslaught of Marine fire, huge fragments falling from it in half-molten chunks as it sagged to the deck, then collapsed.

But the Marine companies were taking heavy casualties. Sergeant Patricia Dayton, with the HQ element, caught a beam that burned away the right side of her armor and body in an instant, dropping her to the deck and leaving what was left of her smoking. PFC Tollindy stooped over her, trying to engage her savaged armor's automatic mindsave, and four energy beams caught him from behind, holing his suit knocking him down in a thrashing tangle of limbs.

Thirty seconds had passed since the *Nicholas* had dropped them here and vanished.

Nal doubted that they would survive for another thirty seconds.

18

Blue Seven
Approaching Objective Reality
0847 hours, GMT

Lieutenant Garwe applied full lateral thrust to his Starwraith as he pulled the craft into a tight, hard trajectory flashing scant meters above the surface of the Xul worldlet. At this altitude, the big enemy beam weapons couldn't track him, couldn't depress to hit him, and his only real concern was Xul point defense weapons.

Those were bad enough, though, as the sky above and around him filled with flickering, darting points of light, pulsed weapons, and near-*c* kinetic kill warheads trying to knock him and the other War Dogs out of existence.

He was looking for a way inside.

The surface below him blurred, a gray-white softness that reminded him of sand on an ocean beach.

An ocean . . .

A beach . . .

Low ocean waves broke to either side of the longboat. He could smell the salt in the air . . . feel the jolt and the rock of the boat as the wave swelled past beneath its keel. He was in a small, white-painted boat with a number of other men, all of them wearing brimmed, cocked hats, clutching their muskets close. Each man wore a green jacket with white facings—lapels, cuffs, and facings—with white waistcoats and breeches and black gaiters worn for the wade ashore. Each had an uncomfortably high, stiff, leather collar intended to protect the throat from sword cuts. *Leathernecks*, some of the men were calling themselves, because of those damned collars.

Private of Marines John Porter was deathly seasick, and each jounce and roll of the small boat threatened to set him vomiting again. Somehow, he managed to hold his rebellious stomach in place. The others in the boat wouldn't appreciate another round of heaves. The beach, thank God, was not far now. Palm trees waved in a fitful offshore breeze; the sky was a deep and impossible blue punctuated by small, fluffy clouds. It was hot, even though it was only early March.

Behind him were the ships of the small Continental Navy squadron—*Alfred, Hornet, Wasp, Providence, Cabot,* and several others . . . including two loyalist sloops captured the day before when they'd arrived off Nassau. A number of other small boats rode the waves in toward the beach around him. The landing force, he'd been told, consisted of over two hundred and fifty Continental Marines and sailors.

His stomach gave another twist. God, were they *ever* going to make it ashore?

Porter was not new to the sea. His father was a merchant who operated a small coastal vessel, the *Mary*, out of Wilmington, Delaware, and John had worked on board her ferrying dry goods between Wilmington and Dover. Three months before, John Porter had seen a broadside proclaiming the Continental Marine Act of 1775, which called for the raising of two battalions of Marines, and for which "particular care be taken that no persons be appointed to offices, or enlisted into said battalions, but such as are good seamen, or so acquainted with maritime affairs as to be able to serve for and during the present war with Great Britain and the Colonies. . . ."

So he'd signed up, receiving the princely sum of seventeen dollars as an enlistment bonus. His two older brothers were already with the army, serving with General Washington up in the siege of Boston.

Unfortunately, his stomach didn't seem to be as acquainted with maritime affairs as his work on board the *Mary* had suggested.

Rumor had it that the two battalions were being raised for a planned invasion of Nova Scotia, but the arrival of British regulars and three thousand Hessian mercenaries at the British naval base at Halifax had put paid to *that* idea pretty damned quick. Instead, the operation had been redirected to the Bahamas. Commodore Esek Hopkins intended to seize large stores of weapons and powder reportedly stored at Nassau, on the island of New Providence.

Protecting the town were two British forts, Fort Montagu and Fort Nassau. Those needed to be taken if the prize was to be won. The tiny armada of ship's boats was coming to shore about two miles east down the beach from Fort Montagu.

The longboat's keel scraped on coral sand. *Thank God!* Another incoming wave picked the craft up and carried it a few feet closer, and then Porter and the others were vaulting over the sides, holding their muskets and powder horns high to keep them dry as they started splashing toward the beach. Captain Nicholas bellowed orders, and the men began falling into marching column. In the distance, a signal gun boomed from the fort.

Some small and deep-seated portion of John Porter's mind marveled at the fact that this was the very first Marine amphibious assault in history. . . .

HQ Section, Second Battalion, Ninth Marines
Within Objective Reality
0847 hours, GMT

Nal rose from the partial cover afforded by a smashed Xul combat machine, laying down a heavy fusillade of fire with his main weapon. The Xul were forming up along the far wall of the cavern, possibly massing for an attack.

The best way to foil an enemy attack, Nal knew, was to hit them first, and harder. "Let's go, Marines!" he called, and he leaped over the wrecked machine, charging the enemy. . . .

Musket fire banged and cracked, and Sergeant of Marines William Derek waved his men on. *"Let's go, Marines!"*

This was it, the climax of a brutal, 500-mile march across the desolation of North Africa, a march marked by sandstorms, desperate food and water shortages, and the repeated near-mutinies of the filthy Greek and Arab mercenaries who made up the main body of the expeditionary force.

General Eaton—the dandy was calling himself *general* now—had picked up a musket and was leading the rush. Derek and the rest of the blue-and-red-jacketed Marines followed, screaming a long, drawn-out battle cry, raw noise and passion from eight throats picked up and amplified by the rest of the force. Ahead, gunfire blazed from the barricades protecting the eastern approaches to Derna. Contrary to the rumors passing through the American camp for the last two days, the Barbary pirates were putting up a fight.

Since 1801, the United States had been locked in a savage little war with the North African Barbary city-state of Tripoli, fighting to end the Arab pirates' demands for tribute and their predations on American merchant ships in the Mediterranean. In particular, a number of Americans, the officers and crew of the frigate *Philadelphia*, were now languishing in Tripolitean prisons since their capture two years before. Eaton, the former U.S. consul at Tunis and now bearing the title of "Naval Agent to the Barbary States," had conceived this bizarre plan to overthrow the pasha of Tripoli, Yusuf Karamanli, replacing him with Hamet Karamanli, Yusuf's deposed brother. Eaton had scraped together a ragtag army of Greek, Arab, and Levantine mercenaries, and several hundred Arab cavalry loyal to Hamet—about five hundred men in all. America, he'd told Hamet, would help him regain his throne in exchange for a pledge of friendship with the United States. Hamet, despite a weak and vacillating nature, had accepted the offer.

There were just eight Marines and one navy midshipman in the American contingent holding the tiny and wavering army together. Under the command of Marine Lieutenant Presley O'Bannon, they'd been detached ashore off the brig *Argus* at Alexandria seven weeks ago. Two days ago they'd reached Derna, Tripoli's easternmost outpost and roughly half of the distance to Tripoli itself. Eaton had requested permission to peacefully enter Derna, but Mustafa, the governor, had refused, scrawling simply "My head or yours" across the bottom of Eaton's message and returning it.

Despite the defiant reply, Derek had been convinced that Derna's defenders would flee at the army's approach. Now they would have to take the place by storm.

Perhaps two-thirds of the town's inhabitants supported Hamet. The remaining third were staunchly loyal to Mustapha, however, and had mustered perhaps eight hundred heavily armed men. A fort overlooking the harbor mounted eight nine-pounder cannons, while makeshift barricades protected the approaches to the city.

Eaton had divided the force, sending Hamet and his cavalry around to the western approaches of the city to cut the coast road to Tripoli and to storm the governor's palace, if possible. He'd also worked to bring a cannon and its carriage ashore from the *Argus,* hauling it with blocks and tackle up a twenty-foot precipice and dragging it into position east of the city. Eaton, the mercenaries, and the Marines, a force of fifty or sixty men all told, had remained on the east side of the city, studying the barricades and the swelling ranks of the defenders behind them. Three American brigs offshore—the *Hornet, Argus,* and *Nautilus*—had opened fire an hour ago, raining shot into the city's defenses.

And the city batteries in the fort at the town's harbor had replied, firing on the ships rather than the shore party, fortunately. While the *Argus* and *Nautilus* fired into the town, *Hornet* had concentrated on the harbor fort, knocking out its guns one at a time. Before long, the fort's defenders had broken and run, joining the governor's troops on the east side of the city. Worse, the cannon Eaton had brought ashore fired one round . . . but a too-eager gunner had accidentally left the ramrod in the weapon's barrel when he fired it. The cannon was useless, now, and the fire from the city's defenders was growing heavier moment by moment. The tiny force of Greek and Arab mercenaries had wavered, had begun falling back.

Characteristically, then, at the most crucial point of the battle, Eaton had given the order to charge.

Now, Sergeant Derek was racing across uneven ground as the bugler sounded the attack. O'Bannon was just ahead, brandishing his sword, as Eaton in his blue general's uniform waved them on with a musket. After a moment's confused hesitation, the Arab and Greek troops had rallied, then surged forward, sixty men racing wildly into a storm of fire from an army numbering hundreds. Derek could see several of the defenders up on the walls behind the barricades, shooting down at them.

And then they were clambering over the barricades. Derek raised his musket to his shoulder and fired, the flash and sharp bang of the flint in the powder pan coming a half second ahead of the deeper, throatier boom of the weapon as it discharged. Just ahead, a mustached face beneath a white turban contorted as the ball slammed into the man's forehead and toppled him backward. Derek kept moving up, his musket unloaded now, but sporting a bayonet over the muzzle that flashed in the sun.

Eaton paused at the top of the barricade, waving his musket over his head. From somewhere beyond, one of the defenders fired, and the shot shattered the former consul's wrist, knocking the musket from his grasp.

O'Bannon, his sword drawn, pushed past the wounded man and ran an Arab soldier through the throat. More musket fire rattled from the city walls behind the barricades. At

Derek's side, Private Edward Steward stumbled and fell, dead or wounded, Derek didn't know.

And then he was over the barricade and plunging down into the streets of Derna. An Arab soldier swung a scimitar, and Derek—in approved, by-the-book response—parried the blow with his musket, recovered, and lunged, putting the bayonet through the screaming man's belly. And from then on the fight was hand-to-hand. . . .

No, hand to *tentacle*. Nal burned down a Xul machine rising up in front of him, then blinked and shook his head. What the hell had just happened? For a moment, he'd been . . . someone else, in strange clothing and carrying a strange weapon, storming the ramparts of a desert fortress. . . .

Garroway, Gold One
Above Objective Reality
0848 hours, GMT

General Garroway was having trouble controlling his Starwraith. The time slip between Objective Reality and the *Nicholas* now drifting in outside universe was proving more than his link systems could handle. He was approaching the surface of the Xul world, intent on touching down what appeared to be the gaping door to an underground hanger or weapons bay . . . but he kept losing the image. The weapons bay shimmered, then winked out, momentarily replaced by a towering stone wall. It was night, and *they* were just ahead. . . .

"What the hell? . . ."

Garroway blinked, then sat up in his link couch back on board the *Samuel Nicholas*. For just a moment, he'd been . . . *somewhere*. Not on the transport. And not in the Starwraith above Objective Reality. He'd been in a city, crouching in a narrow, cobblestone street beneath a brooding, ancient stone wall set with stone steps.

Now, he was back on board the *Nicholas*, and the vast angry whirlpool of the Great Annihilator hung suspended in the projection overhead.

"Give me a wider channel!" he demanded of the techs running his QCC link with the Starwraith still within the Quantum Sea.

"Aye, aye, sir!" one of the techs replied. "We still have your pod. . . ."

"Put me back in there! *Move it!*"

And again, Garroway was within the Annihilator's maw, dropping precipitously over the rugged surface of the Xul worldlet . . .

And then with shrill, sing-song cries, the Chinese mob opened fire from above.

Blue Twelve
Above Objective Reality
0848 hours, GMT

"We've got heavy gun positions," Captain Xander was shouting, "bearing one-five-niner, one-eight-three, and two-one-one!"

"Copy that! I'm on one-eight-three! Firing!" Lieutenant Kadellan Wahrst opened up with her particle weapon, slamming bolts of blue-white lightning into the Xul weapon mount ahead.

"I'm moving for the door!" Javlotel called. "Cover me!"

"Got your back!" Palin replied.

Their goal was invisible optically, but showed up on their implant tactical overlays—a tunnel entrance leading down into the Xul planet.

The Xul weapon, just three hundred meters distant, appeared to be pivoting, its barrel swinging to bring the Marine oncoming strikepods under fire. Wahrst's particle gun bucked with savage, only partially damped recoil and she continued to fire. At first, her bolts appeared to vanish, absorbed by the enemy's shielding, but then, soundlessly, the Xul weapon erupted in geysering light and expanding plasma, as chunks of hot metal whirled in straight-line trajectories into vacuum.

She heard something . . . a shriek, followed by a heavy thud. *Impossible!* she thought. *There's no atmosphere to carry sound. . . .*

But the racket, a fast-swelling cacophony of chattering automatic-weapons fire and dull, thunderous booms, was so loud now she couldn't hear the link chatter from her squadron mates.

"This is it, men!" a shrill voice called as whistles began shrieking. "Over the top!"

She didn't recognize the voice, and there was no ID tag with it to tell her who had spoken. But her vision blurred, and Corporal Edgar O'Malley clambered up out of his shallow hole and joined the assault. To either side, hundreds of other Marines, in khaki uniforms and flat, tin-hat helmets surged up out of the shot-torn earth and moved forward, as machine-gun fire chattered and heavy caliber artillery rounds howled overhead and burst in no-man's land, sending up vast, black fountains of mud and earth.

O'Malley leaned forward as if bracing against a stiff wind . . . but the wind was imagined, a psychological artifact of the storm of lead sleeting past the advancing men, snapping and cracking above their heads, passing to either side. . . .

At the tree line up ahead, at the far end of a chewed-up wheat field, a Hun Maxim gun opened up. O'Malley saw the flicker of the muzzle flash, and then a line of eight Marines just in front of him toppled, twisted, and fell one after another from right to left as the enemy gun swept the line. Lieutenant Agway was still on his feet, standing in front of the line, his back to the enemy, walking steadily backward, arms spread wide, his .45 pistol in his right hand, a cane in his left. He was shouting something, but the roar of gunfire and high explosives was so loud O'Malley couldn't hear a word.

He assumed Agway was shouting encouragement.

It was O'Malley's first time in combat . . . the first time i combat for most of the men of the second Battalion, sixt Marines. A tough Irish-immigrant kid in the streets of Phil adelphia, he'd enlisted the day after America had entere the war, like so many thousands of others, and been shippe by train to the dark hell of boot camp.

The Irish still weren't entirely accepted within certain quar ters of American culture. His fellow recruits had called hin "Paddy" and "Spud" and subjected him to merciless beating in the shower head, while his D.I.s had called him "maggot and worse, promising him that he didn't have what it took t be a Marine and then gleefully setting out to prove it.

He'd proven them wrong, all of them. He'd survived, com ing out tougher than ever. He'd been assigned to the sixt Marines, a part of the second American Division, and sent t France.

O'Malley had arrived just as a massive German offensive had shattered the French Sixth Army along the Marne Rive front. As the Marines had hurried forward toward the crum bling front line, passing broken groups of ragged Frencl soldiers moving to the rear, a French officer had suggeste that the newcomers join the retreat.

"Retreat, hell!" Marine Captain Lloyd Williams ha snapped back. "We just got here!"

The Marines hadn't even had time to dig themselve trenches. From hastily excavated fighting holes—*foxholes* was the apt term coined by some of the men—the Marine: had opened up on the approaching Germans with a devastat ingly accurate fire from their '03 Springfields from eight hun dred yards and brought the enemy advance to a bloody halt.

That had been three days ago, June 3. O'Malley hadn' been part of the turkey shoot, as some of the guys were call ing it, but had been in reserve. Now he was at the very front the cutting edge.

And it was a shrieking, thundering, blood-drenched night mare.

When the brigade had first arrived at St. Nazaire, French army instructors had drilled them in the *proper* form for assaulting enemy positions—falling into line in front of their positions, deploying skirmishers in advance of the main body, and moving forward at a brisk, but carefully disciplined walk. And it was a walk into Hell itself.

Machine-gun fire stitched and rattled, slicing down Marines before they could take their positions. Mortar rounds rained down among them, throwing up huge gouts of earth and mud and torn flesh. Heavier artillery howled overhead, shaking the ground with each savage detonation. Men were falling everywhere as the advance proper began. A mortar round exploded just in front of them and Agway simply vanished in the blast. The Marine line continued forward.

The Marines wavered. The storm of fire grew heavier. . . .

Fuck this shit! O'Malley thought, and he dropped into the dubious cover of the bullet-shredded wheat. Other Marines were doing the same, dropping flat on the ground as men among them continued to die in horrible numbers. French combat training be damned. The French themselves hadn't advanced in massed formation since 1915.

The Marines lay in that exposed position for several horrible moments, taking more casualties. Just a few feet to O'Malley's left, a Marine lay on his back, clutching at the wet spill of his intestines, his mouth wide open as he screamed and screamed and screamed at the sky, and O'Malley couldn't even hear him. Some Marines kept moving forward on their hands and knees, while others rose up to provide covering fire. They were fifty yards from the German positions now, and they continued to die as Maxim rounds scythed down wheat and Marines together.

Stubbornly, O'Malley began crawling forward.

• • •

Garroway, Gold One
Above Objective Reality
0849 hours, GMT

For a few fragile moments, Garroway was in two worlds—
piloting his Starwraith across the surface of the Xul worldlet, and moving on foot through the narrow confines of an
Asian city, a screaming horde of Chinese racing toward
him. He couldn't tell where the illusion was coming from, or
even if it *was* an illusion, or if, somehow, it represented
some twisted aspect of what might be real.

It certainly *felt* real. The Starwraith vanished, a raggedly
shredding dream. He was General . . . no, he was a *captain*,
Captain John "Handsome Jack" Myers, the commanding
officer of a contingent of U.S. Marines sent to protect American and European diplomats inside the walled Legation
Quarter inside the ancient city of Peking. Gunfire banged
and cracked, and the Chinese a few yards ahead shrieked in
shrill, sing-song gibberish.

They were coming. . . .

The situation was desperate, that July night in the year
1900. Within China's beleaguered capital, thousands of foreigners, most of them civilians and many of them women and
children, were crammed into an area less than three-quarters
of a mile square, with little food or water and dwindling reserves of ammunition.

Protecting them were 392 regular troops and 125 civilian
or government service volunteers. The troops were drawn
from the maritime forces of eight nations—Russia, Japan,
Italy, France, Germany, Austria, Britain, and the United
States.

The American contingent consisted of fifty-three enlisted
U.S. Marines and three officers.

Outside the compound, tens of thousands of Chinese—the
murderously xenophobic members of a secret militant group
calling themselves "the Society of the Righteous Harmoni-

ous Fists"—had begun a siege, keeping up a steady bombardment of the Legation Quarter, and vowing to slaughter
every foreigner inside the Chinese capital. They had dedicated themselves to wiping out every trace of foreign influence within China.

Because of their public displays of martial arts, the mili-
tants were known as "Boxers." They wore no uniforms, as
such, but were identified by a single piece of red cloth somewhere on their bodies—a sash, a turban, or an apron.

The so-called Boxer Rebellion had been going on since
the end of the Sino-Japanese War in 1895. The Dowager Em-
press Tzu Hsi, the real power in the Chinese court, had been
using the Boxers in her bid to drive foreigners out of China.

The siege of the Legation Quarter had begun on June 20.

There were rumors that foreigners in the city of Tientsin
were also under siege, rumors that Tientsin had been relieved
and that a relief force was now on the way to Peking, rumors
that Christian missionaries and converts had been massacred
recently at Paotingfu, but how true any of the stories might
be was anybody's guess. The siege had been going on for almost two weeks, now, and the legation defenders were decidedly on their own.

South of the Legation Quarter rose the massive, ancient
Tartar Wall, overlooking the compound with strategic menace. At first during the siege, the German marines had kept
control of the wall, but on July 1, the Germans had been driven
off, and throughout the next day, the Boxers had been high
atop the wall, building barricades and hurling large rocks
down into the compound, while keeping up a more or less
constant fire with antique muskets. The defenders had erected
an inner barricade, but something had to be done about the
Boxers looking down into the compound from the parapets
above.

Now it was two-thirty in the morning of July 3, and Captain Myers and eight American Marines had just gone over
the barricade beneath the Tartar Wall. They'd pulled midnight

raids like this one before when, tiring of the incessant bombardment, they would sneak over the walls and take out Boxer gun positions that were too close for comfort.

Their goal this time was the Chinese position atop the Tartar Wall, consisting of a makeshift barricade and a tower erected the day before. More Marines and a number of Brits and Russians were supposed to be coming over behind them, but they'd been spotted by the Chinese up on the parapets, who'd immediately opened fire, hitting a Russian seaman in the leg.

The raid had been stalled, and Myers lay on the cobblestones, pistol in hand. He could see the Chinese just yards above, yelling like madmen and brandishing a bewildering array of pole weapons and swords, along with a few old muskets. The initial firing had petered out, but if the Boxers elected to rush the Marines now, sheer weight of numbers would roll over the exposed Americans and back into the legation compound.

It was, Myers thought, a choice between lying in the street and being slaughtered or of going onto the offensive. They might all die, anyway, but at least there was a chance. Rising to his feet he screamed, *"Let's go, Marines!"* and launched himself toward a flight of crumbling stone steps leading up to the parapets above. Privates Turner and Thomas raced past him and into the lead, firing their rifles as quickly as they could work the bolts, pounding up the steps. Myers and the other Marines followed, while behind them, more legation troops began spilling over the Allied barricade.

Gaining the top of the wall, Myers found himself just a few feet from the enemy. A handful of Chinese muskets fired across the barricade, and Turner pitched backward, shot through the head. The other Marines kept moving forward, however, firing as they came. Myers brought up his pistol and fired it into the Chinese mob.

The Boxers, he knew, surrounded themselves with superstition and magic, swallowing charms that they claimed made them invulnerable to bullets. One way they picked up recruits out among the peasants was to shoot at a Boxer with blanks, proving the power of magic over gunfire.

For some reason, though, the magic wasn't working here. Myers' shot caught a Chinese militant full in the face, knocking him backward into the arms of his startled compatriots. He fired again and a second Boxer went down. The mob behind the barricade wavered, then broke, the individual rebels beginning to flee toward the rear, colliding with others in the rear who hadn't yet caught on to the fact that a retreat was beginning.

The rest of the Marines, mixed in with Russian seamen in their striped shirts and British marines, came up the steps and poured a devastating volley into the retreating Boxers, killing dozens of them.

And then Myers and a handful of Marines were over the first Chinese barricade atop the wall, knocking aside crates and bags of rice and pushing on. The fighting was fierce and hand-to-hand. Thomas was hit in the stomach and fell, clutching his bloody belly. Myers found himself facing a dozen Boxers armed with deadly trident-tipped spears and pole arms mounting wickedly curved blades. He fired his pistol again . . . and yet again . . . and then felt a keen and slicing pain in his leg as a Boxer lunged forward with a spear.

Captain Myers went down as the Chinese around him rallied. . . .

19

1902.2229

Blue Seven
Approaching Objective Reality
0849 hours, GMT

Lieutenant Garwe emerged from the fog of the illusion, shaking his head. Where was he? For a moment, he'd been somewhere else, some*one* else entirely, on a beach beneath a brilliant subtropical sun, splashing ashore from a small boat while trying to keep his powder dry. He remembered the sand of the beach . . .

But what was beneath the whiplashing tentacles of his Starwraith was not sand, quite, but the powdery gray regolith of the Xul planet. He'd plowed into the surface in a spray of dust, gouging a crater before regaining his senses.

What the hell was going on?

He called up a tactical display projected within his mind, looking for other members of the squadron. There was no one.

"Blue Squadron, Blue Seven," he called. "Where is everyone?"

A blip appeared on the tac display, IDed as Blue Two. That was Maria Amendes. "Gar?" she asked. "Are you there?"

"Affirmative. Where the hell were you? Where were *we*?"

"I was . . . someplace else," she told him. "I was on . . . on one of those funny ancient ships. A seagoing ship, not a starship, with tall poles and sheets of cloth and lots of rope everywhere."

Amendes, Garwe remembered, wasn't much for history. "You mean a sailing ship," he said. "Eighteenth, maybe nineteenth century. . . ."

"I don't know when it was. But I was a *man* in a blue and red uniform. I was on this wooden platform high up on one of those poles with a bunch of other men dressed like I was, and we had these funny, long, heavy weapons, and—"

For just a moment, Garwe caught the echoes of what Amendes had experienced. She'd been a U.S. Marine on board a vessel from the Age of Sail perhaps 2200 years earlier, part of a squad assigned to the mizzentop during a broadside-to-broadside battle with an enemy ship. The Marines were using their muskets to try to pick off their opposite numbers in the rigging of the ship alongside, then turning their fire on the enemy officers on the deck below. He could hear the thunder of big guns, the rattle of musketry, *taste* the sharp bite of gunpowder in the sulfurous and billowing clouds embracing both ships.

He couldn't see enough detail in that one glimpse to determine exactly when that long-ago battle had taken place, but it was close—within a few decades—of his own experience splashing ashore on a sun-drenched beach.

"What was it, Gar?" Amendes asked. "What's happening to us?"

"I'm not sure. It might be a Xul weapon. Close with me, and let's try to reach that opening up ahead. Looks like a way inside."

"What opening?"

"Bearing one-five-five."

"Got it. On my way. I'll meet you there."

"Roger that."

At optical frequencies, there was nothing to be seen but gray rock and dust, the blue-violet mist in the sky, and a thin slash of gold light marking the Xul world's rings. His

Starwraith, however, was processing data from the battlespace net, a far-flung web of sensors, remote drones, and probes that pulled in data from all wavelengths and presented it to his tac display overlays.

Lifting from the ground on his gravitics, he began drifting forward. His AI spotted a Xul point-defense weapon three hundred meters away and he turned his X-ray laser on it. Within his in-head display, a targeting cursor zeroed in on the enemy gun, locking on to it. He thought-clicked the triggering command. . . .

. . . as sand crunched beneath his shoes. The column had been struggling ahead through soft beach sand beneath the hot sun for an hour, now, muskets loaded and at shoulder arms. Behind them came a column of fifty sailors off the *Cabot* under the command of Lieutenant Weaver. Ahead, Fort Montagu rose next to the emerald waters off New Providence Island, a low, deeply truncated pyramid with embrasures for cannon, and a red, white, and blue Union Jack fluttering from a flagpole inside. The town of Nassau lay just beyond, pastel-colored buildings gleaming in the sun. The place, both town and fort, appeared unnaturally quiet, even deserted.

The Marines had hoped to catch the fort by surprise, but a signal gun had boomed out as they'd come ashore, sounding the alarm. Bad luck, there. They would have to storm the fort . . . unless the redcoats could be talked into surrender. To that end, a short while before, Captain Nicholas had sent a runner on ahead with a message for a Governor Montfront Browne, advising him to avoid bloodshed and surrender the town.

A puff of smoke appeared at one of the fort's embrasures, followed seconds later by the far-off boom of a cannon. Porter saw something strike the beach a hundred yards ahead and to the left, sending up a spray of sand between the column and the sea. A second later, it hit again, farther up the beach, and then a third time, the round skipping across the sand as it flashed past. Several of the men in ranks bellowed derisively.

"Damned lobsterbacks!" Private Dolby called out. "Y'ninnies can't hit a barn wall at arm's length from yer noses!"

"Silence in the ranks!" Captain Samuel Nicholas called. "Sergeant Prescott! Have the men deploy in line of battle, if you please."

"Aye, sir!" the sergeant, a grizzled old-timer off the *Alfred*, growled. "Awright, you men! You heard the Captain of Marines! Column, *halt*! Battle formation, *hut*!"

The Marine drummer rattled off a long roll as the Continental Marines broke out of column formation and took up two parallel lines, one behind the other, facing the fort. Porter was in the front rank, feeling nakedly exposed and vulnerable. The fort was still several hundred yards away, well beyond effective musket range.

"The men may fix bayonets, Sergeant."

"Aye, sir! Awright, Marines! Horder . . . *harms!*"

More or less as one, the lines of Marines brought their muskets down off their shoulders, slapped them into port arms, then dropped the buttstocks to the sand sharply alongside their right legs. They'd been practicing and drilling these maneuvers for weeks, getting them letter perfect, but in the excitement of imminent battle, the execution this morning was a bit ragged.

"Fix . . . bayo*nets!*"

Porter drew the slender, 14-inch steel blade of his bayonet from its scabbard, fixed the locking ring over the muzzle of his weapon, and snapped it home.

Captain Nicholas walked in front of the lines, his sword drawn. "Men . . . no fancy speeches this morning. Right now, up in New England, General Washington desperately needs gunpowder for the Continental Army outside of Boston. Over there is the British supply depot for the Bahamas . . . and about six hundred barrels of black powder. We're here to take it away from those fellows. Sergeant, you may deploy the men for the attack."

"Yessir! Huzzah for the captain, lads!"

"Huzzah!" Porter and the rest of the 250 Marines and

sailors shouted in shrill unison. With surprise lost at the landing, they might as well let the British know they were coming. "*Huzzah! Huzzah!*"

"Marines! Charge . . . *bayonets*! At the walk . . . for'ard . . . *harch!*"

Right foot first as he'd been taught, John Porter stepped forward, his musket held stiffly at his right side, bayonet leveled at the enemy. He wondered if they would fire a volley before they reached the wall . . . and how close that might be. He wondered if they would have to storm those sloping stone and wood walls with the bayonet, and how many men might die in the attempt. He wondered . . .

A second puff of smoke erupted from the fort. Another ball struck the sand just ahead, and Porter wondered if he was about to die.

HQ Section, Second Battalion, Ninth Marines
Within Objective Reality
0847 hours, GMT

Nal wondered if he was about to die. For a moment, he'd been locked in a terrible, life-or-death struggle with a nightmare apparition of black metal-ceramic and lashing tentacles . . . but the vision faded and he was back on the barricades outside the city of Derna.

Musket fire crackled from behind the barricades, knocking down several Greek and Arab mercenaries. Sergeant Derek was caught now in a desperate, life-or-death struggle with some hundreds of turbaned Barbary Coast pirates, and for a horrible moment, when Eaton was shot and the assault began to falter, it seemed as though the attack was doomed at last. Derek recovered from his bayonet thrust, then whipped the stock of his musket around to smash the jaw of another pirate rushing him from the left. Just in front of him, a musket boomed and Private John Whitten caught the round high in his chest, sprawling to the ground in an untidy splay of arms and legs and pooling blood. Derek lunged again with his bayonet, cutting down the pirate who'd just fired.

And then, suddenly, magically, the enemy was running, *running*, turning their backs on the polyglot band of Marines and mercenaries and fleeing into the town. The men began cheering, some of them throwing caps and turbans into the air. Against all expectations, against all odds, the rush had carried the barricades and broken the enemy line of defense.

Nearby, the naval midshipman with the column was tying off a rough bandage around General Eaton's wrist. The man gave a thin-lipped smile and drew his pistol with his right hand. "We're not done yet!" he bellowed, pointing with the weapon. "The fort, men!"

Flushed and panting with exertion and victory, the handful of Marines and mercenaries cheered more loudly. After a mere sixty of them had stormed the barricades and set hundreds of defenders to flight, *anything* seemed possible now. As Derek began pulling the force back into order again, though, he felt a dark flash of foreboding. Of the seven enlisted Marines in the party, including himself, three—Thomas, O'Brian, and Steward were wounded, Steward critically— and one, John Whitten, was dead. Over half of the Marine contingent was out of action, now . . . and the Marines had been all that had held Eaton's bizarre little army together for the past seven weeks. Several Christian Greek mercenaries lay dead as well, along with several Muslims, and a dozen men out of the sixty were wounded. The victory at the barricades had come at a high price. One of the wounded men insisted he was still able to fight, but the other two would be left behind with some Greeks to watch over them.

The harbor fort lay just ahead, ominously silent. The naval midshipman raised a pre-arranged signal flag from a city wall parapet, and moments later the naval gunfire from the flotilla offshore slackened; then died away.

"We take that fort and the city is ours!" Eaton declared. "Victory or death!"

Eaton, Derek had long since concluded, was a vainglorious idiot with a penchant for melodrama. But the fort appeared empty, almost inviting.

Gunsmoke clung to the streets of Derna like a thick, New England fog as the ragged army, with four enlisted Marines and one officer in the van, began making its way through narrow streets toward Derna's harbor fort.

Blue Twelve
Objective Reality
0849 hours, GMT

Lieutenant Kadellan Wahrst wondered what was happening. She'd been . . . on her belly in the wheat, as machine-gun fire sliced the stalks inches above her back. Then she'd been crawling, trying to work her way around the Hun gun position. And then . . .

She guided her Starwraith up to the opening, a twenty-meter triangular cavern mouth yawning in the gray surface of the Xul world. Laser beams and particle cannon continued to gouge huge chunks from Xul surface structures, silencing the defensive weapons one by one. In the violet-blue mists overhead, flights of Marine Maelstrom heavy fighters off of the *Nicholas* flew dangerously low across the fire-torn landscape, guided to Xul targets by strikepod Marines on the surface, or by unmanned battlespace drones and recon AIs.

Captain Xander's icon was gone from her in-head display. No . . . there she was. Fifty meters distant and closing. What was wrong with their tracking?

"Blue One! Blue Twelve! Where've you been?"

"I . . . I'm not sure what happened." Captain Xander's voice sounded shaken. "I was . . . in Mexico. *Mexico.* A place called Chapultepec. . . ."

"Fuck," Blue Nine, Misek Bollan said. "I was in some kind of small, open metal boat. Explosions in the water everywhere. And the beach was so far. . . ."

"We may be under attack," Xander said. "Psychic attack. Or possibly through our implants. Shake it off!"

"We've got an entrance to the Xul underground here!"

"I'm coming."

Xander, Bollan, and three other Marines joined Wahrst moments later. Their scanners showed no signs of life or movement within, but that didn't mean the Xul weren't lying in wait, their power systems damped down to near invisibility. Theory said the Xul "pilots" of those war machines lived on their equivalent of the Net, digital intelligences that could animate a lifeless piece of metal with a thought and turn it deadly.

"Nicholas, Blue One!" Xander called over the main QCC channel. "We are entering Objective Reality."

And that was a misnomer if Wahrst had ever heard one, she thought. Whatever was happening around her, it wasn't reality, objective or otherwise. As she entered the cavern's mouth, the darkness faded to bright sunlight, to waving stalks of wheat, to pillars of climbing black smoke and the bellow and howl of artillery rounds.

Corporal Edgar O'Malley was crawling fast now, on his hands and knees, his Springfield awkwardly slung over his back. His destination was the tree line to his left, now less than twenty yards away.

All across the battlefield, tiny groups of Marines, their numbers decimated in those first few bloody moments of the advance, had abandoned their worse-than-useless French training and hit the deck, continuing to move forward but taking advantage of every bit of cover the shell-ravaged fields and woods had to offer. In a way, it was the supreme American military gesture, reverting to Indian tactics to defeat an enemy that expected them to march and maneuver parade-ground fashion in plain and easy-to-kill sight. American colonials had used such tactics to drive the British column all the way back from Concord to Boston in 1775. Now the U.S. Marines were using them to gain a foothold in the woods.

Belleau Wood, the place was called, a tiny comma of forest two miles long and narrowly pinched at the middle. It occupied the center of a triangle marked by three shell-blasted villages—Belleau, Bouresches, and Lucy-Le-Bocage—and its sole importance lay in the German high command's determination to teach the newly arrived Americans a bloody lesson in the realities of European warfare.

Emerging from the wheat, O'Malley crawled over a low hummock and slid down among a small clump of Marines huddled in the scant shelter afforded by a smoking shell crater. Other Marines lay and crouched nearby, trying to return fire against the incessant and deadly chatter of the German Maxim guns. The mangled dead and dying lay scattered everywhere.

"*Fuck* this!" one of the men inside the crater shouted. He rose to his feet, fully exposed now to the enemy fire. With a start, O'Malley recognized him. He'd seen his photograph, and even seen him in person at a military review a few weeks before. He was Gunnery Sergeant Dan Daly, one of the old-breed leathernecks, a two-time Medal of Honor winner from the Boxer Rebellion and Haiti.

Daly waved his bayoneted rifle over his head with a wild forward sweep. "Come *on*, you sons of bitches! Do you want to live forever?"

With a roar, the Marines in the shell hole scrambled to their feet and clambered out, rushing forward with Daly in the lead. Elsewhere across the bloody wheat field, other Marines singly and in small, huddled groups saw the charge, rose up and joined it.

And O'Malley raced forward with the rest of them, shouting wildly.

Garroway, Gold One
Above Objective Reality
0849 hours, GMT

The sharp, cold pain in his leg brought Garroway screaming back to full consciousness. He was again on board the

icholas, lying in his link couch, his Starwraith unattended
mewhere within the depths of the Great Annihilator's
avitational maw. A Navy corpsman bent over him, look-
g concerned. "General? Are you okay? What happened?"

The pain was fading but its memory remained. He also
membered his last glimpse of the battle, the screaming
ob of Chinese Boxers as they closed in on him, jabbing
d lunging at him with their spears and pikes. Sitting up,
e tugged at his trousers, exposing his left calf. An angry
d welt there was rapidly fading. "Son of a bitch."

"What happened to your leg?" the corpsman asked. He
ached for a nanospray therapeutic unit. "Here, let me in-
ct you. . . ."

"Forget it, son," Garroway told him, waving him off. "I
eed to think about this."

He dropped back on the link couch, but not to reconnect
ith the Starwraith. He wanted to talk this over with So-
rates or one of the other high-level AIs, but if the Xul had
ompromised the Associate Fleet's electronic networks, the
Is too might be compromised.

He began linking in with his command constellation. Two,
eisman and Bamford, were still linked to other Starwraiths
t Objective Reality, but the other nine were merely linked in
t the *Nicholas*' end of the data stream, managing the battle.

"Heads up, people!" he snapped over the circuit. "We
ave a problem."

econ Zephyr
Objective Reality's Ring
849 hours, GMT

Lieutenant Amanda Karr was a part of the chorus. Through
uther and a set of translation programs compiled over the
enturies by other penetrations of Xul ships and networks,
he could merge with the litany and follow it.

They were researching the Marines.

*These are ancient enemies. We have faced them be-
fore. . . .*

We have faced them. We have beaten them, absorbe
them. . . .

And they have beaten us, time and time again.

Survival is paramount. We must survive.

To survive we must find their weaknesses and de-
stroy them.

Destroy them. . . .

Karr moved through a sea of chanting voices, unnotice
the penetrator program providing her with a software she
that let her move through the alien electronic network, tas
ing, listening, understanding. Hundreds, no, *thousands* o
distinct data streams carried encyclopedic volumes of info
mation that seemed to relate to the history of the Marin
Corps. As she sampled the streaming data packets, she caug
glimpses of ancient, seagoing sailing ships, of ranks of me
in stiff-necked uniform jackets carrying antique powder fire
arms, of men in cloth uniforms and steel helmets, of men i
various types of space suits and combat armor.

She merged with one stream. She saw a frozen, snow
covered hillside. Gunnery Sergeant Donald Atkins crouche
in his fighting hole, aiming a primitive pulse laser at an ac
vancing wave of dark-clad figures. To left and right, othe
Marines in mid-twenty-first-century combat dress calm
picked out their targets and fired. The heavy backpack ba
teries powering their Sunbeam, Mk. IX lasers had bee
placed in their holes by their feet; winking orange indicato
lights indicated that all of the power packs were nearl
drained dry.

And the Chinese Hegemony hordes kept coming. . . .

Karr could hear Atkins' thoughts. The year was 2061, an
the place was Hill 440 outside of Vladivostok, in eas
maritime Russia. The Marine Third Division had been calle
in to help America's Russian allies repel the Hegemony's at
tempt to take over the entire Russian Far East.

The winking light on Atkins' battery pack went red, then ⸺aded, and his Sunbeam died.

"That's it for my laser," he called over the tactical comm ⸺et. Setting the useless weapon aside, he drew his service ⸺idearm, a high-power 10mm Colt M2015 automatic.

"Same here," Captain Norman said from a nearby posi⸺on. "We hold here, Marines. We *hold!*"

The front ranks of the oncoming army were only fifty me⸺ers away, now. Atkins chambered a round and took aim. . . .

Karr jerked back out of the data stream. The simulation . . . ⸺o, the alternate reality, the *parareality* within the flow was ⸺owerful and compelling. But where was it coming from? It ⸺as inconceivable that the Xul would have enough informa⸺ion about human and Corps history to create such a detailed ⸺lusion. The information had to be coming somehow from ⸺he Marines' own libraries.

A digital scout within an electronic jungle, she began to ⸺nvestigate more deeply.

⸺lue Seven
⸺pproaching Objective Reality
⸺849 hours, GMT

A third cannon shot boomed out from the fort, struck ⸺and, and skipped toward the Marine formation. At Nicho⸺as' shouted orders, the two ranks of Marines parted, divid⸺ng left and right, and the near-spent ball rolled harmlessly ⸺etween them. Another order, and the ranks came together ⸺gain, continuing the relentless advance on the fort.

The guns appeared to be silent, now. Far off in the dis⸺ance, a bugle sounded and, moments, later, the flag hanging ⸺rom the fort's flagstaff lowered.

"Damn my eyes!" a sailor called out. "Th' buggers're *sur⸺rendering!*"

With quickening excitement, John Porter and the rest of

the Continental Marines swept toward the fort, as the gate swung open to receive them.

HQ Section, Second Battalion, Ninth Marines
Within Objective Reality
0849 hours, GMT

And in the Tripolitean town of Derna, a handful of Marines rushed the gates of the harbor fort. Enemy resistance appeared to have collapsed entirely, and Mustafa's troops were scattering everywhere.

To the south and west, Hamet's cavalry had swept into Derna unopposed. The defenders on that side of the town, apparently, had been drawn off by Eaton's assault on the eastern barricades, leaving the way wide open for Hamet's men. They'd occupied an empty castle on the outskirts of town, then moved on to seize the governor's palace.

Offshore, in the harbor, the guns of the tiny American flotilla fell silent.

The harbor fort's gates stood open, and Sergeant Derek charged inside. . . .

Blue Twelve
Objective Reality
0849 hours, GMT

Beneath the eaves of Belleau Wood, Corporal Edgar O'Malley followed Gunnery Sergeant Dan Daly at a flat-out run, as German bullets zipped and buzzed like angry hornets and the ground trembled to the *crump* and *thud* of explosions. The Maxim gun position that had driven O'Malley to ground in the first place was less than fifty yards to his right, on the edge of the forest.

A gray shape rose from behind a tangle of logs and cut

rush just ahead. O'Malley raised his Springfield and triggered off a round, and the gray shape sprawled to the ground. Still cheering, the other Marines swept into the forest, taking more casualties, but sweeping the startled Germans from fighting holes and trenches.

Working his way to his right, O'Malley found himself a scant twenty yards behind and to the right of the machinegun nest. A gunner, a loader, and three other men with the characteristic coal-scuttle helmets of the Imperial German Army crouched in a hole barricaded with timber, their full attention still focused on the sun-drenched glare of the wheat field in front of them. The gunner clutched the twin grips of the deadly Maschinengewehr '08 inches in front of his face, squeezing off tight, professional bursts at the Marines still advancing across the open ground.

O'Malley leaned against a tree, took aim, and squeezed off a single shot. The machinegunner dropped, his helmet drilled at the temple by the .30-caliber round. O'Malley worked the bolt of his rifle, sending spent brass spinning through the air as he chambered a new round, took aim again, and fired. One of the Hun infantrymen, just turning to take the gunner's place behind the Maxim gun, jerked and fell. O'Malley triggered a third round, and a third German lurched to one side, sprawling face down over the barricade.

O'Malley was doing some fast calculating. His Springfield fed from a five-round internal magazine. He'd fired once when he entered the woods . . . and three times more in fast succession just now. He had one round left, and two Germans in front of him, both of whom had finally figured out where the superbly accurate rifle fire was coming from, and who were turning now to face him. He could kill one of the two, but not both.

For an agonizing couple of seconds, O'Malley and the two German infantrymen faced one another. Then one of the Germans dropped his Mauser rifle and raised his hands. "*Kamerad*!"

Coolly, O'Malley swung his aim to cover the second German, who quickly dropped his rifle as well. "*Ve zurrender!*" the second man called in heavily accented English.

And then more Marines were swarming into the wood out of the bloody field beyond.

20

Marine Ops Center
Marine Transport Major Samuel Nicholas
0850 hours, GMT

"It's not just some kind of projected illusion," Janis Fremantle was saying. "We're getting reports that Marines are actually dropping off the tactical scans, as if they really are teleporting someplace else. Some*when* else."

"And Zephyr doesn't think the Xul are doing it?" Garroway asked.

"Oh, the Xul are involved somehow. All of our Zephyr penetrators are tracking the data streams responsible inside the Xul Net. But the Xul may not be aware of what they're doing."

"Maybe they're data mining," Colonel Jordan, the constellation's computer expert, said. "Trying to find out who's attacking them."

"Or they're using it as a distraction," Major Allendes suggested.

"It could be a damned effective weapon," Colonel Adri Carter, Garroway's Executive Officer, pointed out. "If our people are simming as other people, in other situations, other places, they can't pay attention to where they are physically."

Garroway thought again about how real, how all-consuming the hallucination had been, and nodded agreement. He really *had* been a Marine named Myers, really *had* been wounded on the barricaded Tartar Wall above the Legation Quarter in 1900 Peking. His leg was still throbbing with the memory.

"And it's possible the Xul don't know how completely they're scrambling us," he said. "If they did, they might have put up a stronger counterattack. Either that, or we haven't seen their end game yet."

"You mean they're still setting us up for the kill?" Ranser asked.

"Something like that."

"Perhaps," Rame suggested, "it's an attempt to communicate."

"Also possible. But all we can go on now is the effect their attempts are having on us. So far, it's more like a weapon than chit-chat. What kind of command control do we still have?"

Major Den Kyle was the command constellation's senior QCC Network Controller . . . the senior *human*, at any rate. Garroway had ordered all AIs and digital humans to stand down, just in case they'd been contaminated by Xul electronic infiltration. "At any given moment," he said, "we have solid links with perhaps half of our personnel over there. It's like Janis said. They keep popping in and out, as if they're going someplace else. When something happens—like you getting stuck with that spear, sir—to jar them out of it, they come back."

"We need to put more pressure on the bastards," Garroway said. "How long until we can rotate again, Admiral?"

Ranser consulted an inner checklist. "We're ready any time, General. But we're not scheduled to go back in for another—"

"Pass the word to all hands, then execute our next rotation," Garroway said. "Remember, a lot more time is passing out here than in there. The bad guys won't be expecting us to pop up again so soon." He turned away suddenly.

"General?" Ranser asked. "Where are you going?"

"Back inside," Garroway replied. "I need to see this from over there. . . ."

Blue Seven
Approaching Objective Reality
0850 hours, GMT

The gates opened as the Marines and sailors marched up to the fort. Inside, there were only a handful of defenders. The three cannon shots fired from the walls had been a token defense, a means of preserving honor. Honor preserved, they could now surrender.

A painfully young redcoat lieutenant was in charge of the defenders. Nicholas accepted his sword, then returned it to him. His men, Nicholas said, would be paroled on their word of good behavior.

In any case, there weren't enough Continentals there to waste guarding prisoners.

One ceremony was crucial, however. As the Marines stood in ranks at attention in the parade ground at the center of the fort, as the Marine drummer rolled off a sharp tattoo, Samuel Nicholas broke out the Grand Union flag . . . thirteen red and white horizontal stripes, with the red, white, and blue Union Jack inset at the upper corner of the hoist. It was the same flag that had flown over the *Providence* and the other ships of the tiny American Navy.

Porter watched the flag as it climbed the mast and felt a peculiar, almost surging tug at heart and throat. Not the British flag . . . *his* flag. America's flag.

And as he watched, another presence grew stronger in his mind. Porter was fading, Garwe growing stronger. It was Marek Garwe standing there in Fort Montagu, watching the flag-raising ceremony, feeling the sharp rush of pride even though the people he was watching had been dead 2,200 years, and the flag of a long-vanished republic meant little now save as a historical curiosity.

He was still powerfully moved.

HQ Section, Second Battalion, Ninth Marines
Within Objective Reality
0850 hours, GMT

Sergeant Derek raced through the open gates of the fort, close behind O'Bannon, waving his sword, and Eaton, arm bandaged, holding a cocked flintlock pistol in his good hand. Many of the fort's gunners had fled already, and several of the nine-pounder carriages had been smashed by gunfire from the *Argus* and the other American ships, but several cannon remained intact, and a number of Arab gunners still manned them.

Derek bayoneted a Barbary soldier wielding a scimitar just beyond the gate. Eaton raised his pistol and fired at one of the gun crews on the platform behind the fort's palisades. A turbaned soldier dropped his ramrod, slumping over the weapon's muzzle. The other members of the gun crew scattered, running for cover, and the fever caught among the other gun crews as well. In moments, the Barbary troops were scrambling over the low walls, fleeing the fort and leaving it to the cheering Americans, Greeks, and Arab mercenaries.

Most of the cannon had been reloaded in preparation for a massed broadside at the American ships. Shouting, waving his sword, O'Bannon began bullying the Greek Christians and Arab Muslims, getting them to manhandle the heavy guns around to face the opposite direction, down into the heart of the city.

"Sir!" Derek called out. "The flag! . . ."

The Tripolitan flag still hung from the flagstaff in the center of the fort, and firing from beneath those colors would be a serious breach of military custom. "Right you are, Sergeant," O'Bannon replied. Trotting down the stone steps from the parapet, where his men continued to wrestle the captured guns around to the south wall, he unfastened the lanyard and quickly hauled down the flag.

He had another flag tucked away inside his blue jacket. Pulling it out, he attached it to the lanyard, then swiftly hauled the banner up the flagpole. It broke in the offshore breeze, fifteen white stars on a blue field, fifteen horizontal red and white stripes along the fly.

The Marines cheered, then, and, perhaps because it was infectious, so did the Greek mercenaries . . . and then even the Arabs were cheering as well. It took a few moments, but as the cheers and huzzahs died away, Derek could hear more cheering, this floating in across the harbor. The brig *Argus* was close enough that he could see blue-jacketed sailors crowding her ratlines and rails, waving their flat hats, and cheering wildly. A similar commotion appeared to have broken out on board the more distant *Hornet* and *Nautilus*.

Only then did the real meaning, the real *magic* of the moment strike Derek.

The United States of America had been in existence for just twenty-nine years. During that time, she'd fought a Revolution lasting seven years, as well as an undeclared and totally maritime quasi-war with France. Now, America was fighting for her right as a nation of the world, the equal of all others, the right to unrestricted commerce on the high seas without being forced to pay humiliating tribute to foreign princes.

And for the first time in her brief history, her flag had just been hoisted above a bastion of the Old World.

The U.S. Marines had made their mark upon history, and nothing, absolutely *nothing*, could possibly stop them now.

Marine Transport Major Samuel Nicholas
0851 hours, GMT

"Three . . . two . . . one . . . rotate!"
"Initiate dimensional translation."

At Ranser's command, the ten-kilometer bulk of the *Samuel Nicholas* dropped out of normal space and into the eldritch otherness of the Quantum Sea. She materialized almost exactly where she'd been before, perhaps five hundred kilometers from the Xul world-base. Although the *Nicholas* was primarily a transport, she mounted massive X-ray and gamma ray lasers in turrets on her outer hull, and possessed numerous mag-accelerators capable of whipping antimatter warheads or simple lumps of dead mass to near-light velocities and slam them into the target.

For perhaps a quarter of a second, the *Nicholas* hung in empty space, unnoticed. With the difference in time flow within this region, the ship had been gone for less than a minute. Then the Xul began to take notice of her. At the same time, her own fire control computers had located the transponders of Marines and Associative ships in the region, and targeted areas of the worldlet where they could avoid inflicting casualties through friendly fire. Gouts of light began sparking and flashing across the planet's surface as the *Nicholas* main weapons came to bear.

The Associative Fleet continued their ongoing bombardment as well, and in seconds the entire face of the Xul world appeared to be sparkling with a multitude of hits.

The enemy's fire didn't slacken, however, and in seconds both the battlecruiser *Poseidon* and the cruisers *Hesperides* and *Azuran* were savaged by multiple beams from the Xul worldlet. Multiple explosions ate through the vessel's hulls, leaving the *Poseidon* a drifting hulk, the other two as expanding clouds of hot gas and debris.

The surviving Associative ships continued the bombardment, however, working to suppress the Xul surface structures, turrets, and weapons mounts and reduced the volume of enemy fire. After twenty seconds, the huge transport winked out once more, vanished back to four-D space. And, seconds later, it reappeared, drifting in a different direction, this time, hammering the Xul world from a different quarter.

Xul combat machines emerged from caverns and shielded

entrances in black, swarming clouds. They were met by squadrons of heavy F/A-750 Nightstar fighters and A/S-4000 Maelstroms, cutting through the clouds instants after devastating high-energy beams burned through them.

Many of the fighters lost their human components momentarily, as the Marines in their cockpits shifted into simulations coming through the combat Net, but the AIs continued flying them. Some fighters winked off of tactical displays entirely, to reappear moments later, as high-volume data streams interacted with the strangely malleable pseudo-space of the Quantum Sea.

Overall, the Marine and Navy forces were able to keep up the pressure, however.

In the sky and beneath the ground, within the Quantum Sea and at a thousand realities across time and space, the Marine assault of Objective Reality continued.

Blue Seven
Objective Reality
0851 hours, GMT

The gun powder that was supposed to be in Nassau wasn't there.

It took fourteen days to load the supplies captured at Nassau on board the tiny American squadron—eighty-eight cannon, sixteen thousand shells, ten thousand rounds of musket ammunition, and other supplies—but the majority of the precious gunpowder stored there had been moved elsewhere the day before.

During the voyage back from Nassau, the flotilla had engaged a British warship, the HMS *Glasgow*, and Nicholas' Marines had helped man the broadside cannon. The fight was inconclusive, but Lieutenant John Fitzpatrick and six Marines had been killed—the first Marines ever to die in combat—and four others had been wounded.

The powerful surge of emotion, of pride in the Corps and

the Corps' history, was giving way as Lieutenant Garwe began slipping back into control of the simulation.

The raid on Nassau had been a spectacular success by any measure, but there were ongoing debates that tended to cloud the light of that bright victory. Commodore Esek Hopkins, the commander of the little Continental Navy flotilla that had seized the Bahamian port, came under censure. His orginal orders from Congress had been to clear the Chesapeake Bay of British raiders, but he'd disregarded those orders to carry out the raid on Nassau. On his return, his fleet was blockaded helplessly inside Narragansett Bay, and there were allegations of his incompetence and inaction, both at Narragansett Bay and in the action with the *Glasgow*.

In January of 1778, he'd been permanently relieved of his command.

And there were questions . . . *questions.* Tun Tavern, the recruiting station so beloved of the Corps, might not in fact be the actual place where the Marines had first been recruited. The histories suggested that it had been another tavern entirely, the Conestoga, owned by Nicholas's family, where the Marine Corps saga had actually begun. The records from the era were so fuzzy and incomplete, it was impossible to be sure of what was real, what was myth.

Garwe felt himself tottering on the edge of a swirling, dark depression. Who *were* the Marines, anyway? Their history had all been a shabby lie. The landing at Nassau had been almost unopposed, and the powder they'd hoped to seize was gone. Esek Hopkins had been disgraced, and the Marines during the Revolution—aside from recruits enlisted and taken directly on board naval vessels—had primarily served with Washington's army as artillerymen, though a handful had sailed down the Mississippi in 1778 to deny New Orleans to British merchants.

For the most part, the Continental Marines had proven less of a force than Corps legend suggested. Though the modern Corps traced the birth of the Marines back to Tun Tavern and November 10, 1775, the Continental Marines had been disbanded in 1785, and America's Marines had gone out of existence, along with the Continental Navy. They would not be resurrected until President John Adams signed a bill establishing the Marines in July of 1798.

Lieutenant Garwe came out of the simulation within the cavern beneath the surface of the Xul world. One moment he'd been wrestling with dark thoughts, somewhere else, and the next he was taking fire from a Xul position just ahead.

"Fuck!" he screamed, and began returning fire. . . .

HQ Section, Second Battalion, Ninth Marines
Within Objective Reality
0852 hours, GMT

Reality wavered, and Nal tried to make sense of what he was seeing. Sergeant Derek stood above one of the captured Muslim cannons, helping to aim it into the city of Derna. The defenders appeared to be fleeing everywhere, now that the fort was in Marine hands.

Fort Enterprise, Eaton had named it.

Nal's thoughts and personality appeared to be emerging in control of the scenario, however, as Sergeant Derek faded into the background. He felt as though he was seeing the battle, the entire campaign, from an omniscient viewpoint. He was Sergeant Derek, and the date was April 26, 1805. But he was also someone else. . . .

Derek tried to focus. He was . . . he was . . .

He was Master Sergeant Nal il-En Shru-dech, a *dumu-gir* of Enduru, the world called Ishtar.

He was an Associative Marine, proud of his line, of his heritage. . . .

But he could see the Battle for Derna for what it was. Eaton and his tiny command had held off a Muslim counterattack. For a month they'd remained at Derna, with Eaton fretting over the delay.

And then a message from the American naval squadron's

commander had arrived on June 1, announcing that peace negotiations had begun in Tripoli. Back in the United States, President Jefferson—perhaps unaware of the success of the tiny American expeditionary force in North Africa—had agreed to pay the ransom for the *Philadelphia*'s officers and crew.

The entire march across five hundred miles of desert, the wild battle at the eastern approaches to the city, the deaths of poor Steward and Whitten—Steward had died of his wounds two days after the battle, though the other wounded Marines had survived—all of it had been for nothing. The sudden shift in American foreign policy had been a particularly vicious blow for Hamet, who'd trusted Eaton's promises that he would rule Tripoli in his brother's stead.

Eaton died in 1811, in poverty and obscurity. In that same year, Presley O'Bannon was presented with a ceremonial sword for his services by the state of Virginia—a curved scimitar identical to one Hamet had given him. His name etched into the blade was misspelled: *Priestly* N. O'Bannon.

In all, a tawdry ending to a glorious page in the history of the Marine Corps. . . .

No! Nal's fist clenched, and he struggled to push the thought, the emotion, aside. It had *not* been for nothing, had not been tawdry.

Derna had been as meaningful, as *powerful* a symbol as the liberation of Ishtar.

But he was left shaken, as doubt clawed at the edges of his consciousness.

Marine Ops Center
Marine Transport Major Samuel Nicholas
0850 hours, GMT

Garroway fell once more into the illusion, of men struggling across the barricades erected atop an ancient stone wall in the darkness. He could see fires scattered across the city to

the south, hear the shouts and screams of the Boxers, hear
the polyglot battle cries of the legation defenders. The last
volley of fire from the charging Marines had killed at least
sixty of the Chinese, and swept them back from the barricades.

Captain Myers lay on the parapet, clutching his wounded
leg. The Boxer who'd speared him lay sprawled nearby, dead.
Some of the Russian and German defenders were picking up
Chinese bodies and unceremoniously dumping them over the
south side of the wall into the city below.

Curiously, though, Garroway no longer felt as though he
was Captain Myers. The wall, the city, the armed men moving along the Tartar Wall parapet, all had taken on a kind of
mental distance, with Garroway as the observer, watching
events happening to someone else.

At the same time, he was aware of repeated, pulsing shudders passing through the simulation. It took him a few moments to realize that he was somehow sensing the volleys of
high-energy lasers and particle beams, of near-*c* kinetic
warheads and the detonation of antimatter missiles against
the Xul worldlet.

The planet was badly damaged, and the alien electronic
network was faltering. For a moment, Garroway was back
on board the *Nicholas,* the QCC link slipping.

And then a new stream of simulation images and sensations were coursing through his mind.

He was climbing a mountain.

His name was Sergeant Michael Strank, USMC, and he
was trudging up the steep slope of the volcano rising from
the south end of the tiny, pork-chop-shaped island. Below
him, the American fleet stretched away to the horizon, hundreds of ships, many still pounding the island with their big
guns, as aircraft swept through the skies overhead.

The name of the island was Iwo Jima, and it was February
23, 1945.

On the beaches immediately below the base of Suribachi,
landing craft continued to run in up to the beach, and Marines

by the thousands moved about on the black sand. Suribachi, five hundred forty-six feet high, loomed over the tiny island, dominating it.

The Japanese had riddled the mount with tunnels, turning it into a fortress. The island was a part of the Tokyo Prefecture—the mayor of Tokyo was mayor of Iwo Jima— which meant this was the first speck of land in the Americans' long island-hopping strategy that was actually a part of the Japanese homeland, not a foreign possession, not a conquest. The Japanese commander on the island, Lieutenant General Tadamichi Kuribayashi, had decided against trying to stop the Americans at the beaches, but to turn the entire island into an interlocking network of strong, mutually supporting positions for an in-depth defense. Kuribayashi was convinced that Japan could not possibly win the war, but if he could make the invasion of Iwo costly enough, perhaps the Americans could be discouraged from attempting an actual invasion of the home islands.

So far, the strategy had been working well. The first of some thirty thousand Marines to wade ashore on the morning of February 19 had been greeted by an eerie and unnerving silence. As patrols began fanning out into the island's interior, however, they came under devastating fire from hidden gun positions, and naval artillery pieces hidden behind massive steel doors in the sides of Mount Suribachi began hammering the beaches below.

For four days, now, the Marines had been fighting this elusive and dug-in enemy, taking fearful casualties in the process. Even now, the mountain couldn't be called secure. Pillboxes and gun emplacements along the slopes had an annoying habit of coming alive again moments after they'd been cleaned out by grenades, high explosives, and flamethrowers, as enemy reinforcements came in through the tunnels.

Strank's squad in Easy Company, Second Battalion, Twenty-eighth Marines, Fifth Marine Division, had been laying telephone wire up Mount Suribachi when they'd been joined by PFC Rene Gagnon, a Marine runner charged with carrying a flag to the mountain's summit. An hour and a half earlier, a patrol had reached the top of Suribachi and raised a 54"×28" flag, but the banner was too small to be seen easily from the beaches far below. Down on the beach, Colonel Chandler Johnson, the Battalion Commander, had handed a larger flag to Gagnon and told him to take it up the mountain.

The squad of Marines reached the top of Suribachi at around noon—Strank, Corporal Harlon H. Block, PFC Franklin R. Sousley, PFC Ira H. Hayes, and PFC Gagnon. A number of Marines were already at the top, the first flag fluttering in the stiff, offshore breeze. Lieutenant Harold Schrier met them as they approached.

"Whatcha got there, son?"

Strank took the flag from Gagnon.

"Sir, Colonel Johnson wants this big flag run up high so every son of a bitch on this whole cruddy island can see it," Strank replied.

Johnson chuckled. "You'd better do it, then."

"Aye, aye, sir."

The Marines found a length of water pipe and jury-rigged it into a flagpole. A Navy hospital corpsman, Pharmacist's Mate 2nd class John Bradley, joined the five Marines, helped them brace it into the earth with stones and raise it upright. This flag was much larger, measuring 96"×56", easily visible from most of the island.

Thirty yards away, a Marine with a motion picture camera captured the whole event on film. Next to him, a war correspondent was stacking up rocks to provide a better vantage point for pictures of the beach. Catching the movement out of the corner of his eye, the man whirled, scooped up his camera, and snapped off a single shot.

And the raising of the *second* flag on Suribachi entered the Marine Corps legend.

Strank . . . no, *Garroway*. Garroway *knew* that simulation. It was one of the training and indoctrination sims routinely downloaded to Marine recruits. Though he'd never experienced it himself, he was willing to bet that the Captain Myers scenario, during the Boxer Rebellion of 1900, was a standard Corps training sim as well.

Again, the reality of the simulation seemed to waver for a moment, and Garroway found himself fully back in charge. For a moment, he was helping the others secure the flagpole upright by attaching lengths of white line and tying them off. But the reality within his mind was wavering, *thinning*, and he found himself wavering between the Starwraith strikepod and the link couch back in *Nicholas'* Ops Center.

The *Nicholas* was again in space outside of the Great Annihilator, which hung in the dome-projection overhead like a vast, angry blue eye. Garroway tried to sit up, tried to speak, as several staff officers hurried over.

Then he was back on Iwo Jima, but with a kind of God's-eye overview of the entire battle. Emotion poured through the link, paralyzing in its intensity. He *knew* what would happen, what *did* happen. Six days after the flag-raising, Michael Strank would be killed . . . probably by friendly fire from an American destroyer offshore. Two of the other Marines, Block and Sousley, both were killed on Iwo as well, and the corpsman, Bradley, was wounded.

And he felt the controversy over the invasion of Iwo itself as well . . . a kind of depressing atmosphere or weight settling across his thoughts. Theoretically, and according to Marine Corps legend, Iwo had been targeted to provide emergency landing facilities for B-29 bombers flying to and from Japan from their base in the Marianas Islands, and, in fact, over 2,200 B-29s touched down on the island during the course of the rest of the war. The first, *Dyna Mite*, had made an emergency landing at one of Iwo's landing strips on March 4, three weeks before the island was finally declared secure.

But there'd always been a question concerning the need to capture the island at all. The battle had lasted from February 19 to March 26. A total of 70,000 Marines fought for the island, and suffered almost 28,000 casualties—40 percent—and including 6,825 dead, almost one man in ten. Most of those B-29s landing on Iwo had done so for minor technical checks, for training, or for refueling, and there were other, less fanatically defended islands in the region that could have served the purpose just as well. The original invasion plan had been put together because the Army Air Force wanted to stage fighter escort missions off of Iwo to protect the bombers . . . but such operations proved to be both impractical and unnecessary, and only one escort mission was flown off the island before the end of the war.

All those dead and wounded . . . for *nothing* . . .

And in that instant Garroway saw what the Xul were doing.

It was a deliberate and deadly attack, and he needed to block it *now*.

21

Marine Ops Center
Marine Transport Major Samuel Nicholas
0855 hours, GMT

"It's a kind of an attack," Garroway told Ranser and the others. He was again fully awake, mentally back in the Ops Center. The dome overhead looked out into the tormented nebulae of the Galactic Core, with the Great Annihilator a massive blue spiral of gas and dust burning with eerie light.

Around him were the other eleven members of 3MarDiv's command constellation, as well as Admiral Ranser and his staff, and Rame, representing, as always, the Conclave. At least Garroway *thought* it was Rame. Other Conclave delegates had been coming in and out of Rame's body lately like restless ghosts.

"An attack?" Carter, his Exec, asked. "What do you mean? What are they attacking?"

"It's . . . it's a way of attacking our morale," Garroway replied. "A way to attack our core values as Marines. Somehow they're tapped in to our training sims, and they're feeding them back to us, but subtly altered."

"Altered how?" Admiral Ranser wanted to know.

"I was at Suribachi," Garroway told him. "For a Marine of my generation, that was the holy of holies, the single defining image for the entire Corps. They were calling into question the reason for what happened, for the flag-raising on Suribachi."

"Never heard of it, General," Rame said. "An ancient battle?"

"A mountain on an island on Earth. The United States Marines stormed that island over two thousand years ago, and raised a flag at the summit. A photograph, a kind of visual image recorded at the time, became *the* icon of the old Marine Corps." He transmitted the image over the command constellation link so the others in the ops Center could see: the red, white, and blue flag fluttering proudly from a length of pipe, pushed up to a forty-five degree angle by six straining men. "Believe me," he went on. "Marines do *not* like to be told that what happened there was a mistake, or that the battle was fought for no good reason."

"We're getting all these reports from other Marines in the battle," Fremantle said. "You think the Xul are doctoring those feeds, trying to destroy morale?"

"If *my* experience is anything to go by, that's exactly what they're doing."

"What, are they lying about that stuff?" Rame asked, puzzled.

"No, it's not lying, quite. But they certainly emphasized the negative aspects of the histories. It's all in how you tell the story."

Colonel Fremantle nodded. "I don't know about you folks in the forty-first century," she said, "but there used to be a lot of controversy back in our day over news sims. The AIs who put together compilations of data feeds on the daily news had to select which news items to transmit, and how much time and attention to allot to each. Even if you're trying to be completely open and balanced in your presentation, you can slant things pretty hard one way or another just by the focus of your story. That's been a basic problem of news feeds since before the Age of Electronics. I think maybe the Xul are doing that here."

"Exactly," Garroway said.

"Any idea how they're doing it?" Captain Yaren, a member of Ranser's staff, asked.

"I'm not sure," Garroway replied. "But we've been receiving those reports of coded signals riding gravity waves out of black holes and stargates. They might have accessed our Net that way. How about it, Socrates?"

"Possible," the archAIngel replied. The artificial intelligence sounded almost subdued. *"Sentient electronic systems, I remind you, would have no way of ascertaining if they'd been corrupted, however. My judgment may not be trustworthy."*

"Which is why we pulled you guys off-line on the combat net," Garroway said. "Nothing personal, but you *wouldn't* know."

"We're no different than they are," Jordan said. "If our Marines were being . . . tampered with, they wouldn't know it. Not while they were actually inside the sim."

"Agreed. So we need to take them off-line, too."

"Wait," Carter said. "Sir, what do you mean?"

"I mean we need to pull the plugs on their implants. *All* of them."

"General!" Ranser sounded shocked. "You can't do that!"

"That's insane!" Rame put in.

"You could kill them!" Captain Yaren said.

"It won't kill us," Garroway replied.

Major Davenport, 3MarDiv's CC technical expert, shook his head. "No, it won't *kill* us," he said. "But it sure as hell will scare the shit out of us. . . ."

"All of us old-time Marines trained without implants," Garroway told them. "Did you know that? In case we found ourselves fighting somewhere without a local Net, or if our local servers went down. First law of combat: if something *can* go wrong it will, and probably in the worst possible way. So we practice getting along without." He grinned at a memory. "We all woke up out of cybe-hibe without the things, too. We managed okay. Wasn't pleasant, but we managed."

"But all those Marines down there, Gar," Ranser said,

shaking his head, "they reply on their implants for . . . for everything. Linking with their strikepods and weapons! Communications. Navigation. Tactical feeds. Sensory data. *Everything!*"

"I know," Garroway said, his voice grim. "And I wish to hell I could see some other way. But I don't."

"I don't see how we can do that," Carter said. "I mean, we could lose people who are in the middle of a firefight. Or wounded Marines, who are on life support over the Net."

Garroway nodded. Adri Carter cared a lot about the division's individual Marines, which was what made her such a good Exec.

"I don't like it any more than you do, Colonel," he told her. "Maybe we can have them switch off voluntarily, rather than kill the entire Net from here."

"You're talking about disabling every implant in your division?" Rame said, incredulous.

"Yes." He thought about it. "We might get by with having just the Marines on-planet pull the plug. I haven't heard of any reports of simulations or illusions in the Fleet, have you?"

"None, General," Fremantle told him. "The effect so far has been limited to personnel on or within the Xul world."

"I can't even imagine living without my implant," Ranser said, "much less trying to fight a battle." His eyes narrowed and he looked at Garroway with critical appraisal. "Wait a second. Do you need psych support?"

Garroway gave a thin smile. "You think the Xul got to me? Go ahead and have the psychs check me out. But we *are* going to do this. . . ."

Blue Seven
Objective Reality
0855 hours, GMT

Garwe was fully back in reality, now, triggering burst after burst into what appeared to be a living, moving wall of machines. Xul instrumentalities within their base infra-structures had the disconcerting property of shape-shifting. Their combat machines, most of them, were roughly human-sized and more or less fixed in their shape, save for the tentacles that grew and dissolved from their surfaces. The interior walls of their larger facilities, bases and ships, how-ever, appeared to consist of millions of insect-sized devices that joined with one another in constantly shifting three-dimensional patterns. The digital intelligences behind them seemed to move through the shifting surfaces and reshape them at will, creating weapons, sensors, electronic systems, and other less identifiable components at will.

At least the components were macro in scale, and not nanotechnic. Though Xul employed nanotechnology, they apparently used it on a limited scale, preferring the larger, visible units in their massive construction projects.

Which meant that if you vaporized enough of the little buggers, you could eventually wear them down to the point where their electronic ghosts fled, which meant they were no longer *alive*.

Garwe continued to burn through the shifting mass of black robotic insects, but he was still wrestling with the after-effects of his unexpected visit to Earth's eighteenth century. Had he really been there, or had it been entirely a simulation, an illusion? And what had caused it?

He suspected the Xul had had a tentacle in it; there was no other reasonable explanation, though the strange environ-ment of the Quantum Sea could have been a factor. Dreams here, they said, could become *real*. . . .

Space seemed to twist and shimmer to his right, and an instant later Blue Twelve, Lieutenant Kadellan Wahrst, was *there*, firing her particle weapon into the living wall.

"Where the hell were you, Kaddy?" he yelled.

"I'm . . . not sure. Ancient Earth . . . 1918, I think. God . . . the *futility*. . . ."

"It doesn't matter," he told her. "We're *here*. We're *now*. Keep firing!"

The wall was beginning to dissolve, as thousands of black constructs the size of Garwe's thumb began dropping gently to the deck. The Xul worldlet's gravitational field was low—less than a twentieth of a G—and things fell with agonizing slowness.

The digital spirits animating this chamber appeared to be fleeing.

Captain Xander flicked into existence. "Jesus!" she said. "What the hell is going on?"

"Some kind of Xul effect, Captain," Garwe told her. "I think they're tapping into our simulation records. Training sims, but . . . they kind of take over, don't they?"

"Yeah. I was at Chapultepec."

"What's that?" Wahrst wanted to know.

"A fortress outside of Mexico City. First Mexican-American War, 1847. 'From the Halls of Montezuma,' remember?"

Every Marine, Globe and Anchor alike, knew the stanzas of the Marine Corps Hymn. "From the Halls of Montezuma, to the shores of Tripoli." The first was a reference to forty U.S. Marines who'd stormed Chapultepec along with over two hundred other hand-picked American soldiers. The second remembered Captain O'Bannon and his seven Marines at Derna.

"It wasn't like I thought from the general histories," Xander added. She sounded shaken. "There were *kids* there. Some of the enemy soldiers were *kids*. . . ."

Garwe picked up some flashing images of the battle over a side comm band from Xander's implant, along with statistical data as her AI tried to assimilate the data. Chapultepec had been held by a few hundred Mexican soldiers—reports varied from 400 to 832 in all. Once the initial storming party had taken the walls, columns of American infantry, thousands of men, had poured over and down into the fortress, moving through to seize the Belén and St. Cosmé Gates leading into Mexico City itself. Most of the Mexican soldiers had retreated, but six cadets from the Mexican

Military Academy on Chapultepec Hill refused the order to retreat and fought to the last man. The last one alive, Juan Escutia, had wrapped himself in a Mexican flag and hurled himself from the castle parapet to keep the flag out of foreign hands. Some of the cadets were as young as thirteen.

For centuries they were remembered as *Los Niños Héroes,* the heroic children.

"We killed them," Xander said. "We killed them *all.* . . ."

"Not all," Garwe reminded her. "The ones who chose to stay behind and fight. They stood up against overwhelming odds and they died. That's what war is all about, remember?"

"I . . . remember." Xander joined the others as they continued burning out the nest of Xul machines. But she moved slowly, almost hesitantly, and Garwe wondered if she was all right.

HQ Section, Second Battalion, Ninth Marines
Within Objective Reality
0857 hours, GMT

Nal led a platoon-strength formation deeper into the Xul world. Within the weak gravitational field of the tiny planet, terms like *down* and *up* were very nearly arbitrary, but there was pull enough to create a sensation of depth, a yawning cavern opening below the Marines as they descended the uneven walls.

They'd followed a descending passageway for several kilometers, fighting off several successive waves of Xul combat machines. At last, they'd emerged within a vast, open space, a kind of funnel extending far above their heads, and dropping at least five kilometers into the depths.

Far beneath them, a massive Xul instrumentality was coming together, swiftly growing as billions of insect-sized machines flew in from every direction or oozed straight out of the walls, melding together into a squat, vaguely spherical mass unsuccessfully shrouding a dazzling inner light.

Nal didn't know what the thing was, but at a kilometer across, as big as many Xul warships, it spelled trouble.

"Are you getting this, sir?" he called. "Sir! Captain Corcoran!"

There was no reply, and his tacsit readout showed no sign of the company commander.

"Lieutenant Haskins!" Again, no response. Damn it, where were they?

He still couldn't quite credit the idea that when individual Marines began engaging in those training sims, they actually vanished. That seemed to violate all the laws of physics—the rational and intuitive ones, anyway.

But there was no denying that Marines were popping in and out of existence like virtual particles in the Quantum Sea. Master Sergeant Nal il-En Shru-dech was, at least for the moment, in command of the company.

"*Nicholas*!" he called. "This is Company H of the 2/9! We have a target for you!"

Marine Ops Center
Marine Transport Major Samuel Nicholas
0858 hours, GMT

"We have a class-1 priority QCC message coming through, General," Major Tomas Allendes reported. "A master sergeant on command of a company. Requesting a spacial delivery. . . ."

Companies normally were commanded by captains, sometimes by first lieutenants, but in combat the unexpected, the disastrous, and the confusion were the rule. Senior enlisted personnel did the real work of running small units in any case, and any officer worth his insignia listened to his NCOs and trusted their judgment.

"Spacial delivery" was the outrageous pun some joker in the ops planning constellation had invented as the designation for d-teleported nuclear and antimatter weapons. When the *Nicholas* was inside Quantum Space and within 100,000 kilometers or so of the Xul world, she could use dimensional teleportation to toss high-yield weapons through to key target areas inside the objective.

The technique had been practiced in sim, but had never been attempted in the real world. To make it work, a spotter team had to be inside the target taking *precise* measurements of position and local gravitational metrics so that the teleport crews on the *Nicholas* could lock in on the target zone.

It should work in theory, if *Nicholas* could get in close enough, and if the spotter team could come up with accurate positional numbers. The tricky part was getting the spotters out before the warhead blew . . . and being careful that proximity to other Marine elements within the objective didn't become friendly fire statistics.

"Patch him through."

"Aye, aye, General."

A moment later, Garroway saw a grainy image filtering up through his implant. It was tough to decide exactly what it was he was looking at. The image appeared to be originating from a helmet camera on a Marine clinging to the side of a black, metallic cliff. Other Marines in Hellfire armor were nearby, some coming down the walls, some crouched on a narrow ledge.

"*Nicholas!*" a voice called. "We need a fire mission! Priority triple-zero!"

"This is General Garroway." He glanced at the transmission ID. Master Sergeant Nal il-En Shru-dech, HQ element, H Company, 2/9. The man had a good record. A good Marine. "What's the target?"

The voice hesitated, surprised, perhaps, at a connection with the senior-ranking Marine in the operation.

"Uh . . . yessir! I don't know exactly what the damned thing is, but it's big! And I think it's important!"

"Show us."

The helmet-cam view wavered and swung as the Marine let go of the wall and slowly drifted down to the ledge. "I think . . . I think I can give you a view, here . . ."

It looked, Garroway thought, like a black sun.

No . . . more like an ordinary, luminous sun, but one shrouded inside of black armor, with openings here and there that let the radiance shine through.

"We've got remotes going down, General," Nal's voice said. "Should have a better view in a minute. But I'm reading that thing at a kilometer-plus across, and scans show power readings off the scale. I think it may be their power core, sir! A quantum power tap!"

Garroway considered this. The Xul possessed QPT technology, of course. In fact, Humankind had developed its own QPT technologies by studying captured Xul ships like the Europan Singer. A power tap pulled energy from the Quantum Sea by using a small, artificially generated black hole; what was unusual about this set-up was having the black hole technically inside *another* black hole—the Great Annihilator. Simply having the tap physically located inside the Quantum Sea instead of safely within the normal realm of four-D spacetime was enough to give a physicist nightmares.

But he remembered learning how humans had used a quantum converter to turn a 150-kilometer moon of Eris into a microstar bright enough to heat a world from near zero-absolute to warm enough for liquid oceans. This technology might be similar, a source of staggering power.

That black shell surrounding the central furnace, he thought, was a lot like the Dyson shell the Xul had built around the supermassive black hole at the galaxy's center in order to control it and generate power, though on a far smaller scale.

Yeah, it made sense. Nal's unit might have stumbled upon the Xul power generator, or one of them. Take it out and the Associative strike force would do a lot of damage to the enemy.

"Okay, Master Sergeant," he said. "You've convinced me. Do you have the targeting data?"

"Yes, sir. It should be coming through now!"

"Then get your ass out of there, Master Sergeant. Unless you want to see Hell up close and personal!"

"Aye, *aye*, sir!"

Garroway looked at the circle of men and women with him in the Ops Center. The harsh blue glow of the Great Annihilator shone down from the overhead dome, illuminating them in cold, electric light.

"You all get that transmission?"

"Yes, General," Ranser said. "I've relayed the request through to *Nicholas'* weapons center."

"There may be a problem here, sir," Captain Kyrsti Xin said. She was Admiral Ranser's senior tech specialist.

"What is it?"

"What, exactly, is going to happen if we blow that construct up?"

"We'll cripple the Xul base," Allendes told her.

"Maybe. But what if the detonation runs out of control?"

"You mean like the Galactic Core Detonation?" Garroway asked.

"Something like that. The blast could engulf the entire world, maybe take on an extra kick if there are other power centers down there. But the real question is . . . if it explodes, *what happens to Reality?*"

"I don't think we quite follow, Captain," Rame said.

"Look, the whole Quantum Sea is the base state for what we think of as Reality, right?" Xin told them. "Atoms, electrons, photons, the fundamental building blocks for all matter and energy are essentially standing waves within the flux of virtual particles within the Quantum Sea. What happens when we trigger something that might easily be as big as a supernova down there? Will it wipe out all of those waves? Or a significant number of them? Damn it, we could wipe out our whole Galaxy—stars, planets, civilizations, *us*—in an instant!

"How long will it take you to set up a sim to estimate our chances?" Garroway asked.

"I'm not sure. Thirty minutes to an hour, maybe. . . ."

"Jordan?" Garroway caught the eye of his constellation's computer expert. "Link with her and help."

"Aye, aye, sir."

"General," Rame said, "if there is even a tiny chance that this action would erase the Reality of a significant portion of the Galaxy, perhaps we—"

"I know," Garroway said, cutting the Conclave delegate off. "And I don't like it either. But we don't have much of a choice, do we?"

"There's *always* a choice," Rame told him.

"I'm not sure there is this time. What if what the Xul are trying to do down there in the first place is create some kind of doomsday device?"

"Interesting thought," Ranser said.

Rame looked puzzled. "You mean they could use it as a kind of super-bomb, to wipe out Reality?"

"Exactly. We know that the flux of virtual particles within the reality base-state represents a *staggering* amount of energetic potential. Enough potential energy within a volume a few centimeters across, the physicists say, to destroy a galaxy. *Our* Galaxy."

"And that Dyson object they're building down there could be the trigger," Ranser said. "My God."

"If we don't find a way to disarm or safely detonate that device, the Xul may do it themselves. Deliberately."

" 'To save the village we had to destroy it,' " Ranser said, quoting an ancient military adage. "Shit. I don't think I want to write up the after-action report on *this* one."

Blue Seven
Objective Reality
0903 hours, GMT

The wall collapsed, the individual machine-elements dissolving as they came apart in the intense heat. Garwe rose
from cover and moved forward. "Let's go, Marines!"

Captain Xander, Lieutenant Wahrst, and several others
followed across the broken, metallic floor of the cavern.

And then Garwe was someplace else.

No, not Garwe. *Garroway.* He was Major Mark Allan
Garroway, and he was on Mars, back in the Solar System.
Red-ocher desert, broken rock and sand dunes, stretched off
to every horizon beneath a pale, pink-tinted sky that darkened to deepest ultramarine at the zenith.

Crouching in a gulley behind the sheltering crest of a sand
dune with a number of other Marines, Garroway held his
M-29 ATAR assault rifle above his head, using the weapon's
optics to transmit a camera image to his helmet's HUD without exposing his head. The next dune in line was 185.4 meters distant, according to the weapon's range finder. He could
make out black spots along the crest of the dune opposite that
might be the helmeted heads of the enemy. Beyond them
were the microwave tower, several habs, the grounded shuttle
Ramblin' Wreck, and the pale blue of the UN flag hanging
listless in the near-vacuum that was the Martian atmosphere.

High-velocity rounds slashed silently into the sand, throwing up gouts of dust.

The year was 2040, during the UN War, and Garroway was
in charge of the small Martian Marine Expeditionary Force,
the MMEF. The enemy troops over there, crouched in a trench
just behind the top of the dune, were UN troops—French,
most of them—and they'd captured the American base at
Cydonia.

"They're dug in and they're waiting for us," Garroway said.
He pulled his assault rifle back down. "We can't take them
frontally."

"Hey, you think the beer-bombing idea's gonna work, Major, sir?" Corporal Slidell was lying on his stomach, just beyond Lieutenant King.

"It damned well better, Slider," Garroway said. "If it doesn't, we're in a hell of a fix . . . and we'll have thrown away the only beer within a hundred million miles."

"You can say that again," Slider replied. "Sir." His tone stopped just short of insolence. The beer Garroway was referring to had been smuggled up from Earth by Slider Slidell, and Garroway had taken charge of the contraband at Slidell's disciplinary hearing.

Now the beer was being put to a use somewhat different from that which its brewers had intended.

Lieutenant King raised his rifle for a look. "Hey, Major!" he called. "Have a peek!"

Garroway lifted his rifle once more, careful not to expose too much of his arms to French fire. The Martian environment was a deadly arena for combat. One nick from a bullet anywhere on your pressure suit meant rapid and explosive decompression.

There it was, silhouetted against the sky just beyond the enemy lines—a spindly-legged craft balanced atop pale plasma flame, one of the point-to-point Martian suborbital shuttle craft affectionately known as lobbers. As he watched, a black speck fell from the open cargo hatch, tumbling as it slowly fell, spilling dozens of smaller objects in a broad footprint across the surface below.

The reaction was immediate and animated. Men in combat armor with blue-painted helmets were leaping from their trench behind the far dune, some slapping at themselves, some shooting their rifles at the lobber overhead, most running as fast as their cumbersome suits would allow, scattering across the desert.

"You know," King said, "I think we've just added a new secret weapon to the Corps' inventory. Beer bombs!"

"Yeah," Slidell said. "*My* beer! . . ."

"Sacrificed in a good cause, Slider," Garroway told him.

"We were not issued ordnance sufficient to the needs of this mission. We therefore improvise, adapt, and overcome!"

"Yeah, I guess. Look at them blue-tops run!"

Silent gunfire volleyed from the Marine line, targeting the French troops who were shooting at the lobber. Several toppled over, falling back into their trench. More of them dropped their rifles and began running.

"Let's go, Marines!" Garroway called, struggling to rise in the yielding sand. A bullet struck his combat armor with a sharp *spang* audible within the suit. He turned, targeted the French soldier who'd fired, and took him down with a short burst.

French soldiers still in their trenches opened up on the charging Marines. Marchewka was hit and flung back down the back slope of the ridge. Then Hayes took a round through his visor, his helmet exploding in a burst of pink and white vapor.

But another case of contraband beer came spilling across the French trench line, and the remaining UN troops suddenly broke and fled.

Marines were known for their use of close-air support in combat, but this was the first time that the weapon had been aluminum cans filled with beer. The thin containers were under considerable pressure in the almost nonexistent Martian atmosphere, and punctured very easily. When they ruptured, the beer exploded in a sticky, golden cloud that covered everything it landed on, freezing almost instantaneously.

French soldiers stood in the open, desperately trying to clean visors suddenly iced over and opaque. Everywhere the stuff landed and froze, it *steamed*, the ice sublimating into near-vacuum. The UN troops had no idea what was hitting them, and could only imagine that it was some sort of chemical attack, an acid, perhaps, eating away at their combat armor.

By the time they figured out what was really happening, the U.S. Marines were there, disarming them and herding them into small groups of POWs. The base fell swiftly to the Marine assault.

Nearby, at the base, several Marines knocked down the mast bearing the blue UN flag, and raised an American flag attached to a five-meter length of pipe.

As Garroway stood to attention and saluted the flag, Garwe's personality began reasserting itself. The suddenness and the clarity of the sim had caught him completely by surprise.

That had been Mark *Garroway*? His Marine ancestor two thousand years back in the past?

"Sands of Mars Garroway," they'd called him, and he'd passed into Corps legend with Samuel Nicholas and Dan Daly and Smedley Butler and Lewis "Chesty" Puller and so many others. And he'd been there, been *him*. It didn't seem possible.

He felt, too, a strong and negative emotional load linked somehow with the simulation imagery. The fighting on Mars had been to secure certain artifact fields and archeological digs on the planet—the very beginning of xenoarcheology. Shortly after the first manned landings on the Red Planet, the first Builder artifacts had been discovered, evidence that extraterrestrials had colonized Mars and performed their equivalent of terraforming, transforming Mars, briefly, into a warm, wet world half a million years ago.

The xenoarcheologists had also discovered the mummified remains of beings from Earth—not modern humans, but members of the species now known as *Homo erectus*, still wearing uniforms of some sort. Evidently, they'd been trained by the aliens, and some had been transported to Mars as a labor force.

Later, scientists had proven that the aliens had tampered with the *Homo erectus* genome, creating the species later called *Homo sapiens*.

Modern man. Human roots extended farther back in time, and farther out into the universe, than had been imagined.

Humans had been created as a slave species. Not long after,

the Xul had destroyed the Builders, and wiped out the tiny and fragile terraform colony on Mars. A small colony of *Homo sapiens* still on Earth, though, had been overlooked.

And their distant, distant descendents had eventually returned to the frozen desert that was Mars and found those remains. The Americans had tried to grab the fragments of advanced technology still hidden beneath the sand . . . and the attempt had triggered the UN War.

Children, squabbling over advanced technology they couldn't possibly understand, determined only to keep any possible benefits away from anyone else. . . .

"That's *not* the way it happened!" Garwe shouted, staring up at the cavern's ceiling high above his head. "They were trying to take it away from us! We shared, with the whole planet, later! *What happened on Mars made us what we are today!*"

"Gar?" Xander said. "Are you okay?"

"Uh, yeah. Sorry, sir. Was I out long?"

"A few seconds."

"Was that all? It felt like half an hour!"

"Downloads register as memories," Warhst reminded him. "You know, a typical dream you have at night only lasts a few seconds, but it *seems* much longer. I think this is like that."

"There's also the fact that time is running slower in here than . . . outside," Xander said. "You could slip out for a quick drink, spend half an hour chatting, and be back a few seconds after you'd left. Where were you, anyway?"

"Mars," he said. "Cydonia. Get this. I was Sands of Mars Garroway!"

"Don't let it go to your head."

Garwe looked around. They were not under fire at the moment, and seemed to have a long stretch of cavern to themselves. Ahead, the tunnel seemed to open up into a pit leading down. His tac display showed other Marines ahead and below them . . . members of the 2/9.

"We're going to join up with them," Xander said. "They're pulling up out of that pit, and we're going to help."

The ragged column of Marine Starwraith strikepods—nine of them left, now—drifted across the black surface toward the pit.

HQ Section, Second Battalion, Ninth Marines
Within Objective Reality
0904 hours, GMT

"You want us to *what*?" Nal was thunderstruck. The bastards couldn't mean it!

"We want you to cut your implant feeds, take your implants off-line," the voice of Colonel Jordan said with a maddening calm that could not possibly be real. "It's imperative that you do so."

"By the Ahannu of my fathers, are you trying to fucking *kill* us?"

It wasn't the way to talk to a colonel—especially a colonel in the division's command constellation. The old man himself was probably listening in.

"Master Sergeant, the Xul are using a psychological weapon against us. They're feeding our own training sims back at us, but with emotional baggage attached that may be designed to impair the division's combat efficiency. The only way to prevent that is to disconnect from the Net. And *that* means unplugging your implants. *Now*."

"How are we going to coordinate the special delivery with you? QCC requires a Net link to operate."

"By radio."

"This deep underground? It won't penetrate."

"Then get your ass and your Marines up to the surface, Master Sergeant!"

"With respect, *sir.* We won't be able to navigate. *Sir!*"

"We're tracking another group of Marines to the top of that tunnel you're in. They have a navigational lock on the way they came in. You'll hook up with them and follow them out."

"Sir, this won't—"

"Do not argue with me, Master Sergeant! Get the hell out of there any damned way you can! The quicker the better! But *kill* those implants! Ops Center out!"

Nal was stunned. He remembered going without an implant for several weeks during boot camp, about 875 or so years ago. And, of course, on Ishtar, he'd not even had an implant until he was nearly seventeen standard. Enduri kids didn't. But he'd come to rely on the thing in the twenty-three waking years he'd experienced since boot camp, and he didn't like the idea of going without again. It had been bad enough when he'd woken up from cybe-hibe on that station orbiting Eris, and found his regulation implant gone. Those hours before the new one had grown into place had been damned miserable.

And that had been in the security of an Associative orbital, not in the middle of a Xul world twelve hundred kilometers across and packed with Xul hardware and weapons. This was *not* going to be pretty.

"Okay, Marines," he said. The order had gone out over the Net to every Marine in the division. "You heard the man! Disable the implants."

"Fuck *no*, Master Sergeant!" Garcia said.

"That's suicide, man!" Corporal Donovan said. "Suicide is against regulations!"

"How can we trust *them*?" Sergeant Cori Ryack put in.

"*Don't* give me any of your lip, people!" Nal was furiously angry. He didn't want to take it out on the Marines in his command, but the anger had a way of spilling over from the original cause to anyone and anything who happened to be in the way. "We have our orders! Disengage your implants!"

"Shit," Cori said. But he saw her link icon in his in-head display wink out.

One by one, grumbling, most of them, the other Marines thought-clicked the codes necessary to disable their implants and, one by one, their icons went dark. Nal waited until all thirty-four of the Marines with him were disconnected, monitoring them through his own link, before he thought-clicked his own implant and killed it.

It was like throwing a switch and plunging the room into darkness. There was no data feed, no QCC link, no targeting locks for his weapons, no sensor information, no AI guidance, no drone intel, no time indicator, no navigational pointers or battlespace monitors, *nothing.*

"H Company, radio check!" he rasped. His throat was suddenly dry.

"I hear you, Master Sergeant," Cori said out of the darkness. Then, realizing her ID tag no longer showed on Nal's in-head display, she added, "Sergeant Ryack, present."

"Corporal Donovan, present."

"Gunnery Sergeant Boyd, I'm here."

"Lance Corporal Zollinger, yo."

The names continued as, one after another, the men and women of the ad hoc platoon, cobbled together from H Company's HQ element and all three platoons, sounded off.

Nal felt a little better, knowing all of them were there with him in the dark.

Blue Seven
Objective Reality
0904 hours, GMT

Garwe was outraged. "What is this, some old-Marine rite of passage? It's sick!"

"Just do it, Marines," Colonel Jordan's voice said, implacable. "That's an order."

"Do what the man says," Xander told them. "We can manage outside the pods."

"Those HQ REMFs . . ." Bollan began.

"If you ask me," Maria Amendes said, "*they're* the ones who are being infiltrated!"

"Yeah, we can't trust them!" Palin said.

"*Shut up!*" Xander bellowed. "Kill the fucking implants and get out of those pods *now*!"

Starwraith strikepods were completely dependent upon the electronic link between computer and organic brain, moderated through the human implants. With the implants offline, the strikepods would be so much inert plastic, metal, and nanoceramics.

Garwe shared the suspicions of the others. Colonel Jordan was one of the old-time Globe Marines, asleep in cybe-hibe for the past 850 years. It was okay for them to talk about turning off their implants. They'd done that sort of thing in training, according to their stories, and they'd awakened without them at the end of their suspension.

The Anchor Marines had never had to play those sorts of games.

With that thought came another. *We're just as good as they are.*

Which, he realized, might or might not be true. There was only one way to find out.

Angrily, Garwe thought-clicked the code that shut down his implant. Instantly, he was plunged into pitch blackness . . . and nearly overcome by a stiflingly close, claustrophobic sensation. Working his hand up across the front of his body, he found the manual release plate and pressed it.

With a sharp hiss of escaping air, dwindling almost immediately into vacuum-wrapped silence, the Starwraith's two-meter-high body split open lengthwise, and Garwe clumsily rose from the narrow, sponge-lined space within, a space just barely large enough to accept a seated human.

The pod was lying on its side on black, metallic rock that glittered like crystal. Garwe was wearing a pressure suit, of course, with bubble helmet and a small emergency EVA pack holding a rebreather element good enough to keep him alive for several hours. The strikepod, of course, had much better life support, enough to keep him alive almost indefinitely if it found enough organic material for its nanufactories to convert into air, food, and water. In this skinsuit, he would survive for perhaps two to three hours . . . and much less if the radiation flux in the area became dangerous.

His helmet light cast a weirdly shifting pattern of illumination and shadow as he moved. Close by, other patches of moving light marked Xander, Kaddy, and the rest. Which way was the pit? *That* way, he thought. But it was impossible to be sure. He touched a sequence of pressure points on the inside of the open pod, and a meter-long section of the outer hull cracked open, unfolding to reveal a PK-3096 pulse carbine and power pack. Slinging the pack over one shoulder, he checked to be sure the carbine was operational, then set off across the crystalline ground toward the other Marines.

This, he decided, was a fantastic way to get himself killed.

Marine Ops Center
Marine Transport Major Samuel Nicholas
0932 hours, GMT

"We have a better idea of what's going on, now," Garroway told the others. "Socrates? Maybe you should present the technical stuff."

"Full technical specifications are unnecessary and would confuse the issue," the AI said. *"But we now know why Marines have been shifting in and out of the Quantum Sea . . . and possibly where they've been going. And when."*

The basic principles of quantum physics had been laid down two thousand years earlier. Among the stranger implications of the field was the idea that reality itself was some-

ow created by the observer, an implication proven time after
ime in laboratory experiments, and which eventually be-
ame the bedrock of human understanding of the universe.

Within the normal reaches of four-dimensional space-
ime, probability curves represented human perceptions of
eality, bound energy and matter to the moving present, and
reated the experience of time itself. Beneath this perceived
eality, however, was the murky realm of the Quantum Sea,
a vast matrix of interconnected possibility waves generated
within the dance of appearing and vanishing virtual parti-
les. Where possibility waves intersected, they reinforced or
anceled one another; where they were reinforced, a proba-
ility curve within normal space was the result.

The mind affected these possibility waves, a fact demon-
trated repeatedly in quantum physical experiments and
within such art forms as yoga and weiji-do.

In short, reality could be explained as a matrix of possi-
ility waves affected by consciousness; where Mind inter-
cted with wave forms, the waves collapsed and manifested
eality—matter, energy, stars, the entire realm of spacetime
xperience.

Mind, in other words, creates Reality.

The Mind, too, was now understood as a kind of time
machine, with the ability to slow or speed the perceived pas-
age of time . . . and where the perception was changed, the
eality changed as well.

Freeing the mind from the body, again through the prac-
ice of yoga or certain martial arts, or simply through the
ntense and overwhelmingly vivid data feeds of a virtual
imulation allowed a person's concept of self, his *ego*, to dis-
olve. And when the ego-self dissolved, its effect on Reality
hanged, introducing new probabilities within the objective
universe. The enlightenment described by countless religions and spiritual masters through the ages appeared to be
what happened when ego dissolved completely, if temporar-
ly, and Mind and Cosmos became One.

Buddhism had been saying that for forty-five hundred

years. Wiccans and the practitioners of various magical traditions claimed to change Reality by force of Mind, claimed that *this* was what magic truly was ... and according to Quantum Physics it was possible that they did, at least on a small scale. If the scale of magical manifestation was small, perhaps it was kept that way by the limits they themselves placed on their minds through habit, doubt, and fear.

And Marines changed Reality as well, shaped it with their dedication to duty, to honor, to their love of the Corps and Corps history.

"We believe," Socrates told them, *"that the Xul have been attempting to affect reality at two levels. First, and perhaps most obviously, they were using our own historical training simulations as a means of introducing emotionally conflicting data, hoping, perhaps, to affect the performance of our Marines in the field."*

"Won't work," Garroway said.

"Why not?" Rame asked.

"I experienced two simulations ... the Boxer Rebellion in 1900, and the Battle of Iwo Jima forty-five years later. In both cases there were emotional overtones. The Boxer Rebellion involved Western military forces coming in and overpowering a rather backward and technologically primitive people. It was rifles against spears, swords, and a few obsolete muskets. At Iwo, they were trying to convince me that the flag-raising was a political sham, that the invasion of the island itself wasn't necessary.

"But whatever the facts of historical reality, the Marine Corps has its own reality."

"You mean you people made it all up?" Ranser asked, and several of the members of his staff chuckled. Garroway's constellation remained dead-silent.

"No, Admiral. It's a matter of slant, of where the attention is focused. Of what truly *matters*. The reality of the Marine Corps is one created through twenty-two hundred years of service, with old-fashioned ideals such as honor, courage, brotherhood, duty. What we believe, what we *know* to be true is what creates the reality of the Marine Corps through all its succeeding generations. The Xul might try to shade things one way or another—I don't think they can use the sims to lie, exactly, but they *can* attach different shades of meaning that affect how we feel. What they don't seem to be picking up on is that our will, our integrity, our *belief* in ourselves as Marines, are stronger. We experience the alien emotions and shake them off, because we know the *real* story."

"Socrates?" Rame said. "You said there were two ways they were affecting reality."

"The second means is more subtle, and rooted in our understanding of Quantum Physics. We believe that they were . . . measuring, tasting the human mind, and its potential effect on meta-reality. Down within the substrate of the Quantum Sea, they could use simulations lifted from our own data banks in order to temporarily suppress the egos of some Marines by overwhelming them with image and sensation. Suppress the ego-self, and the mind is temporarily freed from the body . . . and from what we perceive as time. In doing so, they hoped to rewrite the meta-reality into something different, something of their choosing."

"Our people were being shifted back in time?" Ranser asked.

"Evidence suggests that the effect pinched off micro-universes within which their separate experiences were manifested," Socrates told him. *"They weren't literally back in history. But they were no longer present within the Quantum Sea, either. They were . . . elsewhere. But as they experience that elsewhere, it becomes stronger, more real. They might remain there, if the simulation of reality is strong enough to overcome their ego-selves."*

"That," Jordan said, "is just a little too weird to be believed."

"If you believe a thing to be true," Socrates told him, *"then it is."*

"Nonsense," Rame said. "I can believe with all my heart that all the Xul out there are gone, poof! It won't make it so!"

"If you believe a thing to be true," Socrates said, repeating himself, *"then it is."*

"There must be other factors," Garroway pointed out. "Like whether or not what we choose to believe is the *entire* body of our belief . . . or just a thin smear of happy thoughts over a planet-sized body of habitual thinking, of business-as-usual. We might limit what we're capable of just by a failure of imagination."

"I don't see that any of this gets us anywhere," Adri Carter said. "Can we blow that . . . that *thing* inside the Xul planet or not?"

"If you believe a thing to be true," Socrates said for a third time, *"then it is."*

"Meaning," Garroway said, "that we *can* drop an anti-matter warhead down its throat and limit the collateral damage out here."

"By what we *believe*?" Rame said, incredulous.

"By what we *know*," Garroway replied. "You're right. We can't just wish the Xul away . . . any more than they can wish *us* away. At least yet. That Dyson object might be designed to give their wishes some muscle. But the Xul world is floating in an incredible sea of potential energy, much more energy than we can even imagine."

"You're talking about the zero-point field," Rame said.

"Exactly. Tell them, Socrates."

"Early calculations," Socrates told them, *"made some two thousand years ago by Feynman and others, suggested that the virtual particle flux within a single cubic centimeter of seemingly empty space represents energy enough to instantly vaporize all of the oceans of Earth. Later calculations—and subsequent experimentation—demonstrated that the actuality of vacuum energy is some seventy-nine orders of magnitude larger."*

"In other words," Garroway said, "the detonation of that Xul world would be the equivalent of lighting a candle within the corona of Earth's sun. No effect."

"Yes," Rame said, "but can we be *sure*?"

"As sure as we can be."

"If you're wrong, you could end existence itself."

"And if we do nothing, the Xul will end our existence for us." Garroway looked at the Conclave representative. "How about it, Lord Rame? What's it going to be?"

"I . . . *we* need time to deliberate."

Garroway consulted his inner time sense. "We're rotating back into the Quantum Sea in another twenty-one minutes. You have that long to decide."

Sweat gleamed on the wide expanse of the H-supe's scalp. His large and golden eyes betrayed his fear. "It's not enough!"

"It *has* to be enough, Star Lord. We won't have another chance."

"I recommend we do it, Star Lord," Ranser said. "If we don't, the Xul push a button soon, and it will be as though we, the entire human race, never existed. They edit us out of Reality. Or, worse, we wake up and find we're their slaves, that we've *always* been their slaves, with no hope ever of breaking free."

"I don't think slavery's an option," Garroway said with a shrug, "The Xul don't think that way. They're more interested in eliminating any possible threat."

"If . . . if we eliminate them," Rame said, "Doesn't that make us as bad as them?"

"Good and bad don't have much to do with it, Star Lord. This is about *survival*."

Blue Seven
Objective Reality
0935 hours, GMT

Feeling almost naked and almost unarmed, Garwe hurried across the black, metallic landscape with five other Anchor Marines from his scattered squadron—Xander, Wahrst, Bollan, Amendes, and Palin.

Digital life forms like the Xul had a distinct advantage here, he thought. *They* didn't need to breathe, for one thing. . . .

They could also power up larger machines and field more powerful weapons. The pulse-carbine he carried used magnetic induction to accelerate plasma bolts—decent enough for a shoulder-fired weapon, but pathetic compared to the compact but powerful x-ray lasers his Starwraith had mounted. An unaugmented human could only carry so much, after all. Besides, an x-ray beam weapon could burn the Marine firing one almost as badly as it burned the target, one reason the Starwraiths were so heavily armored.

Why the hell had the brass ordered them to unplug? Those simulations? That had been spooky, sure, and had left him feeling not quite in control. He could understand why headquarters wanted to keep the Xul from messing with the squadron's heads. But they'd been *handling* it, okay? The pods had been popping in and out of reality, but they hadn't been getting lost, they had been coming back, and the Marines all had been coping . . . even Xander. She'd been badly shaken by her vision of Chapultepec and Los Niños, sure, but she'd pulled herself together and kept on going.

They reached the lip of the crater and peered down inside.

Without their sensors, they couldn't tell how deep the thing was, but it went down a long way. A pale, white glow seemed to emanate from somewhere in those depths.

And off to the right, Garwe saw a line of Marines in combat armor toiling up the side.

"There they are," he said, pointing.

"I see them," Xander replied. She shifted to the general combat frequency. "Marines . . . coming up the side of the crater! This is Blue Flight! Do you copy?"

"We copy," a tired voice called back. "Where are you?"

"At the top of the pit, about fifty meters above you and to your left." She stood up and waved. "Do you see me?"

"Roger that." One of the figures waved back. "On our way."

This is ridiculous, Garwe thought. With their implants,

they could have identified each other easily, without all of that arm-waving and radio traffic.

And then a blindingly hot bolt of plasma energy caught Xander squarely in her upper torso, exploding her in a puff of red vapor, the blast silent save for a sharp burst of static over Garwe's radio. Her skin-suited legs and lower body stood for a second, then toppled slowly forward in the low gravity and into the pit.

Her head, still in a black-scorched helmet, struck the ground and bounced, slowly, toward Garwe's feet.

Garwe had already spun in the direction from which the bolt had come. The wall of the pit, to the left, off beyond the climbers, was writhing, coming alive as Xul combat machines molded in against the rock began to uncurl and emerge. He brought his carbine to his shoulder and opened fire, sending bolts slamming into the alien machines. The other Marines began firing as well, Wahrst and Bollan dropping to their knees as they fired volley after volley into the enemy.

But it didn't appear that the light weapons were having much, if any, effect. A second bolt seared through the space between Garwe and Wahrst, gouging a steaming crater into the black ground. Static hissed and snapped over the Marines' comm channels as human and Xul weapons alike opened up in a crisscross-web of deadly energies.

The War Dogs were exposed and badly outnumbered and outgunned. Within another moment, though, the first of the Marines climbing the wall of the pit emerged over the lip, turning to add his fire to theirs.

Static spat, and one of the climbing Marines was hit and fell back into the pit, but slowly the firefight turned in the Marines' favor. . . .

• • •

HQ Section, Second Battalion, Ninth Marines
Within Objective Reality
0938 hours, GMT

Nal watched Corporal Donovan's body tumble slowly into the depths, bit off a curse, then grabbed the rim of the pit just above his head and dragged himself up and over. The other Marines in his tiny command clambered over the edge as well. For a few moments, they stood in a ragged semicircle at the pit's edge, pouring fire into the slowly morphing surface of the wall twenty meters away. Molten gobbets of metal sputtered and drooled from the wall, and then the enemy fire ceased entirely and the wall went dead.

"Which way?" Nal asked the Marines who'd been covering them from above.

"That way," one of them said. "I think."

"You *think*? You'd damn well better be sure!"

"Hey, we don't have our Nav systems up and running, okay? But we came through from somewhere up there."

"Good enough, Marine," Nal said. "Let's move it, though! This tunnel is going to get distinctly unhealthy in just a few minutes!"

"Aye, aye, sir," the Marine said, responding to the decisive tone of Nal's voice.

"You people in the pressure suits, get in the middle! H Company, form up around the outside! Protective perimeter! *Move! Move!*"

With the Marines of H Company surrounding the others, the unarmored Marines could take cover behind the 2/9's heavier armor.

Nal thought the others must be Anchor Marines, though he didn't ask. They were wearing lightweight pressure suits, however, rather than Hellfire armor or something heavier, and carrying popgun carbines that were scarcely better than sidearms in a firefight. With the Hellfire-armored Marines on the outside, the pressure-suited Marines stood a slightly better chance of living through the next few minutes.

Nal tried to orient himself. This might have been the tunnel he and the others with him had traversed earlier to reach the pit . . . but all of the Xul's underground works looked pretty much alike, and they might have emerged into the pit farther down inside its mouth. If these newcomers said that they'd come *this* way, it was good enough for him.

"What's the damned hurry?" one of the Anchor Marines asked. It sounded like a woman.

"Did HQ tell you what we found back there?" Nal asked.

"Nope," another Anchor Marine said. This one was male. "Just said to find you and get you out."

"Figures. Truth is, I don't know what we found . . . but it's big and it looks important. The *Nicholas* is going to try a d-port bombing run in a few minutes. We do *not* want to be anywhere close when that happens!"

"Shee-it!" the other Marine said with considerable depth of feeling. "Let's step it up, people!"

Nal noticed that one of the other Marines was carrying a pressure helmet, and that a woman's head was still encased inside. The eyes were open and staring behind the partially char-frosted visor.

"Who's that?" he asked, curious.

"Captain Xander," the Marine holding the head replied. "Our CO. She was hit just before we joined up with you."

Nal refrained from asking why they were dragging the head along. He *knew* why.

The tragedy was that without their implants, the Marines could not save the woman's personality.

Mindkeeping, the technique was called. If a Marine's brain was more or less intact, mind and memory and personality could all be recorded in the implant, allowing for a full reconstruction later . . . even if the Medical Department had to clone a whole new body. Without the implant, all they could do was clone her from some of the undamaged tissue. Captain Xander would start off her new life as a newborn baby, an exact clone of the original, but with none of the original's memories. She would be an entirely new person.

The original Captain Xander was irretrievably dead.

Carrying the head wasn't harming anything, though, at least so long as they weren't being shot at. Nal decided not to make an issue of it.

He also considered asking one of the Anchor Marines who was in command now. He had a feeling that these Anchors were part of one of the Starwraith squadrons that had been assaulting the Xul worldlet from the outside. If so, these eight people were all lieutenants—officers—while all of the Marines in Nal's group were enlisted personnel.

None of them wore visible rank tabs on their suits or armor, however. That sort of thing had always been handled through the implants, identifying a speaker or an icon on a tac display by his rank and position. There'd been no need to physically mark their suits.

If they were going by the ancient Book, those eight lieutenants should have sorted out who was senior—by graduating class, if necessary—and that one would have taken command of the entire group. Nal didn't want to take the time to do that, though, and it was simpler, and safer, for the experienced NCO to simply take charge now, and work out the niceties of rank later.

If there *was* a later.

He thought he could see a spot of light in the distance up ahead.

23

Marine Ops Center
Marine Transport Major Samuel Nicholas
0954 hours, GMT

"Translation into the Quantum Sea in one minute, thirty seconds," a technician announced.

Garroway, Ranser, and their staffs stood in the Ops Center beneath the glowing blue eye of the Great Annihilator. *Once more into the breach, dear friends,* Garroway thought, quoting an ancient text. *Once more into the breach. . . .*

"So why was this flag-raising you were participating in so important?" Rame wanted to know.

"A politician—James Forrestal, the secretary of the Navy—was on the beach on Iwo Jima that morning when the first flag was raised," Garroway told him, his voice low. It was as though he were remembering the incident first-hand. "Even though it was a smaller flag than the one they put up later, and not easily visible, it *was* seen. Marines all over the beachhead started yelling and cheering their heads off. Ships offshore began sounding horns.

"Anyway, the politician turned to the Marine general standing next to him, a guy named Holland Smith, and said, 'Holland, the raising of that flag on Suribachi means a Marine

Corps for the next five hundred years.' It became an icon of the Corps."

"That was what, two thousand years ago?"

"Something like that."

"More than the five hundred years predicted by this James Forrestal."

Garroway shrugged. "It wasn't a prediction, and the number of years is irrelevant. He was commenting on the public relations of the event, on how important it was for the Marine Corps."

"Public relations? I don't understand."

"Over the years, plenty of presidents—the leaders of that country—tried to eliminate the Marine Corps to save costs, to be efficient and end redundancy in the military services, that sort of thing. There were key battles and campaigns, though, that made the Corps so famous, so popular with the citizens of that country, that they were never able to kill it. The March at Derna. The storming of Chapultepec. The Battle of Belleau Wood. The raising of the flag on Suribachi. They're all part of who and what the Marines are."

"Maybe that's why those simulations the Xul were broadcasting didn't have much effect," Rame suggested. "They weren't telling your Marines anything they didn't already know!"

"That's possible."

"Speaking of those simulations, sir," Fremantle said, "are we *sure* it's a good idea to keep our implants on for this rotation?"

"Those transmissions were aimed at the Marines near and inside the Xul planet," Garroway said with a shrug. "I don't think anyone experienced them on the *Nicholas*, did they?"

"No data yet, General," Carter said. "No reports of it, anyway, except for you, Narayanan, and Davenport."

Major Davenport and Colonel Narayanan had been the other two members of the command constellation who'd linked into Starwraiths with Garroway earlier. Both had broken free at the same time as Garroway. Davenport had reported slipping in and out of the mind of a Marine sergeant fighting Muslim insurgents in Egypt in 2314. Narayanan had been with the Marines in Operation Heartfire, the assault on the Xul Dyson sphere at the Galactic Core in 2887.

"And we were linked through to our Starwraiths," Garroway said. "The sims seemed to switch off when we cut the link and woke up back here. I suspect we'll be okay, at least for the few minutes it'll take for pick-up and launch."

I hope, he added to himself. Things *always* went wrong in combat.

"If *you* want to switch off your implant, Colonel, I'm sure that would be fine with the rest of us," Carter told Fremantle, grinning.

"Um, no," the intelligence officer said. "I don't think that will be necessary."

"Rotation into the Quantum Sea," the Ops Center tech announced, "in five . . . in four . . . in three . . . two . . . one . . . *initiate!*"

And the *Nicholas* dropped through into the violet-blue haze of Otherness.

Again, the ringed dwarf planet hung suspended in front of the transport, twenty thousand kilometers distant. Five naval vessels remained; they'd pulled back out of range after taking heavy punishment from the Xul world, but began closing with the planet once more when the *Nicholas* appeared.

"Give orders to take those ships on board," Ranser said. "Let's get them out of here, too." No one knew what would happen to this bizarre space-that-was-not-a-space beyond the throat of the Great Annihilator if the Xul world-base exploded. *Nicholas* would pick up all of the ships and men it could . . . *if* the Xul let them.

"Aye, sir."

"Sir!" Carter said. "*Nicholas*' teleport department reports they've begun establishing viable links. They request permission to begin bringing our people aboard."

"Do it," Garroway said.

He was thinking about his many-times-great grand nephew.

Nicholas' teleport crews would only be able to pick up Marines they could positively locate on the surface. Any Marine units that had penetrated the planet would be blocked by layers of rock.

There were nearly six thousand Marines on the surface of the Xul world now . . . and most of them would be underground. An hour ago, Carter had projected over five hundred electronic clones of himself to the various Marine commands down there, ordering them to unplug their implants and to begin making their way back to the surface. How many Marines had managed to do so was anybody's guess . . . and with their implants switched off, *Nicholas* couldn't ping them to establish contact or even to conduct a tacsit census.

Young Lieutenant Garwe had been with one of the groups underground, Garroway knew. He hoped his distant relative would be able to make it out.

"Teleport department reports we've begun bringing Marines back on board," Carter reported.

"And Weapons Department reports the special package is ready for launch."

"Good." Now it was in the laps of the gods. He turned to Rame. "How about it, Lord Rame? What do your Conclave friends say? Are we going to do this or not?"

Rame drew in a ragged breath. Although they weren't being IDed through Garroway's implant, Garroway could sense other minds, other eyes, watching through Rame's. How many? There was no way to tell.

"I've not been able to reach everyone within the Conclave," he said. "Only a few thousand . . . perhaps twelve percent?"

"Okay. And how do *they* vote?"

"Forty-three percent are in favor of delivering the antimatter warhead, as you suggest, General. Thirty-nine percent are against. Eight percent either have no opinion, or they are still debating the matter."

Garroway wondered how any intelligent being could *not* have an opinion about the possibility of destroying all of

Reality. Some of the intelligences with whom Humankind had made contact across the Galaxy were pretty strange, with a philosophical detachment or simply with an alien point of view Garroway found difficult to understand, but even *so.* . . .

Democracy, an ancient politician had once humorously noted, was absolutely the worst form of government in existence . . . except for all of the others. It had the advantage of being confused and disorganized enough that the freedoms of its citizens could be more easily preserved. The disadvantage, though, was that when something *had* to be done, and done quickly, it was almost impossible to create a consensus in time to do anything about it.

Historically, the Marines had carried out the government policies set by others, but this time, in the face of a clear and present danger as the ancient formula had it, Garroway was going to give the orders he knew to be right. "Forty-three to thirty-nine," he said. "Time's up, Lord Rame. The ayes have it."

Rame hesitated, then nodded. "I agree. What else can we do?"

"We could do nothing and die." He turned to Carter. "How are we doing?"

"It's going to take a while, General. We have a lot of men out there, and not all of them are back at the surface."

"Ten minutes," Garroway said. "Then we launch."

The order to teleport the antimatter warhead into the Xul worldlet might well be the death sentence for more Marines than Garroway cared to think about now.

The volume of fire from the Xul planet was greatly reduced, now, but still fierce. *Nicholas* was taking numerous hits as she drifted slowly toward the Xul base. The surviving ships of the squadron continued to fire as they moved slowly out toward the *Nicholas*, and began maneuvering to be taken aboard. Nicholas targeted the Xul batteries one after another, pounding them into hot plasma, and the enemy fire was reduced still more.

Garroway thought about other targets of the Marine Corps over the past two thousand years. There seemed to be a sharp escalation built into the history of the human-Xul war.

In 2170, a Naval task force with a Marine element embarked had gone through the Sirius stargate to emerge in Cluster Space, at a Xul node out beyond the rim of the Galaxy. They'd destroyed an asteroid there which housed another stargate, in order to keep the Xul from discovering Earth.

In 2323, another Navy-Marine task force had accelerated a transport filled with Martian sand to close to the speed of light, releasing the cargo to literally sandblast an entire planet, and the Xul fleet nearby, at Night's Edge.

In 2877, with the help of the alien Eulers, Marines had used a faster-than-light ship to disrupt the core of a star, creating a supernova that wiped out a Xul node in Starwall Space.

And just ten years later, in 2887, Marines and a naval squadron had assaulted the Galactic Core itself, collapsing the Xul Dyson sphere into the supermassive black hole at the Galaxy's center, and initiating the Core Detonation itself.

With that kind of history, it seemed almost inevitable that now, twelve hundred years later, the Marines would be poised to end all of Reality itself. . . .

Blue Seven
Objective Reality
0949 hours, GMT

Garwe struggled on across the broken metal-rock-crystal of the cavern floor. The boots built into the feet of his pressure suit were not thick-soled, and though the material was too tough to tear on the rough surface, fortunately, it was *not* comfortable to walk on. All of the War Dogs were slowing, as exhaustion and blistered feet became harder and harder to ignore.

Even so, it was tough to resist the urge to break into a run.

Purple-blue light was shining up ahead—a tiny patch marking the cavern opening.

The Xul began emerging from the walls and floor around them.

Garwe raised his carbine and began firing, burning down the black, biomechanical tentacles growing out of solid rock, a fast-growing mass of tendrils trying to reach the struggling Marines. The outer perimeter of armored Marines took the brunt of the first assault, but then the floor seemed to soften, to melt into the consistency of thick tar, and tentacles and less identifiable appendages began growing from the plastic mass at their feet.

For a time the battle was at knife-fighting range, as tentacles wrapped around individual Marines, lifting them from the ground, as Marines fired at the Xul mechanicals at point-blank range, as Xul plasma beams snapped and burned from the nearby walls with shrill bursts of static over the radios. One of the armored Marines was grabbed and pulled down by a mass of finger-thick tentacles like the business end of a sea anemone. As more and more tentacles closed over the Marine, they began merging together, encasing the armored form in a black mass that seemed to be dissolving back into the cavern floor. Garwe took three steps and reached the struggling Marine, firing his carbine into the black mass with his right hand, while using his left arm to haul the man free. Another armored Marine came up beside Garwe, and together they pulled the trapped man up and out of the tarry ooze.

Then, with blinding suddenness, Misek Bollan was lifted off the ground by a black, jointed tentacle as thick as Garwe's thigh, growing up out of the ground itself. For a horrible instant, Bollan was suspended above the other Marines, screaming, as his squadmates turned their fire on the shimmering thing coiled about his hips . . . and then the tentacle convulsed and tightened, pinching the Marine in half. It gave a shake, and Bollan's body flew apart, legs going one way, torso, arms and head the other, trailing blood and gore.

Before he could react to the sight, something grabbed Garwe by his right ankle and yanked him hard to the side, hoisting him. The biomechanical tentacle had flowed up out of the ground itself and wrapped itself around him, jerking him bodily from the ground. Dangling upside down, he tried to bring his weapon to bear, but the slender black arm writhed and pulsed and twisted, impossible to target. Garwe hesitated. If he fired too close to his own leg, he could breach his suit, and then it would be all over.

Then one of the armored Marines was there, throwing his arms around the lurching tentacle, using his suit's flamer to burn through the black, metallic coil. With a shock, the tentacle parted, and Garwe landed on his arm and shoulder. The piece of tentacle wrapped around his leg continued to move and tighten with a life of its own. The other Marine burned it away with an expertly timed pass of the flamer, melting most of the coil, but leaving Garwe's suit intact.

"Thanks!" Garwe called. Terror clutched at him. His heart was pounding; he was having trouble breathing.

"Not a problem," the other replied. For the first time, Garwe was close enough to the other man to read the name stenciled on the chest of his armor: NAL, S.

He would remember that name, Garwe promised himself, so he could buy the guy a drink when this was over.

The Xul assault appeared to be breaking off, as more and more of the biomechanical appendages and robotic machines were melted into slag or vaporized in high-energy bursts from lasers or plasma weapons. Garwe decided the fighting at Nassau had been a hell of a lot easier. At least there the enemy didn't ooze up through solid rock and assemble itself in front of you.

Bollan, horribly, was still alive. The interior of his bubble helmet was smeared with blood, and air was bubbling through the opening in his suit where it had been torn apart, but his arms and torso were still twitching, still soundlessly writhing. If he'd still been in a Starwraith, the assault pod's medical suite might have plugged into him and kept him alive—at the very least his implant would have been able to pull off a mindkeeping save.

There was nothing they could do for him now, however, save the final peace. Garwe shoved the muzzle of his carbine against the side of the blood-smeared helmet and pulled the trigger. Bollan gave a final, convulsive shudder, then lay still.

Two Marines were dead—Bollan, and one of the armored Globe Marines. GARCIA, F was the name on the second man's armor. He'd been disabled by a volley of plasma fire, completely enveloped in living black tar, pulled down against the rock floor, and finally crushed to death.

Garwe noticed that Kaddy had left Xander's head behind, somewhere.

It seemed better that way.

In a very real sense, the entire minor planet was a single Xul organism. The Xul intelligences had reworked the rock itself with their equivalent of nanotechnology, creating a near-infinite maze of channels, ducts, and pathways throughout the world's volume through which sub-microscopic machines could flow like liquid. The analogy made Garwe think of himself and his fellow Marines as bacteria, as microscopic invaders fighting a macroscopic life-form's immune responses.

"Wait a second," Garwe said. He stooped, putting his gloved hand to the ground. "You feel that?"

"Feel what?" Nal asked. In that heavy armor, he wouldn't be able to feel it . . . a kind of faint, trembling vibration coming up through the rock.

"I'm not sure," Garwe said, "but we need to get *out* of here. Now!"

Turning, he looked back over his shoulder in the direction they'd come from. There was something there, something huge, massive, and moving swiftly toward them out of the darkness down the tunnel.

Marine Ops Center
Marine Transport Major Samuel Nicholas
0959 hours, GMT

"Ninety percent of the Marines are on board," Carter reported.

"And the last of the ships is being brought in now," Admiral Ranser added. "Our teleport crews report bringing the last of the *Poseidon*'s crew on board as well."

Ninety percent. Did that reflect Marine casualties in the assault, Garroway wondered, or were there still substantial numbers of Marines inside the Xul planet, their radio signals and tracking IFFs blocked by tens of meters of rock?

"Is there any indication that we still have people over there?" he asked.

"D-teleport crew 10 reports a weak signal," Major Kyle reported. "It appears to be being relayed through several combat drones from a large cavern on the surface."

"Get them!"

"Working on it, sir!"

Garroway felt a shudder run through the *Nicholas'* deck. Time was running out. With the naval squadron now safely inside the phase-shift transport, the Xul had only a single target. The *Nicholas* would not be able to endure this punishment for much longer.

Garroway used his implant link to slip through *Nicholas'* internal network, focusing in on the d-teleport department, and finding team 10. In a moment, he was looking over the navy techs' shoulders at the squat ellipse of one of the teleport gates.

He could see movement, but it was dark and confused, a flashing of bright suit lights and deep shadow. It looked like people, and they were running.

And suddenly, Garroway was somewhere else . . . some-*when* else. He was Gunnery Sergeant Robert Lowery, and he was clinging to the gunwale of a small, open boat plunging ahead through the surf. A geyser of white water erupted ten

rds to the left, threatening to capsize the landing craft and
enching the already soaking men on board in a cascade of
ray.

Then the Higgins boat hit the reef, the bow lunging up
d out of the water. The ramp dropped, and the Marines on
ard surged forward, jumping down off the dangling ramp
d onto the exposed reef.

Everything was going wrong, Lowery thought, *every-
ing.* The pre-landing bombardment was supposed to have
iminated the Japanese shore batteries and machine guns,
t both were still very much alive. The tide was supposed
have been high enough to let the landing craft pass over
e reef that encircled Tarawa's landing beaches, but it was
t.

Lowery hit the reef, then dropped into the water of the
goon beyond. Ahead and to left and right, hundreds of
arines were moving forward, rifles held high above their
ads as they struggled to reach the beaches. Everywhere,
en were falling in ones, in twos, in whole lines as gouts of
ater snapped up with the impact of machine-gun bullets
ashing out from the jungle-masked pillboxes behind the
aches.

Slightly to his right, Lowery saw a long, spindle-legged
er jutting out into the water, and he began angling toward
. A mortar round went off to his left, a thunderous blast
ith a savage underwater concussion that pounded his chest.
He kept moving. . . .

No! He was *not* Lowery! He was Trevor Garroway, *Gen-
al* Trevor Garroway, and the thunder and blood around him
as an illusion . . . an *illusion.* . . .

Gasping, he dropped to the deck of the Ops Center, land-
g on his hands and knees. Ranser and the others stared at
im, startled and worried. "General!" Ranser said. "You just
anished and came back!"

"I am *not* going anywhere!" he replied, rising to his feet
ith Adri Carter's help. "How long was I gone?"

"Only a second or two, General," Carter told him.

It had seemed like forever.

He considered unplugging his implant. He was *not* goin
to let them drag him away now! But without the implant h
wouldn't be able to link through to the other departments o
the *Nicholas*, would be effectively out of the battle.

He would stay linked. He could feel the simulation sti
running, a kind of ghost in the back of his brain. If he let him
self, he could still hear the roar of heavy artillery, feel th
spray and the surge of the seawater through which he wa
wading, smell the—

No! He pushed the sim aside, focusing instead on th
d-teleport crew that was trying to lock on to his Marines.

"Shit!" one of the techs said. "We've got something con
ing up the tunnel!"

Garroway saw something at the far end of the Xul tunne
big enough to blot out the faint light coming from the fa
end. "Get those Marines on board!" he said over the link.

"Yes, sir!" a startled tech replied.

"Ranser!" Garroway said, switching channels. "There's
Xul ship coming out of that tunnel. Be ready for it."

"I see it." Ranser had linked into the combat net as wel
"Tracking . . ."

Blue Seven
Objective Reality
0959 hours, GMT

Garwe stumbled and fell. Someone in armor grabbed hi
arm and lifted him to his feet. "Double time, Marine!"

He double-timed.

Although the rock of the Xul world was laced with path
ways and conduits for flows of microscopic nano-machines
there were still numerous larger caverns and tunnels, lik
the one they were moving through now, which allowed th
larger Xul combat machines—their warships, some two ki

ometers long—to pass in and out. This tunnel was only about fifty meters wide—far too small for the largest Xul needleships—but it was large enough, just barely, for something big coming up out of the darkness behind them.

They weren't going to make it. A Xul ship of some sort was barreling up the tunnel behind them, and they *weren't going to fucking make it*. He considered turning and opening fire on the thing, but hand-held weapons wouldn't even scratch the outer nanocoating of a starship, so he did the only thing he *could* do and kept running.

And suddenly the cavern floor dropped out from beneath Garwe's feet and he tumbled head first into dazzling light, along with the other Marines.

"Got them!" a voice nearby yelled. *"Kill the gate! Kill the gate!"*

Marine Ops Center
Marine Transport Major Samuel Nicholas
1959 hours, GMT

"Got them!" a technician yelled, as Marines tumbled through the ellipse and into an untidy tangle on the deck. Some wore heavy Hellfire armor, while the others were in lightweight pressure suits with bubble helmets. *"Kill the gate! Kill the gate!"*

The large something flashing toward the d-teleport gate winked out as the dimensional twist linking the teleport crew with the interior of the Xul world vanished, and just in time. Garroway wondered what would have happened if that huge, black machine had tried to come crashing through the ellipse into the *Nicholas*. Only part of it would have fit through the gate, but there would have been a *lot* of kinetic energy in the part that made it.

"Our people are on board, Admiral," Garroway said. "Fire the warhead."

"Teleport Three!" Ranser called. "Send the package!"

"Package is released," a voice called back.

"I suggest," Garroway said, "that we back out of here."

"I think you're right." Ranser began giving orders.

And *Nicholas'* bridge crew began making the final prepa rations to translate back into four-D space.

24

1902.2229

Objective Reality
0001 hours, GMT

Within the throat of the funnel-shaped pit beneath the Xul worldlet's surface, an elliptical opening winked on, seemingly hanging unsupported in space. A moment later, a canister some four meters long and two wide emerged from the gateway and, in the low gravity of the planet, began to drift downward.

The ellipse winked out. The canister began picking up speed, dropping faster and faster into the heart of the Xul world. Below it, an enigmatic, artificial sun less than one kilometer across gleamed brilliant behind the black opaque armor of the shell surrounding it.

The Xul became aware of the danger scant seconds before the detonation. Amanda Karr in all of her iterations lurking within the Xul world's ring heard the alarm, saw the sudden focus of attention. Five digital Amanda Karrs emerged from hiding at that instant, disrupting communications channels and taking several banks of internal weaponry off-line.

It was probably too late in any case. The cylinder struck the protective shell, the magnetic bottle inside switched off, and

five tons of antimatter came into abrupt contact with norma
matter in a spectacular and lethal blossom of pure, annihilat
ing energy.

The black, protective shell about the central sun was th
generator for a large quantum power tap; the tiny sun wa
vacuum energy drawn from the Quantum Sea and focused
within the shell, which also harvested it. The antimatter blas
not only disrupted the magnetic fields holding the sun i
place, it nudged the entire shell to one side, bringing it int
contact with the sun.

As with the far larger Core Detonation centuries before
the infalling matter generated a runaway cascade, momen
tarily drawing *more* energy from the vacuum, and igniting
a catastrophic explosion that swiftly began devouring th
nearby walls of the cavern. Safeguards and baffles wer
vaporized. The power tap was running now out of control
an avalanche of unimaginable energy pouring through from
elsewhere to fill and consume the shuddering, crumbling
minor planet.

And throughout the tiny world, digital life forms, the Xul
beings who had as a CAS collective ruled the Galaxy for per
haps ten million years, died by the hundreds of millions, by
the billions, by the unimaginable trillions.

Amanda Karr, all of her, along with the iterations o
Captain Valledy and the AI Luther, did not have time to
escape the holocaust. Instead, they broadcast all that they'
experienced and recorded back to the *Nicholas*, until th
surface of the world beneath them dissolved into blue
white brilliance, and then the out-rushing plasma shell ig
nited the trillions of objects comprising the world's ring
and wiped them away, snowflakes before the blast of a
blowtorch.

A three-hundred-meter long ship just emerging from one
of the minor world's tunnels was overtaken by the blast and
consumed. Other Xul warcraft in the immediate vicinity were
overwhelmed before they could escape.

Silently, its cratered and blast-pitted surface brilliantly illuminated by the swelling and brightening micro-nova, *Nicholas* rotated out of the Quantum Sea.

Marine Ops Center
Marine Transport Major Samuel Nicholas
1002 hours, GMT

"My . . . *God* . . ."

The flash of the exploding minor world had been dazzling, blinding in its intensity. An instant later, they'd felt the stomach-dropping sensation of the transition up out of Dimension^0, and the light had been blotted out.

Now the great, blue-hued spiral of the Great Annihilator hung against the radiance of the Core Detonation.

Garroway looked up at the spiral. His first thought was, *We made it!*

His second was, *how many of our people got out?*

It was not immediately clear that the battle was over, however. The Xul planet had grown intolerably bright, but at the moment they could only assume that the enemy was destroyed. There might be more of them around, like hornets after their nest has been knocked down.

Something rippled through space. . . .

"Hey," Ranser said. "Did you see? . . ."

The Great Annihilator turned bright, and Garroway was, again, someplace else.

He stood again on the shores of an alien sea.

At first, he thought it was the illusory world where he'd first met the Tarantulae. There were similarities—a dark, purple-blue sea, and masses of vegetation in the distance, the edge of a jungle, perhaps. The sky was dark blue, deepening to indigo overhead.

A single yellow sun, tiny against the sky, hung above one horizon.

The world he'd seen before had circled a double star, red and green.

And the buildings in the distance—massive constructs, like smooth-sided mountains—were unchanging, static.

"Do you recognize this world?" a familiar voice said, speaking within Garroway's thoughts. "It's changed a lot in five hundred thousand of your years."

Garroway was about to say that, no, he didn't recognize it. But . . . half a million years. That gave him the clue he needed.

"Mars," he said. "The fourth world out from the sun in my own solar system. As it was when the Builders were here."

The Tarantulae materialized in its column of gold-glowing motes. "Very good, General Garroway. Impressive."

"And *you* are the Builders."

"*Very* impressive. What makes you think that?"

"You're showing me Mars as it was then. When you were there." He shrugged. "Natural assumption."

"Keen insight, rather. Tell us, please . . . what do you know of us?"

Us. Like Rame, the being in front of him was a composite, an assembly many minds within a single artificial body. If, indeed, this simulation had any bearing on reality at all.

"We know the Builders—we also call them the Ancients, sometimes—had a fairly large interstellar empire half a million years ago. We've found their . . . *your* cities, empty, mostly in rubble, on worlds as close as Chiron, around Alpha Centauri A, and as far away as several thousand light years. We know you came to our solar system when my species didn't yet exist. You terraformed Mars—gave it oceans and air and enough of a greenhouse effect to be shirtsleeve-comfortable. And you civilized some of the savages you found living on Earth, trained them, and brought them to Mars as workers."

Archeologists at Cydonia, on Mars, had found the skeletons of *Homo erectus*, still wearing jumpsuits of some synthetic material that had survived the millennia.

"We also think, *think* you tampered with the genome of those early proto-humans. *Homo sapiens* appeared suddenly, almost as if out of nowhere, half a million years ago. A much bigger brain. More powerful intellect. You did all of that, didn't you?"

The being said nothing, and Garroway continued.

"At some point, you encountered the Xul. You fought a long and terrible war that left your worlds devastated by planetoid bombardment." Garroway had seen the ruins on Chiron—crumbling, broken ruins extending from horizon to horizon. "We think there was a battle over Mars, that the Xul dropped an asteroid there that blasted away the air and upset the delicate balance of your artificial ecology. Mars died.

"But the Xul overlooked Earth. They went elsewhere, chasing you, and the early humans on the planet survived. We thought they'd wiped you out. Apparently we were wrong."

"A natural mistake. We left the Galaxy. Most of us."

"Most of you?"

"Some stayed behind."

"How?"

"We built . . . new bodies for ourselves. At the time, we were housed in machine bodies. Very much like the Xul, in fact. Cybernetic organisms are a logical next step in sapient evolution. Once a species learns to pattern minds and upload them into a machine brain, they effectively achieve immortality. Of course, the Xul were hunting for machines. We needed to develop . . . organic bodies."

"Organic . . ." Garroway stopped, his eyes widening. "You . . . were *us*."

"Again, you show admirable insight. We designed the species you refer to as *Homo sapiens*, and a number of us uploaded our minds into their brains."

Garroway snorted. "So it was the Adam and Eve scenario after all!"

"I don't understand?"

"A lot of things about where we came from never quite

added up," Garroway said. "There used to be a popular idea, in fact, that speculated that the first humans might have been the survivors of an interstellar shipwreck. 'Adam and Eve' is a reference to an old religious creation myth. The first humans.

"But once we developed our various sciences, and began taking a close look at ourselves, we realized that we *had* to have evolved on Earth. Humans share over ninety-eight percent of our genome with our next nearest relatives in Earth—the chimpanzee. We share sixty percent of our genome with *starfish*, for God's sake. There's no question that we evolved on Earth, within Earth's evolving ecosystem."

"And the *physicality* of *Homo sapiens* did indeed evolve on Earth," the being said. "We just helped it along a little. But the mind . . ." The being paused. "Tell me, General Garroway. Have you wondered, ever, at your species' fascination with the heavens?"

Garroway nodded. It seemed that humans had always been looking at the stars, weaving them into their stories and their religions. Stonehenge—a colossal calendar and astronomical computer. Religions that placed heaven in, well, the heavens. A feeling that *home* was *out there*, somewhere. . . .

"Half a million years ago," the being said, "Earth's moon orbited your world considerably farther out. Before we left, we adjusted your moon's orbit."

"Why?" Garroway asked, puzzled. Then the answer struck him, and his mind reeled for a moment. "Oh. Eclipses."

"Exactly."

One of the great and unlikely coincidences of history was the fact that, from Earth's surface, both the Sun and the Moon appeared to be about the same size in the sky—about half a degree across. The distance of the Moon varied in the course of its orbits about the Earth. Sometimes farther and smaller, and an eclipse was annular—a ring of sun in the sky. On average, though, it was just far enough to *exactly* cover the face of the Sun when it passed directly between

Sun and Earth, creating the spectacular and awe-inspiring display of a total solar eclipse.

"We felt," the being continued, "that the occasional total eclipse would help focus the descendents of those we left behind on the stars."

Of course. Solar eclipses had been important business thousands of years ago. Court astrologers in China had been executed when they failed to predict one. One of the purposes of Stonehenge, he remembered reading, had been to predict eclipses, and the same was true for numerous other Neolithic constructions in both the New and Old Worlds.

They'd *moved* the fucking *Moon*. . . .

"If you could do something like that . . ." he began.

"Why didn't we stay and fight? A number of reasons. The war was wrecking many of the more habitable worlds across the Galaxy, worlds on which intelligence was either then emerging, or would emerge one day. The Xul are . . . were paranoid sociopaths. As your xenosophontlogists have speculated, they evolved with a strong bias toward xenophobia. Any species they encountered that might one day pose a threat, they eliminated. By chance, they encountered us after we'd already established a large and fairly secure interstellar empire, one embracing some tens of thousands of worlds, and so the war of extermination was long and it was bloody. We elected to migrate—most of us—to other galaxies, where we could continue to develop and grow in peace."

"What galaxies? The Magellanics?"

"Outposts," the being told him, "from which we could keep an eye on things. I don't think you need to know precisely where we live just now."

"Of course not." *But we know you're out there*, he thought. *And one day, we'll meet you again.*

"By that time, we will be happy to welcome you," the being said.

Damn. Garroway had forgotten how easily the thing read minds.

"So why are you talking to me now?" Garroway wanted to know. "You could have just let us go our way, thinking you guys were just another super-human intelligence out among the galaxies."

"For one thing, we are related, as you have just discovered. For another, the elimination of the Xul has freed certain communications channels that have been blocked to us for some time."

"Communications channels? Oh, the black holes."

"The black holes. The Xul have been using a number of them, as well as the singularities within the star gates, for their own communicative experiments."

" 'Communicative experiments.' You mean spreading their xenophobia?"

"The Xul worldview, yes. That different is a threat. That alien must be destroyed. I see your Associative has been having trouble with this."

"To tell the truth, we were having trouble with it long before the Xul started tinkering with our heads. Humans don't need help fearing *different*."

"You seem to be adapting well, overall." The glowing being hesitated for a moment. "There is a third reason for this . . . interview, General Garroway."

Something in the way the words hardened in his mind stirred fear. "And what would that be?"

"With the end of the Xul, the Associative is the dominant cultural group within your galaxy. And meta-humanity— *Homo sapiens* and all of the newer branches of your family, *Homo superioris, Homo telae,* and the rest—is currently the driving force within that culture. How will you handle that?"

"I don't think I see what you mean."

"It is the natural order of things, that sapient species evolve from the nonsapient. Despite appearances at time, intelligence is a survival trait in what you know as Darwinian selection. Given enough time—three to four billion years is usually enough—and sufficient stressors within the environment, the ecosystems of most habitable worlds develop intelligence, usually several times in their histories.

"Of those, only a fraction develop technology, of course. Many intelligent species are restricted by their environments, unable to discover fire, for instance, and through fire, the smelting of metals."

Literally tens of thousands of Galactic species, Garroway knew, lived under water, or in world-oceans locked beneath global ice caps, or in reducing atmospheres where open flames were impossible.

"Some of them overcome those restrictions," Garroway suggested. "The Eulers, for example."

The coleoidian Eulers, evolving within the abyssal depths of their ocean, seemed unlikely prospects for interstellar voyagers. Over the eons in their lightless depths, however, they'd genetically altered creatures not unlike crabs and used these as surrogates to explore the land, to develop an advanced technology, and, eventually, to explore the stars.

Such dogged persistence in the face of evolutionary adversity, Garroway knew, was the exception rather than the rule.

"Indeed they do," the being said. "Many more choose not to leave their own worlds. This may be for philosophical or religious reasons, for astronomical reasons, or for reasons that we may categorize as a failure of vision."

"They become too involved in their own planet-bound problems, you mean."

"That would be one possibility, certainly. But for that fraction, that tiny, precious fraction of technologically gifted sapient species that leave their worlds for the ocean of space, *nothing* is impossible."

"Unlimited resources," Garroway said, nodding, "as they learn to mine asteroids or planetary satellites for raw materials. Abundant living space in orbital habs or other, terraformed planetary surfaces. Sooner or later, a space-faring species will develop solar power, fusion power, antimatter, and quantum power taps. Literally unlimited energy, which is *the* key to technological growth."

"Precisely. Spaceflight is a key marker in the development of any intelligent species. Without it, a species is doomed to senescence and decay . . . and in any case will become extinct when its world dies or its sun explodes. With it, a species will ultimately fill its home star system, then move on to other stars, exploring, colonizing, utilizing. As your species is doing now, General."

"What's your point?"

"That any technological species *will* overrun the entire Galaxy—four hundred billion suns, billions of habitable worlds—in the space of a few million years."

Garroway had heard the argument before. "You're talking about the Fermi Paradox," he said. "Until we reached the stars, we wondered where everybody was."

"And you discovered the answer to the paradox."

"Yes. The Xul. Every time a species achieved space flight, they tracked it down and destroyed it." He cocked his head to one side. "How did you guys escape?"

"The Galaxy is quite large. The Xul were not perfect. In fact, by the time we met them, the Xul were more a network of adaptive systems than intelligence. A force of nature reacting to key stimuli."

"We've seen that as well. They missed plenty of opportunities along the way to destroy us."

"And you were able to destroy them."

The being was driving at something. Garroway wondered what. "So intelligence is free to spread through the Galaxy again."

"Is it?"

"What do you mean?"

"What will you do, General, when your species encounters a young race, one with aggressive and expansionist tendencies, one that, for whatever reason, decides to take what you have and make it theirs?"

Garroway started to answer, stopped, then shook his head. "I was going to say that the Galaxy is big enough for everyone."

"And it is not. Life and intelligence will grow and reproduce and evolve, and it will fill every niche, change every world, fill the Galaxy and beyond with itself. It might take a few million years . . . but that is a scant moment, an eye's blink compared to the billions of years of the Galaxy's lifespan.

"There is also the matter of cultural differences. You will meet intelligent species who care nothing for your worlds, but who are driven by such powerful belief systems that they will feel compelled to either force their culture upon you, or to destroy you."

Garroway nodded. The Xul were proof enough of that. And just within the history of Humankind there'd been so many religions demonstrating the being's point: the Fascists, the Soviets, the Muslim fundamentalists, the Hegemonists, the Pan-Europeans, the Technophobe extremists, the Divine Sons of God. It was a *very* long list, and a bloody one.

"How will you respond the next time your way of life, your very survival, is threatened?"

"I . . . don't know. I don't speak for the future."

"But you *do*, General. The future is *you*."

"It's in our nature to fight to survive," Garroway said. "Are you asking for a promise that we *not* defend ourselves?"

"No. You don't have the power to make such a promise, for your species or for yourself. But I do want you to consider . . . options."

"What options?"

"Come with me."

The landscape of ancient Mars vanished. In its place hung the hurricane vortex of a giant black hole.

The sky in every direction was an opalescent smear of radiance. At first, Garroway thought he was looking at the Great Annihilator . . . but then his sense of scale shifted. What he was looking at was far, far larger . . . the supermassive black hole at the Galaxy's center, cleansed of the Xul Dyson cloud that had surrounded it.

Garroway and the Tarantulae were disembodied viewpoints, dropping toward the titanic singularity's event horizon.

"Do you feel it?" his guide asked. "A kind of thrumming, a vibration?"

"Yes." It was as though the fabric of spacetime itself was trembling with precisely timed pulses or ripples, spreading out in concentric shells from the Core singularity.

"Merge with it."

Garroway wasn't quite certain what his guide meant, but as he focused his awareness on the vibrations, he became aware of . . . images. Sensations. *Memories.*

And he remembered. . . .

He remembered things he'd never experienced, never even guessed at. He remembered an Intelligence that thought of itself as the One Mind. It had arisen out of myriad lesser intelligent species long ago. How long? Thirty million years? Fifty? He didn't yet have the frame of reference to translate what he was experiencing. But a *long* time.

The One Mind had tamed the Galaxy. After eons of struggle among its component species, it had united as an amalgam of intelligent organic superconductors existing as a hive mentality. The One Mind, Garroway now remembered, had created the network of star gates across the Galaxy and beyond. And it had built . . . something else. Something within the depths of the Quantum Sea, but interacting with four-D spacetime through the instrumentality of the black holes and star gates.

"The Encyclopedia Galactica," Garroway said, awed. Then, wondering if the words had made sense to the Tarantulae at his side, he added, "We always wondered if a sufficiently advanced species might find a way of recording galactic knowledge—the science, the technology, the history, the culture of an entire galaxy—so that others could tap into it and learn from it."

"So newcomers wouldn't repeat the mistakes of the older species," the being said.

"Yes."

"The One Mind did that. Unfortunately . . ."

More memories arose in Garroway's mind. It was a little

ike the simulations of the Boxer Rebellion and Iwo Jima, his effortless emergence of memories he'd never known before. The difference was that he was still Trevor Garroway. Still human, despite the strange and alien history he was encountering.

He remembered the Psychovores, malevolent, photophobic entities called the Children of the Night that somehow fed on the minds, the psychic energies, of others, beings that organized whole worlds of less advanced sapient life forms as farms for the breeding and harvesting of their property. How long ago? They'd replaced the One Mind perhaps thirty million years ago, possibly when the One Mind transcended all material instrumentality.

And ten million years ago the Children of the Night had been supplanted by the Hunters of the Dawn—polyspecific pantovores driven by an intense xenophobia, a fear of others quite possibly planted by their nocturnal predecessors. Eventually, the Sumerians of Earth would call them "demons." Xul.

In time, the Builders had created their empire, struggled with the Xul, and failed. Or had it been a failure? Garroway watched, in his memories, the Builders' exodus beyond the spiral arms of the Galaxy. And behind them they left their legacy—the uploaded minds of some of their own within artificially engineered bipedal beings on the world that one day would be called Earth.

Garroway felt . . . small. He wondered if Humankind itself wasn't simply another tool, a weapon in the hands of the ancient Builders against their enemies.

"Not deliberately so, no," the being next to him told him. "But we are pleased that things worked out as they did. Your intervention here at the Galactic Core freed the instrumentality—what you call the 'Encyclopedia Galactica'—for use once more."

Garroway understood. The Encyclopedia existed, if it could be said to have a material existence, as probability waves nested within the vaster, deeper pulse of gravity waves emerging from the supermassive black hole at the Galaxy's center. The Xul had taken over the Core black hole for their own purposes, and in so doing had shut down the Encyclopedia.

With the Xul threat eliminated, the Encyclopedia Galactica was broadcasting once again. Garroway was immersed in it, sensing the pulse, the tides of data stored for tens of millions of years.

"The Encyclopedia's records only go back as far as the One Mind," his guide explained. "But the pattern recorded here is the same as it has been across the eons. We believe the first intelligent species achieved interstellar travel within this galaxy well over four billion years before your Sun came into existence, a mere two billion years after the formation of the Galactic disk . . . though it's possible older species still inhabited some of the oldest star clusters, in a distant epoch when the supernova seeding of heavy metals through the interstellar medium was still new. They spread through the Galaxy's worlds, meeting others, merging, warring, conquering, destroying. Occasionally something like your Conclave would come into existence, a cooperative of mutually alien species united for their common protection and technological and cultural advancement.

"Then, inevitably, one species would arise with the simple Darwinian imperative: *survival requires the elimination of all competitors.*"

"We used to call it 'the empty sky.' The Galaxy should have been buzzing with advanced civilizations. It wasn't."

"The Xul are only the last of a long, long list of sophont species who attempted to maintain their existence by exterminating any and all who might one day challenge them. It's easier to do that when the target species is still young and planet-bound, of course. But the galaxy is a big place, and there are always a few who are overlooked. Fortunately."

"I take it you—your species, I mean—are wondering if Humankind is going to do the same. If we'll try to survive by crushing all opposition."

"The Galaxy has been locked in a bloody and self-destructive cycle of violence for some eight billion years, twice the span of your Earth. Each cycle of violence begets the *next* cycle of violence. Can you humans break the cycle, here and now?"

"I . . . don't know." He wondered. He thought of the Associative bringing the errant Dahlists into line, all the way out in the Large Magellanic Cloud.

He remembered the Legation force bringing the Chinese dissidents to heel.

He remembered crushing the Japanese Empire—Humankind's first use of nuclear weapons, at least in modern Earth history. There were hints that nukes had been used before, in the dim, remote past.

He remembered the fall of the Soviets, the destruction of the Muslim extremists, the crushing of the Hegemony . . . and so many, many more.

"You're asking me if Humankind can survive without becoming as bad as the Xul. I can't answer that. But I *do* know that the desire is there. The Xul were driven by a kind of hard-wired response to threat: if it's different, kill it. We're not. We're a social and cooperative species. We *want* to get along." He grinned. "Even when we can't stand the other guy's guts."

"And that may be the best answer we can hope for," his guide replied. "At least for now."

Garroway's surroundings shimmered, rippled, then vanished, and he was back on board the *Nicholas*. He blinked. "Was I gone long?"

Rame looked at him curiously. "You were not gone at all."

"I . . . see. . . ."

"Our little raid into the Quantum Sea has had one effect," Admiral Ranser said. "The Great Annihilator is gone."

It was true. The *Samuel Nicholas* drifted alone within the sea of fast-moving charged particles, a hot and luminous cloud expanding from the center of the Galactic Core, 350 light years away. The fifteen-solar-mass singularity of the Great Annihilator, however, had quietly rippled into nothingness. Somehow, the Xul worldlet down in the Quantum Sea and its power taps had been inextricably linked with the singularity. When the one had vanished, so had the other.

He could still sense the ripples of probability, of *possibility*, from the Galactic Core, however. Was that real, or imagined? Or . . . an implanted memory?

"We might want to go back in and explore the central Galactic Core," he told the others. "The Central Library is open for business again."

"What?" Rame said. "What are you talking about?"

"You'll see. . . ."

Garroway was remembering a quote, something from a late-nineteenth-century philosopher named Friedrich Nietzsche who'd written a book called *Beyond Good and Evil*. He wasn't sure where he'd picked it up, but he knew it had perfect relevance for Humankind:

He who fights with monsters might take care lest he thereby become a monster. And if you gaze for long into an abyss, the abyss gazes also into you.

The abyss might be gazing into Humankind. What it saw there, however, along with all the faults and follies and foibles of the human species, was a singular organization, a brotherhood of warriors dedicated to honor and to one another.

The Marine Corps.

Forever vigilant.

Forever human.

Semper humanus.

Epilogue

North America
Earth
0800 hours, GMT

The Marine Corps would continue.

There was, of course, considerable question about that continuance once the Associative Conclave understood that the Xul menace, at long last, was gone. There was no need for a Marine Corps now—neither Globe nor Anchor Marines—with peace at hand.

But the Corps had lasted for 2230 years so far, and had long ago acquired a distinct life of its own. It could not simply be turned off when it was no longer needed.

And many felt that there would *always* be a need, so long as Humankind remained human.

Marine Master Sergeant Nal il-En Shru-dech had given a lot of thought to a return to cybe-hibe. That, after all, had been one of the options. Eight and a half centuries before, Marines of the Third Division had been given the choice of disbanding, or of going into cybernetic hibernation. Many Marines, disillusioned with the culture of the day, had opted for cybe-hibe, and the chance of either serving again in the future . . . or of emerging one day in a more tolerant culture willing to accept the Corps and their admittedly non-civilian way of looking at things.

The Corps faced such a decision point again, now, over 2200 years after they'd first waded ashore from small boats onto the beach at Nassau to face the guns at Fort Montagu. Many Marines had opted for the future. Captain Corcoran. Corporal Zollinger. PFC Brisard.

Nal had made a different choice . . . as had his current domestic partner, Cori Ryack.

Lieutenant—now *Captain*—Marek Garwe had made the same choice, as had *his* partner, Kaddy Wahrst. One good thing that had come with the reorganization of the Corps: there were no longer Anchor Marines or Globe Marines. *All* of them were the same—*Marines*.

General Trevor Garroway, of course, was now the commandant of the reorganized Corps. There'd been no question about that. Some of the men and women now in the Corps would have elected the man as *God* if that had been an option.

Garroway was here, on the speaker's gallery, together with the Associative and national dignitaries who'd actually chosen to attend this ceremony today *live*, instead of via sim.

There'd been the question, though, of what to do with those Marines who'd opted not to enter cybe-hibe for a distant and uncertain future. *This* had been the logical, perhaps the only possibility.

The color guard approached the flag staff. "Atten—*hut!*" Nal barked.

At his back, one hundred twenty Marines came to crisp-snapping attention. They wore the current full-dress uniform of the Corps. The tailoring of those uniforms would have been strange to Marines at Nassau, or Tarawa, or Khe Sanh, or Enduru, but certain elements remained constant. *Eternal.*

The stiff collars that gave Marines the name *leathernecks.*

The curved ceremonial swords carried by the officers, in memory of the march to Derna.

The blood stripe—the red strip down the leg, in memory of Chapultepec.

The color guard reached the flagstaff. "Present . . . *harms!*"

Ceremonial rifles came to the present, and Nal rendered a hand salute. An ancient, ancient anthem played as the flag, red and white stripes, field of blue, went up the mast.

The ancient United States of America had never died, quite . . . but it had dwindled away, first as a piece of the North American Commonwealth, later as a member-state of the Galactic Commonwealth and, later still, of the Associative.

But it existed still—seventy-five semiautonomous states stretching from the Bering Strait to the Floridian Sea. Sadly for traditionalists like most Marines, global warming across two millennia and the Xul bombardment of 2314 had long ago submerged or scoured away many of the Corp's most sacred sites—Parris Island, Quantico, Nassau, Camp Pendleton.

But *this* area went back at least two thousand years. It was heavily forested now, a tropical rainforest close beside the ocean, but then it had been a high and barren plateau, a major Corps training and air station in the decades before Humankind had first left its world.

An odd name. Twentynine Palms.

The flag reached the top of the staff, fluttering in the stiff offshore breeze, and the anthem ended.

"Order . . . *harms!*"

As one, with an echoing crack, the rifles snapped back, butts to the ground.

The Corps retained its presence out among the stars, of course. The Marine Corps now had the very specific mission of guarding the Galactic Core, deep within the cloud of the Core Detonation. Scientists from a thousand cultures were out there now, investigating, experiencing the eons of history transmitted from the Encyclopedia. The Marines would make certain that all had access, that none would censor. The free flow of information, of truth, was the single absolute for any culture that sought to avoid the Xul Solution.

But back on Earth, a grateful Associative had established a new military enclave for those who'd volunteered to come here. And . . . who knew? One day, the ancient United States might unfold itself again among the stars.

"Parade . . . *rest!*"

Trevor Garroway, Commandant of the Marine Corps, stood to deliver his speech at the formal opening of the USMC base at Twentynine Palms.

The United States Marine Corps had returned home at last.

IAN DOUGLAS's
MONUMENTAL SAGA
OF INTERGALACTIC WAR
THE INHERITANCE TRILOGY

TAR STRIKE: BOOK ONE

978-0-06-123858-1

lanet by planet, galaxy by galaxy, the inhabited universe has
llen to the alien Xul. Now only one obstacle stands between
em and total domination: the warriors of a resilient human
ce the world-devourers nearly annihilated centuries ago.

ALACTIC CORPS: BOOK TWO

978-0-06-123862-8

the year 2886, intelligence has located the gargantuan hid-
en homeworld of humankind's dedicated foe, the brutal Xul.
e time has come for the courageous men and women of the
t Marine Interstellar Expeditionary Force to strike the killing
ow.

EMPER HUMAN: BOOK THREE

978-0-06-116090-5

ue terror looms at the edges of known reality. Humankind's
ternal enemy, the Xul, approach wielding a weapon mon-
rous beyond imagining. If the Star Marines fail to eliminate
eir relentless xenophobic foe once and for all, the Great
nnihilator will obliterate every last trace of human existence.

THE BATTLE FOR
THE FUTURE BEGINS—IN
IAN DOUGLAS's
EXPLOSIVE
HERITAGE TRILOGY

SEMPER MARS
978-0-380-78828-6

LUNA MARINE
978-0-380-78829-3

EUROPA STRIKE
978-0-380-78830-9

AND DON'T MISS
THE LEGACY TRILOGY

STAR CORPS
978-0-380-81824-2

n the future, Earth's warriors have conquered the heavens. But on a distant world, humanity is in chains . . .

BATTLESPACE
978-0-380-81825-9

Vhatever waits on the other side of a wormhole must be confronted with stealth, with force, and without fear.

STAR MARINES
978-0-380-81826-6

Planet Earth is lost . . .
but the marines have just begun to fight.